ZOMPOC:
HOW TO SURVIVE A
ZOMBIE APOCALYPSE

ZOMPOC:
HOW TO SURVIVE A ZOMBIE APOCALYPSE

BY
MICHAEL THOMAS
& NICK THOMAS

Published in the UK 2009
by SwordWorks, UK

Distributed in the United Kingdom by
SwordWorks, UK

ISBN 978-1906512330

Printed and bound in Great Britain
by SwordWorks Publishing, UK

To all members of the Zombie Abolition Service (ZAS), of whom civilisation will be relying upon in its biggest crisis to come.

ACKNOWLEDGEMENTS

We would like to thank the many individuals who have provided assistance with artwork, proof-reading, editing and posing for various parts of our book. This book was a substantial undertaking that could not have been achieved without the kind assistance of many people. These people include Pamela Jary for her many photographs, editing and constant support, Sophia Jones for her Zompoc party preparation, the White Tigers MCC and The Patriots MC for their riders and bikes, The Academy of Historical Fencing for their weapons and martial arts demonstrations, The Grange for their military vehicles, Paul Edwards for his zombie make-up, Steven Thomas and Rosie Thomas for props, assistance and proof reading.

Additional thanks to, John Shears, Natalie Richards, Dave, Carol 'Caz' Baker, Lorne Purnell, Carl Phillips, Dave Cable, Abigale Dodge, Liz Bridges, Jake Free, Jenny Hallas, Martin Cazey, Carlo Parisi, John Gavan, Steve Galton, Paul Edwards, Tom Parks, Matt Parks, Neil Hamilton, Jamie Hall, Philip Hazelden, Shreiff Benaziza, Jay Hooper, Keith 'Brum' Coley, Tim Gulson, and many others who all provided valuable time and assistance to the project.

CONTENTS

PART 3

PART 4

PREFACE

Will a zombie or zombie-like scenario ever occur? As this book shows, science-fiction is fast becoming science-fact. As the human race searches for ways to overcome illness, advanced technology to do things we could only previously dream of and concoct deadly amounts of chemical and radioactive pollutants. Who knows what the potential side effects of any of things could be?

There are several important points to remember if, or when this uprising occurs. Understanding these points is vital in helping you with your planning and later actions during the unfolding crisis. Zombies are new and something of which we have no experience, and that the authorities, laws and various procedures designed to keep us safe will be useless in the event. Local councils, government, police and military forces are not equipped, trained or expected to deal with these types of scenarios. Studying this book will help ensure that you are not taken by surprise and increase your chance of surviving the Zompoc.

INTRODUCTION

Zombies are not currently a reality but are the stuff of horror movies, myth and legend, right? But what if they were to become a reality? What if that scraping at the window and that low moaning isn't the wind or a branch? Would you know what to do if the zombie hordes were at your door? As you will find explained in this book, with the rapid advances of science, medicine and technology there is the potential for many types of zombies; not just the ones you have seen in films from the 1960s onwards. So, would you, in short be able to survive the 'Zompoc', or zombie apocalypse? This book is designed to help you, the industrious and prepared citizen, to survive a Zompoc and to help others to do the same.

This book has been painstakingly created using information from the worlds experts on survival skills, martial arts, combat training, biology and self sufficiency. It contains information on all possible zombie types such as classic 'undead' zombies through to virus infected fast zombies and explores the potential for other causes. With clear guidance on what to do and what to avoid should you find yourself dealing with the fall of humanity, this book is your key to surviving the zombie apocalypse, fighting back and helping to rebuild society again afterwards.

Start by working through the manual to help you prepare for the worst and consider all options. However, after an initial read it can be used as a handy reference text that can be dipped into as needed. Starting with background information and biological research on zombies this book then continues with masses of information, giving you 15 detailed chapters, all well illustrated and designed to make understanding this topic as clear as possible. These comprehensive chapters include pre-apocalypse preparation, survival strategies, preparing and defending your home, dealing with the living, travel and movement, environments, combat & tactics, operations, supplies & logistics, weapons, personal equipment, vehicles and vehicle preparation. The final chapter is a detailed look at long-term rebuilding and covers detailed sections on trading, self-sufficiency, setting up your own military and militia and lastly, possible uses for zombies after the Zompoc. Together with a detailed index and a useful information section which gives you extra places to check for emergency information or to join anti-zombie groups this is the only zombie apocalypse survival manual you will ever need. We look forward to welcoming you as a member of the ZAS (Zombie Abolition Service) soon.

Michael G. Thomas

Nick S. Thomas

CHAPTER 1: THE ZOMBIE APOCALYPSE

Learning is not compulsory... neither is survival.
W. Edwards Deming

The zombie apocalypse refers to the horrifying and very likely scenario of a general uprising of zombies hostile to human life that engages in a general assault on civilization. This is not as farfetched as it may seem, especially with modern scientific advances. You can read more about zombies, what they are, where they come from and their primary traits please read the 'Zombies' section. The primary reason that a zombie uprising is expected to lead to an apocalyptic conclusion is that victims of zombies may become zombies themselves. This infection may take place in a variety of ways from biting through to airborne contamination. This creation of new zombies could create an exponentially growing crisis, one that would become worse as the numbers of non-zombies drops to a critical number.

it is almost certain that the spreading zombie infection would swamp military and law enforcement organizations whom under normal circumstances are ultimately reliant upon the civilian population for supplies, power, support and other resources. With a lack of central control and authority the panicked collapse of civilian society will be

accelerated until only isolated pockets of survivors remain, scavenging for food and supplies in a world reduced to a pre-industrial hostile wilderness. Of those studies made into the threat of a Zombie Apocalypse or Zompoc, the following basic stages are acknowledged as being likely and these will require your action and initiative to survive.

Likely ZOMPOC Outbreak Stages

❖ The zombies will be created in some way

❖ The uprising will start once the number of zombies reaches a critical level and are too numerous and so break out of their initial containment

❖ The zombies will reach populated areas and this is where the uprising will reach the final stage where it can possibly be halted

❖ Authorities will attempt to control the spread. If they are successful the uprising could be stopped but if they fail then the uprising will spread to epic proportions.

❖ A sudden, catastrophic collapse of all large-scale organisation will take place after the authorities initial failure

❖ With all large scale organisation gone, the general population will be left to fend for themselves resulting in violence, arson, robbery and rioting. This coupled with large scale looting and evacuation will make spread of zombies harder to control.

❖ The surviving populations will have to defend themselves against the ravages of the zombie uprising, and also against the confused masses and terrified people trying to escape.

There are several important points to remember if, or when this uprising occurs. Understanding these points is vital as they will help you with your planning and later actions during the unfolding crisis.

The first threat concerns zombies themselves; they are a new threat. This is something we have no experience of and so the authorities, and the usual laws and procedures will not keep us safe. Local councils, government, police and military forces are not equipped, trained or expected to deal with these types of scenarios. The second point is that the main motivation of the zombies will be to attack living humans. The third is that initial contact with zombies will shock, confuse and surprise people which will stop effective control and aid the spread of the outbreak. People may attempt to help those injured and behave in ways which will generally result in nothing

positive. The fourth and final point is that the response of the authorities, military and police to the threat will be slower than the rate of growth of the zombie population, giving the outbreak time to expand beyond containment.

The ultimate outcome of these points is the collapse of society. Without law, structure, power, water and organization you can expect anarchy. Throw into this mix a growing number of flesh eating zombies and you will be left with pockets of violent and desperate groups of survivors. These small groups of the living all have to fight for their survival using any means at their disposal, defending against both the zombies, the environment and also against other survivors! By now you are probably thinking, Zombies are simply fictional, however, advances in science mean that the creation of something resembling a zombie is actually now a possibility. It might sound crazy but there are so many ways that this side effect could occur that you really want to study this manual and prepare!

WHAT IS A ZOMBIE?

A zombie is a creature that appears in folklore and popular culture, typically as a reanimated corpse or a mindless human being. Stories of zombies originated as part of the Afro-Caribbean spiritual belief system of Vodou, which describes people as being controlled as labourers by a powerful sorcerer. Zombies became a popular device in modern horror fiction, largely because of the success of George A. Romero's 1968 film, 'Night of the Living Dead'. Shockingly, modern science and technology has potentially created conditions that make the creation of various virulent infections and strains very likely.

While the idea of a re-animated corpse traditionally has existed in the realm of fiction there are now many ways a corpse could potentially be brought back to life. It is possible that various viral attacks and nano devices could turn normal cells and therefore ultimately people into slavering, blood thirsty zombies. This means that there are a number of ways a zombie could be created and propagated in the living community.

IDENTIFICATION

- ❖ Lack of emotion and facial expression
- ❖ No need to sleep
- ❖ Does not feel or react to pain
- ❖ Does not breathe
- ❖ Can continue even after sustaining injury
- ❖ Speed and movement <u>should</u> be impaired due to atrophy
- ❖ Weakened limbs
- ❖ Poor hearing and vision
- ❖ Smell – first of poor hygiene and then of decay
- ❖ Pale skin

ZOMBIE CREATION

Zombies do not just pop into existence; they have to come from somewhere. Here we will examine the most common and possible ways in which these creatures could be created. These include such things as re-animation of the dead, disease, radioactive mutation, viral warfare and even monsters and creatures described as a part of religious Armageddon. Though there are many ways they could be created, they all possess similarities with the classifications of undead or infected zombies presented here.

RE-ANIMATION/NEUROGENESIS

The classic idea is of the undead zombie as depicted in the movie, 'Night of the Living Dead'. Stem cell research demonstrates us that we can re-generate dead cells. This idea of re-animation is known as neurogenesis and the concern is that it seems this area of science may be able to re-grow, repair and re-animate dead brain cells. The biggest problem with this research is that the core of the brain is damaged first thus leaving us with the parts that controls basic motor function and primitive instincts behind. Thus the body can function but the capacity for higher level reasoning and morality are lost. This means that you can get hold of a dead or recently dead body, re-animate the brain and get the classic, base zombie that has only basic functions but is able to move and control its various physical functions. A re-animated zombie would in all likelihood not have an infection or problem to pass on via a bite. This is not guaranteed though!

Remember that their reason for existence is being raised from the dead and maintaining this existence through meeting their need to feed. It is reasonable to therefore assume that in order to become one of them you must first die. If death is the only way to be made into the undead then simply not dying is how to stay alive! Yep, logical, we know!

What happens if you are bitten by the undead? If something enters the bloodstream that causes re-animation you will probably not know until somebody dies. Quite simply burn the dead to ensure they do not rise as the undead. If somebody is bitten then assume they will at the very least turn on you when dead. Make it your mission to watch what happens to the newly bitten to get a good idea on how the problem is passed on. Use this to create standard procedures when facing the injured or dying. These zombies should be able to lose limbs and other parts of their bodies without loss of blood or major function; this will make killing them difficult and require precise infliction of damage.

One final point is the possibility of re-animation bringing dead animals back to life. This is a potential concern and could of course lead you to the crazy scenario of where you kill an animal to eat, it re-animates and then attacks you. If this happens then the zombie apocalypse could continue with all kinds of life being brought back from the dead. What will they feed from? Will all undead creatures come knocking on your door? Observation is the only way we have of knowing as this is all conjecture.

COSMIC RAYS AND KILLER ASTEROIDS

This was a popular idea back in the 1950's and is simply the idea of something from space causing some kind of a change to the living on Earth. This was originally the subject of many films, but even in recent years there have been worries about bacteria and other living things being present on asteroids hurtling through space. We all know what happened to the North American Indians when they met Europeans so could the same happen to us on a global scale? For example, in the classic novel 'Day of the Triffids' by John Wyndham, an asteroid shower is seen across the globe throughout the night. The next day the population that saw the bright asteroids are found to be blind. Of course, the story then progresses to giant killer plants, but it could just as easily be zombies! This cause would create the effects outlined in the nanobot, infection and brain parasites sections.

The 'cosmic ray' idea is not a terribly likely cause and primarily the work of fiction writers and filmmakers. What actually are they? Well, cosmic rays are energetic particles originating from outer space that impinge on Earth's atmosphere. The term 'ray' is a misnomer, as cosmic particles arrive individually, not in the form of a ray or beam of particles. Their effects range from altering ambient radiation to electrical interference. Earth is currently bombarded by various particles on a daily basis with no ill effects to date.

LOSS OF SENSES

One theory postulated is based on the idea, as described in 'Day of the Triffids', that a large part of the population is faced with a serious, debilitating problem, such as overnight blindness that will cause a swift collapse of society when coupled with something like a zombie outbreak. Ideas such as solar flares or special weapons are possible culprits here. In this scenario there will be a strong distinction

between those left unaffected (a small number) against the impaired. If the impairment is caused by something 'other worldly', will the affected eventually turn into zombies? Will the large numbers of the sense-impaired turn psychotic? Perhaps the thing that caused the impairment could have other effects on their mind or senses?

BREAKDOWN OF SOCIETY

Following a catastrophic event such as a comet colliding with the Earth, massive disease outbreak or global war it is possible that society could fall back into a more primitive, violent system. Groups of humans, affected by the breakdown could be turned mad or violent in some way. This kind of breakdown is not really a zombie apocalypse though might have many of the same consequences, however the breakdown of society is a very real possibility if a Zompoc should occur.

SCIENTIFIC EXPERIMENTS

Scientific advances do not stop and our understanding of all forms of science are progressing at a geometric rate. Work on stem cells, genetic modification, cloning, disease control and much more are taking place across the globe. There could be unforeseen side

effects to many of these advances and this could result in certain treatments, drugs or trials being used for years before the true problems are revealed. There are plenty of possibilities for these experiments to leak out into the public domain. Accidents do happen and there is always the possibility of deliberate sabotage or terrorism.

TERRORISM

Since the attacks on the United States in 2001 and subsequent attacks in the UK, Spain and the rest of the world, the threat of international terrorism is greater than it ever has been. Terrorists have shown a total disregard for human life, no matter what their race, religion or creed. If these people are able to get their hands on biological or

chemical weapons then we can be sure they will use them. Terrorists are likely to make use of scientific resources and assets in unethical ways and if they are able to gain access to scientists that are sympathetic or blackmailed into helping then who knows what disasters they would be able to release upon us. There is also a chance that if a zombie apocalypse started, some terrorist organisations could actually help the zombies spread in certain areas, perhaps even move them to populated areas to use as weapons and cause chaos.

ATOMIC/NUCLEAR RADIATION

Many of the greatest fictional monsters of the last fifty years or so have been created by the testing of atomic weapons. How many giant lizards have we seen climbing out of the oceans to devastate yet another city? The

basis for this argument is that radiation is known to cause all manner of mutation. This in itself is not likely to cause the types of zombies we would describe as undead, but radiation can damage the skin, tissue, organs and potentially the brain, especially if exposed to excessive amounts. If sufficient radiation was inflicted upon an individual it might be possible to induce various forms of mutation and damage. The probability of creating a violent, dangerous individual are very remote and the odds of this person being able to pass on these traits via bite or fluid contact are nigh on impossible.

However, there is of course the ever present worry of contamination and radiation poisoning. One thing that is possible is that through mutation, a person's offspring could exhibit strange traits and characteristics that might share some common traits with an infected zombie. In the end though, to get a true, animalistic, amoral creature, the brain must be badly damaged. Hopefully, if this

were to ever happen we would find the creature would not be able to pass the mutations on and thus the zombie apocalypse would just be one zombie, the kind of odds we like!

OCCULT & MAGIC

What place does magic play in creating the zombie apocalypse? Well, in our opinion, no part. For completeness we will investigate the options. What actually is magic? Simply put there are two types of magic, neither of which is likely to be a factor in creating zombies. The first is the idea of paranormal magic. This is the use of supernatural methods to manipulate natural forces, such as witchcraft.

Voodoo is the obvious example of supernatural magic but there are other darker magicks throughout the world. Magic enters the realm of the unknown and therefore the creatures it could create are the work of fiction and not something we can truly plan for. This doesn't mean that the rituals, drugs and other

unknowns couldn't be involved in creating or be used to help to spread other types of zombies such as those caused by infection or mind damaging drugs. The second type of magic is the art of appearing to perform supernatural feats using sleight of hand or other methods. Though this may look impressive it will luckily do nothing at all as far as creating zombies goes. This is great news though a fake zombie might cause the odd heart attack!

END OF THE WORLD

The idea of the end of the world is an ancient one and something lots of mainstream religions use as a sword over our heads to keep us in line. Nonetheless there are many predictions, accounts and judgements recorded with regards to this day. Is there any justification to any of this material? Well, that is for you to decide though the predications put forward so far seem to slip past us with nothing happening. 2000 was supposed to be the end of the world for many people, with the 2012 predictions being a worry for some. Religious practice, the apocalypse, judgement day or simply the Act or Will of God are all touted as possible reasons for the creation of slavering beasts, monsters, zombies and other foul creatures.

All major religions have a view on death and the end of the world. Let us consider one most of us are all familiar with. According to traditional Christian interpretations, the Messiah, the "Lamb", will return to earth and defeat the Antichrist or "Beast", in the battle of Armageddon. Then Satan will be put into the bottomless pit or abyss for 1,000 years, known as the millennial age. After being released from the abyss, the Beast will gather Gog and Magog from the four corners of the earth. They will surround the holy ones and the "beloved city". Fire will come down from God,

out of heaven and devour Gog and Magog at the Armageddon, and the Devil who deceived them is thrown into Gehenna (the lake of fire and brimstone) where the Beast and the false prophet have been since just before the 1,000 years. This period is often considered to be the occasion where the dead will rise and fight with the legions of the Devil. Whilst this is a little farfetched it is still one of the potential causes sometimes cited for the creation of zombies. These monsters would presumably be similar to the re-animated dead but who knows when you are dealing with religion! One might ask where the information for this detailed and somewhat disturbing vision comes from. Presumably if you believe in the dogma of Christian belief then you must also believe this account of the end of days?

Think back to George A Romero's classic zombie films and his immortal line, 'When there is no more room in hell, the dead will walk the Earth'. Though this is a work of fiction it does tie into the idea of the religious Armageddon and there are many that are convinced that no matter what types of creature we end up facing on this Earth it will be because it was sent by God. One last thought is that if this is all pre-ordained by God, what can we mortals possibly do against the word and will of the Lord? Good question!

END OF THE WORLD SCENARIOS

❖ Apocalypse, concept in the New Testament, referring to the final revelation
❖ Armageddon, site of an epic battle associated with end time prophecies
❖ End time, eschatological writings in the three Abrahamic religions (Judaism, Christianity, and Islam) and in doomsday scenarios in various other non-Abrahamic religions
❖ Eschatology, part of theology and philosophy concerned with what are believed to be the final events in the history of the world, or the ultimate destiny of humanity
❖ Last Judgment, religious concept

NANOBOTS

This is a very new area of research and maybe another potential cause of zombieism. Nanobots are simply miniature robots that are self replicating and can invisibly build, alter or destroy anything from within a system such as the human body. The concern is that they can be used to construct or repair all manner of problems from weaknesses in metal to performing surgery in critical operations.

month. This is literally science fiction becoming science fact. The technology is currently being created and within a matter of years there is the potential for these nanobots to repair and rewire connections in the brain with the intention of treating many illnesses and disorders such as helping to fix neural problems and brain damage.

So, what happens when they alter a normal, healthy brain? All manner of things could potentially go wrong, maybe even creating the Infected Zombie. An actual living, mind altered psychotic monster infected with microscopic cyborgs! How long does it take for an 'infected' person to turn on you? There is no way to know; only experience will tell.

The really scary thing about nanobots is the variety of ways in which these little machines could jump from zombie to person or possibly spread without assistance from zombies. Depending on the type of devices they could pass through bites but could also be passed through simple bodily contact. The best way to avoid this is to ensure you wear sealed, quality clothing and ensure you are decontaminated after contact. If these nanobots have the ability to move and work through clothing then quite simply, we are all screwed! If you are facing nanobots you must stay well clear of Zombies and ideally, well out of the area they inhabit.

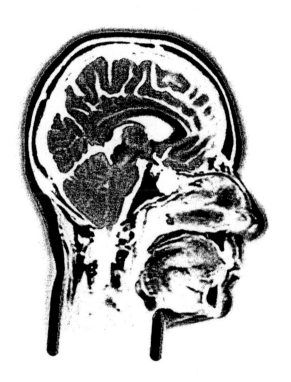

Already research has been conducted in creating a fusion of nano and flesh to create what we might call a nano-cyborg. This bizarre idea is realised by fusing a tiny silicone chip to a virus. One of the first findings was that these tiny cyborgs can still operate for up to a

A victim of nanobots could theoretically have the same life expectancy and food requirements as an uncontaminated human. This assumes that the nanobots will not be programmed to repair damage or to create energy in a non-standard way. If the latter it possible then you might be looking at a form of super zombie that can last longer and maybe even self repair! Be afraid...be very afraid!

INFECTION

Infection is the detrimental colonization of a host organism by a foreign species, in this case a human body. In an infection, the infecting organism seeks to use the host's resources to multiply, usually at the expense of the host. The infecting organism, or pathogen, interferes with the normal functioning of the host and can lead to chronic wounds, gangrene, loss of an infected limb, and even death.

Infection is one of the conventionally accepted causes of zombieism. A brain disorder, spread through traditional infection is already a problem, such as Creutzfeldt–Jakob (CJD) disease, otherwise known as 'Mad Cow' Disease. This disease turns a normal cow into a confused creature, but most worryingly it can be passed to humans that suffer the same fate. This ultimately raises the question, what else is out there either natural or manufactured that can affect brain function and can create a new breed of infected and violent creatures?

The frightening thing about such infectious brain disorders is that they can be both adaptive and can also be spread in a variety of ways. Rabies, for example is spread through exchange of bodily fluids, in this case through a bite wound, and can turn a placid animal into a mad and dangerous one. The same can be true for humans as well as rabies is communicable to humans. Furthermore what if these diseases make it into the water supply? You could end up with the horrifying scenario played out in the movie, 'Cabin Fever' where the youngsters become affected by the diseased water and turn on each other. This is not dissimilar to the strain of 'Rage Virus' in '28 days later'. It shows many of the same symptoms of rabies and is spread through infection of the blood. What if such a virus makes it into the eco-system?

Another thing to consider is whether an infection that starts in humans can be passed to other animals. Based on known science we can find many examples of species specific diseases as the norm but there are those that can sometimes adjust and make the jump to another species. Bearing in mind the nature of infection to spread themselves to their hosts, you would want to avoid contact with the diseased as much as possible. This means avoiding both proximity and also contact with the infected. Also, do not eat or feed from those that have been contaminated or have eaten from contaminated food sources. Again, the mad cow disease example is a good one. Don't eat the beef from an infected cow!

Zombies with an infectious brain disorder can live the same length of time as any human, as long as it is able to fend for itself. They will need to feed and will suffer the same ailments as anybody else. Another important point is how long does it take an infected person to turn into a zombie or enter a zombie like state? Again, this is down to the individual and also the incubation period of the disease or ailment. Currently these problems take time to surface, usually months or even years. That doesn't mean the changes will not happen in a matter of days though with something new and nastier. As with other types of zombie, you need to wait and monitor others to get a good idea as to the means of spread, disease control and mortality.

POISON

Poisons are substances that can cause disturbances to organisms, usually by chemical reaction or other activity on the molecular scale, when a sufficient quantity is absorbed by an organism. The use of poison to damage or control people dates back many centuries and is where the idea of the zombie originates. There are certain kinds of poisons that slow your bodily functions to the point that you would be considered dead, even by a doctor. We have all seen plays where the hero takes

poison to simulate death to get out of awkward situations such as, 'Romeo and Juliet'. The poison from fugu (Japanese blowfish) can induce a death-like state and it is easy for people to be convinced by this. The problem is that to bring them back to life you need to use an alkaloid and this can leave them in a trance-like state with no memory, but still able to perform simple tasks like eating, sleeping, moaning and shambling. Does this sound familiar to you? Does this resemble a Zombie?

Again, this isn't completely fiction as something similar has happened in Haiti. There is a famous case of a man who died from poisoning and was administered an alkaloid to counteract it. He was buried, but amazingly the locals found him wandering around the village 18 years later. This case of an actual zombie had been created with naturally occurring chemicals.

BRAIN PARASITES

Parasitism is a type of symbiotic relationship between organisms of different species where one organism, the parasite, benefits at the expense of the host. It is possible that these frightening microscopic parasites could turn victims into mindless, zombie-like slaves. Believe it or not these microbes are fairly common in nature. You might think the bugs in Star Trek II were bad enough but these parasites can be truly scary. For example, there's one called toxoplasmosagondii that infects rats, but can only breed inside the intestines of a cat. The parasite actually forces the rat to seek out cats so they can kill and eat the rat, thus allowing the parasite to live and breed inside the cats intestines. Pretty sick huh? Imagine if something similar to this moved onto humans, what kind of sick, violent tendencies could these bring out in the living? Flesh eating perhaps?

TYPES OF ZOMBIE

From information in films, literature and other sources, most people think the only kind of zombie is a slow moving, shambling corpse. We have already shown that a re-animated corpse is possible but further research can show that there are many other types of zombies with many different and very dangerous traits. From our research we can simplify our study of these creatures into two broad categories or groups of zombie; we will call them the Undead and the Infected and understanding the differences will become critical to your survival.

Be careful as there is on occasion some overlap between the types of zombies and in some cases you will start with an example of the infected and then move onto undead! If you consider the example of a person that is mortally injured and then attacked and bitten by undead zombies you may find that they slowly slip away, possibly exhibiting some of the symptoms of the zombies before they die. Once they are dead they would presumably rise as a brand new, reasonably fresh zombie. In the first minutes, hours or days these zombies may even have partially functioning bodies; this could result in the undead zombie sharing some of the features such as speed or strength of the infected zombie. Another possibility is that the undead zombie; when fresh may retain more of its mental capacity and thus be able to problem solve, recall past memory or even operate machines and equipment. Could you face a number of fast, strong, weapon wielding zombies that can work together and problem solve?

We need to look at the key strength and weakness of these two creatures to help us formulate our survival plan and hopefully save the remnants of humanity. Read this with care!

UNDEAD ZOMBIES

The traditional Undead zombies are typically depicted in popular culture as mindless, unfeeling monsters with a hunger for human brains and flesh. Typically, these creatures can sustain damage far beyond that of a normal, living human. Generally they can only be killed by a wound to the head, such as a headshot, and can pass whatever syndrome or infection causes their condition onto others. The key element of this monster is that it is dead, either because it is reanimated after a natural death or was infected, died and then re-animated. Why are they called undead? Quite simply they are dead but somehow the remains have been made to move and attack.

IDENTIFICATION

❖ No need to sleep
❖ Does not feel or react to pain
❖ No need to breath
❖ Can continue even after sustaining injury
❖ Speed and movement <u>should</u> be impaired due to atrophy
❖ Smell – poor hygiene and decay
❖ Poor hearing and vision
❖ Pale skin

SPREAD

❖ Fluid transfer through bite or other physical contact
❖ Zombification upon physical death

Notes: The time from bite to zombification is uncertain and must be observed in several cases to determine.

Though they can move their organs no longer work and their bodies continue to rot. How can we spot an undead zombie in a crowd or out on its own? Well, by default a zombie is nearly identical to a regular human. They shouldn't be sprouting extra limbs or horns but if they do then take necessary precautions such as either running like hell or shooting them, then running like hell!

In the first few weeks the infected will look exactly like a human, their bodies are the same and they will be wearing the clothes they were originally found in. The changes will become more evident over time as their clothes rot or fall apart and their bodies will start to take damage and deteriorate, the rate of which will be determined by the environment. A zombies flesh will rot far more slowly in cold climates or winter than in the warm temperate climates of summer or the tropics. Even more noticeable will be their smell, eau de rot is not nice!

What motivates an undead zombie? How long will they 'live' and what keeps them alive? An undead zombie will have impaired or reduced reasoning due to brain damage upon death. Higher reasoning is located in the neo-cortex and is the first part of the brain to become damaged with starvation of oxygen upon death when someone dies. The longer they have been dead the less of a threat they should be. Note the word, should as this is not necessarily a given!

Recently converted zombies are possibly a whole different breed compared to the long term dead coming back to life and may actually exhibit more of the traits of the infected than the undead! A long term re-animated zombie that has been converted immediately after death could in theory have full use of their major organs and body parts and therefore be as quick and as strong as the living!

A long term undead zombie however will suffer problems in a variety of ways. For starters they will not be able to swim as without air in their lungs they will sink. Zombies will also find climbing and jumping difficult due to wasted muscles and poor vision do to degeneration of the eye. Due to the much reduced mental capacity and damaged senses the zombie will find problem solving to be difficult though not impossible. In theory the longer the zombie was dead before being 'raised' the weaker they should be due to the damage to their muscles and body parts. This is all theory though and as always, actual observation of the undead is the safest way to be sure.

STRENGTHS

An undead zombie has a few things in its favour, the first being the fact that it is dead. This makes the zombie impervious to attacks that would kill a living creature. Poisoning of the air supply, excessive heat, chemical or biological attacks would have no or limited effect on the dead. It would certainly no affect them in reaching you. Another advantage of being dead is there is no need for a circulatory system. This means the zombie can take substantial punishment to the body and limbs without actually stopping the creature. As the brain is the only thing providing the re-animated creatures with control, then destroying it is the only thing that will stop them.

WEAKNESSES

The most obvious weakness to the undead zombie is the same as their strength and this is the fact that they are dead. Being dead means that organs, muscles, tissue and tendons will rot, collapse and atrophy. The end result is that large parts of the undead zombie will perform poorly or not at all. Motor skills are going to be diminished over time due to decay and loss of brain function. Remember, they have to die first and the longer they are dead before they rise again, the more their brain will

be damaged. If the body has been dead a long time then there is little chance of any useful motor function being retained?

A human suffers increasingly irreversible brain damage every minute after the first 3-5 minutes without oxygen, so brain damage is quick and permanent. Once the victim dies they can be without oxygen for quite some time before the virus takes hold and resurrects the host as one of the undead. The loss of blood flow to the brain carrying oxygen causes massive amounts of brain damage and this accounts for most of the flaws inherent to the undead zombie. Simple decay also causes the zombie to be weakened as they lose the ability to move and grasp hold of their prey over time. This also causes them to be vulnerable to elements and physical damage as their flesh loses elasticity and its ability to maintain shape. Also, as the decomposition process continues a zombie's senses will deteriorate as the required hearing, smelling and sight organs begin to rot away. In short, time is on the side of the living if they can try to outlive the undead. Keep in mind that the physical ability of a Zombie depends on the condition of the host before infection and also the condition

after taking damage from falls, bumps and attack by the living.

You can expect undead zombies to be slow though exact speeds should be determined through observation. Ask yourself how well you would run with bruises on your knees and a stressed iliotibial band? Well imagine both legs are rotting and one foot is broken and twisted, your speed and control will be substantially reduced.

INFECTED ZOMBIES

Infected zombies may well share many similar attributes with the undead zombie. In fact it is possible that after being bitten by an undead zombie, the living may 'turn' into an infected zombie before finally dying or possibly even remain as an infected zombie, thus creating another strain of creature. An infected zombie, just like an undead zombie will look essentially the same as any human, the defining characteristics are those created by the infection itself and its associated effects. Look for violence, animalistic behaviour, symptoms of brain damage and possible damaged flesh or clothing. Zombies will not take care of personal hygiene so look for the stench of the dead, decaying and unwashed.

As seen in recent films such a Zack Snyder's 'Dawn of the Dead' remake and '28 Days Later', these zombies are sometimes known as running zombies or fast zombies. This is simply down to the fact that these zombies are still living, breathing creatures with at least the same physical abilities of any other human.

Some further important questions about the infected are what motivates an infected zombie? How long will they 'live' and what keeps them alive? An infected zombie will have a variety of motivations depending on their original character, the extent to which their judgment and mental capacity has been damaged and how animalistic the infection makes them. Assume the worst and hope for the best! You can probably assume at the very least that the infected zombie will treat you as hostile; the worst case scenario is that they will actively seek out the living either as food or as simply an enemy or competition to eliminate.

IDENTIFICATION

- ❖ May not feel or react to pain
- ❖ Torn or damaged clothing
- ❖ Blood coming from the mouth
- ❖ May have untreated injuries
- ❖ May fight after injured
- ❖ Unable to communicate

SPREAD

- ❖ Bite or other physical contact
- ❖ Contamination may be fatal
- ❖ Zombification could take place when alive or dead

Notes:
The time from bite to zombification is uncertain and must be observed in several cases to determine.

STRENGTHS

An infected zombie is going to have advantages and disadvantages due to their altered state. These zombies will demonstrate acts of what appears to be super human feats of strength but this is simply their ability to function without the restraints that confine

human behaviour daily and also their greater tolerance or disregard for pain. Absence of pain or certainly the ability to act without the debilitating effect of pain can make zombies appear massively strong. Humans can exhibit super-human feats of strength when motivated but will eventually succumb to pain and fall victim to simple body mechanics. They may be able to perform these feats of strength simply because they cannot feel the pain that causes us humans to cease our actions. Thus they continue to pursue through all obstacles simply because they do not know to stop as their motivation overrules their pain sensors.

Another side-effect of this absence of pain or weariness is that a zombie can continue way past the physical levels expected from a living human. Whilst a fence or secure door might hold against a sustained 30 minute assault by a living human pounding their fists into the door, what would happen to a zombie? These creatures could strike until their hands crumple and rot whilst their bodies will keep them going until they are physically unable to stand. It is possible than a single zombie could actually keep up this assault for hours or days. If you then increase the zombie numbers from one to one hundred then you will find all but the most secure door and fortifications will succumb to their relentless assault.

The other senses may also appear to be super human simply because they do not analyze information the way humans do. While a human will observe and study something till they are aware of what they are looking at, a zombie will see it, smell it, hear it etc, and instantly "investigate". This may come across as a zombie somehow behaving in a more intelligent manner than they really are.

WEAKNESSES

The greatest flaw of the infected is that they will act on their animalistic tendencies and investigate anything that interests them. This tendency will be handy for the living in the creation of traps and plans to avoid and destroy them. Do remember though, that the infected can easily retain parts of their previous lives depending on the damage the infection to the brain that the infection itself causes. It is also fair to assume that over time, neglect, poor diet and damage will be enough to weaken and damage the infected to a sufficient level to render them impotent. For example, if you injure an infected zombie, it will not attempt to fix itself or seek medical attention. It will succumb to infection, disease and further damage making them even more susceptible than the living to medium to long term damage. This knowledge is useful when planning your defences, as they can be structured to inflict further damage, making it much harder for the infected zombie to reach you. An example is creating a layered defence for a building. Rather than just reply on sturdy wall you can erect various barriers that can inflict minor damage that will slow down the infected making finishing them off at your walls much easier and safer.

KILLING ZOMBIES

Once zombies are a reality and roaming the street and countryside it is important to know how to stop the menace both in the short and long term. The eventual aim is to eradicate the threat forever. Both types of zombies, whether undead or infected can be weapons sections will provide detailed information on specific weapons, equipment and techniques to kill these creatures, whatever the type of zombie, quickly and efficiently.

neutralised. The common theme with all zombies is to destroy the brain; this will render a zombie ineffective and unable to cause further harm. It is still important to ensure the destruction of the motionless corpse. The most important thing to know before you can kill a zombie is to identify what you are dealing with. If you are facing off an undead zombie there is no point in stabbing it in the heart unless you get a kick out of sticking a pointed weapon into a shambling thing. You must therefore be able to identify the threat and know how to neutralise it quickly and cleanly with minimal danger to you and your party of survivors. Reading the equipment and

FIGHTING UNDEAD ZOMBIES

Undead zombies are very different to other creatures you may have experienced. They are no longer human and thus no longer subject to the human limits of morality and other higher behaviours. The only way to be sure of killing them is by destruction of the brain stem. Due to how the brain is constructed, this means that sword cuts or bullet impacts to the brain may not be enough to completely kill a zombie. Decapitation will of course separate the head from the body and thus leave only a head that could cause you a problem. The actual brain stem itself must be shot, cut, crushed or burnt to be 100% certain of the death of the zombie. It is worth remembering that no matter whether you have successfully killed the zombie or not, fire is your friend and by burning the body you can be certain of keeping yourself and your friend's safe. It is possible that a reanimated zombie could be destroyed using large quantities of acid, though obtaining and using dangerous chemicals is probably not a good idea. Freezers are also a way of stopping the undead though this is perhaps not the most practical method! The most important thing concerning killing zombies, as previously stated, is that destroying the brain stem or burning the zombie is a guarantee of a good kill. Just make sure when you go for the head that you aim for the brain stem which is situated at the rear of the brain, at the top of the spinal column. When shooting, aim between the eyes and you will have a better chance of hitting it, even better hit them from behind at the base of the skull with a heavy object or sharp weapon.

FIGHTING INFECTED ZOMBIES

Infected zombies are easier to understand than other zombies because they are in fact still human and subject to the weakness of any human. Simply put they can be killed by anything that will kill an uninfected human and as quickly as an uninfected human. This means that weapons, ammunition and other equipment designed to be used against people will work on those infected just as well. Remember though, it is of paramount importance to avoid the infection yourself. This is spread through transfer of bodily fluids such as blood, saliva or sweat. So you do not want bits of zombie hitting you if you use weapons like shotguns or explosives. to actually kill the infected zombie, a shot or blow to a major nerve junction will stop them immediately. You can also kill them effectively by aiming for major organs such as the heart, lung or brain. Destruction of a major organ will kill them after a short period of time, dependent on how good the hit is! Note

though, aiming for specific organs such as the heart and lungs is not always easy. As previously explained, you need to be careful about spreading the blood of zombies as it will help spread infection. Extra care then should be taken using edged and blunt trauma weapons in close combat. Strikes to the spinal column and neck are great ways to bring this type of creature to the ground. Remember that the infected could be faster, stronger and more powerful than you so engage them in close quarter combat with weapons at your peril. Always observe the zombie so that you are familiar with its physical traits and limitations. Something else to bear in mind is that an infected zombie will eventually succumb to death if it is not able to keep its body working. Therefore starvation, lack of oxygen or water can also help cull the menace of the infected.

There is a possibility that an infected person may be treatable as an antidote may exist or one may be created to reduce or remove the problem. This is unknown though and something that cannot be relied upon in the short term. It should not stop you from dealing with the menace at hand as you could be infected next. Remember that with vaccines comes the possibility of new strains of the virus becoming more tolerant, perhaps making it even worse than the original! Drugs may also be used to halt the progress of the infection for some time, possibly even keep it under control until your drug supply runs out. Keeping an infected person around is a big, big risk to take and you need to consider this very carefully as you can guarantee they will always turn on you at the worst possible moment! If a member of your party becomes infected, you must consider your survival and that of the rest of your healthy party first.

Difficult decision may have to be made, so make sure you consider such possibilities in advance so that you may deal with it effectively no matter what choice you make.

ZOMBIES IN WATER

Most of the globe is covered in water and in many cases the idea of fleeing to the sea to escape the zombies is a good idea. Either staying at sea or finding safe, secluded islands is a popular plan and one of the ideas outlined later in the Survival Strategies chapter. There are however some important questions that need to be answered with regards to zombies and water. The first question is simply, can zombies swim? Well, this depends on a couple of factors, the first one of course is whether the zombie itself is infected or one of the undead. An infected zombie is a living creature like any other human and so in theory can do anything a human can. Depending on the type of infection and its effects you may find a zombie will be unable to co-ordinate breathing and swimming motions without drowning. The best way to find out is to observe a zombie in water. If the zombies can't swim safely then you have found a new way to kill them!

As far as undead zombies are concerned, there are different considerations. For a creature to float it must contain some kind of buoyancy. For the living, the air in the lungs provides this

buoyancy. The undead have no working lungs and thus no air in them to float. The undead may have rotting organs and flesh though, and these will emit methane gas. This gas can form in pockets and may allow them to float. In the long term though the zombies will sink like a stone but will still be able to move. Yes, that's right, the undead zombies could potentially sink to the bottom and then walk along the sea or river bed. Take care when setting anchors and mooring lines as these could potentially be climbed by zombies that have the physical ability to pull themselves up the lines and onto your boat. Never, ever let your guard down.

UNDERWATER COMBAT

So, if zombies may be underwater then, how do you fight them there? This is a good question. First of all, why are you in the water? If you fall in or are swimming across a river, you will encounter several problems. The single biggest one is lack of visibility under the water. Not all of us live in the tropics with warm, clear water. If you live in the UK you can expect cold water with limited to almost zero visibility, especially in rivers. From this murkiness a zombie could reach out, grab, bite and attack you. Basically keep out of the water unless you have absolutely no choice. If you are forced to fight them either on the surface

or underwater you need to use their weaknesses against them. The undead can't generally float so you have a height advantage and can attack from above. Against the infected you have a big problem unless you can get them underwater and hope they drown before they realise the danger.

In terms of which weapons and equipment to use underwater, there are only a few truly effective options available to you. First of all you will need breathing equipment and ideally a wet or dry suit to keep warm. Decent scuba kit is recommended as well as the knowledge and skills to use it safely,. Don't dive only to find your kit doesn't work and you have too many weights! Edged weapons can be used, though the water will reduce your speed and effectiveness. The traditional underwater weapon is the harpoon or spear. These can be found in diving and marine specialist stores. There are many types, some of which are gas powered. Shooting zombies underwater is ineffective and not highly recommended. Guns of course do not work underwater but even if you are on a boat, hitting a zombie underwater can be tricky. One other weapon that may be of use in an emergency is the propeller of your boat though you can expect to take damage and possibly love the ability to continue travel in this craft.

THE ZOMBIE BRAIN

As they were originally human, both types of zombie possess the same physical body parts as living and uninfected humans, though the physiological characteristics may be altered and various organs and systems may be compromised or become redundant. Of all the organs the brain is the most important to consider as it is the root of what separates humans from zombies.

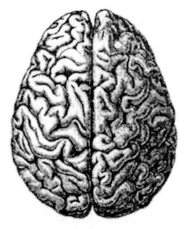

The ability to conduct complex behaviours, such as higher reasoning, which is found in highly developed animals such as man, apes and dolphins are located in the cortex, which is the outermost layer of the two hemispheres of the brain. If you were to remove the cortex in animals, their behaviour would become purely instinctive and 'stereotyped'. They would simply react to certain stimuli in a predictable and consistent manner and their behaviour would be based purely on instinct alone. Such is the behaviour of the zombie, who loses the capacity to exhibit higher social behaviours as the cortex is the first part of the brain to be damaged when starved of oxygen, as in death. It can easily be affected by infectious disease that is able to cross the blood brain barrier that encases and protects the brain.

When a zombie is created a form of incomplete brain death occurs. The higher brain functions are disabled and the mechanical and motor control centres remain, complete with a small amount of memory function. This results in the limited aspects of zombie behaviour; they can move around and exhibit other motor skills, such as eating and drinking, but lack coherent consciousness or higher functions such as speech, morality or table manners! To kill a zombie, as has already been emphasised, you must kill the parts of the brain that allow it to function. This includes the cerebellum, which is the centre for motor skills and co-ordination, and the brain stem which controls breathing. Both are situated at the rear base of the brain, beneath the cortex and immediately above the spinal column.

> "The cerebral hemispheres are the two largest structures at the top of the brain which enfold (and, therefore, conceal from view) most other brain structures. [...] The top layer of the cerebrum (about 1cm at its deepest) is the cerebral cortex (usually just called 'cortex' which means 'bark'). [...] About three-quarters of the cortex does not have an obvious sensory or motor function and is known as the association cortex; this is where the 'higher mental functions' (cognition) - thinking, reasoning, learning, etc. - probably 'occur'. [...] There is no doubt that the cortex is not necessary for biological survival [...] as some species do not have one to begin with (e.g. birds) and in those that do, surgical removal does not prevent the animal from displaying a wide range of behaviour, although it becomes much more automatic and stereotyped."
>
> "Psychology: The Science of Mind and Behaviour" by Richard Gross, p55-56

FALSE POSITIVES

You might be wondering what false positives are? Quite simply this refers to recognizing those that look like zombies but are in fact human. We've all met people who act, smell or look like zombies, but in fact might simply be homeless people or those that play MMORPGs too much, and in the longer term is likely to be those who do not keep up with personal hygiene and have become weak. Believe it or not you might think someone suffering from fatal alcohol syndrome might be a zombie or how about a catatonic schizophrenic? Either of these could be easily mistaken when in fact they are a wandering, mentally ill stranger. We have all encountered our fair share of glassy-eyed drooling vegetables but who's to say whether these people are zombies or not? Do also remember though that though they may not actually be a zombie do you really want them in your team? If they are family members of friends you may not be able to leave them behind but if they are strangers or those that you find on your travels they may prove to be more of a hindrance than a help. Later sections of this book cover whom you may want in your party and more importantly, whom you don't want in your team of survivors! In a post-zompoc world, euthanasia for people unable to contribute or fend for themselves may be a kinder alternative than leaving them to starve, or worse still, become a zombie victim.

CHAPTER 2: PRE-APOCALYPSE PREPARATION

A wise man in times of peace prepares for war.
Horace

Surviving the first day of the Zompoc will be partly do to luck and partly to do with preparation. You cannot affect your luck, but you can be prepared. Many natural disasters, such as Hurricane Katrina, Mouth St Helens and more recently, the earthquakes in Sumatra have shown that most people are not remotely prepared for any kind of disaster. They rely on their country's emergency services and infrastructure to look after them, which in most cases clearly hasn't worked very well. It is a well known fact that people who survive such disasters are willing to do anything to stay alive. They are prepared to fight as hard as they can and refuse to roll over and die. This mindset can massively improve their odds of survival. Combine this with a decent survival kit and a bit of preparation and you will have a fighting chance, quite literally. This type of preparation is also recommended by the Dept for Homeland Security in the United States as preparation against all kinds of disasters.

SURVIVAL KIT

A survival kit, or 'bug-out' kit is a pre-prepared kit of basic items that you can grab within a few seconds and contains everything to prepare you for survival, typically for around 72 hours. The 72 hour period is a vital one, as this will be the most dangerous hurdle that you face initially. Surviving the first onslaught and establishing your new way of life will be a huge shock to the system. There are many considerations to be made in a survival kit, but most of it is related to personal hygiene, food and warmth, as well as basic utilities.

This kit needs to be completely accessible at all times. This may mean putting together several kits to keep in different locations. The first most obvious location for a survival kit is in your home. Whether you decide to hold up in your home, or 'bug-out', this kit will be extremely useful. Consider keeping a second kit in your car and possibly one at work also. When finding a location to keep the survival kit, make sure it is easy to remember and always to hand. Do not let it become piled under junk in a storage room. Typical places to keep a survival kit would be under your bed, in the boot (trunk) of your car and under your computer desk (at home or work).

A list of items to include in your kit follows. This list isn't exhaustive but remember that you must be able to carry it.

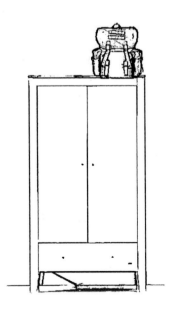

KIT CONTENTS

- ❖ drinking water
- ❖ a first aid kit that includes extra items such as Neosporin ointment, gauze rolls and extra tape
- ❖ a box of antibacterial wipes.
- ❖ a bottle of antibacterial hand sanitizer. It is a good idea to include a small bottle for each family member or friend.
- ❖ toilet paper
- ❖ feminine hygiene products (can be used to dress wounds and stop nose bleeds)
- ❖ clean white towels and face cloths
- ❖ an alcohol or gel fuel stove and a pot large enough to boil water and wash towels and clothing.
- ❖ toothpaste
- ❖ Toothbrush
- ❖ hydrogen peroxide.

- ❖ isopropyl alcohol.
- ❖ Flashlight and spare batteries
- ❖ 36 Hour Emergency Candles - These can also be used for a emergency stove
- ❖ Green Emergency Glow Sticks - These typically last 12 hours each
- ❖ Survival Whistle
- ❖ Compass
- ❖ Signal mirror
- ❖ Flint starter - for starting fires
- ❖ Waterproof containers or bags
- ❖ Box of 50 Waterproof Matches
- ❖ Lighter
- ❖ Warm Jacket
- ❖ Multi-Function Knife
- ❖ Leather Palmed Working Gloves
- ❖ At least 45 Feet of Nylon Rope
- ❖ Roll of Gaffer Tap

After putting together these essential items, you should also add items that are important to you personally, such as prescription medications that you would need to keep taking or a spare pair of glasses. Your survival kit should be packed in a robust and easy to carry pack, a hiking day pack. You may also want toad some food items, though be sure these are not perishable and lightweight. Survival kits are intended to keep one person equipped for three days, but what about others around you? You may well have other friends, family members or fellow survivors making camp with you, but what if they do not have survival packs? If those around you are not as prepared as you are then they will drain your resources, reducing your chance of survival. Make sure all of your friends and family keep at least basic survival kits to hand at all times, as it is important to your survival as it is to theirs.

LEAVING YOUR HOME BEHIND

No one ever knows when a life-changing emergency might occur. When and if it does take place you must be ready to act immediately. Whether you hold up inside your own home, or you evacuate and become

mobile you need to be prepared. As previously stated, the first 72 hours immediately following a disaster are critical. It is likely you will not have electricity or running water. In the case of the Zompoc, emergency services will be in chaos and will not be able to respond to you, so you will be on your own.

One of key preparations you can make is to have an evacuation plan in place should you need to leave your home immediately. Each family member or occupant should have a responsibility and a function to optimise the departure process and eliminate duplication of tasks. Rehearsing this, even just the verbal plan, on a regular basis is good practice and can be a good way of checking everyone knows what to do and keeping plans up to date if things change. Be sure that you and all those around you are familiar with all potential entry and exit points in the building, whether that is your own home, work or that of other family members or friends. This also means knowing where all keys are kept, how window locks operate and where your survival kit is located along with quick routes to vehicles among other considerations.

MEETING POINT

If you need to leave your home for safety reasons, another preparation you can make is to have a prearranged meeting place away from home where your friends and family can reunite in case an emergency prevents you from returning to your home. If communication lines are not working, a known designated location can provide a rendezvous point to gather. This meeting point needs to be a sensible one, well placed and secure, as well as accessible when need be. Motorway/highway junctions are a possibility, as they allow for good visibility and easy escape options. A building rooftop is another, easily defended and with access to other adjacent buildings if need be. Out of town petrol (gas) stations are also a potential meeting point as they typically feature roofs or shelters which you can climb on to for safety

while you wait and also allow a place for your car to be parked nearby in emergencies.

Your choice of a sensible meeting point will depend on where you live and what is best for your circumstances. It may be beneficial to designate several meeting points in a priority tiered system, so that if one is compromised you can still find each other. If you have a tiered system for meeting points, ensure that each of them is quite different to the other, as if one is compromised it is likely that other similar locations may also be so. Ideally, choose three locations and order them by priority of distance from you. So if you live in a town or city, one would be nearby, one would be in the suburbs and the final one would be on the outskirts or in a semi-rural area.

If you often work away from home or your friends and family live apart across a large area, set nearby meeting points for those local to you for initial emergencies, and regional or national meeting points for the others. This will of course depend on where you live and how much distance is between the various friends and family you have. If there is more than a 100 mile gap between people then you are better off not trying to meet up initially, unless the distance between you are rural or barren and easily crossed.

AWARENESS IN NORMAL LIFE

It is impossible to predict when the Zompoc could start and where will you be. You could be at home, at work, in the street, or in a pub. Learning to be aware of all that happens around you is a vital skill in identifying when things will start to go downhill. When you are in unfamiliar territory, try and face the entrances of the room so that you can see all around you and keep a good eye on all that is happening around you when outdoors. Do not day dream as you walk through the street, but have your wits about you and use your peripheral vision. Other simple awareness and observation skills can also make all the difference in a survival situation. Whenever you enter any building, make a mental note of where all potential exits are, which will include doorways, fire exits and windows. Also know where any potentially useful items are, such as fire axes which can be found in some buildings for example.

IF YOU ARE ABROAD DURING THE OUTBREAK

Depending on how often you leave your own country or travel long distance within your own within it, there will always be a risk that the Zompoc may start in your home town, region or country, or that it starts right where you are. Preparing for either of these eventualities is very difficult. If the outbreaks begins in or near your home area, do not attempt to return there, use the time you have to prepare as best you can or 'bug out'. Having to survive away from familiar surroundings such as your home or work and possibly culture puts you at a distinct disadvantage. It is

likely you will be without a survival kit and without an extensive knowledge of the area. The best course of action is to band together with local survivors, who can provide the knowledge you have not got. If the zombie outbreak begins near to where you are while you are a long distance from home, then 'bug out'. Attempting to get home may or may not be a possibility depending on distance and accessibility to transport and roads. You will have to decide on the best course of action dependant on your location and circumstances. Do however, bare in mind that the outbreak is likely to spread very quickly and getting home will not necessarily make you any safer, and it could waste potential preparation time.

COMMON SENSE PROTECTION

The knowledge and ability to protect yourself can be the difference between surviving the initial Zompoc strike and becoming a victim of it. Firstly, do not leave your house or work doors open and unlocked at night or if you do not have an unobstructed view of them. Equally, do not leave windows open. This kind of common sense advice is applicable to normal everyday life anyway, yet some people still do not follow it. Ensuring that your vehicle is always in good working order and that it is at least reasonably appropriate to escape in if need be. For example, a convertible is less than ideal due to its soft top so at least have it as a spare car only.

Do not rely on the internet or television for all of your knowledge. When people face power cuts, they truly realise how cut off and helpless they can be. When you want to check something, such as a location, an ingredient or a review, you may normally go online but this is not a luxury you will have during any apocalypse. After having read this manual you should have a good idea of what sorts of information you are going to need to know. Do some research on your local area and things that will be close to hand, like store types, petrol/gas stations and suchlike. Knowing your area is vitally important. Too many people today rely on satellite navigation. Satnav will likely still work while you can power it, but without internet access it is likely be difficult to find the address of where you want to go anyway. Familiarize yourself with your area and the surrounding areas also. Know multiple routes of getting to the same places in case certain roads are impassable for any reason.

Having this knowledge readily to hand could save you valuable time and ensure you stay ahead of the zombie horde and the panicking crowd fleeing them.

SURVIVAL TRAINING

Traditional survival training includes many elements, typically revolving around surviving in hostile, volatile, native or barren environments. Much of this survival training may not be helpful to you in the short to medium term; but in the long term it could mean the difference between life and death. If you survive long enough, you will have to learn to look after yourself and others without the logistical support of a modern government and the society that you know today. However, in

the short term certain survival skills could also be useful to you, dependant on your situation. If you live in a remote location or happened to be in one when the Zompoc starts, then this training will be especially useful to you.

Survival training covers a huge array of subjects and topics and you should consider further independent research and training if you can. This training often revolves around self-sufficiency which is a skill that few people possess today. Even if the exact skills are not relevant to you, the philosophy can get your head in the right place and help a lot when you are up against the wall. At the very least it will provide you with information on sheltering, finding food and staying out of trouble!

FIRST AID

In any kind of apocalypse you are going to have to look after yourself and those around you. It is certainly beneficial to know basic first aid, including dressing wounds, splinting broken bones and treating other aches and pains. In today's society we have access to a huge wealth of highly advanced medical treatments, but during the Zompoc your access to these

will most likely be cut off or severely limited so first aid will be more useful to you than anything high tech or medically complex. Unless you happen to be a trained doctor, paramedic or nurse then you will not know what you are doing anyway. Consider a weekend or day course on first aid to give you a basic grounding in the subject. Remember though, that should a member of your survival party become wounded and infected by a zombie, then there is little you will be able to do to save them.

CUSTOMISATION AND BODGING

Once the apocalypse has begun, you are going to have to rely on your own skills and abilities. In reality most people today have very few skills and abilities that will be of any use when society breaks down and they are on their own. Knowing how to use tools, repair cars, mend clothing and equipment and maintain your house with your own hands and tools are all important. Simple DIY skills will ensure that you are capable when the time comes. Being useful with a hammer and welding equipment is especially useful. Knowing through habit how to assemble and build a variety of objects and a core understanding of constructing strong joints and attachments will be of great use, particularly when it comes to beefing up a vehicle or barricading your home.

OBSTACLE MANAGEMENT

When walking, climbing and running for your life it is vital to your survival to understand how to overcome various terrains. Keeping healthy, fit and strong will certainly assist you in this task. There are additional ways in which you can improve your speed and effectiveness over terrain. Military style training will keep you in shape and assaulting obstacles on a regular basis while parkour is another fine example. Parkour, which loosely translates as free running, is a French developed sport whereby the objective is to tackle obstacles in the fastest and easiest fashion possible. It is certainly a rather specialist and unusual hobby,

but there are other alternatives. Gymnastics will provide fantastic overall body strength, as will climbing, but the regular practice and hobby of any serious physical activity will greatly improve your odds when you need to tackle any terrain.

CHOICE OF HOME

It is highly unlikely that many people will have enough money to upgrade their home to one better suited to the apocalypse, but it can be a consideration if you are already moving. When looking for a new home, consider its security, beyond the normal deterrents to humans such as house alarms (zombies disregard these), and consider things like actual barrier defences. As well as the obvious security features, location is just as important. Cities will be where an infection spreads the quickest and will make survival hardest due to the overwhelming odds. Also give some consideration to the neighbours when looking for a new property. Are they capable people? Do they own weapons and other resources? Could you rely on them for help? Certain locations may give you better immediate protection than others, such as structures built high off the ground, apartments, gated communities, castles and other defendable buildings.

DO NOT RELY ON ELECTRONIC INFORMATION

In society today we largely rely on getting our information electronically, including storing it that way. But what happens when you lose power? For example, imagine that you decide to get a survival manual such as the Zompoc guide, but not having given it proper thought and planning, you go to the internet, click a few buttons and voila, save it on your hard drive, ready for when you need it. But what happens when there is no power or you don't have access to a computer or portable reading device? Any information that could be useful to you must be readily available in a non-electronic format, which includes keeping resource and information books handy, such as ones on first aid, survival techniques, DIY, car repair and other manuals as well as maps which are especially useful.

FORMING GROUPS

Creating a local militia may beyond the realms of realism for many, but forming solid bonds between groups of reliable people is not. Make sure you establish a good relationship with strong reliable people within your community. This could be as simple as joining a local martial arts or sports club, a local gun club, neighbourhood watch and all manner of other groups. Look at your daily and weekly routine and identify who you are likely to be with when the Zompoc hits. The chances are that you will be at work or home, so ask yourself if you are friendly with a good number of active and useful neighbours. Could your work colleagues hold their own in a fight? Having solid, helpful and trusted people around you will be vital for survival.

YOUR HOME, WORK AND CAR

These are the three most likely places that you will be during the start of the Zompoc, so are those three areas ready and prepared? For detailed information on preparing your home for the apocalypse you should check out the section devoted to it later in this manual, but what of your work? Here it is likely that you will not be able to make modifications in advance. What you can do to be prepared at work will of course be dependent on where you work and the type of work you do. Having a survival kit nearby is the most basic change you can make. Put one under your desk, in your locker, and/or in the boot of your car if you travel a lot. The next consideration is to check if you have good visibility from the place where you do your work, such as your desk or work station. Facing away from the door or being too close to a ground floor window could be your downfall. Do what you can to be in the best position as possible when at work at all times so that you will see any potential developments when the Zompoc hits and be prepared to act at all times.

Your car is potentially your main asset for 'bugging out' in the short term. It is possible that when the outbreak occurs that many roads will be completely blocked by those trying to escape, but you have to hope that some options will be available and be prepared to exploit them. A large amount of this will rely on knowledge of the area and potential alternative routes. It is rather unlikely that you will have a vehicle prepared for the Zompoc beforehand as few can afford to kit out and armour their vehicle. However, there are considerations which can make all the difference. Having an off-road vehicle will greatly increase your options when 'bugging out' as well as being better suited all round to travelling during the Zompoc. Making sure your car is well maintained and kept with a good amount of fuel in the tank at all times will ensure that you can rely on it when the time comes. Also, keep a basic tool kit in the trunk or boot of your vehicle for emergencies. This is good practice anyway and a tyre iron can also double as a good makeshift weapon if needed!

EMERGENCY SERVICES

In everyday life we take emergency services for granted as a safety net for everything we do. When considering preparation you need to give plenty of thought to how you can fulfil all of the tasks necessary that you would currently expect of the emergency services. How could you take on their roles when they no longer exist? This may require learning new skills or simply just having some common sense and making do with what knowledge, skills and resources you have to hand.

AMBULANCE/MEDICAL

In the short term you will have nothing more than first aid supplies, so forget things like complicated medication and life support equipment. The biggest risk of injury comes from carelessness and the infected. If somebody does become infected then medical attention will be useless. Euthanisation might be the kindest option in this situation. The other major risk during the Zompoc is from everyday infection due to poor hygiene. Learn to sterilize and clean both injuries and any items of clothing that you have contact with. Aside from this, basic first aid techniques such as using straps and splints and dressing wounds will be of help. Normally, when someone is hurt, the basic response is (or should be) to go and help them, but in many cases during the Zompoc running will be the better option for everyone. They may be infected or violent and may cause you harm.

POLICING

The police maintain law and order which are two elements that will no longer exist, at least on a large scale during an apocalypse. The law will no longer have meaning or use, so forget relying on it, but maintaining order can be considered. This can be maintained by having a strong community with competent leaders. Consider creating or joining a neighbourhood watch scheme or forming a militia (where

legal). At the very least you could gain some leadership training and experience through work, a club or other means that could stand you in good stead if you need to lead or deal with difficult people.

FIRE SERVICE

If any fires are created during the Zompoc then they are almost certainly deliberate and necessary. The best and most likely response should be to run as whatever is on fire may be running at you! In the event of building or vehicle fire that affects you, make sure you are familiar with and have access to hand held extinguishers. Beyond that, if the fire does not threaten you, leave whatever is ablaze and move on. Other tasks of the fire service can be effectively achieved with an axe and crowbar; items that you would be well advised to have to hand.

MOUNTAIN/SEA RESCUE

If you are stupid enough to get stuck up a mountain, on a cliff face or in trouble at sea during the Zompoc, no one will be coming for you. Recreational trips are not recommended so you will have no reason to be in these places. Survival is key during the Zompoc and mountains are treacherous places which increase the chance of sustaining a serious injury and may result in death. If you have got to the point of needing to be rescues at sea then you will already be a gonna. Consider prevention your greatest tool, and if you take to a boat to escape, stay away from rough seas and learn how to swim.

PRODUCIING POWER

You have access to regular and easily accessible power because you live in a developed society. It is provided through a complex network of systems which most will never have to see or be aware of. But how then, will you get power when it's not provided by the national grid? Power is required for a variety of means, from lighting your house to running power tools and cookery. There are an endless number of reasons you will need

power during the Zompoc.

If you choose to lead a nomadic life then water power is unlikely to be useful to you, but portable wind generators and solar panels could provide a solution. Whichever way of life you choose to lead post-zompoc, you should have some understanding of your options in terms of power generation and consider implementing one or more of them.

GENERATORS

Petrol driven generators are relatively common and easy to use. They do however have two draw backs; noise and the need for a fuel supply. Generators will burn through fuel at quite a rate, meaning you will have to keep them topped up regularly. This is not a problem as long as you have good access to fuel and the structure set up to acquire it. In recent times a growing number of people have been buying larger generators as a secondary power source for their homes. These would be excellent in a Zompoc if you decide to hold up at home and can keep them re-supplied. The noise of a generator however is a big problem, as they will draw a lot of attention to yourself as well as reducing your awareness to danger from approaching sounds.

WIND POWER

This source of power is free (after the initial outlay of cash for the equipment), and easily attainable, though not always reliable. Wind power, in the form of domestic windmills are fairly quiet and low maintenance, though power production can be low and weather dependant. The fact that they require no fuel

however, makes them a very valuable option.

WATER POWER

This form of power is rather dependant on your location. Water wheels are complicated to set up unless you have the knowledge and skills, though they do produce good power. Either you are in the right location and know about them or you don't. If not, then discount this option.

SOLAR POWER

The sun is a very powerful source of energy and nearly all living things depend on its

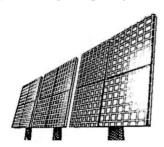

energy. Solar power is the process of converting sunlight to electricity. Solar power can be an intermittent energy source, though fortunately it is fairly predictable when you will and will not have it over a 24 hour period! Solar panels can be fitted to both buildings and vehicles but will currently yield only small amounts of power quite slowly. It is typically used to recharge batteries so that electricity is then available when needed. Solar power will clearly be more useful in some areas than others due to the amount of sunlight and cloud cover.

STAYING FIT AND HEALTHY

Being able to run quickly for a prolonged period, or having enough strength to hoist your entire bodyweight up and over a high wall can make all the difference. Getting the strength and fitness of a world class athlete is not a realistic goal for many, but staying fit healthy and strong is perfectly do-able. Many people today live very sedentary lifestyles due to the nature of office and desk working and

this problem is compounded by the easy access to large quantities of junk food. There is more information in 'The Living' section but joining a gym is a good choice. Even just walking, jogging n or doing some form of exercise every day can help you prepare. Do anything as long as you do it regularly. Supplement this with sensible eating and you should stay in reasonable shape.

In terms of health, you should also give consideration to intoxication and other altered states of mind. If the Zompoc starts when you are intoxicated by alcohol or drugs (whether prescription or illegal), your chances of survival are severely diminished. Severe intoxication is bad for your health and fitness anyway. Moderation is the key to both staying in shape and being alert and aware when disaster strikes.

COMBAT SKILLS

Do not wait for disaster to strike before learning to defend yourself as it will probably be too late. Ideally, you want a good all round knowledge of all the potential options available to you. Joining self-defence clubs, martial arts groups and fencing clubs will all be of benefit in producing a well rounded and aware individual who is able to handle themselves confidently.

Learn to handle any guns that will potentially be available to you. This could be as simple as going Clay pigeon shooting and it will give you a good grounding in the basics of shotgun shooting and usage. Developing gun skills will depend on where you live and what is accessible to you. For example, joining a gun club is easier in the US but in the UK the rules on gun ownership and use are very restrictive. Pistols are banned completely but you can still go clay shooting with shotguns or target shooting with rifles. The best skills are those that you can learn whilst enjoying them as this will encourage you to practice more. Playing Counter –Strike or Halo on the computer do not count towards combat skill training! Learn to use more simple projectile weapons such as longbows and crossbows, even if you do have guns available. There are plenty of archery clubs in most countries, so this is another skill you can develop to prepare.

There are also likely to be times when you don't have a weapon to hand and you will need to be able to handle yourself in this situation. Unarmed combat training is easy to acquire anywhere in the world. Try to concentrate on the more martial of the fighting systems as you need to be able to

actually fight and neutralise an adversary, not just score points in a competition. For example, some forms of karate are orientated for combat while others are geared towards sport competition. Some martial arts training features no sparring at all and this is of little use to you in preparing to defend yourself. You need to practice in a realistic situation and not just go through the moves as it is imperative that you get used to dealing with different combative scenarios with all kinds of people. Close combat weapons based training is slightly more difficult to find, especially in terms of getting regular and realistic sparring practice as opposed to sport derived or form based training. Despite this, there are still plenty of options such as Kali (Pilipino stick fighting), HEMA (Historical European Martial

Arts) and some of the Japanese and Chinese based weapon systems.

Learning tactics will be much harder in civilian life as it simply isn't taught on any kind of regular basis to civilians. Do not worry too much about this, study a few books on the subject and focus your attentions on turning yourself in to a good all round fighter.

DISCUSS YOUR ZOMPOC PLANS

Most people, in particular men, will have given thought to their own personal survival plan in the event of a disaster such as the Zompoc, but only some of what they give thought to gets any serious consideration. Thoughts alone will not save your life if the worst should happen. Share your thoughts and ideas with friends and family and develop the best possible solutions together if possible. Having a shared common knowledge amongst those you know will give you a great source of survivors when the time comes and will assist all of you in becoming effective as quickly as possible.

You can study and read information on surviving the Zompoc, and it is highly recommended that you do, but survival will vary greatly on the location you are in and the people that surround you. Take the best of the information you have researched and apply it to your situation. At the same time, do not widely communicate any plans you might have to work colleagues or casual acquaintances that you do not trust. You do not want the whole world to know where you're going to hold up and get your supplies!

WHAT YOU WEAR

The clothes and items you have on you every day could potentially be what you are stuck with wearing on the first day, or even for the initial first few days of the Zompoc. Have a look at what you typically wear throughout the week from work wear to casual clothes and formal wear. Ask yourself, how would it perform during the Zompoc?

Clothing may seem a trivial consideration but the right clothes can make all the difference to being able to run, climb and fight properly. Your work wear is likely dictated by your job, but that does not mean it has to be restrictive. Most people wear some variation on a suit or a uniform relating to their employer.

The first most obvious element to consider is footwear which will need to be fit to use for any purpose. Shoes to be worn with a suit do not necessarily have to be uncomfortable or restrictive so the key here is to buy decent quality shoes that you can walk long distance in without discomfort. Make sure you wear shoes that will grip well on a variety of surfaces; leather soled shoes for example, will

slip easily on many surfaces. Many women wear heeled shoes to work or when out, or strappy sandals, but most women's formal footwear is incredibly impractical. Forget improving it and just ensure you have easy access to something like trainers at work and in your car. When wearing casual clothes it is common for most people today to wear some variation of trainer or boot which is excellent for general purpose usage.

Ensure that your work wear, even if it is a suit, is not restrictive. Make sure you have full articulation of all your limbs. This also applies to formal wear as it is no good wearing a pair of jeans so tight you can't run, nor so loose that they fall down and trip you up. Be practical with what you wear.

Formal wear tends to be the most restrictive of all clothing and the least practical. The same rules apply to most formal clothing as work clothing. The best option is to ensure you have access to more practical attire nearby. It is probably wise to keep a change of such clothing packed at all times and in your car or with your survival kit, just in case!

QUICK PREPARATION GUIDE

❖ **Find food and water** - You will want to plan for this in advance. If everything breaks down, one of the first things you'll need is an immediate supply of food and water.

❖ **Find a group** - First, there's physical safety in numbers. Second, your immediate family and friends may be to hand and can hopefully be relied upon.

❖ **Pick a leader** - Don't believe, even for a second, that you can survive chaos without installing some kind of order and power structure. You will need this if you are to have any chance of surviving.

❖ **Shelter** – Consider where you plan on hiding out. Is it possible to stay at home or is it untenable to stay there? If you live in a densely populated area, it will probably not be a good place to hide. You will need somewhere defensible and also somewhere that will keep you warm and dry.

❖ **Heating and cooling** - Is the electricity working? If not you will need alternative power sources as it may not come on again, ever! Are there any heat sources available? If not, you will need fire, which of course requires something to burn.

❖ **Fortify your area** - You could use vehicles to build your defence and line cars, busses, or trucks around you for protection. You could try to build a wall if time permits. You could even attempt to build a fort of sorts.

❖ **Collect weapons** - This is an obvious one. Ensure that you know how to use them and practice. Just remember that if someone wants to be a part of your group, their weapons are too.

❖ **Long term** - Finally, think long term when it comes to survival. How are you going to find food and sustain yourselves in the long term? Consider the following:
    a. Rationing the food you have
    b. Freezing food that might go bad (if you have the means). If not, then eat perishable food first
    c. Gather and store seeds for farming possibilities (present and future)
    d. Cattle, pig, chicken and other farm animals availability
    e. Winter rations

CHAPTER 3: SURVIVAL STRATEGIES

*Victory at all costs, victory in spite of all terror, victory however long
and hard the road may be; for without victory there is no survival.*
Winston Churchill

Your survival plan should be essentially divided up into three phases where each is based upon a time period during the Zompoc. Read through these sections and give yourself a rough idea of the plans available to you because when the Zompoc hits you won't have time to debate which are the best options; you will need to act fast.

Luckily, there has already been substantial work done on this subject and this can help you formulate effective plans and strategies for dealing with and surviving the Zompoc. The most recent research is by P Munz, Ioan Hudea, Joe Imad and Robert Smith in their detailed 2009 research piece entititled, 'When Zombies Attack! Mathematical modelling on an Outbreak of Zombie Infection'. In this paper they analysed the mathematical outcomes of various approaches to deal with a zombie outbreak. There are a few provisos that need to be considered with this research, the most important being that it deals with the classic, slow moving undead zombies. They avoided the Infected strain of zombies and

thus do not include a large number of variables. Nonetheless, we can use some of their ideas to help us consider the options. There are many possible strategies you can adopt during the Zompc, from hiding and fleeing, to starting a holy war against the undead. Some of the more common scenarios are presented here. Note that not all of them require going on the offensive.

According to the research carried out by Munz et al, the only possible way to survive in a Zombie uprising is for a co-ordinated and scaled series of military action offensives to cull and force back the numbers. Trying to live alongside the Zombies is impossible due to the fact that overtime the human birth-rate (required to keep the population stable or expanding) will keep the zombie population supplied with fresh subjects to convert.

This chapter deals with possible overall strategies that you can adopt. Refer to additional chapters for details on vehicle preparation, environment, convoys, supplies and weapons, while the Operations chapter deals with specific missions such as raids, re-supply, intelligence, culling and rescue. Assuming you make it through the short and medium term, make sure you check the rebuilding chapter for more information on long term plans and for rebuilding your fledgling society.

YOUR RESPONSIBILITIES

As with all things in life, people have both rights and responsibilities. During the Zompoc your rights are not really of much interest to the shambling zombies but your responsibilities to your fellow survivors is very important. When you include thinking about your responsibilities to others, you will need to come up with a personal survival plan which considers what is important, not just for yourself but also for other people and humanity in general. Yes, you can hide out and wait but what will that do for the rest of the living? It is your responsibility to first keep yourself and your close family and friends alive. Your second responsibility is to ensure that you protect who is left and ultimately remove the zombie menace. Ensure your personal goals are compatible with your long-term plans as you cannot, and will not be able to survive the Zompoc on your own. More importantly, it would be supremely selfish to do so.

SUICIDE

This isn't really a survival strategy but it is an option some will choose to turn to rather than fight or try and survive. There will be some of you for whom the Zompoc will be too much. Either mentally, physically or emotionally you may be unable to do what needs to be done and therefore may decide to end it. If this is a route you find yourself considering once the Zompoc starts, there are a few things to consider. First of all, will your suicide help or hinder those around you? If your family are trying to escape and zombies are battering down the door definitely don't start acting like

---

ORDER OF RESPONSIBILITY

- ❖ **Yourself**. Pretty obvious, if you do not ensure the safety and survival of yourself you will be unable to assist anybody!
- ❖ **Family**. These are your closest relatives that live with you or nearby.
- ❖ **Friends** and colleagues. People you know and are on good terms with.
- ❖ **Pets**. Certain animals can be very useful during the Zompoc.
- ❖ **Strangers**. People you do not know but are alive and potentially useful.

Denethor in 'Lord of the Rings' and start erecting your noose. If you are trapped and have no chance of escape it might be a simple choice between that of avoiding being bitten and becoming a zombie, being eaten alive or a choice of killing yourself. The latter option can obviously be done quickly and painlessly if done correctly. If you are already bitten or infected in some way then you must also consider how to end your life so that you cause the least danger to those around you. Don't be a coward and simply create another zombie with a friendly face that could gain the sympathy of friends or family. It is best for the survival of your family and friends if you take the selfless route; however get an agreement from your comrades that they will burn or destroy your body immediately afterwards.

If you are on your own and you become infected, you need to make sure your conscious brain can never lose control of your soon to become zombie body. This will not be easy but in times of the Zompoc, desperate decisions must be made. If you are forced to take this option, try and take as many zombies with you as you can. A homemade bomb directed at the largest concentration of the enemy will give you a quick death plus help your friends.

72 HOUR SURVIVAL

In terms of survival, the first 72 hours will be the most critical and dangerous times you will have to face. The Zompoc will spread quickly bringing death, destruction and panic to your life and those around you. The decisions you make here will determine both whether you survive the first days and also decide which future options might be left available to you. For example, if on the first day you hide in the top of a skyscraper in Manhattan, you will find that escaping from the building and the city in a Zombie infested locale will be nigh on impossible. If you escape to an island in the first 24 hours you might be safe, maybe even long-term but what about everybody else? This is why the first 72 hours are so important, they will shape your survival and those around you for weeks, months and even years to come.

Should I stay or should I go?

The Clash

STAY OR LEAVE?

Your first decision during the Zompoc is whether you should leave or stay where you are. Depending on your circumstances and the nature of the Zompoc, the first important decision is based upon what is happening and what is likely to happen. You should understand and plan for both scenarios. If the Zompoc strikes hard and fast you may have no time to escape, even if you want to. For example, you may wake up at home to find your entire neighbourhood has turned into the undead and your home is surrounded and besieged. The same could also possibly happen at your workplace as home and work are where most people spend their time. There is of course also a chance you might be at a mall, or other public place when it happens. If the Zompoc uprising occurs quickly, but is effectively dealt with it may be safer to barricade your home and wait it out for a few days. If on the other hand the Zompoc is out of control and zombie hordes roam the streets unchecked then you could end up trapped. You will need information but could find that local authorities may or may not immediately be able to provide up to date information on what is happening and what you should do. Nonetheless it is important to monitor all forms of media communication for the latest news as much as possible. There are other forms of communication that will be important such as word of mouth, CB radios and short wave radios.

STAY

If you choose to stay where you are during the first few days or are forced to stay, there is a list of things that you need to ensure is done to keep you safe and alive. Please remember that hiding out indefinitely is not the same as this short-term measure. See the section covering medium term strategies for staying or hiding for longer periods of time and refer to the chapter on fortifying your home for immediate ideas on how to beef up the security of your home or workplace to last the first few days. You may only have minutes or hours to get things ready once the Zompoc strikes so your first job is to make sure you and your family are safe. Lock all doors and windows and ensure there are no easy ways into your home. Your next job is to secure weapons and supplies. While the water supply still works start filling containers and bring in any valuable supplies that are in unsecured areas of the house and move them to where you can access then safely. If the power is still running. use it to check for news and information and put fresh food in the fridge or use your freezers.

EVACUATE

If you decide that it is time to evacuate your home or workplace you will need to make sure you can do it in an orderly and safe manner. Plan how you will assemble your family and anticipate where you will go to rendezvous. Make sure you have several destination options available to you in different directions so you have options in the Zompoc. Make sure you have your 72 hour survival pack with you and that you have all the important materials you could possibly need for the next few days, such as a change of clothes, food and anything else useful that you can transport readily.

IF YOU TRAVELLING

Though it is better for you to be near your home or workplace when the Zompoc strikes there is always a chance that you may be travelling. If this happens and you find yourself on the road, a boat, airplane, in a car or on foot, there are certain things you must consider.

The most likely form of transport most people will be using is the car. As already stated, no matter what you do, one of the first things you need to do is get as much information as you can. Turn your radio on and do your best to get as much as you can on what is happening, where the dangerous areas are and if there are roadblocks, quarantines, safe areas being set up and the nature of the threat you are faced with. The more information you can get at this early stage the better. The next thing is to get somewhere safe as quickly as possible. Depending on where you are and how well you know the area, this might mean heading home, otherwise you might want to head to those areas outlined in the reports you have been listening to. If you decide to go home then refer back to the section covering staying at home and prepare.

Unless you are very well prepared when on the move, you will be lacking weapons, clothing and basic supplies. It is best to try and grab what you can as quickly as possible, before your immediate area becomes untenable. If for some reason you are already in a hostile region, definitely don't try exploring buildings. You really don't want to be one of those killed on day one! If you are on foot then it is fair to assume that you will be lightly equipped. Again, you will need information, supplies, weapons and a plan. If you are close to home and it is safe, get back there but if you are in a hard to defend location far from home then you will need to find a safe location with access to supplies and weapons as soon as possible. Consult your maps or road signs and work out an early strategy.

If you are travelling by public transport such bus or rail, then your options are limited in some ways as you will be travelling between urban areas. Trains are obviously on a fixed route from station to station. Get information and work out where the station with the best chance of keeping you alive is. Don't get off at the nearest busy city, it might even be wise to stop the train and leave outside of the main urban zones. Once again, it cannot be iterated enough that you need as much information as possible before you start running around. Buses can be redirected to safer areas, abandoned or commandeered for your own use. Those travelling on watercraft are in a pretty good situation as you should not be under immediate threat. If this is the case you want to consider your situation very carefully as most options could worsen your odds and not improve them. You should either find a safe place to dock or moor so that you can obtain information or head out into open water and keep away from the land if you have enough resources to survive. Jump straight to the medium term water based strategies in this case. If you are travelling by aircraft your options are very limited as you will have to wait and see where you land. This means you will essentially be in the same position as somebody travelling on foot or by bus so the same rules apply.

MEDIUM TERM STRATEGIES

So, you have managed to escape and formed a band of equally motivated people. You have some resources including supplies, weapons and a place to hide out. What is your strategy? Will you hunker down and hope somebody else will come and save you or will you step out and start reclaiming your world, one zombie at a time? The answers lie in medium term strategies and it is your job to find which one is best suited to your plans and objectives.

What is a medium term strategy and how does it differ from the one which covers the first 72 hours? The biggest differences are concerned with travel, communication and supply. After the first days you can expect travel to be made difficult due to abandoned vehicles, crashed cars, rubbish, the dead and other detritus to be scattered in the streets. On top of these obstructions you can also expect to find large numbers of zombies as well as the potential problem of other survivors scrambling around, drawing attention to themselves or even interfering with your own plans. After the first 72 hours have passed you can expect most or all of the major communication platforms to

be inoperable. This includes television, radio, most telephones and internet based communication. Also expect a reduction or complete lack of electrical power and the resulting problems associated with this. With reduced or no power you will find street lighting will not exist, security alarms will be set off until they run out of battery power and water systems that rely on pumps will all grind to a stop. Shops will be ransacked in the first few days and people may already be stockpiling items for the coming weeks and months. After 72 hours your own food, water, batteries and other supplies may be running low. If at this point there is no sign of things improving you are going to need a secure place to survive in if you haven't got one already; one that will last the next few weeks and then months. If you are thinking of escaping to the sea then the time to make your move is as early as possible. Don't start thinking about it three months down the line as by this time the boats may already have been taken or the zombies may be in such massive numbers it will be near suicide to try and make it there.

THE PLANS

Quite simply these medium term plans all assume that you have been successful in your initial survival. These strategies will take place after the first few days and are the critical gap between the first few hours of the Zompoc and the ultimate long term survival and rebuilding plans that you will need to make. These strategies are often considered to be the most crucial as they require you to learn how to procure food and supplies, travel and shelter safely, defend yourself and provide security among other things whilst having no time to train or make mistakes. Those than can make it though this period will be the true survivors and will be responsible for helping rebuild what is left of society. Do not leave planning your medium term strategy too late. Ideally start thinking about it the minute the Zompoc hits. Even better, plan it now!

There are three main types of strategy that you can expect to use in the short to medium term. This of course depends entirely on where you were at the start of the Zompoc and what you did. For example, did you stay in your home, fortify it and wait or did you get in your car and 'bug out' of the city to the countryside? Assuming you and your comrades survive the first days, months or even years you will eventually need to establish something more permanent to allow the continuation of humanity. For this later, long term plan see the final chapter on Rebuilding. At this point it is very important to get as much information on your immediate area as possible: What is happening around you? What are the characteristics of the zombies? What resources do you have access to? What routes are open to you? You will need to know all of this before you start making plans. If you live in the centre of a large metropolis and learn that the zombies have overrun the city and that your block is the only one likely to be left inhabited do you really want to start planning a rebuilding strategy in the middle of this? Likewise, if you live on the coast and have access to boats and other vessels it might be unwise to look at moving back into the cities right away. Make sure your plans are compatible with your situation. One last vital thing is to always have a disaster plan in your pocket, ready for when everything goes wrong and you need to make a break for it.

RECOMMENDED PLANS

CITY DWELLERS – PLAN 4

The huge populations in cities will make zombie infection, like any other form of infection, spread astonishingly quickly. The large populations of a city will soon be your enemy, you cannot hope to face those odds with anything short of an army, so leave, before you become one of the masses.

COUNTRY FOLK – PLAN 1

Those that live in rural areas stand a better chance of survival simply due to the small populace and therefore number of enemy; zombies will come at you in a trickle. Rural dwellers often own guns and have vehicles well suited to the Zompoc, as well as a better understanding of self sufficiency. Unless you choose to find a boat, amassing your rural community in to a militia will be your best option.

NEAR WATER – PLAN 3 or 5

By no means the only course of action, but finding a boat and doing a runner is a good possibility when you live near the coast. Whilst roads might well be clogged, the sea will always be free to roam. If however, you live more than 10 miles from the ocean, think again; you probably won't make it without serious preparation.

HIDE STRATEGIES

These are basic strategies that are your default, no-brainer options. Take note though, that simply hiding in a cupboard and being quiet is no guarantee that you will be alive in the next 24 hours! Here are some of the more common defensive strategies based upon finding somewhere safe and hiding from any dangers that may appear. These are quite often the first plan you will think of, especially if you are lacking information (intelligence) on what is going on around you. Are the zombies localised? How far have they spread? What are the living doing?

Though these are not always the most dynamic plans you have to consider your position if you are already in a good, strong, secure and well supplied location. Always consider location, supplies and danger levels before selecting a strategy.

> ## PLANS
>
> ❖ PLAN #1 HIDE AND WAIT AT HOME
> ❖ PLAN #2 QUARANTINE

ESCAPE TO SAFETY STRATEGIES

These strategies are essentially of the same nature as the hide and wait but include one major difference, the requirement to find a safe place. This may mean moving to the other side of a town or city, it may also mean getting a convoy of vehicles and travelling across the country to find a safer, more secure place to base yourself. Your place of safety doesn't necessarily require an actual physical space; it may be simply the ability to keep moving so that you are never pinned down to a particular location or region.

> ## PLANS
>
> ❖ PLAN #3 LIVE AT SEA
> ❖ PLAN #4 ESCAPE AND REBUILD
> ❖ PLAN #5 ISLAND RETREAT
> ❖ PLAN #6 START A NOMADIC LIFESTYLE

OFFENSIVE STRATEGIES

These strategies may include components of the previous ones but feature a much greater emphasis on taking personal responsibility for ending the Zompoc. This can range from an escalating cull of the Zombies right through to full-scale additional warfare against them. These strategies put you and your people at greater short-term risk but also give you the greatest long-term chance at survival. Remember, you cannot co-exist with Zombies, at some point they will find a way to turn on you. Here are the offensive strategies that offer a much greater chance of success though with greater individual risk.

> ## PLANS
>
> ❖ PLAN #7 FIGHTING COLUMN PLAN
> ❖ PLAN #8 MILITARY OFFENSIVE
> ❖ PLAN #9 FORTRESS OFFENSIVE
> ❖ PLAN #10 START A HOLY WAR

PLAN #1 HIDE AND WAIT AT HOME

This is a default position and the one you would adopt when you have no other plan or if you have made no preparations. There are occasions where this option is useful though such as waking up to find your home totally surrounded and if you are in a good defensible location. Ensure your home is safe, look for supplies and look after your friends and relatives while keeping quiet and waiting for things to improve. You should find a small number of people to hide out with but not too many. If you start trying to house large groups of people in your home you will find supplies will run out in hours and sleeping space and sanitation will quickly become an issue. The important thing about the hide and wait plan is that you do not want to travel too far or leave yourself exposed to ambush by the zombies

and thus need to either stockpile supplies early or establish a few safe routes to load up on supplies.

The biggest draw back with this plan is primarily linked to location. Houses are rarely located on their own and are usually situated in areas with other houses and people. Where there are people there will be zombies and this increases the risk of becoming a victim yourself. Another consideration with staying at home is that as time progresses your ability to find supplies, people and information will be reduced and you will have to take the risk of foraging further afield. Quite simply, this is a short term plan that will require others to come to your aid or for the Zompoc to end quickly whilst you hide.

IMPORTANT NOTE:

Always check group members for any sign of infection or contamination by zombies. If they have cuts, bites or wounds you really do not want them around. This seems harsh but one zombie in your home can spoil your day. It is important that you observe both zombies and those that are injured or bitten right from the start so you can watch for signs of those that might turn. Don't forget that anybody can fall or scrape an arm. It is even possible that they could be bitten by an animal rather than a zombie. As always, information and caution are paramount.

PLAN #2 QUARANTINE

Similar to the previous hide and wait strategy, this plan features one additional and somewhat dangerous change. Whilst trying to keep alive you will also be placing the newly infected into quarantine. For this strategy to work you must be ruthless with the quarantine procedure. The type and duration of the quarantine will be determined by the Zombie type and its characteristics so once again observation is paramount. Quarantine is your default option for newly found people and it will be most popular with those that find people they either know or feel sorry for. Remember though, that this strategy is only of use if you have some kind of cure for those infected or want to be sure new people are clear. If the exposed have any real possibility of becoming a zombie then you are risking the lives of all those in your care if you don't act accordingly

WHAT IS QUARANTINE?

Quarantine is voluntary or compulsory isolation, typically used to contain the spread of something considered dangerous, such as infectious disease. Quarantine usually consists of two main types: The first is simply a way of keeping the subject out of the general population until their clothing, items and hair can be decontaminated. A good example of this is quarantine from anthrax. For this type of quarantine persons are allowed to leave as soon as they shed their potentially contaminated garments and undergo a decontamination shower. The second type of quarantine is of more importance during the Zompoc and is used to keep an individual separate from the group until the incubation period of the disease has safely passed. The length of segregation should be slightly longer than the known incubation or 'conversion' time of the disease causing the zombie problem. For example, if you are facing an infected zombie problem and know that to convert from dying human to zombie takes 12

hours you will want to add at least 50% to the quarantine time. To be on the safe side you can easily double or triple the quarantine time. The problems you might face will of course be the initial indignation by those being kept locked away and also the possible complaints of deprivation or violation of human rights. Just remember that these niceties are designed for more civilised times before the Zompoc. Sentimentality is for another day...well into the future. The bottom line for this strategy is that any plan requiring you to co-exist with potential zombies is VERY, VERY dangerous and contains a probability of failure. Use this strategy at your peril!

PLAN #3 LIVE AT SEA

Simply put, the live plan to live at sea is the idea that you will move yourself and your immediate entourage to an ocean going boat and avoid land as much as possible. If you are in the Navy or Merchant Navy or have spent a good deal of time at sea then this will probably be one of the first ideas you will think of. There are of course some problems with this plan and you must carefully weigh up the pros and cons before rushing off to the first boat you can find.

Why should you look to the sea? Well, first of all the sea is a harsh, uncompromising part of the world and an area that is difficult, if not impossible for a zombie to make use of. If you are anchored in the middle of the English Channel on board a medium sized vessel you are pretty much safe from Zombies. Yes, there are still risks but they are much, much lower than being on the land. The sea is more often calm (depending on location) and you will have decent visibility most of the time. If your vessel is of a sufficient size it can have all the

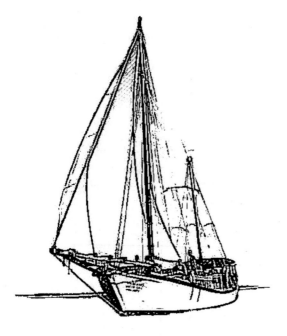

AT A GLANCE

☑ Isolated environment
☑ Easy to defend
☑ Plentiful food source
☑ Quick to relocate
☒ Limited access to supplies
☒ Life at sea can be dangerous
☒ Maintenance is substantial
☒ Boat capacity limited

major features of any home with the massive added bonus of being able to relocate at a moment's notice including the ability to move to completely different parts of the world with relative ease, as long as you have the skills and knowledge. The larger, more sturdy vessels are best for long term occupation. Remember that some are optimised for deep sea travel while others are intended for coastal and inland waterways. There are also many off-shore platforms such as oil rigs and scientific research stations that are hard to access and designed to operate independently of the land and these are perfect for medium term hiding and survival. Moored cargo ships, ferries and cruise vessels are also good for use as semi-permanent bases; just make sure they are clear of zombies beforehand. See the relevant sections on specific water craft, travel and supplies to understand this idea more fully.

The biggest problems with this plan are for those who have no previous experience at sea. Commanding a ship with no idea on navigation, safety or meteorology could spell a quick and wet death for you and those accompanying you. Selecting a suitable craft that you can command with confidence will determine the difference between short and long term survival.

PLAN #4 ESCAPE AND REBUILD

This plan involves finding somewhere safe from zombies and then starting to rebuild. In this scenario you make a concerted effort to find a safe, secure area as quickly as possible after the Zompoc and then work on becoming self-sufficient.

The first question you need to ask is where are you planning on going? As with most things during the Zompoc, you want to avoid areas where zombies may be located. This will of course be determined by how zombies spread, their range and the likely contamination zone. Reconnaissance and intelligence gathering will be very important here. Don't climb in a bus and head off into the unknown but take your time and make sure you choose a path that won't get you all killed. Once you have chosen a location and are reasonably certain on its likelihood of safety and its ability to support your group you will need to organise your assets and resources and then travel there. You will need all your healthy people plus the right vehicles, equipment and supplies to sustain you in a long and dangerous trip. See the relevant sections on vehicles, modification, convoys and travel for further information.

Once you have arrived at your safe and secure location you will need to get your new home habitable as quickly as possible. There is no

point in planting crops and building farms if your people only have supplies for a month. In the first months you will have to raid the surrounding area to find and accumulate materials and keep doing this until you have something more long-term established. In the long-term you will be looking to build farms, workshops, provide amenities such as power and water, and supply sufficient security for your people. If this proves successful you may then want to move on to one of the offensive strategies to start clearing your immediate area of the zombie infestation and start making life a little more reasonable. Once you are at this point the final chapter on rebuilding will be useful, where you can learn about becoming truly self sufficient.

PLAN #5 ISLAND RETREAT

The island retreat plan is one of those ideas that usually occurs to a group of survivors in a film after most of their number is dead. They've tried the mall, police station, and gun store and eventually arrived at the conclusion that they need to leave what is familiar behind and find a place that is free of zombies to start with.

With this plan you will need to get all your uncontaminated people, equipment and supplies to a self-contained island that is free from zombies. Remember, that if people lived there before the outbreak then there could already be zombies on the island, or the current inhabitants may be aggressive towards you. Once you successfully gain access to an island you will need to set up a base that will allow your people to thrive whilst keeping zombies away from you. If your island is far from the mainland you will need to become self-sufficient. This will require you learning how to provide all the basic functions and amenities without outside assistance. If you are close enough to the mainland then you can raid territories for supplies. This is where light boats and transports will come in.

For those that are not 100% sure, an island is simply a landmass that is completely surrounded by water. It can be a few hundred feet in the middle of a lake to a country like Ireland. Depending on where you live and if you are anywhere near a large mass of water, there are likely to be islands. They come in all different shapes and sizes so it will be very important to select one that is big enough to manage with the people you have but that is small enough to defend. There are key questions that will need answering, such as where will you get your food from? Do you have access to clean water, power and transport? In the UK for example, there are hundreds of islands, most of which are in the North. The majority of these are windswept, inhospitable places to live and could prove a tough life for those of left living. Other islands

AT A GLANCE
☑ Safety in isolation
☑ Quite easy to defend
☒ Good based of operations Travel required to reach islands
☒ Potential for being trapped
☒ Difficult to resupply
☒ Limited size for expansion

such as the Isle of Wight in the south are relatively large and only 3-5 miles from the south coast of England. This island already houses a modest population of 120,000 with many facilities. Assuming the population is not contaminated you could relocate to somewhere similar to this and have access to a secure base with many people of different skills. If the population has already turned to zombies then you will face a large but not impossible number of foes to eradicate to leave the island clear and safe for the living.

Security and quarantine procedures will be very important on your island as it will be easy to become lax if you haven't faced a zombie or infected person for some time. If a zombie makes it to your shore you will need to be ready to repel them. Use time honoured techniques as used by the US and Japan in World War II and clear the beach line of cover so that you can easily spot problems before they are inside your complex. Set up alarms, watch posts and other security measures so that you will be warned of any problems and make sure you have several well stocked and well armed defensive bastions to retire to in an emergency.

Last but not least, you must have an escape plan. If somehow your island becomes untenable due to lack of food, supplies, sickness or zombie invasion you may need to leave in a hurry. Have boats with stocked provisions ready at key areas.

PLAN #6 START A NOMADIC LIFESTYLE

Nomads are communities of people who move from one place to another, rather than settling permanently in one location. Believe it or not there are actually 30-40 million nomads in the world today. This style of mobile living is quite well suited to a variety of apocalyptical events, the Zompoc being one of them.

There are three mains types of nomads, the hunter-gatherers moving between hunting grounds, pastoral nomads moving between pastures, and "peripatetic nomads" moving between traders.

NOMADIC HUNTER GATHERERS

The nomadic hunter-gatherers lead, by far the longest-lived subsistence method in human history which is that of following seasonally available wild plants and game. This is a potentially successful way of living but can prove difficult to those not used to the harder way of living. This also assumes that your food supply will not require you to head into areas that are possibly infested by zombies or that the very game you seek is not affected by whatever created the zombies in the first place.

The peripatetic nomadic lifestyle is also a possible system that you can utilise but it assumes both availability of people and resources to trade with. You will need reliable means of transport and must be very wary when visiting new places and traders. Do this by obtaining vehicles and then keep moving away from infested and dangerous areas. Pick up people and supplies on the way. This way may prove successful to start with but is vulnerable to vehicle problems as well as resupply issues. The lack of a permanent base means you are less likely to be surprised and overrun but you will also lack the long-term facilities for medical care, crop growing and weapon modification and building that are essential for long term victory.

PLAN #7 FIGHTING COLUMN PLAN

This is very similar to the nomadic plan in that it is based heavily upon a strong, mobile column that contains all your people, vehicles, weapons and supplies. Your column is essentially a mobile commune, carrying everything you could ever need whilst fighting zombies wherever you find them. Take care to never stay in a place too long as this increases the risk of exposure to zombies and other threats. It is a hard lifestyle, living off the land whilst taking the fight to the enemy.

Your fighting column will move from place to place, stripping towns, farms and shops for supplies and then moving on. You will not be able to completely destroy all zombies, but you should be able to destroy a large number. At each new location you will have the chance to

take on new people if they are uncontaminated or dispose of those that are. It will be very important to include many armoured transports with large amounts of food; fuel and water. If you run out of any of these you are in big trouble! Like the ancient Mongols, your mobility will be your saviour. The chapter on vehicles contains more information but stage 3 prepared vehicles are essential here along with scouts and assault vehicles. The ability to tow spare vehicles and carry the lighter ones such as bikes and quads is also important.

In terms of strategy, you must continue to eradicate zombies rather than avoiding contact all the time. It is risky to pile straight into a contaminated zone so you will need to follow the outer routes and urban areas, cleansing what you can as you move through the area and moving quickly on so that you don't become surrounded as zombie hordes move in behind you. You can expect to sustain casualties over time as exposure to zombies and continued combat will ultimately mean people will be injured, bitten, infected or killed.

This lifestyle will not be for everyone and you will need to adapt. Ideally, you and your group will possess some combat skills and weapons training which you can put to good use from day one. If not, then you will need to learn quickly as you go along. You will need to keep morale high, enforce discipline and keep the fight going. If anybody shows signs of wanting to do something else you will need to stop the insurrection fast; a fractured convoy will leave you weakened and could potentially cause the loss of your people and all your hard work. Encourage focussed aggression against your common enemy and an esprit de corps to keep your people's spirits up. You are the mobile crusaders with a mission.

PLAN #8 MILITARY OFFENSIVE

If by some lucky reason you are able to obtain access to military hardware, supplies and a base then you can consider entering a conventional war. This is a likely outcome if you are a member of the Forces, a National Guard or Territorial Army unit. Assuming you have the skills and training you can adopt a variety of military strategies. Just remember to secure your bases and supplies otherwise you will be no different to the rest of the living trying to survive. Military land vehicles are well suited for anti-zombie operations. Air support is less useful though great for scouting and search missions.

Waiting for zombies to come to you might seem a sensible way to fight them, especially when you have access to hardware, people and ammunition. This isn't actually the case though. The problem with letting zombies come to your base is that they force you onto the defensive and leave your last safe place as your frontline. Take the war to the zombies and keep them away from your supplies, people and resources.

Good communication is required for offensive operations along with strict discipline and leadership. Select your areas and attack them carefully. If you are expected heavy resistance use an offensive strategy but with defensive tactics. A good example of this, is when

AT A GLANCE

- ☑ Powerful weapons and equipment
- ☑ Access to useful vehicles
- ☑ Positive approach to resolving the problem
- ☒ Frequent combat will use up resources fast
- ☒ Exposed to greater danger by contact with the contaminated
- ☒ Reliance on modern weapons, supplies and equipment

sweeping and clearing a built up area such as a town. Rather than swooping in and operating an urban battle, use the zombie's weaknesses to your advantage. Move into a defensible part of the town and make sure you have safe exit routes if it all goes pear shaped. Get your troops dug in with clear arcs of fire, ideally up and out of reach of grabbing arms and biting teeth. Make lots of noise, possibly send in some decoys and encourage the zombies to follow or attack you. From this position you can thin out the ranks and then continue shooting till they are all eliminated. If you are still fighting when it becomes dark you can retire and come back the next day to a different part of the town and repeat.

PLAN #9 FORTRESS OFFENSIVE

This involves establishing a strong fortress that you can use as a safe base of operations and then fighting back. This plan assumes you have access to some weapons and personnel and have the skills and motivation to fight. As you lack the heavy equipment and hardware you will need to take a more cautious approach than the military offensive plan. This is similar to the 'find somewhere safe' strategy but with a strong military angle.

As well as finding a safe place you will need to start a coordinated programme of culling and steady expansion. Each day select a specific target and then strike hard and fast. You will need to increase the number killed daily, whilst slowly increasing your own numbers. Careful planning will be required for this to work. Do not waste people and resources on unrealistic missions. You will not see immediate results but slowly and surely you will start to expand, increase your own numbers and push back the zombies. It is imperative that you fight this war

AT A GLANCE

- ☑ Minimal travelling required
- ☑ Easy access to tools and household supplies
- ☑ Useful local knowledge
- ☑ Access to own car/vehicles
- ☒ Limited options if anything goes awry
- ☒ Likely to be near populated areas and zombies
- ☒ Dangerous if fortress is breached

methodically. Ro do this you must keep their number down and yours up so you cannot take prisoners or leave wounded, bitten people behind, they must be euthanized. If this is too slow for you them move on to the Holy War scenario that is next but just remember that the holy war scenario is for the truly dedicated!

PLAN #10 START A HOLY WAR

In this scenario you gather your living comrades, supplies and weapons and launch yourself into a bloody and violent confrontation that ends in one side achieving total victory. It goes without saying that this is a very, very risky plan and is best left to either the suicidal or for when you have reached a balance between successful operation and zombie expansion and want to finish things off quickly. If there is a time limit that requires you to defeat zombies then you will have no choice but to do this. For this to work you will need secure vehicles, lots of weapons and supplies and most importantly of all, a large and fearless group of people who are dedicated to the cause.

A holy war will be fuelled by numbers, yours and theirs. Select major targets that contain survivors and zombies. These are dangerous but contain the resources you need. Conduct aggressive operations using the high ground, use traps and other tactics described in the other plans. You will take casualties and must therefore attempt to recruit new people during the war.

Make sure your people are equipped and capable of fighting at close quarters as you can expect to fight in all kinds of circumstances. Those that fall in battle must be finished off to deprive their bodies to the enemy. It is every person's duty to even the numbers game in your favour! Locating potential hiding places for the living is a priority as they are your replacement soldiers. Either you find them or the zombies will. Both sides will need more soldiers! There is little time for rest and you should waste no time establishing workshops, factories and farms. Each and every day will be continuous action until you reach the final stage. This is bloody work but should you undertake this route then the only option is to fight and win! No guts, no glory!

WHO TO LOOK FOR?

There are groups of people who already exist and have much to offer other survivors during the Zompoc. As to how many are left and whether they are willing to help you, remains to be seen. The best groups of people are those that have a working hierarchy, leadership and basic structure. This works best if well established and will make planning and survival much easier. You want to look for groups than can offer either skills or equipment, but ideally both. These groups can include the following types of people:

MOTORCYCLE GANGS

These gangs are usually groups of people with a shared interest, namely motorcycles, drink and good rock music and already have an established hierarchy. They often have their own clubhouse, which is secure from robbery and usually outside of the centre of major towns and cities. On top of this they have access to large numbers of motorcycles including trikes and custom vehicles. You can expect a variety of skills from them including welding, mechanics and potentially combat related skills too. Another bonus of these groups is that they wear decent protective gear by default. It is hard to find a biker

without good leather clothing, helmets and sturdy gloves and boots. If you know any of these guys or even just a small number then they can really be of great help. The only real problem with a group like this is actually persuading them to let you join with them if they are feeling safe on their own. Motorcycle

clubs often have a core group of members that come from shared backgrounds. For example, there are some clubs that are based purely on ex-forces personnel. These groups can provide excellent skills, knowledge and equipment as well as a sense of order.

SPORTS TEAMS

Useful sports teams include groups which focus on physical fitness such as football (soccer), rugby, baseball, American football, hockey, lacrosse and cricket. These teams of people are selected based on their skill and physical ability. Sports people like golfers do not have to be so physically fit and the vast majority are hobby players so these are not what are being referred to here. Most serious teams are usually well trained, physically conditioned and used to a form of hierarchy. One downside is that sportsman, especially professional sportsman often require a substantial calorie intake including drink, food, protein and supplements. Keeping these guys in the field could cost you a lot of supplies. Another problem is that team members can be very competitive and this could be a problem with them wanting to take over or change your well laid plans.

MARTIAL ARTS GROUPS

Unarmed Martial arts groups are very popular throughout the world and include excellent systems from Europe and the East. The most popular martial arts are Boxing, Karate, Thai Kwon-do, Kung-fu and Muay Thai kickboxing. There is also aresurgence in Historical European Martial Arts groups that work on grappling, throwing and knife based techniques. It is very important that you choose a martial art that is suitable for surviving the Zompoc and not one that is just for fun. Be wary of sport based martial arts as many, such as Karate actually practice a competitive version of what used to be a more martial system of combat. The same applies to Judo, which has the added drawback in that you don't really want to be holding a zombie to

the ground! This doesn't mean martial arts like karate and judo are bad, you just need to find a combat orientated club.

On the face of it these people seem perfect for your plans but in the end you really don't want to be arm wrestling zombies and kicking them in the head. You need to kill them ideally without being touched by them and it is very easy to be scratched or bitten whilst in the middle of your latest Chuck Norris technique. However, it is worth noting that there are few unarmed martial arts groups that have protective kit worth using in the Zompoc.

ARMED MARTIAL ARTS

Armed martial arts, such as those practised in the US or Europe can be of real use during the Zompoc. These groups train in a variety of

hand-to-hand combat techniques and unlike most modern martial arts systems they actually train in techniques exactly as they were intended. That is, their full martial intention remains intact and as such the techniques are meant for combat. In the UK, Europe and the US there is a resurgence of Western Martial Arts based upon the traditional fighting systems of Europe. These martial artists train in the use of dozens of types of weapons including single sword, two handed swords, sword and shields, spears, quarterstaff and much more. These weapons can be found throughout the globe and can also be fashioned or improvised quickly and easily if the need arises. These groups often have access to large amounts of training armour, protection and blunt weapons (which can be sharpened easily when required). This is an excellent core of equipment and knowledge to use to help prepare your people and to join with. Again, be wary of sport fencing as this is not the same thing and is purely based on a sporting points system. A zombie really won't care who has precedence or how many points you have from poking him!

Another very handy benefit of these groups is that they are often involved in substantial amounts of study and research both in old manuscripts and also in actual physical interpretation of the techniques. This interest in research and study is a useful characteristic for people during the Zompoc. These people can therefore provide you with organisation, skills, knowledge, weapons and training. Check out groups like the Academy of Historical Fencing for more information on the weapons, equipment and training in these effective arts that served Europeans well for literally hundreds of years..

VEHICLE COLLECTORS

Vehicle collectors and enthusiasts are the groups out there that have an interest, some would say obsession with particular types of motor vehicles. These groups are actually pretty damned handy during the Zompoc as they have access to a wide variety of traditional vehicles, often military ones, plus the skills to use and maintain them. These people may be interested in classic British sports cars, off-road and all terrain vehicles such as Land Rovers, Jeeps and amphibious vehicles or trucks. Even those that use and run classic buses will have their day in the sun. Buses, as you will see in the vehicle section have many uses in the Zompoc.

RE-ENACTMENT GROUPS

These groups are essentially groups of people that act out the part of historical figures, armies and battles for the general public. They might play the part of a German paratrooper, a Roman soldier or a Viking. Though they do not always have the best combat training or fitness, they do have access to equipment, clothing, armour and other people with the same interest. A group of fully equipped Vikings might not seem perfectly suited to a Zompoc, but they will give you access to clothing, armour, tents, weapons (even if blunt they can be sharpened) and much more. This kind of equipment is not easy to find in numbers and could prove very handy. Even better, in some countries you will find groups with actual live firing weapons such as American Civil War groups. A minie bullet firing percussion cap rifle is extremely accurate and powerful and would definitely put a nice hole in a zombie's skull! Some World War 2 groups often have access to large numbers of military vehicles, all usually lovingly restored and cared for. It may not seem very modern but a column of armoured cars, trucks and jeeps could really help you.

SHOOTING/ARCHERY CLUBS

It goes without saying that numbers of people with weapons and shooting skills have a lot to offer during the Zompoc. These groups are much more likely in the US as opposed to the UK where pretty much all weapons are banned and many enthusiasts have had to give up

shooting since the handgun ban. However, there are plenty of other gun clubs including clay pigeon shooting groups. The ability to obtain weapons and ammunition will be of great importance as well as the shooting and gun maintenance skills that can be passed on.

You will also find archery clubs dotted around and they can keep fighting for a long time due to the ease in which ammunition can be constructed or reused. Talk to them about the optimum arrows against soft targets like zombies as you don't want to just puncture them, you want to put them back in the ground, permanently. Remember to always ensure that you follow the laws of your country and do not purchase or use anything that is considered to be illegal in any way when preparing pre-Zompoc. What is the point in buying weapons for the Zompoc only to find you are stuck in a cell when it starts!

SURVIVALISTS

These people have been preparing for this kind of doomsday scenario for decades. Some of the common preparations undertaken includes preparing a clandestine or defensible retreat or safe place and stockpiling non-perishable food, water, water-purification equipment, clothing, seeds, firewood, defensive/hunting weapons, ammunition, and agricultural equipment.

Some survivalists do not make such extensive preparations but instead merely incorporate a "Be Prepared" outlook into their everyday life. Many of them have a bag of gear that is often referred to as a 'Bug Out Bag' (see Pre-Apocalypse preparation for more information)

holding basic necessities and useful items weighing anywhere up to as much as the owner can carry. A variation on the 'bug out' bag is the 72-hour kit. In most emergency situations, it will take at least three days for help to arrive. Therefore, there should be three days worth of food, water, and personal items for each member of the family. The 72-hour survival kit also includes first aid kit, small toys (for children), important numbers and papers, as well as a plan for making contact and a meeting location. The most ardent Survivalists aim to remain self-sufficient for the duration of the breakdown of social order, or perhaps indefinitely if the breakdown is predicted to be permanent such as an unending Zompoc.

The only real problem you will face is that survivalists will probably not be interested in you as they have their own survival plan that isn't based around you! These guys have tonnes of supplies, weapons and training and can expect to be left on their own for years at a time.

MILITIA

A militia is military force composed of ordinary citizens to provide defence, emergency law enforcement, or paramilitary service in times of emergency without being paid a regular salary or committed to a fixed term of service. They usually respond to an emergency threat to public safety, usually one that requires an armed response, but which can also include ordinary law enforcement or disaster responses. The main feature of a militia though is that the militia member is armed and thus the status of the person is changed from peaceful citizen to soldier citizen. This is not the same as the traditional military militia used by the United Kingdom and United States over the last few hundred years. It is against the law in the United Kingdom to carry an offensive weapon and therefore if you attempt to create some form of militia you will almost certainly get a knock on the door from your local constabulary. Quite simply, if you live in most European countries, just forget the idea. This doesn't mean you can't join online organisations like the ZAS (Zombie Abolition Service) where you can make plans, swap information and get ready for that dreaded day. In the US there are many militia organisations, some of which are connected with survivalist groups. The great benefits of these groups are that they have access to the skills, equipment and organisation of military forces.

USEFUL LOCATIONS

Lastly, remember that successful strategies will require careful use of terrain, buildings, supply routes and defensive structures to keep you and your people safe. Some buildings might seem impregnable but in the wrong circumstances a super strong building can actually turn into your own prison or worse still, your coffin. Refer to the 'Environments' section for more information on this as well as the building preparations sections for ways to improve the defensive capabilities of your base. For the nomadic strategies you will find your vehicles will become your homes so make sure they are sufficiently prepared for this task. The section on 'Supplies and Logistics' describes useful locations with regards to supplies and materials. Always remember that where there used to be people there may now be zombies so always choose locations with care. If you are hunting zombies then you will of course need to know where they are.

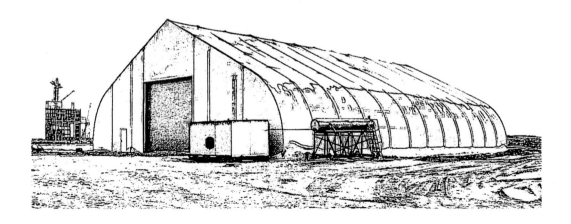

CHAPTER 4: PREPARING AND DEFENDING YOUR HOME

To be prepared is half the victory.
Miguel De Cervantes

WHAT ROLE DOES YOUR HOME PLAY?

During the Zompoc, the role of your home, if you happen to be in or near it when the outbreak occurs, will be very much the same role as it was in normal life before the Zompoc. Your home is not a place to hold up as a fortress and wait out the storm. If you do this, the number of undead will continue to rise beyond your manageable limits and you will be overwhelmed. Whilst you do not want to sit and hide in your home long-term, in the initial outbreak it might well be the best course of action. Later on, your home will likely serve as a base of operations, at least in the short to medium-term. This means that your home needs to be as safe and secure as you can possibly make it.

Whether or not to stay in your home for the first few hours, days, weeks or months will depend entirely on your location, your defences, the number of enemies and your chosen method of survival. Your home will only provide safety and security to a small number of people. If the streets have become a war zone then you may have no choice to stay there but even later on, it is unlikely to be the best place to stay. But this is of course your decision.

For those of you that live in the countryside, your own home may be a much better place to stay than inner city areas. Country homes typically house small numbers of people, and therefore potential zombie numbers are low. These homes can also typically sustain a more self sufficient lifestyle.

PRE-APOCALYPSE PREPARATION

You can do all the research on fighting zombies that you like, but if you don't survive the first day because you didn't prepare your home, it will all have been useless. As we go about our normal lives, it is not really practical to convert our own home into a bunker, which is unfortunate. However, many preparations can be made that will improve your chances of surviving the outbreak of zombie infection. It is quite likely that when the zombie outbreak, you will be in, or near to, your home. Therefore, get it ready to fulfil its new purpose of survival.

There are many ways to improve the security and protection of your home, much of which will be dual purpose. In some disaster areas in America people have resorted to building their own safe rooms in which to survive extreme conditions such as hurricanes and tornados. Such safe rooms will often have thicker walls and shutters for windows and these can provide excellent security from the zombie. But as ever, make sure you have an exit strategy.

BASIC SECURITY

In a world with human crime we place an emphasis on alarm systems, lights, cameras and guard dogs which will deter thieves and alert police to a break in. Unfortunately many of these features are designed to deter human thieves and will not work on the population whom are now dead. Luckily, some modern security features will fulfil a dual role and should be considered over normal human specific prevention measures.

EXTERIOR DOORS

These are the primary point of entry into your home so start reinforcing them. Many exterior doors have large panes of glass which is no good at all. Get a new door which has little to no glass at all. The priority here is your front door, as your back door will likely have other barriers such as fencing for protection, so that this can be dealt with afterwards. Also make sure that you have strong locks on your front door, ideally combined with strong bolts on the top and bottom of the door. Once this is done turn your attention to any other exterior doors and make similar improvements.

WINDOWS

Old fashioned single pane glass is very weak. A simple strike with the arm can break through it, which makes this very poor security. Get double glazing as quickly as you can at least to the ground floor windows. This will provide a huge increase in security. Even if the undead can smash through your double glazing, it will take them much longer to do so and make so much noise that you will be alerted to their presence and ready for them. Also acquire window security film for all windows. This will further strengthen all windows and make entry much more difficult. Security film is also an excellent cheap solution if you cannot afford double glazing. Once the Zompoc begins, boarding the windows up is an option but in normal everyday life this would not be possible, nor a nice way to live. However, there is nothing stopping you from being prepared for this by having all the boards pre

cut and ready to fit on ground floor windows. Fitting them would take a matter of minutes with the right tools ready to hand. This is an idea which has been taken up by many people in potential hurricane and tornado risk zones. It is also an excellent method of preparation for the Zompoc.

INTERIOR LOCKS

If your doors and windows fail, you need to be able to section off areas of the house quickly in order to stay alive. Install sturdy locks on all key interior doors and also consider this for any bedrooms that are in use. Lockable bedrooms will allow you to quickly barricade yourself in when an emergency arises. Just be sure you have an exit strategy from that bedroom, such as ropes or ladders to escape out of the window or into the loft.

EXTERIOR WALLS AND GATES

Once your building has increased security measures, your outer walls can be improved to create a first line of defence where possible. Many houses have brick walls around their perimeter while others have simple wooden ones. If you have brick walls, extend their height with strong railings, such as wrought iron or strong wood. Barbed wire can also be used which will help tangle any zombie attackers, but be sure to comply with current rules whilst law and order still exist. If you have wooden fence panelling around your house then there is little you can do that will improve security. Just be sure that the fence panels are in good condition and not rotten and split so they will give at least some extra barrier of defence.

LOW LYING ROOFS

Be sure that none of your upper floor windows are accessible by low lying roofs or any other objects, such as sheds, garages and wheelie bins. If you have a permanent low lying fixture which could lead to entry of first floor windows then secure the area with fencing, barbed wire, bird spikes and anything else necessary to close off entry to upper floors.

WEAPONS

In Britain you are not legally allowed to own any weapons for self defence, but that does not mean that you cannot have items in your house that could potentially be useful in the event of zombie attack. Just never tell anyone the reason why you bought them. Check out the weapons list later in this book, but legal items such as a fire axes, shovels, crow bars, machetes and crossbows are all potential items.

EMERGENCY LIGHTING

In the event of the apocalypse it is likely that you will lose electricity very quickly. The dark can be very scary when you know maybe a zombie looking to bite you and you can't see where it is! Generators can be used to power lighting and other facilities, but be aware that they will also draw attention to yourself from both zombies and opportunistic humans. Carry a regular stock of candles, lanterns and torches, with plenty of spare batteries and whatever other fuel you need such as gas or oil. Being able to see in the dark can be a matter of life or death.

MAPS

Keep a stock of maps in the house, including highly detailed local ones. When the power goes out and you no longer have internet access, you'll be glad that you did. Also familiarise yourself with the local area; more than just knowing where the local pubs and supermarkets are. Have a good general knowledge of where the hardware shops are, sources of useful vehicles, police stations, army barracks, gun shops and potential escape routes.

WARDROBE

Keep some gear in your wardrobe that will be useful like a leather biker's jacket, motorcycle gloves, sturdy boots and that kind of thing. Ensure that you have gear that will provide some protection, as well as be easy to move in, fight in as well as run in. Refer to the personal protective equipment section for more detail.

If the Zompoc strikes at night when you are in bed and you find yourself under attack with just a few minutes or even seconds to defend yourself, the wardrobe may be all you have access to. Storing weapons in the wardrobe, or near it may be a good option but you must of course adhere to the current laws of the land. Keeping items that can be used as weapons in your wardrobe in the UK, such as a crossbow is not illegal; only having them for home defence is. Simply choose your wardrobe or nearby storage area as the crossbow's home and only use it as a weapon during the Zompoc.

LOFT AND CELLAR

These two locations are some of the obvious places to secure as they typically only have one entry point, but you must give it more consideration. Being underground provides you with excellent protection in the short term as one entry point is easy to fortify and defend. But sadly it could also be your undoing. If the number of zombies becomes too great outside and is more that you can realistically kill, you will be trapped in your cellar and die of starvation. The loft/attic is a better proposition as it is high off the ground and usually has only one entry point of stairs or a ladder. Many homes have removable or pull down ladders meaning that you immediately have a very safe environment. Despite there being only one entry point it is not difficult to make a hole in the roof and escape that way. Making it a much better bet than the cellar. Most British and American houses have an accessible loft. Be sure to deck it out with simple floor boards and store some useful tools there as well as other key items like torches. Also be sure to have an exit strategy planned, such as ropes or a ladder should you need to leave through the roof.

SUPPLIES

In the short-term you are still going to need to have some supplies to get you started. Always keep several litres of bottled water in the house as well as food that does not need to be cooked and has a reasonably long shelf life. Also consider keeping filled fuel cans in the garage, as these will be very useful in an emergency for your car or for Molotov Cocktails - a quick and dirty solution to arming yourself.

Most people only keep stocks of food in the fridge and freezer but that will be of little use unless you have your own generator. Shelf stable foods are the answer here. Keep good stocks of canned and bagged foods which do not need any special storage methods. Many of these have long shelf lives, often years. Other consumables such as batteries, matches and candles are well worth keeping in stock.

STAYING TOOLED UP

Always keep an extensive supply of tools in your home, as you may likely need them at very short notice. A well stocked toolbox with screwdrivers, hammers, pliers, cutters, nails and screws is an excellent start but what about power tools? Power tools make many jobs much quicker and easier. A drill, electric

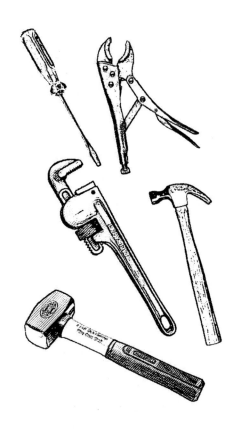

screwdriver and disc cutter are an excellent start. These power tools will typically be mains powered, which could potentially be a problem. Consider stocking wireless power tools that can be charged from your car battery or a small generator. This could be a good idea, but brings with it a few new problems.

A good set of tools can be vital during the Zompoc. They will enable you to beef-up security, get access to locked and nailed down premises and items, improve and maintain vehicles and can even be used to defend yourself. Consider having multiple sets of tools, as they so often go missing or get forgotten.

As well as tools, you will need a supply of building materials to use to build your defences. Consider keeping a stock of panels of thick wood. Cheap chipboard is fine as long as it's the thicker stuff as well as metal bars or strips, corrugated iron, and plenty of fittings, brackets, bolts and wall anchors. If you have to quickly fortify your home there will be no time to go looking for DIY supplies. Have them ready. Such supplies can also be used to quickly modify your vehicle. If you can weld, consider keeping plenty of supplies for that purpose. If you cannot then drills, bolts and ropes can go a long way to fitting items.

IF YOU LIVE IN A CARAVAN/TRAILER

Caravans and Trailers, whether they are static or mobile homes are very poor for defence in a zombie situation. Windows are frequently weak and door locks minimal. Even the walls of most caravans are very thin.

If you have a static trailer, the best thing you can do is pack up and abandon it. Hit the road and head in the safest direction or find the nearest location to hold up with better security. If you have a mobile caravan, it is a different matter. Mobile caravans should be treated in the same way that you treat vehicles in terms of armouring them up. A caravan can be great as a home as you can lead a nomadic life easily. Look to the vehicle preparation guide on more advice for this. If you have a Motor home or RV, even better but again see the 'Vehicle Preparation' guide.

Do bear in mind that although a caravan or motor home in itself may not be ideal for defence, it can quickly and easily be moved within the safe confines of somewhere that is. Get a few caravans within the confines of a castle for example and you have a very nice defensive and comfortable place to survive indeed.

FORTIFYING YOUR HOME DURING THE APOCALYPSE

Surviving the initial wave of zombie attacks will revolve around either 'bugging out', or having a secure location in which to hold up. Your home is the most likely spot as you will probably be in it or nearby when the attack starts. Your own home is familiar and you know what its weaknesses will be, how to solve them and what useful items are contained within it. You must consider however that if it is in an area with a large population, holding up in your own home could trap you and be your demise. This very much depends on what type of zombies you face and where you live. Refer to the 'Survival Plan' section for what is most suited to the situation.

If you do decide that your own home is the place to stay, the first stage is to establish sections of the property in order of priority to defend and the work required to secure them. If you have a house, shutting off the staircase is usually the fastest way of doing this, securing all upper floors immediately. Securing the ground floor against zombie invasion is much more difficult due to the number of accessible doors and windows. When you have shut off access to the stairs, be sure to check that none of the windows of the upper floors are accessible from other rooftops or exits such as ladders or fire escapes. The easiest way to quickly plug the staircase is by removing an unnecessary door, or two, from anywhere in the house, and fitting them in place on the staircase. This door will need to be movable for your own passage so use ropes, hinges or weight to keep it in place. You can use a portcullis style of fortification here, or fit a board from the landing, flat across the stairs, like a floor over the stair well. This needs to be easily secured in case of emergency and have hinges and locks for easy access and lockdown.

Once you have sectioned off the upper floors of the building, move anything useful upstairs,

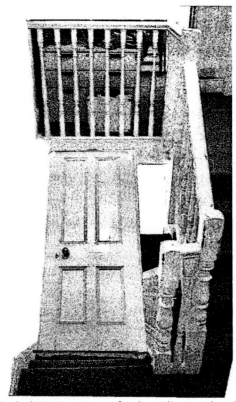

including weapons, food, radios and other useful items.

The next stage will be to secure the ground floor, by barricading all windows and doors. Leave only one doorway active and strengthen it. At this stage you may be better off looking for an improved base of operations. Forget nailing odd planks of wood in a haphazard fashion over the windows. This never works in the movies and it doesn't work in real life either. You'll run out of planks too quickly anyway.

If you have a bungalow move everything you need to the loft as that is probably your only safe option. If you live in a flat or apartment ensure that the front door is secure and that the balcony is blocked off and secure.

FORTIFYING FOR LONG TERM SURVIVAL

If you are unable to find a suitable better location or are forced to defend your home long-term further improvements should be made. DIY/hardware stores are your friend here and most people live within just a few miles of one. Stock up on thick MDF boards, hardwood beams, strong metal bars, typically dexion, doors, cables and ropes as well as all fixtures and fittings that you will need to make everything strong. Don't think that a hammer and nails will make things strong enough. You will ideally need power tools or the clever application of ropes and cables. In this case, get a generator, or make good use of cable free tools which can be charged from your car.

EXTERIOR

For short-term survival you must section off the upper floors of your house. Once this is done, its time to reclaim the ground floor. The way to do this is to start reinforcing the ground floor and surrounding area as follows.

WINDOWS

The obvious thing to do is to start fixing large boards over all the windows, or bricking them up if you have the time and skill. Remember, a certain quality of life must be considered. If you have got this far then you are thinking beyond just surviving until tomorrow. In this respect you want to try and maintain some light through your windows if possible.

THE QUICK AND DIRTY OPTION

MDF, chipboard or equivalent boards bolted to the walls is a simple solution and one which is regularly used in normal life when houses are unoccupied as it is simple and effective. Get the thickest boards you can from your local DIY store or timber yard. Cut them to shape with power tools and secure in place with sturdy bolts or brackets. You can consider strengthening these boards by bolting full length wood or metal slats along the length. This is not a pretty solution and will cut out all

light to the rooms. It is however a very quick and simple fix to the problem.

THE SMART OPTION

Use the MDF as above, but leave 10" gaps at the top of each of them for light but fill those gaps with strong wire mesh as is often found around schools and commercial premises. Be sure that this is all firmly secured with additional strengthening poles. This solution will be as strong but still allow natural light in the rooms for a better quality of life. If you have enough wire mesh consider covering the entire windows with it rather than using any wood and strengthen with additional bars to

stop zombies getting enough leverage on the

wire to pull it from its mounts.

THE LUXURY OPTION

In an ideal world you want as much light in the room as you do with normal everyday living and yet still being able to relax in safety. The way to achieve this is through steel bars bolted to the frame of the house. The one potential weakness of this system is that the bars themselves are something for the undead to hang on to and wrench at. With that in mind, these have to be secured down extremely well with many high quality wall anchors. Also consider support bars that go down into the ground or fix to an outer wall, making it impossible to pull out. Also consider digging trenches in front of the windows to make access to them even more difficult.

DOORS

Front doors on modern houses tend to be fairly strong but many also have large glass sections. The first thing to do is strengthen the locks on your door. Add a large strong bolt to

the top and bottom of the door. Do not secure these bolts with the small screws that most come with but fix the bolts with high quality strong fixings where possible. Also consider a traditional hook and bar system. Then add a sheet of wood or metal to the front door by screwing or bolting it on for extra reinforcement.

The back or side doors of most houses are much weaker than the front door and this needs to be resolved. Zombies are not picky as to which one they use. Take the same approach to these doors as with the front entrance. Use extra bolts and an extra layer of material on top of what is already there.

HOUSE WALLS

Almost all houses in Britain are made of bricks which are stronger than any zombie will be able to smash through. This is heartening. You should not have to worry yourself with the exterior walls of the house. If however, you have wooden walls, make more thorough checks. Wooden walls to houses are fairly strong but if the wood is old and rotten it can be smashed or torn apart. Consider extra plating with wood, metal or corrugated iron.

INTERIOR

Even though you should now have secured the downstairs of the house, the upstairs will still be by far the safer location. Consider a traditional portcullis style gate over your stairs. This will provide a really strong fortification for the upstairs and will be especially useful for night-time. This is much easier to construct than you may think. A garden wrought iron gate (the tall type) can be excellent for this as well as metal fencing, a wooden door or a spring base from a bed etc. A simple rail or rope and pulley system can work a treat to provide a quickly opening but secure boundary to the stairs.

There are other ways to quickly produce an initial barrier defence. Parking high sided vehicles in front of your house, or banking cars up to obstruct the entrance to your property may not keep the zombies out completely but will provide a choke point allowing you to safely take on smaller numbers at a time. This is an excellent and quick solution which should be considered early on whilst you make the necessary improvements to the house itself.

FLATS AND APARTMENTS

The fact that most flats and apartments only have one entrance which is one door that is usually very strong is a good thing indeed. However, that one entrance could also be your demise. Fighting your way through an endless corridor of zombies could quite likely be an impossible task. If you do have a flat or apartment, be sure you have other ways out. Keeping ropes or ladders handy should hopefully ensure you can escape to the ground or surrounding buildings. Flat and Apartment

EXTERIOR WALLS

It is not likely you will ever have the time or opportunity to reinforce your outer walls but if you have time to do so consider building a good perimeter and first line of defence. Anything permanent like a brick wall is not a realistic option unless you already have one. Improvised walls however can be built using corrugated iron, wooden planks, cars, sandbags and in fact anything substantial that can be piled high.

Wire grid fencing is incredibly good at holding the hordes at bay but it is rarely ever used around residential buildings in the UK. Such fencing however is commonly used around schools, sports facilities and various businesses so consider getting hold of some. This could be done pre-Zompoc and combined with your wood fence panels if you want to maintain a discrete image.

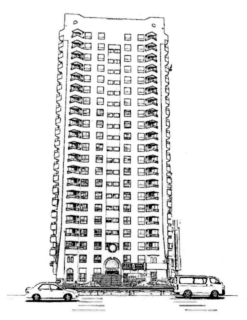

blocks are potentially excellent for defence due to the tall nature of their construction and limited ground floor entrances but getting back out of them could be a real hazard.

Ground floor flats and apartments will typically suffer from all the weaknesses of a normal house but this is all dependant on the building. If the ground floor apartment windows are accessible then take the same approach as a house. Focus initially on sectioning off upper floors, then barricading ground floor windows if you can. The great thing about flat and apartment blocks is that you have a good source of potential survivors to assist you. In this respect you must also be very careful. Firstly team together and section off the upper floors, then do an extremely thorough sweep of the entire building. It is entirely possible that in an apartment block that one or more people could be infected before you get the barriers up so sweep and clear.

BEYOND PHYSICAL BOUNDARIES

We have now looked at many ways in which you can improve your security and defences. In fact with a day's work and the appropriate items you can fortify most homes pretty much indefinitely from the zombies but what then? It is rather unlikely that the infected/undead will get bored and leave. If they can die of starvation it will probably take a lot longer than you can last. Starvation has been the cause of many losses at sieges throughout history so how do you stop it? Initially you need to ensure that you have a very well stocked building in terms of water and food as well as other items to keep you warm and clean. Ultimately though, even the best prepared survivalist will have to leave his fortification.

If the zombies know where you live, and they probably do, they will likely keep amassing beyond any number you can expect to fight. This means you will need a safe way in and out of the building. There are lots of ways of dealing with this problem but it will depend greatly on the location of your home as well as the equipment you have available. You should know by now that you are going to have to be putting a regular dent in the zombie population so having a system in place of culling those around your premises is essential. Keeping the outside of your house clear would be ideal, but not always necessary. Ensure you have other means of getting out of your house other than the front door. This can include ladders and ropes, or even vehicles parked outside with roof access from upper floor windows. How exactly you do this is very dependent on what kind of zombies you face and what sort of house you have so use the information contained in this section to establish the best method for your situation.

WEAPON ACCESS

When fortifying your home, it is extremely important that you have the ability to safely attack the infected outside without having to open your front door to them. Their number will not reduce by itself! This is going to be achievable initially by having weapons suitable for the job and later by having areas in which those weapons are useable from. Depending on the weapons you have and the way your property is set up, the way in which you set up fighting areas will vary. If you have decent guns with enough ammunition then an upstairs window will provide an excellent shooting spot where you can put your feet up and do a little culling.

Molotov cocktails are without a doubt an excellent Zompoc weapon. They can be made anywhere easily and getting new ammo should never be too much of a problem, providing you can get it into the safe confines of your home. The trouble with the Molotov cocktail is that it is very dangerous to you and any vehicle or building that you are in. Your home must be carefully looked after in this respect. Throwing Molotovs out of the first floor of your house can work well but be very careful that you do not spread any of the fire towards your own building. If you have brick walls and metal covers on your windows this will be less of a problem, but having wooden walls or wood covering on your windows is potentially a life threatening problem.

If you have nothing but hand-to-hand combat weapons at your disposal then you will have to give consideration to weapons like lengthened spears and pole weapons which allow you to fight from the safety of a high position.

Never consider using ground floor windows or doors as weapon positions as even small firing slots can provide enough grip and leverage for a zombie to wrench your fortifications apart. Balconies provide the best positions for those fortunate enough to have them Just be sure that they cannot be accessed by lower roof tops or supports. Balconies provide excellent visibility and will allow you to sit and enjoy the sun whilst you do some work.

SALLY PORTS

A sally port is essentially a door in a structure that allows people to make pass and make sallies without compromising the defensive strength of the building. Historically a sally was a military manoeuvre, made typically during a siege by a defending force to harass isolated or vulnerable attackers before retreating back behind their defences. Sallies were a common way for besieged forces to reduce the strength and preparedness of a besieging army. Targets for these raids included equipment, which could be captured and used by the defenders, labour-intensive works such as trenches and mines, and siege engines and siege towers. Sometimes enemy labourers were also targeted.

Is any of this relevant to defending your home? Well, of course it is! What if you have two or three zombies milling around outside and light is starting to fade. Do you want to leave them outside, so that they could possibly break in during the night? A quick, discrete raid by a small group of people could quickly eliminate the zombies without compromising your basic security. You can then retire back inside and remain safe and secure.

How can you make a sally port then? Well, first of all, this doesn't mean you need to modify your home to a crazy level. Though sally ports in castles were prebuilt affairs it doesn't mean you cannot get the same effect with a little imagination. The basic idea is to have a way of leaving your building quickly and to be able to reuse it. A fire escape or lowering a sturdy ladder is a good example for during the Zompoc. Be sure there is somebody to lift you and it back up or you might end up in a rather unfortunate situation!

For the more astute reader you may also have noticed that a sally port makes a very handy escape point for emergencies. For obvious reasons, don't have a sally port right next to the place zombies keep targeting if possible. What is the point of escaping, only to drop into the middle of a zombie mob!

CHAPTER 5: THE LIVING

When considering a Zompoc, most people put the emphasis of their thoughts and plans to dealing with the zombies and too often forgetting the living. The living are a huge priority to you as you will unlikely survive on your own. The first thing to bear in mind is that safety in numbers is an idea that definitely rings true. Despite this, the larger the group the more organisation is needed and the harder it is to manage safely. The zombies may be the catalyst of the apocalypse but you will have more to worry about than just them once it has started.

WHO TO LISTEN TO

Once you no longer have the structure of your normal life you will have to listen to those around you and decide whether or not their information is valuable. Not everything everyone says is useful so remember this quote:

With this in mind, you must at all times give considered thought to every action and learn to recognise who is worth listening to and who is not. In the short-term many people will panic and those people are likely to be of little use in anything they say or do. Mid to long-term panic should be less of a concern but inexperience, ignorance and stupidity will be.

Be sure those who you take advice from are savvy in the sort of subjects you are now researching. Do not automatically trust everything that anyone has to say!

EMERGENCY SERVICES

With an outbreak as large as the zombie apocalypse, the emergency services will be in tatters within days if not hours. Do not rely on them for anything. This will be a difficult task for many as civilised society has grown used to having help at hand with nothing more than a phone call. The phones will be useless due to demand anyway and the emergency services will be swamped and very shortly lost. There is a definite possibility that elements of the military could survive, particularly those at sea or on isolated islands, but you will be waiting months or even years to see them, if ever. Do however bear in mind that members of the emergency services can be very useful to you and any team you have in your new life.

FORMING GROUPS

Let those who once fought against brothers and relatives
Now rightfully fight against barbarians.

Pope Urban II

You cannot afford to be picky here so try and group together with any humans you find and put all squabbles behind you. Groups will need a leader. If you are that sort of material, take the lead but if you're not support whoever is best suited to the job. Despite the need to gather together there are some people which must be avoided. Even during the Zompoc some people will be dangerous to be around. These people can be stupid, misguided, suicidal or egotistical among other things. There are many reasons why people can be dangerous and best avoided and you will have to learn to judge this yourself. You cannot be as careful choosing your friends as you might like, but don't accept any old idiot that happens your way either.

POLITICS WITHIN A GROUP

When people get together to form a group there are always politics involved together with indecision, distrust, competition, animosity and hatred. This needs to be avoided at all costs. Decide on the best leader and support them in every way you can. Keep petty disputes out of the picture. In a survival situation you will find that one of three people will become the natural leader: The physically strongest, the most intelligent (as an overview in life as opposed to pure IQ), or the most savvy (good with people and natural leaders). Sometimes these attributes will crossover of course.

The thing you should bear in mind is that in the short to medium term you should focus only on survival for the maximum number of people. Personal gain should be forgotten entirely. You can worry about politics in the long term if you survive that long. Initially follow a strong leader and only consider leadership challenges if that leader is making decisions that will lead to the destruction of your group and other survivors unnecessarily.

COMMUNICATION

Phones and the Internet will be two luxuries that you will very shortly be without. This will initially shock many people leaving them feeling alone and scared. Get over it. People have managed for thousands of years without

internet access and mobile phones, and so will you. You must first establish the best ways in which to communicate with the survivors around you and then find ways to maintain that communication whilst attracting the least attention from the zombies as possible.

WAYS TO COMMUNICATE WITH SURVIVORS

Communication is key among survivors and there are several aspects to this. There are different types of communication with different people, different ranges and with different parameters. No one communication method is perfect for all situations so give consideration to using a variety.

C B RADIOS

The CB (Citizen Band) Radio is probably the best all round means of communication with

survivors. These radios can be found in some vehicles such as lorries and trucks, as well as emergency service vehicles. Hand held devices are readily available in high street shops but be sure to keep a stock of spare batteries. For these you can also use headsets which will free up your hands for fighting, driving and general utility work. Using a headset also solves the problem of speaker noise attracting attention because all the sound is fed straight in to your ear though the head set.

Consider setting up a fixed C B Radio in your base of operations as well as vehicles and using hand held among personnel. These radios can make all the difference to survival, allowing easier co-ordination of teams and resources. These radios will also allow you to find other survivors in your area.

Consider using vehicles that have C B Radios already equipped. If they are not accessible they can always be fitted with relative ease. You will find C B radios at electronics shops, both large table top models as well as hand held. You will also find more limited selections at retail stores and supermarkets. Keeping these radios going is very important to keeping your community alive so round up plenty of spares as well as large stocks of batteries.

LOUDHAILER

Over moderate distances the loudhailer is very effective at carrying your message to many people at once however, it will draw huge attention to yourself. Only use the loudhailer in situations where you do not mind giving your position away to the surrounding zombies or you have no choice. The loudhailer is an excellent emergency alarm to surrounding survivors when trouble is imminent and unavoidable. Loudhailers can be found at electronics, hardware and similar shops.

DUMMY BOARDS

You will have surely seen Dawn of the Dead (2004). When survivors are stuck on opposing roof tops without radio communication boards do the job. Large boards with hand written

messages such as whiteboards are best as they are easily re-used. This is a simple and effective solution to communicating across short distances that cannot be travelled due to the zombie population. Binoculars/telescopes will assist and increase the useable distance. Dummy Boards are a basic and easy solution in certain circumstances as well as especially useful when you need to communicate across impassable areas and one party do not have radios.

ADVERTISING YOURSELF

You will want other survivors to find you and join the fight for survival. Therefore a strong public profile is important. Consider spray painting messages on your facilities and vehicles so that other survivors can easily locate you. Also, mark any road signs or public city maps with your location. The great news here is that zombies will merely ignore them but survivors will know easily how to find you. There is however one risk of such a public profile, hostile and opportunistic humans. Despite the dire situation of survival you jointly face, some people will attempt to take your supplies and facilities from you. If you cannot defend your facilities then do not advertise

them. However, if you cannot defend them to start with, you have a problem. See the section on hostile humans for further information on this subject.

LIGHTS/SIRENS
Both of these will draw the attention of anyone in a several mile radius or more towards you which is why they are lumped together. Lights and sirens are great for alerting other survivors to your presence or warning them quickly so consider making use of them on vehicles as well as in buildings. Radios are a good means of communication but there's no better way to alerting a lot of people very quickly than a siren which is especially useful at night when many people are asleep.

DEALING WITH INFECTION
Dealing with infection is something you are inevitably going to have to do, initially on a large scale and later with individuals. When all hell breaks loose everyone will be looking for shelter but be careful of whom you help. The type of zombies will affect how bad a problem this is. If they turn within seconds then the risk of not noticing infection is greatly reduced but if it takes hours or days the risk increases. When you meet new people ask them to show you all susceptible bite areas of their body.

This may not be dignified but can be a matter of life and death.

HIDING INFECTION
You should have seen enough movies to know that people will hide wounds from you in the hope that you will not notice or that they will be okay. Friends and family may also protect each other by hiding known wounds and infections. This is the height of stupidity. Always be sure to check everyone out when you first meet them. This also needs to be taken into consideration for your home or base whenever anyone enters it. No matter who they are they must be checked for bites, wounds and infections. If there is any potential risk of infection confine that person to a secure place until you are absolutely sure that they are not a problem.

EUTHANISING FRIENDS AND FAMILY

Many people will inevitably find it difficult to euthanise a friend or family member. Having read this manual you should be aware of the inherent risks of this situation and will be able to overcome them but other, lesser prepared humans may not. Never leave a single person to euthanise their friend or family member alone. Allocate someone to be with them or offer to do the job for them. This is a situation where you have to be objective. Never let infected family members or friends go as you are only increasing the number of enemies you have to face when you could have finished it simply to start with. Be aware that when you 'kill' a friend or family member different situations can arise. If you euthanise them once they have already turned, then all normal 'rules' apply. If however, you euthanize them whilst they are infected but still human they will likely re-animate. This process could be immediate or take up to several hours. The only way to be sure that the body does not re-animate is to euthanize through destruction of the brain or decapitation.

THE RISK OF INFECTION IN YOUR HOME AND BASE

If you are thoroughly checking everyone who enters the building you should minimise the risk of infected people entering the premises, however there is another risk. Do people who die of natural causes or misadventure also re-animate or do they have to be infected with something first? There is no definite answer but potentially this is a big risk. If you go to bed one night in your base and one person has a heart attack or slips and falls to their death then you potentially have a zombie within your perimeter.

This problem needs to be dealt with in two ways. Initially section the property to limit danger to people and secondly be prepared for a fight at all times. How this is done is linked more to preparing your home or base but the risk from the living is relevant here. Always sleep in a locked room where possible and have your comrades do the same. Then, post watches and guards working in shifts each night to patrol and guard the whole building. Those on guard must awaken the occupants of every room each morning to ensure that all are still human. With this in mind keep weapons close to hand at all times and have your wits about you. Know where your spare ammunition is, how to access it quickly and how to load and use your weapons properly.

There are other ways in which infection can get in to your base than just via humans. Animals can potentially be carriers of disease and they can also psychically transmit infected material. Be sure to check any pets or animals that are brought in to your home or base thoroughly. Also, barricade your walls, not just from zombies but also smaller animals that could transmit infection such as mice and rats. This is no easy task but you must do what you can to prevent infection, both from zombies as well as common infections.

Additionally, anything which comes in to contact with the outside world much be thoroughly cleaned on a regular basis which includes you, your clothes, tools, weapons and other equipment. For those fighting the zombies this will be of special importance. You might do well to allocate one or two people whose entire job is cleaning and sterilisation.

PLAY TO YOUR STRENGTHS

Everyone is different so accept that and establish the best job for each person. The physically strongest and able bodied will clearly be the best for fighting, the nimble and fast best suited to foraging, and the less able bodied to guarding and driving. Equal opportunities will be an idea of the past. Establish what you are best at and do it. Some people are naturally gifted at certain things while others train and practice till they reach a certain proficiency at a task. Always take advantage of the strengths of individuals and also try and strike a good balance. A group of lumberjacks will be good at one thing but perhaps not great at other tasks!

Initially when you are on your own or with but a few allies you may have to fulfil tasks which you are not best suited to. Unfortunately, there is little that can be done to assist in this situation other than simply rising to the task, being correctly prepared and quickly establishing larger groups in which you can focus on your strengths.

EDUCATE OTHER SURVIVORS

Not all survivors will have such a well thought out and developed understanding of Zompoc survival as you are quickly learning. Having knowledgeable, sensible and well educated (in survival) people around you will greatly increase your chances. Bestow the knowledge of this book to team mates and fellow survivors and see the training section in particular to improve the combat effectiveness of your team. Education for your fellow survivors is a lot more important than you may realise. Just because some things are obvious to you, they may not be to others. Trying to teach things which are obvious to you can be difficult as many things which you would consider as basic may go unsaid or overlooked because of this very reason. Always start from the beginning. There is no harm in going over old ground so be sure that everyone knows what the deal is. It can make all the difference when your life is on the line.

HEALTH AND WELLBEING

Staying alive is the first concern of course but you have more to consider than just the bite of a zombie. Initially we will look at the short to mid-term situation.

NUTRITION

As most of the population is now dead, there will be a large food supply and a reduced demand meaning you can forage from shops and homes as you please. This will be do-able for at least the foreseeable future whilst you become established. All foods which perish without refrigeration or freezing will decay within a matter of days unless you can provide power to run the equipment to keep them in a stable state which is unlikely. Other food stocks however will be edible for months, years and even decades.

Canned, tinned and dry foods will be your staple diet as they are easily stored and do not easily perish. Such foods are known as shelf stable. To a reasonable extent you can manage without any cooking facilities at all, but for your own sanity and health, get something to cook with quickly. Gas camping stoves or equivalent are readily available, with plenty of supplies to keep them running for years. They are also quick and simple to use. Getting cooking equipment sorted quickly and a good stock of food supplies to go with it will go a long way in keeping spirits high and your body strong.

MEDICINE

Medicine is the art and science of healing. It encompasses a range of health care practices evolved to maintain and restore health by the prevention and treatment of illness. Complex medicine will go out of the window on a short to medium-term basis. Your concern here should be with all things available at the chemist.

You need to keep common minor injuries under control and free from infection. Quick recovery times are essential. No medicine will cure injuries from zombies so focus on other aspects. Be equipped to deal with broken and sprained bones, joint damage, common colds and standard infections and fatigue. Medical supplies should be easily available from chemists and supermarkets.

ESSENTIAL MEDICAL AIDS

BANDAGES/PLASTERS

Covering wounds (that weren't caused by zombies) is absolutely essential in preventing infection. Infection of open wounds can lead to weakness, disease, and even death. Covering of wounds is also vitally important when you live among the dead as any contact between them and an open wound could result in infection of the worst kind. Be well stocked in these items at all times and cover all injuries thoroughly.

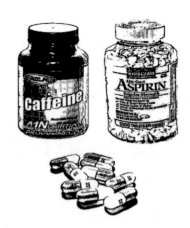

ANTISEPTIC WIPES AND CREAMS

As well as covering all injuries thoroughly you will want to clean any open wounds to prevent infection. Clean all cuts and grazes before dressing them. Change the dressings regularly and clean wounds with sterile wipes or alcohol every time.

FATIGUE RELIEF

When survival is the order of the day rest may just not be an option. You need to be at the best of your ability for as long as is needed. Keep a good supply of fatigue relief. This can come in the form of caffeine pills such as 'Pro Plus', as well as energy drinks, coffee and any form of sugary product or stimulant.

PAIN RELIEF PILLS

This may seem a petty consideration when there are flesh eating monsters at your door, but pain of any kinds can mean the difference in fighting or running to the best of your ability as well as being able to make the best calm and calculated decisions when needed.

JOINT SUPPORTS

There are all sorts of ways to injure joints, particularly the wrists and knees. An injury such as a sprain can reduce your chances of survival greatly by not allowing you to move or fight to the best of your ability.

CLEANLINESS

When your life is at risk every day cleanliness may not even occur to you anymore but this could be the very thing that kills you. Infection from both dirt, grime and bacteria as well as zombie infected elements are all a risk. Keep everything you touch regularly clean, such as

your bed, your cooking equipment and eating implements, the steering wheel of your car, your weapons and clothes and everything. When you fight in close proximity with the undead it is entirely possible that you will come in contact with their blood and this can be a major problem. Of course hand-to-hand combat should be avoided for this very reason, but that is not a luxury you will always have. Whenever you can clean and cleanse all equipment that you come into contact with. This is just as relevant for your car and base.

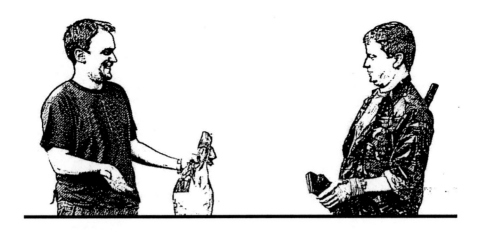

Stock up on plenty of spare clothes and equipment as well as strong cleaning products such as bleach. If you ever end up fighting a zombie in your vehicle or home be sure to do a very thorough clean up job. Cleaning is boring but it would be pretty lame to have such a great base and to be killed by infection (zombie or not) because you didn't do the dusting.

SANITATION

Not a particularly pleasant subject but one that must be considered none the less. Clearly your toilet facilities may no longer and even then there will be no local authority keeping things going and water supply will be short. Likewise the local council will not be collecting your rubbish each week. Sanitation is highly important for medium to long-term survival in preventing infection and disease. The problem of sanitation when you no longer have public services is compounded by the zombie danger. You need to get rid of waste, both human and solid somehow.

MENTAL STATE

Keeping people psychologically healthy is going to be a really important issue both in the short and long-term. Initially the shock and trauma of the Zompoc may stun some people and this can lead to inefficiency and even suicidal tendencies. You, and all those around you must stay focused and whilst that may sound

easier said than done the majority of people have a will to survive. In the short-term you need to keep an eye on all those around you to look for symptoms of extreme depression (beyond the expected normal depression about the world ending). Keep people active and they will stay focused and avoid depression. This is also useful as you need people working and fighting on a regular basis.

Psychology is an important aspect to all elements of your survival. If you have to face a zombie(s) in combat and are fearful you will likely die. Go in fighting with the mindset knowing that you are going to destroy them and you have a much greater chance of survival.

As a survivor, whether you are a leader or not you have a responsibility to keep an eye on other survivors, not just to defend them physically but also to ensure that they stay as mentally healthy as possible. An apocalypse situation can put people under more pressure than they can usually handle resulting in serious depression, under performance and even suicide. Suicide is a danger on two different levels. Initially you lose a survivor, and that is a very bad thing. You need all the help you can get but additionally that suicidal person may shortly become a zombie. Be watchful of those around you and do what you can to keep spirits high.

FITNESS AND STRENGTH

When the Zompoc starts you are going to want to be in as good shape as possible and generally fit, healthy, strong, with muscle and stamina. You do not need to be an Olympic athlete (though it would be nice), but being healthy and strong could make all the difference when you are running for your life or defending yourself in hand-to-hand combat with nothing but a broken bottle and a broom handle. In terms of preparation for this eventuality, do regular exercise and try and keep your body fat down to a healthy level. Smoking is not good for stamina but if it keeps you sane then fair enough. The zombies are more likely to get you than cancer.

In the Initial phase of the Zompoc, fitness and strength will no longer be your focus, only survival. If you hadn't prepared yourself in advance it's too late now and if you are still alive you will likely be running, fighting or working hard enough to keep fitness up. At this stage, concern yourself more with staying healthy by getting as good a diet as possible and not getting bitten.

In the medium and especially long term, fitness and strength is going to be a real concern. You and all those around you need to be kept in good physical and mental condition. For some, such as those commonly fighting pr practicing to do so, this might already be achieved. But for others, such as guards, drivers and those who work mostly within the confines of your facility, exercise will be doubly important.

Traditionally, most people do the majority of their exercise either outdoors or in a well maintained and equipped gym facility. Exercising outdoors will be difficult unless you have a very well established and defended region, this is something you can generally rule out. Certain indoor facilities such as swimming pools will also have to be ruled out due to the maintenance requirements of keeping them clean and healthy. How then can you provide a means and motivation for your people to stay fit?

Providing means for people to exercise will not just keep them fitter and stronger but also keep them happier and mentally healthier. The two best ways to cater for this are initially through establishing a basic supply of free weights. A room full of free weights will bring people together with a common interest; it will keep them focused and away from depression and anxiety. Consider finding some kettle bells, they will keep your people fit and strong and with no maintenance required and no other equipment. They were introduced by the Russians as a very cheap and simple way to train hard with little space and money. Kettle bells are also great for those living a nomadic lifestyle. The next stage is to establish a larger indoor area where sports can be played such as football (soccer), basketball, tennis, squash etc. Any game that can easily be played indoors that is good for fitness but with the minimum chance of injury is excellent. This stage is only going to be relevant once you have a fully established community.

HOSTILE HUMANS

The human race has a long history of fighting each other and this will not stop simply because we have a common enemy in the form of zombies. The threat from other humans will typically be the most basic primitive one that has existed since we lived in caves; someone has something another wants such as a bigger cave than they have or items they want. They hit them on the head and take it, simple.

Everything you acquire or build, such as a strong home or base, vehicles, supplies and weapons is all very valuable. There will be others out there who would rather take it from you with force or cunning rather have to do the work themselves. There are several ways that you can do to reduce the risk of violence or opportunism from other humans. The ways in which you fortify your base and vehicles from zombies will mostly and hopefully also work well against living humans too.

Never leave your base or home unguarded. If possible when you do, lock it up or make it discrete. The two main ways to protect what you have is to hide it or guard it. Hiding will only work whilst you are a small group, after this protection is the key. A show of force will be enough to deter most opportunistic humans until they can show more force than you. It is always a risk that a group of humans with more manpower, guns or bigger guns turns up and wants what is yours. This will always be a concern and is hard to defend against. Remember, do all that you can to keep alive by avoiding the fight altogether. This is the best option and in this respect, the deterrent of looking strong is your best option.

Additionally, when you are away from your base in vehicles, always keep them guarded. Locking vehicles is an option but most are quickly and easily stolen. Also, locking your vehicles could be risky as you want quick and easy access to them in emergencies.

In terms of keeping supplies out the hands of thieves and vagabonds you should be storing all essential supplies within the safety of your compound, home or base. Do bear in mind that whilst you will have zombie-proofed your area, humans can still use other means to breach your perimeter or building. Those looking to steal from you can drive vehicles through gates, fencing and walls, blow holes in areas and more. All of this can leave you completely exposed to the zombie hoards, whilst the thieves make their getaway. This is another reason why keeping guards active is so important.

KEEPING PETS

As of 2006, 63 percent of all US households own a pet. Clearly many people enjoy having the company of a non-human companion, why would that change in the Zompoc? There are

however a number of considerations which must be made. The first most obvious one is can non-humans be infected? The chances are unlikely as few diseases transmit across species, but it can happen of course. If non-humans can be infected then it is going to make survival that much more difficult, actually nigh on impossible.

Let us then work on the principal that the zombie infection only affects humans, this is after all most likely. Is it safe to keep a pet? There are many risks of keeping a pet during Zompoc, the main being infection. Animals can transmit infection without knowing it, making

them potentially lethal to you. Pets will also require feeding, meaning additional supplies will be required.

Keeping pets is not all bad. As companions they can add a lot to people's lives and during the Zompoc that could mean the difference between losing your head and staying sane. Some animals such as dogs may also assist you. They can alert you do intruders and presence of trespassers. In fact, a dog will likely be the best pet you could have as they will help you if trained properly and show affection to keep your spirits high. Horses may also prove useful, but few know how to look after them.

A horse is not just a pet but also a method of transport. It doesn't need to be refuelled but will need frequent food and care. Also be aware that horses can quickly tire if you require prolonged speed from them.

Others pets that are of use in the Zompoc are birds and small mammals. Birds come in all shapes and sizes and can offer handy early warning of threats or in the case of raptors, the ability to help with food and hunting. Mammals such as ferrets can also help with hunting underground for prey.

DOGS

The dog is a domesticated form of the Gray Wolf. The domestic dog has been one of the most widely kept working and companion animals in human history and is useful for a huge variety of roles in the Zompoc as well as being a loyal and friendly companion. Over centuries man has bred dogs for different traits that make them more suitable for different jobs. Whilst most dogs are great pets there are specific breeds that have important benefits that you will need to consider. If you already own a dog then you may want to try and train it to perform certain jobs, at the very least as a guard animal or use its ability to carry light objects. Remember that a dog is a pack animal by nature and wants to be part of a group. If you let it, the dog will take over as pack leader and this will reduce the effectiveness of the animal. Being the pack leader doesn't mean shouting all the time. It simply means that you have to provide the leadership and energy of the group. There are a few myths with dogs like the fact that you need to train German shepherd dog by speaking in German or that showering your dogs with treats will make them love you. A dog is happy and contented when part of a structured pack.

BIRDS

Birds are popular pets though in the Zompoc you will find only a small number of them will be of use to you. If you currently own and fly birds of prey then you can use these animals for hunting and catching killed prey. Birds like canaries can be used for gas and enemy detection though a dog is probably better.

FERRETS

These friendly little animals are mainly kept for hunting rabbits. When using ferrets the rabbit holes are covered with small purse nets fixed to the ground with a small wooden peg. The ferret enters one of the holes and although a completely domesticated animal they have retained the instinct of their ancestor and will hunt through every nook and cranny within that warren, using their highly developed senses of hearing and scent to locate any rabbits present. The rabbit, with the ferret behind it, will bolt out of the nearest exit hole and be caught in the purse net. They are then despatched quickly by the ferret owner.

LONG TERM SURVIVAL

If you can survive long enough to establish control and an area and regain ground then much of the information containing in this section will begin to change, as you begin to re-establish society. For more information related to the living long-term, see the 'Rebuilding' chapter at the end of the book.

DOG BREEDS

❖ **Sporting - Gun Dog.** Perhaps the most intelligent of the breeds, resulting in their wide variety of uses and their ease of training.

❖ **Non-Sporting Dogs.** No longer perform the tasks they were originally bred for. These dogs vary in every conceivable way from size, temperament, features and coats

❖ **Working Dogs.** Developed to perform a wide variety of tasks, such as herding, droving, pulling, hauling, herding, hunting, rescuing and guarding.

❖ **Herding Dogs.** Perform a variety of tasks relating mainly to the herding of livestock.

❖ **Terrier Dogs.** Developed to hunt and kill vermin. The vermin included control rats, mice and other predatory animals.

❖ **Toy Dogs.** Developed to ease the lifestyle and provide pleasure to rich people.

❖ **Hound Dogs.** Chase (or hound) a quarry by sight or smell, or a combination of both senses. They have exceptional eyesight, combined with speed and stamina.

❖ **Scent Hounds.** Specialise in following the scent or the smell of its quarry.

❖ **Sight hounds** . Also known as Gazehounds as their gaze focuses on the horizon seeking game, specialise in hunting their quarry by sight rather than scent.

❖ **Hunting Dogs.** Bred primarily to work with people to hunt animals. fish and birds.

CHAPTER 6: TRAVEL & MOVEMENT

Quick decisions are unsafe decisions.
Sophocles

At some point you are going to need to move. You may be travelling on foot, by truck, boat, plane or bicycle but however you do it you will be doing one big thing, leaving the safety of your fortified safe place. Travel on land is dangerous and must be undertaken lightly. The first and most important thing to remember is preparation. What is your objective, what are your resources and what is the timescale? You may need to travel a short distance to retrieve a person or you move all of your people to a new location hundreds of miles away. Maybe you just need to run one block for supplies but whatever the reason you need to be prepared for the unexpected and make it back alive and uninfected.

TRAVEL BY LAND

Travel on foot is always going to be necessary no matter which vehicles you use or where you are hold up. Even if you have a helicopter you will need to leave it at some point. Travel on foot is the most dangerous as you immediately lack the speed and protection of a vehicle and

leave yourself vulnerable to the infected. Travel by vehicles as much as possible but when on foot make sure you plan and then plan again. Refer to the sections on clothing

and equipment and team selection before venturing out into the unknown. You are going to need vehicles unless you plan on hiding in your fortified safe place surrounding by death and decay until you die. With most of the population looking to take a sizable bite out of your throat you will find a plethora of vehicles available to you. Obviously if you already own suitable vehicles use them, you will probably find more suitable and better vehicles with some quick scouting. Vehicles include all forms of motorised transport and include aircraft, land vehicles such as cars, trucks, buses and motorcycles and finally watercraft such as boats, jet skis and ships.

OBTAINING VEHICLES

Your first job with vehicles is obtaining them! If you don't have access to vehicles then look to the general public who will have abandoned them in massive numbers due to the fact that they are now dead. There are several places you can look for vehicles during an outbreak. The most obvious places to search are car parks and parking garages, car dealerships and public service stations. Though these will have lots of vehicles there are a few big problems, the first being that car parks are often dark and secluded, also the vehicles usually don't have the keys left in them! It is much easier to look for vehicles in open areas since they allow faster escape and smaller chance of being ambushed whilst still offering you a vast array of types to choose from.

Main roads, motorways, freeways and busy streets are a good place to find abandoned vehicles, though remember that just because you've found the perfect truck if it is stuck in the middle of hundreds of cars you will never get anywhere. Look around the side streets, slip road or for vehicles with space near them so you can escape safely. By looking for cars in smaller parts of your city you will help mitigate

the risk as less population means fewer zombies. Always take a friend when searching for vehicles. See the 'Travelling on Foot' section for advice here. Land vehicles are common throughout the world and used for almost every job on the planet. You will be using them for a variety of uses that will probably start with your quick exit to a safe place when the Zompoc breaks out. After this initial rush to safety, what else might you use vehicles for? Well, collection of people and supplies is one important area, scouting and rescue is another. For each task there is a suitable vehicle and it is important that you use the best vehicle for a specific task. See the 'Vehicles Chapter' for more information on vehicle types along with their benefits and flaws.

PLANNING TRIPS

Unless you are planning on hiding in a coal bunker for months or even years you will at some point have to travel somewhere. It is critical that any journey no matter how small is carefully planned with regards to goods, supplies, people, clothing, weapons and objective. If you are not careful you could find your next shopping trip ends with you ending up as the meal!

Short distance travel is necessary and also very dangerous. By short distance we mean a distance that can be measured in minutes or hours. This is likely to be where you forage for supplies, investigate a nearby building or help a friend. These operations, whilst seemingly simple, can easily get your people killed as you may be on your own or in small groups making you easily blocked, trapped or ambushed. If you are going to be moving on foot it is imperative that you are equipped and with a group, even if it is just one other person. You need to choose your objective, your place to return to and emergency options for when everything hits the fan. Refer to the relevant chapters on clothing, equipment and supplies for foot travel and make sure you are mobile. Under no circumstances arm yourself up like a tank and walk out into the street on your own with all your weapons, yes it will be fun for a while until you are finally buried under a pile of corpses. Remember, Zombies are unlimited - your ability to fight is not.

At the other end of scale is long distance travel, this is where you expect to be travelling for more than a single day. As well as the precautions that you take for short distance travel you must also plan for rest, sleep, maintenance, repairs and refuelling. This makes long distance travel very dangerous and susceptible to failures in planning. Depending on your situation you may find you will have a well organised, equipped and modified outfit ready for long distance travel or you will have to cobble something together hastily to get out fast. Either way, for long distance travel it is imperative that you make use of the convoy system. The idea of a convoy is a group of vehicles (of any type, but usually motor vehicles or ships) travelling together for mutual support and protection. Often a convoy is organised with armed defensive support, though it may also be used in a non-military sense, for example when driving through remote areas. This use of multiple vehicles will provide assistance and effectiveness whilst providing redundancy in people, equipment and resources if anything goes wrong.

CONVOYS

If you are planning on moving a number of people from one place to another, especially over a long distance, you will need to organise a convoy. At its most basic level a convoy is a group of people or vehicles travelling together. During the Zompoc you will find your convoys will become both critical for survival and also something you will need to spend time and effort organising.

You are likely to need to move a small group, probably family and friends first, hopefully later on you will need the ability to move larger groups. In the early days your convoy will probably consist of nothing more than a couple of vehicles, following a lead car. As time moves on and you get more people, better prepared vehicles and have a little more time to prepare there are things that can be done to make your convoy safer and effective.

Moving people and supplies works best with stage 3 prepared vehicles but in an emergency you can do it in any vehicles. At the most basic level this is making sure your vehicle is as safe and reliable as you can make it. With time and resources you can improve and modify your vehicles to make them safer, faster, more reliable and better suited to specific tasks in your survival during the Zombie apocalypse. We make uses of the three stage system for vehicle modification. See the vehicle preparation chapter for more on this subject as it covers everything from re-enforcing windscreen to adding extra armour, beefing up the engines, adding additional cargo capacity and also the addition of offensive and defensive weaponry.

CONVOY VEHICLES

When travelling as a convoy there are certain vehicles than will be used to perform certain roles. Obviously your early, hastily assembled columns of vehicles that you use at the start of the Zompoc will consist of anything you can find. Even in these early days you will find vehicles like trucks and buses are best used to haul people and supplies whilst motorcycles are better suited for scouting and escort duties. There are four broad classifications for vehicles and it would be wise to identify their

CONVOY VEHICLES

- ❖ SCOUT VEHICILE
- ❖ ASSAULT VEHCILE
- ❖ WEAPON VEHCILE
- ❖ TRANSPORT VEHCILE

roles as early as possible so that you can prepare them for convoy work and ensure your convoy works effectively and reliably.

SCOUT VEHICLE.

Every convoy needs to make use of information; this is where your scout comes in. If you do not know what lies ahead then you may be driving into a world of pain, this is where a scout vehicle comes in critical. These vehicles need to be crewed by your more experienced and independent people as they will need to think fast and on their feet in an emergency.

Vehicles suitable for scout work usually consist of small, fast machine such as a motorcycle, ATV or convertible. The key requirements are that they are light, quick and manoeuvrable. Obviously two wheeled vehicles have a major advantage in that they can easily move around obstacles and even travel off the main routes. The scout's job it is to go ahead of everybody else and find any dangers, look for possible safe spots, supplies and to generally keep the convoy safe and secure. Vehicles such as trikes and quads do have additional benefits though that can outweigh their disadvantages. Firstly, they can carry greater loads and are thus handy for emergency extraction, carrying small valuable supplies and even people. The

second advantage is that they are a much more stable, slower speed platform for weapons and combat. Stick somebody on the back of a trike with a firearm and you have a quick, handy attack vehicle. This vehicle will need a driver and a spotter at the very least. Communication gear is important so they can get back in touch with the main convoy. If you have one, you should have radios. No weapons other than the driver's small arms and light, easy to access firearms. Anything more than this might encourage them to get bogged down in a fire fight. If using trikes or quads then you can add extra crew and up the weapons as these become support vehicles with a scouting component.

ASSAULT VEHICLE

The assault vehicle is something every convoy will want. This is a cross between a combat vehicle and a heavy utility. If you have only one vehicle in your convoy it needs to be this one.

The main function of the assault vehicle is its ability to protect the front of a convoy by moving road debris out of the way, clearing zombies out of the path of the transports and essentially being the armoured plough. The roads may have all kinds of crap on them, not including the undead themselves. You need to be able to keep the road clear whilst still moving.

Though critical to the convoy this vehicle will be the one taking damage and always in action. Because of this you can expect a constant erosion of armour, tyres, clutch and engines on these vehicles. If you are going to beef up the armour or add reinforcement to some of your vehicles this is the one that

Suggested Modifications

- ❖ ARMOUR PLATING
- ❖ JERRY CAN HOLDERS
- ❖ RADIO
- ❖ FLARE GUN
- ❖ PLOUGH/COW CATCHER
- ❖ WEAPON MOUNTS
- ❖ ARMOURED WINDOWS
- ❖ EACAPE HATCHES
- ❖ WHEEL/TYRE GUARDS

needs to be at the front of the queue. Any snow ploughs or cow catchers definitely need to be fitted to this beast. At the very least you need a decent bull bar fitted. Only combat crews in this vehicle and they need to be armed appropriately for the mission. It is also highly advisable to fit this vehicle with escape hatches and any extra weapons and armour you have the time to fit. Suitable vehicles for this are large trucks and buses.

WEAPON VEHICLE

The weapon vehicle is quite flexible and can be any kind of vehicle that can carry people and weapons. Make sure these vehicles are pretty tough and carry people that have and know how to use weapons correctly. It is their job to help protect the convoy, guard broken down transports and in an emergency can perform the role of transport vehicle.

At the most basic level a weapon vehicle can be a minibus with the windows knocked out to provide shooting positions to a pickup truck with several people on the back with rifles. The primary job of these vehicles is to provide combat power wherever it is needed and you therefore don't want to use your largest vehicles for this job.

A good weapons vehicle is small enough to be able to get around obstructions and traverse rough roads or terrain whilst being big enough to carry a useful number of people and weapons. Ideally you want strong, reliable

Suggested Modifications

- ❖ ARMOUR PLATING
- ❖ JERRY CAN HOLDERS
- ❖ RADIO
- ❖ FLARE GUN
- ❖ TURRENT OR PINTEL MOUNT
- ❖ HEAVY WEAPONS
- ❖ ESCAPE HATCHES
- ❖ LOTS OF SPARE AMMUNITION

vehicles like Land Cruisers, Land Rovers and Jeeps for this kind of work. Make sure they have basic armour protection fitted and that their fields of fire are clear. Easy access to ammunition and supplies is also important. As these vehicles are going to be racing around helping people and vehicle in emergency situations they need to be flexible. Extra space inside for emergency seating and spare cargo will add to the versatility of these vehicles.

TRANSPORT VEHICLE

This is any vehicle being used to carry cargo, people or any combination. Though not as exotic as the other vehicle classifications you will find this is a very important vehicle, possibly the most important. Almost every mission you ever conduct will need one.

A transport vehicle is obviously designed to carry heavy weights over long distances. This means you need to use vehicles designed for carrying heavy loads over their axles such as trucks, lorries, buses and coaches. A decent, high torque engine is also very helpful when moving heavy weights. Diesel engines tend to be very tough, reliable and get much better fuel economy than an equivalent petrol engine.

The transport vehicle may often be the same type of vehicle as the assault vehicle. The big difference is that the assault vehicle is a fighting platform and designed for blunt force

Suggested Modifications

- ❖ ARMOUR PLATING
- ❖ JERRY CAN HOLDERS
- ❖ RADIO
- ❖ FLARE GUN

impact. There are different types of cargo and you need to have the correct vehicle to move your items. Buses and coaches are great for small items and people and are difficult for zombies to get access to. Flat back lorries are great for larger, heavy loads but are obviously quite easy to climb on and are therefore risky for carrying people.

Due to the critical nature of hauling people and supplies it is critical that you keep your transports out of danger; they are literally your lifeblood.

CONVOY ORGANISATION

The important thing to consider with convoys is how you are going to organise them. There is no point taking 50 motorcycles cross country and then trying to carry tonnes of cargo, spares and weapons on vehicle not designed for the job. Depending on the size of a convoy you will need different types of vehicle to perform different roles. Most of the vehicles will be carrying people and supplies but you will also need scouts, weapon vehicles etc.

SMALL CONVOYS

These are for small groups of 5-10 people and might be your first convoy or perhaps a raiding party or scout group looking for supplies. It is small and light so do not linger in Zombie infested territory.

The ideal vehicles are:

- ❖ 1 scout vehicle
- ❖ 1 assault vehicle
- ❖ 0+ Supply vehicles

With the two basic vehicles you will have one that is armoured up or at the very least of strong and sturdy construction. This vehicle needs to go at the front when you need to brush through obstructions or to run through groups of zombies. The second vehicle will be a scout vehicle, this could easily be a bike or fast car and whilst out at the front scouting should not engage targets or attempt to break through barricades. Retreat to the assault vehicle and let it do that job. If the scout vehicle is lost for any reason you can carry its crew and equipment in the assault vehicle. It is advisable to find at least one supply vehicle as soon as possible so that you have a backup and the ability to carry all your people if you lose one of the main trucks.

Notes:

You have only one main vehicle to carry people and supplies so don't do anything stupid!

Don't let the scouts travel too far on their own. It is critical that all vehicles are able to communicate with each other, ideally with radios, if not with hand signals, coloured flags etc.

MEDIUM CONVOYS

Medium sized groups of 10+ people, all the vehicles should have radios. This could simply be a convoy doing the same job as the small convoy or it may be your long distance convoy heading to a new location or home. Notice that the number of gun and transport trucks is not fixed. Optimise this number based upon whether you are long term transport or combat operations. Obviously if you are travelling 1,000 miles you don't want most of your vehicles only be used for firepower, you need to haul people and supplies too!

The ideal vehicles are:

- ❖ 1+ scout vehicles
- ❖ 1 assault vehicle
- ❖ 1+ gun trucks
- ❖ 1+ transport vehicles

LARGE CONVOYS

Large sized groups of 50+ people, all the vehicles should have radios. This is a large, powerful convoy that could easily be the entire remnants of a city during an evacuation through to an all out assault column. There is an unlimited size to this convoy though it is still important to include useful support vehicles. With such a large, moving feast you need as many scout vehicles as you can find, there is no way you can afford to lose this critical number of people, vehicles and supplies.

The ideal vehicles are:

- ❖ 3+ scout vehicles
- ❖ 2+ assault vehicles
- ❖ 3+ gun trucks
- ❖ 3+ transport vehicles

POTENTIAL DANGERS

The formation in which the convoy moves can be a type of passive defence. The convoy commander has three options when confronted with dangers ahead. These are to halt in place, continue to advance or disperse quickly to concealed positions. Regardless of the option selected, the actions should be taken and the signal directing the action should be explained to all members of the convoy beforehand.

The primary consideration is the immediate departure from the impact area. The convoy should only be halted when a substantial and unexpected danger is ahead of the convoy. The convoy commander should look for an alternate route around the impact area and the convoy should remain prepared to move out rapidly. The mission or terrain may require the convoy to continue. If this is the case, increase speed and spread out to the maximum extent the terrain will allow.

No single defensive measure or combination of measures, will prevent or effectively counter all problems when travelling in convoy. The best defence is to avoid dangers to start with road block is simply where the route you are using is blocked in a deliberate manner, This could be down to other survivors placing debris, damaged vehicle etc in the way or possibly the Zombies blocking a route through weight of numbers.

When an element of a convoy is halted and is unable to proceed because of disabled vehicles, a damaged bridge, or other obstacle it is advisable for trained personnel will dismount to remove obstructions or damaged vehicles. The road must be cleared and convoy movement resumed as soon as possible. Wounded personnel are evacuated using the fastest possible mode. When disabled vehicles cannot be towed, their cargo should be distributed among other vehicles if time permits. When it is not feasible to evacuate vehicles and/or cargo, they will be destroyed upon order from the convoy commander or hidden/covered until they can be recovered later. If at all possible, radios and other critical items will be recovered before the vehicles are destroyed.

Here are some suggestions to improving the safety of your convoy.

1. Select the best route for the convoy. Decide this based upon the type of the vehicles and materials being transported,. Don't choose narrow roads with lots of obstruction when you have a ten truck convoy. You can easily get stuck and find you are unable to move.
2. Make a detailed map reconnaissance. Do this in conjunction with your reconnaissance operations and keep it as up-to-date as possible. Ensure all drivers have maps and working communications.
3. Make an aerial reconnaissance before and during the operation if you have access to aerial units. Even a micro light or para-motor will prove critical for long range observation.
4. Obtain current intelligence information from forward units or previous operations.
5. Do not travel at night with valuable cargo. The night offers many advantages to zombies but seriously degrades your effectiveness due to your impaired visibility. This will also reduce the speed at which your convoy can therefore travel.

THE LIVING

Other survivors can present a serious danger to your convoy as they are both an unexpected value and have the potential skills and equipment that could be as dangerous as or more dangerous than the zombies themselves. Read previous sections on the living for additional information on how to avoid them and to stay out of trouble. Just because you are living doesn't mean your life or efforts will be valued or rewarded. Your duty is first to yourself and second to your immediate comrades.

Additional consideration when facing the living includes those listed above as well as:

1. Do not present a profitable target unless absolutely necessary. The more food or fuel you carry the more likely you are to be hit.
2. Never schedule routine times or routes. This will make it much harder to work out when you will be passing through and thus hit.

TRAVEL BY AIR

Vehicles that travel by air have one massive and obvious advantage over other vehicles and especially travel on foot. Quite simply they lift you up and away from the infected. These vehicles include light aircraft, air balloons, dirigibles, helicopters etc. The most common will be light aircraft, usually found at smaller airports and aerodromes. The downside to most aerial vehicles is the maintenance required and the fact that they require dedicated landing and takeoff location. On top of this you need to know how to fly them! You will also still need a way to travel short and medium distances and be able to access building to collect people, supplies etc.

OBTAINING VEHICLES

Aircraft are obtained for airbases, airports, hospitals and police head quarters. Don't expect to visit aircraft collections or museums for aircraft. They may look serviceable but they are guaranteed to fail and let you fall to the earth in a somewhat unfortunate fashion

SCOUTING

Due to the height and speed of aircraft they make ideal vehicles for scouting areas.

Another benefit of flying high is the excellent all round view that you will receive of the area. Slower aircraft such as balloons and airships are perfect here as they can loiter quietly and slowly in an area whilst providing excellent intelligence on the ground.

RAIDS

Raid operations are explained more fully in the operations section and involve all kinds of vehicles and resources. The speed and ability to ignore terrain make aircraft excellent for raid operations. They do suffer though in that they use up valuable resources and have a much lower cargo capacity than either ground or water based transport.

COMBAT OPERATIONS

These operations either make use of the aerial vehicle itself as a weapon or as a means to insert fire teams into hostile area. The former required either modified aircraft or military aircraft.

ESCAPE

Travel by air, even in the most primitive of machines, is still usually faster than travel on foot due to the fact that you can avoid terrain and move completely free of roads, highways or rails. Couple this with the often greater speeds and range, you will find travel by air to be probably the most effective way to get out of a dangerous or infested area. The usual caveats about maintenance, flying skill and the possibility of crashing still apply though when you have a pack of 50 zombies on your ass. You will probably find maintenance is not something you will be quite so concerned about. Save that for when you are heading towards the ground at a high rate of kn0ts!

TRAINING

If you try and fly any aircraft without knowing what you are doing you will quite simply die. Realistically it is probably best avoided as you can manage perfectly well using land or sea vehicles. If you really need to train then you can make use of flight simulation equipment or hardware, though gaining access to this kind of equipment is not always easy. The best way though would be to find an actual pilot and get them to train you in the use of gliders or light aircraft. Make sure you train several people so you have redundancy of skills in case anybody is injured or unable to fly.

MAINTENANCE

Aircraft maintenance is notoriously complicated and like the flying it should only be conducted by those with prior skills, knowledge or experience. People with this kind of experience are going to be either civil aviation personnel or military aircraft personnel. Also remember that aircraft use more refined aviation fuel and this is not normally available from the usual outlets for fuel. This will also mean you will need to keep petrol, diesel and aviation fuel at your depots.

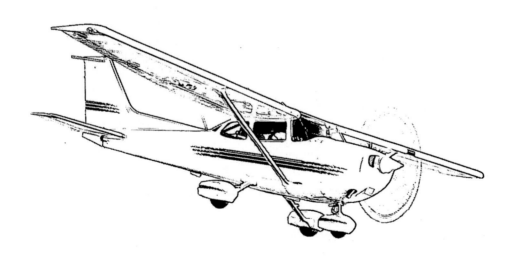

TRAVEL BY WATER

Can Zombies swim and do they float? These questions depend completely upon the type of zombie we are talking about. As discussed in the chapter on Zombies and their background we examined the major differences between the undead and the infected. Undead are basically dead creatures and after the initial expulsion of gas from rotting flesh they will have no gas to help them float. The infected will be the same as you and me and thus able to float and possibly even swim. Based on this it is very important that guards are always posted on your vessels and that you operate an effective a careful and permanent system of watches. You are most vulnerable when moored as the undead may be able to ascend an anchor line whilst the infected may be able to swim across to you. Never stay moored for too long!

Travel by sea offers many of the benefits that land vehicles offer plus some of the benefits of air travel without the prerequisite training and maintenance. Boats come in all shapes and sizes from rowing boats and small riverine craft through to cargo ships, transports and hovercraft. Larger boats and small ships have

several big advantages when compared to other forms of transport; the most important of these is their ability to carry massive amounts of supplies and personnel over a long period of time. This feature means than the vehicles can actually plan the part of an actual mobile, secure base of operations. A good example of a usable vessel is a three-masted schooner like the one shown on the previous page. This type of vessel can easily carry 20-50 people along with supplies, weapons, ammunition and other equipment. With a few light boats on board this vessel can sail the safe waters of the world, dropping anchor near useful ports and stop off points and sending in small raiding parties to collect survivors and supplies. For more information on boat types, uses and availability see the 'Vehicles chapter'.

OBTAINING WATERCRAFT

Boats and ships are much more easily obtained than aircraft and can be found in rivers, inlets, ports and marinas. Remember that smaller

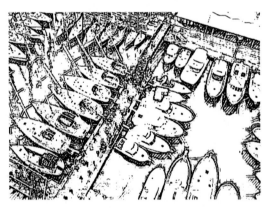

vessels are often available in marinas or even ready loaded on trailers in people's gardens or in the streets. It is very important that you know the difference between boat types and how to power and control them. If there is an outboard motor make sure you are familiar with the control system as it will be the reverse of what you expect. Marinas usually feature fences and basic gate locks to restrict access. The boats themselves pretty much always require the use of a key to actually start them

up. Make sure you plan for this before you try and use one!

USES

Watercraft have a great variety of uses, most of which can be even more effective than land based vehicles. Note that water craft come in a great variety of shapes and sizes. Make sure you can crew and operate them effectively.

SCOUTING

Small vessels can be used for scouting along rivers, canals, estuaries or coastal routes. Your access is limited to the waterways though and it is quite easy to hide from water based scouts. You might be wondering why you need to worry about hiding from the boat. Well, it is not just Zombies that you might need to avoid. What if you are scouting an area and it is being occupied by looters or scavengers? What if they try and take your supplies, interrupt your plans or even worse actually attack you.

RAIDS

Boats and ships are excellent vessels to use for raiding as they can carry substantial cargo and also provide safety in your escape. Make sure you use suitable craft for each stage for example, power boats for the actual operation, whilst mooring a larger vessel that is well armed and features decent storage onboard for supplies and materials. If you are raiding land targets you will need to carefully select landing places so that you can bring your boats up to the land so you can drop of people, weapons and equipment. Traditionally you would make use of ports harbours and quays. Remember to check tides and make sure you don't try to leave at low tide and find your boat is sat in the mud.

COMBAT OPERATIONS

Combat operation can be performed from the water but are obviously limited by the access to most locations. For example, the water routes into a city are never as varied as the road routes. There are advantages to this though in that the less routes the easier it is to plan your access and withdrawal routes. This will result in less chances for ambushes or surprises. Don't forget that you don't have to actually disperse your personnel directly into the combat area, you can ferry people and equipment into a holding area and then carry the operation on from there. Basically you use the boats for transport and then build small, short-term forward bases to operate from. Make sure you can easily reach the boats if things go wrong or you need to withdraw in a hurry.

Watercraft can be used as assault platforms by fitting them with boarding plans or winch lowered platforms like the *corvus* used by the Romans. This will allow you to move a boat alongside another or to move near land and then access it without having to use smaller boats. Be careful to guard the access platform or planks to ensure zombies don't make it onboard. These must be dumped ot raised quickly in an emergency.

ESCAPE

Water based vehicles are an excellent means of transport to use for escape as they make use of waterways that will be far less congested than the main road routes. On top of this Zombies will find waterways either difficult or even impossible to traverse. For escape you want a vessel that is simple to use, handle and power out of a situation. There is no point in racing an armed convoy to a harbour to then try and escape in a fuel tanker. The best vehicles for fast getaways are powerboats, speedboats, small cruisers and dinghies etc. If you are escaping you need to have an idea of where the hell you are going. Just heading out into the Atlantic Ocean will just guarantee your early demise. Are you heading to another larger vessel or are you going to an island? Also note that you can escape to the sea and then simply head down the coast to a safer or more defensive position.

CHAPTER 7: ENVIRONMENTS

When there is no more room in hell, the dead shall walk the Earth.
George A. Romero

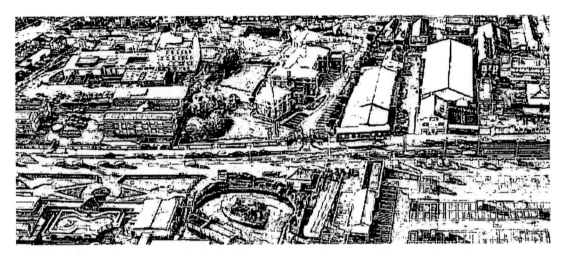

Whether you are holding up where you live, bug out and go on the run, or on the offensive, terrain has to be a major consideration. Each kind of terrain and environment will have varying characteristics which will greatly vary the required tactics and means of survival. Modern day survival enthusiasts take terrain and environment into consideration all the time and prepare themselves for life under various conditions. Surviving in some environments can be challenging at best, but you have even more to concern yourself with than the survival enthusiasts of today.

CHOOSING AN ENVIRONMENT

On the following pages you will find a significant analysis of various location types and their qualities, but how do you go about choosing the right one? This is going to rely very much on the individual. If you are very much a city person and know little of the countryside you are best staying with what you

know, for example not veering further than the suburbs, though sheer enemy numbers may not always make that a possibility. Sticking with what you know would be a good idea since you are comfortable with it and know your way around.

Sadly, you may not always have the luxury of choosing your environment, in which case you need to have a working knowledge of making the most of your situation. If the cities are very quickly overrun, which is likely, bugging out may be the only answer. If you live a very long way from supplies then you may want to consider moving closer although your location may lend itself well to defence providing you have enough fuel for re-supply runs, it could be a good place to stay.

In terms of weather, even the area you have lived in could really catch you off guard when common services are not available to you. We get used in towns and cities to gritters laying salt on the roads before the ice is about to strike, a luxury you will no longer know.

There are a number of key factors that must be considered with environments, these are:

1. Defence characteristics
2. Number of enemy
3. Desirability to other survivors
4. Availability of supplies
5. Transport access
6. Escape options
7. Weather conditions

How you choose or use locations will depend largely on what your purpose for them is. You may consider the use of buildings for raiding of supplies, for defence, or for supplies with the potential of defence in the short term. Consider all aspects and attributes of different locations, as you will likely make a wide usage of many different environments.

GET UP OFF THE GROUND
This is a key principal as ground level is the most dangerous all round to you, as you have no defence at all. Getting off the ground can be as simple as a high topped and equipped vehicle such as a bus, being on a roof top or in a high sided boat.

Underground areas are fantastic for security but only for short term uses. They will typically have you trapped very quickly by overwhelming odds. Avoid any underground areas where possible. By far the best way to make yourself safe is getting high off the ground in a place that cannot be climbed or reached by the zombies. Just always have an exit strategy of some kind.

URBAN AREAS
Urban areas are those locations that feature a number of people and associated building, structures and facilities. These areas range from small housing estates and towns through to massive cities like London and New York.

TOWNS & CITIES
In terms of sheer number of enemies, large population areas present the biggest risk, as you will be facing humungous odds. Unfortunately, seeing as towns and cities are where the majority of people live and work, you will likely be in one when the Zompoc starts. It is not all doom and gloom however. When stuck in a dense population centre you will have access to a great variety and quantity of resources as well as buildings and shelters. In many respects cities can present a dilemma in just choosing which location to occupy, whether short or long term, for the sheer number and variety of them. Deliberately entering a city is unlikely to be a good idea, but may come out of necessity.

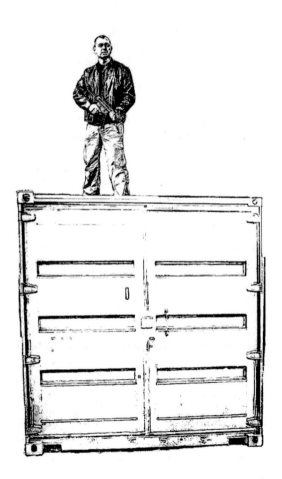

If you can organise a large number of survivors quickly then towns and cities are a place you may likely be able to stay and fight, but with only a handful of people you will quickly be over run. Access to supplies in a major town or city will never be much of a problem, at least not in the short to medium term.

APARTMENT BLOCKS

These share a lot in common with office blocks, but with better sectioned areas internally due to individual apartments. These buildings can provide excellent security for a lot of people at once, but also a hive of infection if you are approaching one that is not safe and already held by survivors. If you live in an apartment block then securing it with other survivors could be an excellent idea for a base. Entering an apartment block for the raiding of supplies will be difficult, with many individually locked rooms and few exit points; it will yield few supplies for a lot of risk.

SCHOOLS

Most schools are no more than two, three at the most storeys high, with a large number of ground floor windows and few useful items inside. A school could potentially be a good place to set up in the medium to long term with larger numbers, but initially most will have too many weak points. However, more and more schools are being fitted with all round high fencing; meaning their potential for defence is excellent. Take it on a case by case basis.

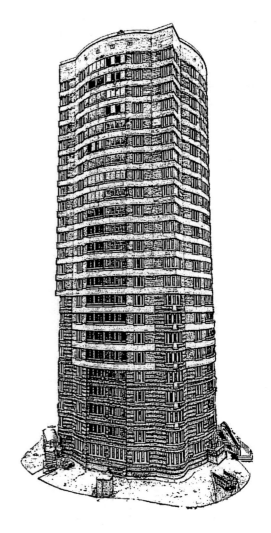

GATED COMMUNITIES

These areas are residential areas containing strictly controlled entrances to both vehicles and pedestrians. They are intended to keep undesirables out. In this respect a gated community works much like a toned down military base, with excellent outer walls and fences and typically some form of security force.

Gated communities stand a much better chance of survival during the apocalypse than regular residential areas for obvious reasons so you may well find large groups of survivors within them, however they may not be welcoming to you. Gated communities will survive because they have decided to keep unknown people out of their area, this may make them less than welcoming should you approach them. If however you can find a welcoming gated community or have the ability to clean one out, they can make an excellent new home.

MALLS

You have of course seen Dawn of the Dead, hopefully both of them, so what would a mall really be like? Most malls would in fact be

excellent for defence as they feature so much in the way of barrier defence security, hardened glass and shutters. Malls, when fortified, will also provide you with an excellent source of supplies. The downside to a mall is their vast size, safely securing them is a logistical nightmare and even with good sweeps you could miss something and get caught out badly. Only consider a mall if you have a group of over ten people, ideally plenty more.

With the large number of people who have seen Dawn of the Dead (both original and remake), it is likely that it would be the logical point to head for. This meaning that a large number of people could accumulate at them. This could provide an excellent base and source of survivors but also a massive risk of infection unless it is handled carefully.

American malls may feature gun shops and hardware stores, but British ones do not. Despite this, food supplies are typically plentiful, as is clothing and often sports equipment. Malls are often surrounded by other out of town stores which can provide the things which the mall does not. If you can get to a mall which is safe from the undead and free of infection great; but be sure to section it off quickly and bring in excellent safety measures to stay free of infection, such as permanent guards and quarantine facilities for anyone entering. In terms of raiding a mall it is a tough task, for its rather good security will also provide you with few exits should things get ugly. Be very careful when entering such a large building with so few exits.

BANKS

These buildings are built to withstand attack, meaning they can offer very good protection. The downside is that they will also keep you in, offering few escape routes and no useful supplies. You can't bribe the undead.

Most banks have very strong security glass, the older style buildings are best as they feature lots of stone and smaller windows. Few banks will offer good firing positions from upper floors and they may have very limited access in or out. If you do occupy a bank, be sure to choose a one with good escape exits, ideally roof access. If you are looking at a bank as a secure location make sure it is a traditional place with strong walls and a decent vault or safe area. Many modern banks are actually quite weakly built and rely upon guards and complex arms for security. This works fine in normal, everyday life. In the Zompoc you will find few of these places with working alarms and 24 hour a day guards patrolling them.

Even then, of what use is an alarm when fifty zombies come shambling in to bite your arm off?

NIGHTCLUBS

You will find plenty of these in the centre of towns and cities, they typically feature few, if any ground floor windows and excellent security. Typically very secure, though often featuring no access to high level shooting galleries and very little natural light. With little of nutritional value, most will suffer the same problems as banks.

POLICE STATIONS

They are likely to be a hub of activity during a disaster and British stations feature little of use in terms of protection and weaponry. Avoid them! The risk of infection with the number of people that will flock to these places is very high and could result in them falling within hours if not minutes.

If you can get in to a police station that has a good supply of weapons, it will likely have very good security, more than you can overcome. However, many police stations are very secure and also offer convenient cells which are excellent for quarantining any one you suspect of infection.

OFFICES

Most offices are part of tower blocks, these feature the same attributes as flats and apartment blocks. There will be few useful supplies inside and too much glass, not enough walls. Despite this, many are only accessible though strong and secure ground floors, making for a safe environment with excellent visibility and access for shooting galleries.

Other than potentially being easy to isolate as a protective area, office blocks feature nothing that is useful to you, meaning all supplies will have to be brought in, bear that in mind. Despite this, the sheer defence characteristics alone and large secure space offered may be enough to warrant bringing all the supplies to it that you need.

and using them for raids or reclaiming ground later.

Most suburbs are made up of large areas of residential housing and low level shopping areas, none of which are good for defence, though some fully enclosed warehouse style environments may suit. Typically suburb areas will be good for access and supply raids, but poor for defence.

HOUSES

For securing of houses see the 'Fortifying your Home' chapter. In terms of using houses to forage supplies, they are easy to access but will yield only small results for the time required. Each home is potentially occupied by the undead. Where possible avoid them, they are not worth the hassle.

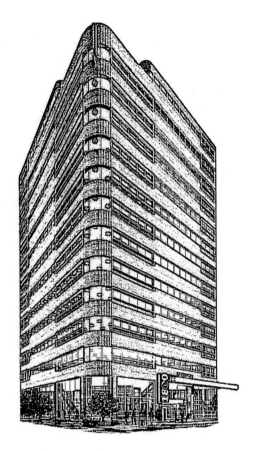

SUBURBS

The outskirts of city areas typically feature as many resources as the city centre itself, and yet it is much easier to access from the outside and get free and clear. These city rim areas do house large numbers of people, but with better road networks and access. Out of town shopping areas will provide an excellent source of supplies with relative easy access and security.

Like the inner city areas, the major concern of the suburbs is the overwhelming number of enemies, this will have to be taken in a case by case basis. It is entirely possible that bugging out of them short term could be a could idea

PUB

Fancy heading to the Winchester? A public house is something found in every single town, village and city in the United Kingdom. Most countries have something similar. Pubs in the UK are intended to be welcoming places with typically low lying windows and easily accessible areas. They feature little useful nutritionally or for defence purposes, though they are very well built with thick walls and very strong doors. Treat pubs like houses, only useable with a good number of modifications.

SUPERMARKETS

These are essentially a mini version of a mall, typically great security and access to supplies, but easier to handle for smaller numbers of people. A supermarket will supply even a large group of people for months, the only downside being that they can rarely be sectioned, so only one line of defence. Out of town supermarkets are definitely a good location, rather than the inner city ones, due to access and number of people.

Raiding supermarkets for supplies is likely to be on your agenda whether you intend to stay there or not. As with malls, they rarely feature many exit points, so only enter if you are sure you can get back out. Always be aware of your surroundings.

AIRPORTS

Potentially an airport could offer a fantastic base of operations, as they almost always have good high fences around the entire perimeter as well as excellent security from one building to another. However, the biggest problem with them is that millions of people go through airports on a regular basis. They will likely be one of the earliest areas to be struck by the

infection, meaning they will be overrun. If you find an airport the best thing you can likely do with it is shut the gates and trap all the zombies inside. Despite the problem with airports, smaller private airfields and historic airfields will often be much more manageable, yet still with good fencing and security. Bear them in mind.

HARDWARE STORES

These stores are essentially the same as a supermarket, with no supply of food, but a huge supply of quality tools and building materials. All of the good hardware/DIY stores are found in the suburbs and out of town. They all have great security and drive-in

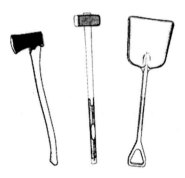

facilities to the actual buildings themselves, meaning you can work on your vehicles in the confines of a well secured facility. The only thing you will be lacking is food. Fortunately many hardware stores are placed very near to supermarkets, they are an excellent choice for defence. The downside to hardware stores is that few will have any kind of good roof access or areas to fight from, meaning culling the hoards will be tough.

RURAL AREAS

SEMI RURAL

These are typically villages surrounding larger towns and cities; far enough out to be among the countryside, but close enough to be commuter areas and not dedicated country based lifestyles. Some of these semi rural villages and small towns can have many

thousands among their populations, but rarely more than 10,000. There will rarely ever be buildings over three storeys high and roads in and out will likely be small and restrictive. The one advantage you have in these areas is that they will not be so overcome by the hordes as the cities and suburbs. Unfortunately, semi rural areas feature a much more limited amount of well stocked shops for you to acquire supplies, as well as rather limited cover and useable buildings

CHURCHES

You can find churches in all kinds of urban and rural landscapes, though the majority of inner city churches have been converted for

alternative uses now, whilst rural and semi-rural ones are typically still churches. Being in God's house will not protect you from the infected, but their typically high strong walls and robust doors will. Most windows on churches are high off the ground and beyond reach, whilst church towers provide excellent defence.

Sadly when such a cataclysmic event like the Zompoc begins, people will flood to churches in the hope that God will save them, making them a hive of undesirables – beware!

PRISONS

Some prisons are located within city limits but most are in the middle of nowhere. They provide excellent defence against the world outside for both a large number of people and vehicles. What must be considered is, who is in the prison when you find it? In the Zompoc scenario a prison could very likely be taken over by either the guards or the prisoners, or could be one big enclosed zombie horde. Approach with extreme caution. If however you have the possibility of using one as a base of operations, excellent.

It is entirely possible that many in a prison could survive due to the high levels of security, though if they were locked in then they would soon die of starvation. Beware that violent criminals will likely want to rule whatever group you have and could lead you to death and destruction, whereas lesser prisons housing thieves and white collar criminals will be much less of a risk to you and other survivors.

The design of modern US penitentiaries is based upon a layered defence with much less emphasis on thick walls and more on security equipments and observation. This makes them less well suited for defence use in the Zompoc.

RURAL LOWLANDS

These areas will typically offer the best visibility and in that respect are very safe, or course large areas of woodland will negate this, though most areas of Britain have been kept flat and clear. Rural areas of pretty much no good natural defensive locations beyond the odd country house and barn, they are however an excellent place to hold up the night in your vehicles as your guards will be able to see any trouble well in advance and there should be few zombies about.

OTHER AREAS

MILITARY BASES

There are a fair number of military bases around the country, most feature at least reasonable perimeter fences and potentially an excellent supply of hardware. They will however be an obvious choice for many people, so expect to find either a lot of infected or few supplies left. It is of course possible that any soldiers inside may have fortified and survived just hope they are still helpful.

Old military bases, ideally those built before the Second World War tend to be very strongly built, some of them even rival castles and other fortifications with respect to their defensive capabilities.

BARNS

Typically large and without windows, barns, providing they have sides and doors, will provide a good level of protection as well allowing you to drive vehicles in. The downside is that there will rarely be firing or guard positions. You're better of sleeping in your well prepared vehicle.

The barn is a common location for Zombie games and movies, but it has little use, as is seen in those fictional works. Many barns can simply be smashed or pulled apart and offer only very basic protection.

CASTLES

Providing a castle is still in reasonable condition, which many across the country are, they will be impregnable to zombies as well as incredibly safe from potential rival humans. Rural castles, which most are, will typically have no current resources or supplies that you can make use of, unless they have a good museum, but the quality of defence alone means they should be given serious consideration. Some castles are located in the middle of towns and cities, whilst their defensive capabilities are often just as good, their location means that you could be overwhelmed by the masses and trapped there. Many surviving castles to not have much of their interior left, so be prepared to pitch tents inside. Fortified manor houses can work in a similar fashion and often feature much better creature comforts.

Even though inner city castles could see you surrounded by large numbers, providing you have good access to weapons and a number of survivors to defend it you would likely do very well. Remember that when most buildings require you to be very careful with things such as fire and Molotov Cocktails, the castle does not. Purpose built castles were designed to withstand much more than zombies or anything you can throw against it.

The central feature of the castle was the keep, or donjon, the main commanding tower. The primary function of the keep varied; usually it was a residential structure functioning as a redoubt in times of trouble, but it could also be used as a secure storage area, or, later, as a prison. The curtain walls of a castle are another recognizable feature. Essentially, a curtain wall was a second layer of fortification, separate from the keep and bailey. In some cases, this was a simple defensive barrier. The gates were a weak point in the defences of castles, so gatehouses could be strengthened with flanking towers, a turning or removable bridge, doors, and a heavy portcullis. Another optional feature of a castle was a moat of some kind. Moats were ditches, typically filled

with water, which were dug around the perimeter of a castle to provide a preliminary defence.

Castles are only found in countries where these kinds of fixed, strong fortifications were built. Castles were common throughout Europe whilst other types and styles were used in the Asia and the East. Though there are no castles in the traditional sense in North America there are a good number of military bases built ready for the war of 1812 and after that have many features in common with castles.

Due to wanting to keep unwanted trespassers out, most castles maintain strong and secure gates at every possible entrance, meaning they are useable with immediate effect so give them serious consideration.

MANOR HOUSES

Over five hundred of these homes exist in the UK. They are country houses, which historically formed the administrative centre of a manor. The term is sometimes applied to country houses which belonged to gentry families, as well as to grand stately homes, particularly as a technical term for minor late medieval fortified country houses intended more for show than for defence.

Whilst fortified Manor Houses came under the castle category as they were at least partially intended for defence, manor houses, or stately homes are built only for lavish luxury. They are typically vast stone structures with grand entrances and surrounding grounds. 28 Days later saw the famous usage of a manor house by the ruminants of a British army unit, of which they appeared to be holding up pretty well. Manor houses vary greatly as they are each quite unique, their weakness is in their windows. Most manor houses feature very large strong doors and walls, but relatively low lying and weak windows. If you can secure these windows then the manor house would be excellent to hold up in, with open fires making heating, at least for small areas, fairly simple. Sadly manor houses typically feature few high shooting positions, limited simply to upper floor windows, but the luxury of the building would indeed be a high class way to survive.

Manner homes that are privately owned are usually still surrounded by open flat fields meaning that you can see everything coming from a good distance. This is excellent for defence, but nothing a castle does not typically feature. The biggest advantage is that there are far more habitable stately homes than castles and they are also more likely to still be part of an estate whereas most castles are now ruins and much of their land has been taken up for development.

MOUNTAINS

Gaining the high ground has often been considered a major military advantage in the past. Sadly, it does not carry through to the Zompoc. Zombies are relentless, they do not get tired nor lose hope when their friends are being cut down. They will keep coming. Getting up to high ground is slow and tiresome, which you are then stuck upon. Simply put, ignore the mountains, they are no help. The only useful element of this high ground is sheer visibility, as you can get a reasonable grasp of what is in the surrounding area. However, only go to the high ground for this reason if it is easily reachable by a good quality road. Do not go on foot, it is too dangerous.

DESERT

A desert is a landscape or region that receives almost no rain. As if you do not already have enough to worry about, the desert will put extra wear and tear on your vehicles and increase the rate at which all of your supplies are consumed. The lack of water is a big problem. Like rural areas, visibility and enemy presence is good, but in all other respects the desert is awful. These areas can also easily get even the best off-road vehicles stuck without much warning. Avoid them. If you do have to travel in desert or semi-desert areas, keep to any roads that do exist and get through them quickly. When travelling across deserts, ensure that you have plenty of extra water, as well as fuel. Never travel across any such territory without at least several vehicles in convoy. The risk of breakdown or get stuck in the sand is too great.

Fortunately in Britain we do not have any desert areas at all but many areas of the US do, and you may also be unfortunate enough to be stuck in an area of desert. Despite the clear visibility and shooting areas, it is rather unlikely that you would be carrying enough ammo to survive the Zompoc, the best advice would be to get out of it as quickly as possible.

SMALL ISLANDS

As to whether islands are a good location or not rather does depend on the attributes of the zombies. The question always remains, can zombies cross water? They may be able to swim, float or walk across the sea bed, who knows? If zombies can in any capacity travel across water then that is a concern, but not necessarily one to make them avoidable. Even if zombies can travel across water, they are never likely to come at you in great numbers and therefore an island could be a good isolated and strong position, when combined with fortifications. The big issue that islands have is re-supply, it is going to have to be done by boat, which in turn will still mean foraging for supplies on the mainland areas. In this case, it is likely that you will still have to then keep land vehicles on the mainland. Islands are potentially an excellent place to hold up and start again, just do not rely entirely on water for defence.

WATERWAYS

If water is a barrier to zombies, excellent. British waters are very tidal, meaning that water rises and falls at quite a rate, our rivers are fast flowing and extremely variable. Due to the tide issues, only smaller boats are able to typically be kept moored on British rivers. It is not recommended that you use these. Canals are another big no-no, with only a few feet of water and space between the boat and shore, forget it. It is not all doom and gloom for the waterways though. Docks are a good possibility, as well as lakes. Lakes maintain high water levels and stay fairly calm, the only limitation being the size of boats, which is generally small. Lakes offer no useful terrain to travel, but do offer potential places to hold up.

Due to the tidal nature of Britain the major docks have locks to ensure that water levels stay high. This means a controlled environment of high water levels and few variables, allowing much larger boats to stay moored. They could provide an excellent base of operations from their moored positions. Many docks have just one or two gates defending the entire docking area for a number of boats, meaning they are already easily defended. Ships that are moored in docks can provide an excellent base. They offer loads of protection and can be secured very quickly. They will give most of the advantages of being at sea in terms of protection, but without having to worry about

navigation and keeping the vessel fuelling and running, treating the ship simply as a secure base. House boats are another potentially excellent base, but they vary greatly. Be sure only to choose the ones with a single access point from the land/jetty, not ones moored directly to the shore itself. Ultimately though any large boat or ship will do the same job.

THE SEA

Of all areas the sea offers by far the best level of protection. It is rather unlikely that zombies can actually swim, meaning the only risk could come from your anchor chain if you did stay put. Larger boats and ships also have high sides meaning that climbing aboard is an impossibility. Large boats and ships can house a huge number of people and supplies and allow travel to wherever you want to, providing you can keep the vessel maintained and supplied. To many people the sea is a dangerous place and rightly so, it can be, but in the Zompoc few places will be safer. The only issue of life at sea will come from re-supply, but with good organisation this should not be a problem.

Bear in mind that smaller vessels are not so well suited to the sea and their low sides and small capacity for people will not be good. Sail boats/yachts are excellent in terms of supply as they only require a small amount of fuel, you just need the skills to manage them. Boats are an excellent means of bugging out, as no matter where you moor up if it all goes to pot you can simply set sail again for a new location, rather than being stuck inside a building for example.

Despite boats being an excellent idea be sure that you know what you are doing at sea, as it can be a very dangerous place. Ideally travel in convoy as you would land vehicles; this will give a much greater chance of survival. Just because the sea is a much safer place than land, never put your guard down, always keep guards on duty at all times of day. Zombies may still be able to climb aboard as well as jump from one vessel to another in an infected boat or ship colliding with yours.

ROAD NETWORKS

The roads are most people's principal route of transport for most things they do in life, but there are many considerations. In the Zompoc you will not want to be on foot too often, with small load bearing ability, low travelling speeds and a lack of protection. A vehicle is the key. However, how useable will the roads be?

During any kind of panic the road networks flood and get bottlenecked by the overwhelming number of people trying to do the same thing. Whether this would happen when the Zompoc begins will rather depend on the rate of infection and therefore how much time people have to clog the roads up.

Other problems will also arise. The roads will no longer be maintained, quickly becoming strewn with all kinds of debris. Weather conditions will also seen the build up of ice, mud, dirt or sand fairly quickly in many areas.

Therefore, when travelling on the road networks, which you will want to, you will ideally want a tough 4x4 vehicle which will provide you with the ability to tackle most conditions. The ability to ram objects out of the way, including whole cars, will mean that

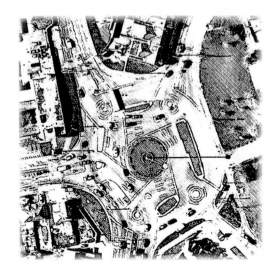

you will quickly want to modify your vehicle if possible, or find something already suited to the job.

Another consideration you should make is other motorists. Initially this will come from the panic of the Zompoc starting, but later from survivors. Once society no longer enforces the driving on the correct side of the road, abiding by the speed limits and stopping at intersections you simply won't care. This is fine, but do bear in mind that an unexpected collision between your vehicle and another in motion could disable or destroy both. The simply rule for safety here is to have your wits about you, as you should anyway. Awareness to everything that is going on around you as well as keeping an eye out for potential hazards will keep you safe from not just the undead, but also the living.

TEMPORARY SHELTERS

When you are out travelling or if you need to stay somewhere overnight or due to bad weather you will need a temporary shelter. No man can stay awake all the time so you will need somewhere that allows you an opportunity to rest without being attacks. Depending on where you are you need a location that is safe, dry, has multiple escape routes and good views. If possible set up some objects to operate as a rudimentary alarm.

WEATHER CONDITIONS

Types of locations and terrain must always be considered in any kind of survival situation, but weather is equally as important. Britain is a temperate zone and that means the weather is fairly mild all year round with an average level of rainfall, making it one of the easiest countries in the world to survive in. Having said this, without everyday luxuries such as gas central heating and the structure of a country to keep roads and paths free and clear, you are going to have to learn to look after yourself and be prepared. Severe weather conditions such as ice and snow can easily have you trapped both in vehicles and on foot. When you consider weather conditions, lowland areas with mild to dry climates are clearly by far the safest to survive in. The weather conditions in which you are in when the Zompoc strikes will severely effect choice of vehicles, clothing, protection and plans generally. The wide variety in weather conditions mean that you will have to decide on the best course of action yourself, but it is very self explanatory once you know to be prepared for it.

CHAPTER 8: COMBAT & TACTICS

If you are not prepared to use force to defend civilization,
then be prepared to accept barbarism.

Thomas Sowell

It is without doubt that in a Zompoc you will have to fight for yourself, unless for some reason that you managed to be in a nuclear bunker before the attack with enough supplies to last whilst others do the clean up for you. When it comes to fighting the zombie hordes you must give more consideration to the war than just finding weapons and ammo. In the short term you will have to consider how to fight one on one or one against many,

therefore you have to rely on your own hands and feet.

With the humans ability to use advanced and complex tools and the zombies likely inability to do so, do not play them at their own game. Zombies can only hurt you in close combat, so where possible, avoid it. Saving ammunition by fighting with hand weapons is not remotely sensible or safe, hand-to-hand combat of any kind is only done when there is no other choice. There are too many risks of being injured, as well as infected. Just think of all the infected blood being spread around when you cave in a skull or take the head off. Luckily for you we have spent thousands of years training and practicing warfare, this knowledge will be of great importance in the Zompoc as you will have to fight. Fighting is divided up into two key areas, those of combat and those of tactics. The combat side is the actually death dealing part and includes unarmed techniques, using close quarter combat weapons like knives and swords and finally using ranged weapons like bows, rifles and machine guns.

UNARMED COMBAT

Initially you may not have access to any weapons at all, and if you run out of ammo or lose a weapon at any time you may also have to fight with nothing but your own body. Unarmed combat should be avoided at all times, used for last resort situations only. If it is possible, running is always preferable to fighting in unarmed combat. The first best option if you get entangled with a zombie is finding a way to bug out, use slips of the body and strikes wherever you have to just to create an opening to dash. Killing a zombie in hand-to-hand combat with no weapons is an incredibly difficult task. Typically in hand-to-hand you can disable an opponent with strikes, asphyxiation, locks and breaks etc. There are only two techniques that will kill a zombie without weapons, striking the brain stem hard, and breaking the neck. Striking the brain stem hard will immediately kill your target, breaking the neck will immediately incapacitate the entire body. Do however beware that just because you break the neck it does not mean that the head will not keep trying to bite you. Zombies, most probably, do not need the bodies functions nor blood supply, so there is no reason why their head would die just because the body has. Wild kicks and punches just give the zombie something to bite or grab onto. You might think a swift kick to the head could provide sufficient energy and damage to kill a zombie but what about the practicalities of kicking something that is trying to bite or gauge you. Hand to hand combat is very, very dangerous. Please don't do it!

WHAT TO DO WHEN UNARMED

❖ **Run** – If you are unarmed and attack the first option is always to run
❖ **Shove** – If you are attacked and cannot immediately escape, shove them and run
❖ **Strike** – If you are held, strike them hard with a closed fist, then run

ARMED COMBAT

Since the dawn of time we have been using tools. The use and construction of tools is in fact one of the defining features of our evolution. When fighting zombies you will find tools and weapons will be critically important and will give you the edge in combat, especially when faced with a foe that can potentially absorb more damage than you. Don't forget a cut or a bite to a zombie is nothing, the same for you could mean death and zombification. The simple lesson is to get armed as soon as possible, ideally with weapons that keep you as far away from zombies as you can.

THE BODY

The torso is the largest target available to strike when fighting zombies and in living humans houses the important organs such as the heart, liver and kidneys. The loss of any organ will ultimately cause death in seconds, hours or days. In the undead the rules change and you will probably find there is no circulation and that the lungs and major organs serve no purpose. It is therefore important to understand your foe before plunging a blade into the heart of the undead. If the zombie is vulnerable to organ damage then you want to take out the lungs or heart, either will stop and then kill the zombie quickly.

DECAPITATION

This is one of the most efficient ways to kill a zombie, but also one of the most difficult. Even during public executions throughout history many executioners have not struck the head off with one, or even two swings of the sword, and this was when their target was kneeling and still using a purpose built heavy bladed executioner's sword. A zombie is unlikely to be so compliant. Other heavier bladed weapons, such as axes, make decapitations easier, but no simpler to set up. If you can work in teams then consider decapitation, but as a rule destroying the brain is easier. To give an idea at how difficult decapitation with the sword is you just have to look at the development of the guillotine, as it was the only way to guarantee to a proper clean decapitation. The only time you are ever likely to have a situation as simple as a traditional execution is when euthanising an infected human. Despite this, you may still be able to achieve a decapitation with the shovel of all things, as its edge is designed especially for cutting into objects straight on. It is never recommended that you take on zombies with nothing but a shovel, but in Britain it may be the only weapon you have to hand.

DESTROYING THE BRAIN

This guarantees an immediate and safe kill, an excellent choice. Anyone with even the slightest bit of zombie knowledge will know that a gunshot to the head puts a zombie on the ground for good, but is this always true? Sadly not, the bullet must penetrate the skull and strike the brain, for that is the only vital target area for a zombie. This type of shooting requires a high degree of shooting skill as well as the ability to perform well under pressure. Smaller calibre guns have also been known to have their bullets bounce off the skull, this is likewise a problem for typical shotgun ammunition beyond close range firing. Despite the difficulty in making head shots and having those shots be effective, the luxury of fighting from a distance is always preferable to having to do it up close and personal. It is likely that you will at some point have to fight in close combat with the undead. As a rule, destroying the brain is by far the best option here. Any implement capable of delivering a high degree of blunt trauma can destroy the brain, this could be as simple as a cricket bat, ala Shaun of the Dead, but that's really just an emergency solution. Axes, maces and hammers are all excellent at this job. Remember from chapter 1 though that you need to destroy the brain stem, so make sure you aim for it, it is at the base of the brain!

DISMEMBERMENT

Removing a limb from a human disables them as an opponent in almost every situation. This is not the case with the undead, they do not feel pain or fear. When fighting the infected you will be able to inflict impaired mobility as well as massive trauma and blood loss that could kill them in minutes. There are major arteries in all the limbs and no zombie with a working circulatory system will survive against limb removal. Removing a limb can make an undead zombie less combat effective but still very much a threat. Lopping off an arm will make them easier to fight against, but still 90% combat effective, removing a leg will severely slow them down and make them quicker to finish off. As far as which part to aim for, well this will determine how effective the creature will be after your attacks. If you strike the ankle or wrist you will still cause major blood loss or mobility reduction but then could still move towards you or strike with a damaged or bleed arm, not good! Take the arm off above the elbow and the leg off above the knee and put them down for good. Despite dismemberment being an effective solution to reducing your enemy's combat effectiveness, it is an unnecessary and wasteful procedure that should generally be avoided unless it is absolutely necessary. Always go for the head if you have the option or take out the limbs and then go for the head. Make it your rule to never end a fight until you have destroyed the brain!

FIGHTING MULTIPLE OPPONENTS

Even the bravest cannot fight beyond his strength.
Homer

This is the biggest fear for any survivor, but sadly an almost certainty. If you are using projectile weapons you will almost certainly run out of ammunition very quickly, whether that be overall or simply reload times being too slow. Facing large numbers of shambling zombies is a situation that requires careful thought but is doable. Fighting large numbers of running zombies is often going to be suicidal.

Modern fighting and self defence has shown that even the best fighters can only handle two, perhaps three human attackers at once, with any reasonable chance of victory. Now imagine you are fighting the undead, who have no fear, do not feel pain, cannot be incapacitated with locks and breaks etc. If you are unarmed, run, until you can find some kind of shelter or barrier.

Certain martial arts have dealt with fighting multiple opponents quite effectively, one of these is Gatka, Indian martial art created by the Sikhs of the Punjab region, it is still commonly practiced today. Gatka revolves around the principals of being able to learn to fight quickly and easily with any type of weapons and against multiple opponents'.

Gatka's key principal of fighting multiple opponent's is to never get embroiled with a one-on-one fight with any one attacker, for you will then be totally exposed to the other assailants. Keep moving, keep striking. It is as simple as that. You fight almost in a frenzy, but a controlled one, not allowing any opponent to close with you and keeping continuous motion of the weapon to strike all around against many targets. If you have got to this situation with zombies then the chances of survival are slim, but better to do the best you can and stand a chance than not. Against slow moving zombies this technique can be extremely effective, and when combined with a good level of protective gear, you could fight much greater odds. Do however be aware of fatigue, even if you are in a fit and healthy condition, fighting more than twenty in this manner will likely be too much.

TAG TEAM FIGHTING

Having friends when it comes to survival against huge odds is always a good thing. If you can work in pairs to take down individual zombies that is great. The fact that you are facing much greater odds means that this will not always be a luxury you have, that will depend on location and situation. Fighting one zombie with two survivors makes the odds of infection much smaller and the chance of success much greater.

Certain weapons can be perfectly suited to this style of fighting, such as the boar spear, where one person can ensnare the zombie by thrusting the spear through its chest, whilst the other destroys the brain from a much safer position. In actual fact, whatever weapons you have, two against one is a good thing. The technique of two or more survivors using a boar spear is an excellent one for dealing with running zombies, providing you can catch them out individually. It is probably the safest hand-to-hand method of doing so. Against shambling zombies however, don't bother; you would be over complicating the situation. Just smash their head in

GROUP TACTICS

Got a team of heavies to back you up? Nice. Working in larger numbers is fantastic, you can hold off larger numbers, assist during reload times or fatigue, defend a greater number of entry points, have specialist weapons and roles etc.

The most important factor of group combat is organisation. What made the ancient Roman and Greek soldiers so great was not necessarily their individual training but their discipline and

highly trained ability to work together. You need a clearly set up organisation to a group, even if that is just four people. A leader must be decided upon and individual tasks established where necessary. Team members need to know how to work together and assist each other. One of the biggest concerns as your numbers grow will be from friendly fire. This is especially a concern with a large

number of projectile or thrown weapons. Discipline and structure is the best way to defend against this.

USING COVER

In a modern police or military context this tends to mean utilising buildings, trenches, cars and any other barriers as a defence against gun fire, explosives and detection. Survival against zombies however means something quite different, being in that respect much closer to ancient and medieval warfare. Unless the undead really start to develop intelligence you are not going to have to defend against projectile weapons or explosives, though be aware of threats from other humans in this fashion.

The first most basic objective in the use of cover against the undead is creating a barrier, one that is not easily overcome nor worked around. This can be a strong door to a building, a large wall, fighting from a rooftop etc. Be sure that the barriers you use are as strong as possible, for zombies will exploit any weakness that exists. Fighting from cover is much safer than not, you have weapons, they do not. To hurt you a zombie has to close the distance and use their own fists and teeth, but you can strike them at a larger distance with whatever projectile thrown or hand to hand weapons that you have.

One of the biggest considerations that you must make when using cover is have an exit strategy. It is no good locking yourself in a bank safe if there's only one way out and too many opponents to fight through. High ground is always a good idea in the fight against zombies, vehicle roofs, building rooftops etc. When fighting from cover, be sure that you have weapons that enable you to fight rather than just survive. It's no good being on a roof top with nothing but an axe. Certain weapons are excellently suited to fighting from cover, the Molotov Cocktail being a primary one.

Another good use for cover and obstacles is to use them as long range cover to slow down an attack. Rather than hiding behind a wall you can actually use the wall or similar physical obstacle to make it easier to shoot and kill zombies. A classic example of this is by setting up a perimeter at a range of 50 yards (whatever is your farthest accurate shooting

range) from your buildings outer walls. You don't need a high wall, just a decent obstruction, perhaps with broken glass, rocks, cables, barbed wire and anything else that can cut, main or injure. When the zombies move towards your house they will become entangled and start to hurt themselves trying to break free. At this moment you will have plenty of time to shoot at them whilst keeping at a safe distance. You can take this idea even further and copy what the Eastern Romans did and use a defence in depth system as used at Constantinople. This idea is to have the lowest walls on the outside with them increasing in height to the centre. To copy this idea you can create multiple layers of obstructions with the final, tallest and most substantial near your final fortification or building.

FIGHTING FROM VEHICLES

A well prepared vehicle should allow you to fight from relative safety, but the safety of your vehicle has to then be considered. Molotov Cocktails have to be used in a far more careful fashion when fighting from a vehicle, as the flames can spread to the vehicle, or be brought to them by the zombies. Molotov's should only be used from vehicles when you are on the move and thrown in the opposite direction to which you are travelling.

The relative safety of a well prepared vehicle will mean that you can fight to a certain degree in your own time, rather than be concerned about the continuous hoard bringing you to your knees. With this relative degree of comfort and safety should also come more consideration to ammunition. If you are safely able to cull the undead without wasting valuable ammunition, do so. Bows and crossbows are excellent in this respect as the ammunition is easily replaced or improvised. Certain hand to hand combat weapons can also be very handy. Spears and other pole weapons can be extremely effective from a vehicular weapons platform, as the undead cannot close the distance with you anymore and having to be accurate and efficient under pressure is less of a concern. Remember that when fighting from a vehicle you can fight from both the inside and the outside. To facilitate this you can add access hatches and fighting platforms to the vehicle and then use firearms and pole arms to strike at range. You will have a better field of fire, viewing position etc, but will also make your people more exposed to enemy attacks.

DEVELOP WEAPON SKILLS

Ideally you would have already developed skills in both projectile and close combat weapons. However some people do not have access to such training, do not want to do it or are pacifists. It's all very well being a pacifist right up to the point when a zombie wants to bite your head off. Just remember what John Rambo said,"When you're pushed, killing's as easy as breathing". Even if you did develop weapon skills in readiness for the apocalypse, you will want to continue to hone them. You should hopefully have realised now that keeping ammunition supplies up for any weapons is going to be no easy task, so you cannot afford to waste it practicing against targets. At the same time, it's no good going in to the field 'green'. The answer to this dilemma is airguns and BB guns. Pellet and ball bearing guns are easily available with few legal barriers, they also serve no useful purpose in fighting the hordes, so wasting ammunition in training is no problem. Pellet and BB guns are not completely representative of a real gun, in respect to recoil and sometimes ammo capacities, but for closer range target and tactics practice they are excellent. Look out for gas powered semi automatic and full automatic BB guns and bolt action pellet and BB guns, they will be really useful to your training. The next level of training will be with live ammunition from a safe position, such as a rooftop or secure vehicle, allowing you to finish off your training on real targets.

TACTICS

Military tactics are the techniques for using weapons or military units in combination for engaging and defeating an enemy in battle. It is your job to ensure you can use all the assets at your disposal to effective fight and defeat zombies where ever you may find them. Tactics include basic manoeuvring training, using vehicles, conducting fighting withdrawals and assaulting enemy positions.

USING VEHICLES AS WEAPONS

In 2005, in the UK, a total of 4,881 pedestrians were killed in motor vehicle accidents, what does that tell us? It tells us that a vehicle is a very dangerous animal! In today's society we all have to give serious consideration to the safety of those around us, but when the Zompoc hits, you will be wanting to cause as much damage as possible!

With the average civilian vehicle weight being around two tonnes it is no surprise that they can be very effective against the human body, but what of vehicle damage? Over the last few decades cars have focused more and more on pedestrian safety, with large crash bumpers, low fronted bumpers, the banning of flip up headlamps etc. This has all improved the chances of survival for the pedestrian, which is not good during the Zompoc. Also, what have these changes done to the vehicle itself? Modern safety features mean that vehicles crumple on impact, that's no good when you will be doing it on a regular basis and need to keep going.

Certain vehicles are better suited to striking zombies than others, high fronted ones for example. When an average family car hits a person they will likely be thrown on to the windscreen, that is not ideal when facing zombies, larger 4x4's will keep them down on the ground. Traditionally built ladder chassis vehicles like the Land Rover Defender are also better suited to deliberate rams. When using your vehicle as a ram, be sure you have beefed up the protection as to not damage your means of transport.

The biggest mistake that many people make when striking targets with vehicles is that they go too fast. Evasive driving skills will teach you for example that to ram another car out of the way you want a well maintained steady pace, rather than high speed, using torque and power rather than momentum, which will see greater damage to your own vehicle. Using custom vehicle weapons such as spikes and scythes is rather specialist and relevant to each vehicle, as well as rather self-explanatory.

With vehicle protection and durability in mind, the question must still be asked, will hitting a zombie with a heavy vehicle kill them? Of course killing a zombie in this fashion will still rely on destroying the brain, the simple answer is that with steady good speed and a substantial high fronted bulbar, as you should have, yes, almost every time.

DEFENISVE POSITIONS

Historically a wagon laager was created by circling all of your wagons and placing people and animals inside the circle, often attaching the wagons together in sequence This tactic was also famously used in America by pioneers in case of Indian attack. In a modern military context forming a 'laager' has a slightly different meaning, but we are interesting in the traditional usage, also called a Wagon Fort. A laager is a quick way to make an improvised fort when on the move, the question is, how useful is it against zombies? When setting up camp you are unlikely going to want to be out on the ground, especially at night, joining the vehicles together could also risk being stuck in a disaster situation. Despite the laager in a traditional sense being a bad idea, there are certain elements that can be useful. Keeping your vehicles close together is indeed a good idea as you can support each other, also, having some kind of connection is also a good idea. When using vehicles as stationary weapons platforms you can join them with ramps or ladders, enabling fighters to quickly move between each vehicle for sharing supplies, quickly strengthening certain areas of defence, or bugging out if one vehicle is compromised. This idea is clearly only suited to high sided vehicles that cannot be easily climbed, such as buses and lorries.

LEARNING TO BEHEAD

Taking the head clean off is not as easy as you might think it requires a lot of skill, accuracy and the appropriate application of force and blade alignment. Most noted beheadings have been through execution where your target is not moving, and even then, many have failed.

Many in the sword based martial arts communities' regularly practice 'test cutting', whereby you cut targets with sharp blades in order to practice technique, edge alignment and accuracy. Test cutting is an excellent way to practice these skills and will give you an excellent foundation in understanding how the sword can be used to its best effect. Training with a pele can also be good for practicing your accuracy. Finally learning to strike against a moving target, this is far more difficult. With any luck you will face slow moving, shambling zombies, in which you stand a chance, but against the runners, simply use a better suited weapon. In pairs, you can practice hitting the shambling zombies by having one person act out the part of the zombie, walking continually towards you, whilst the other strikes when possible to the neck to behead. Be sure to use a high level of protective gear when hitting your friends!

INDIVIDUAL TACTICAL TRAINING

This covers a range of techniques from quick target acquisition to hitting moving targets, quick reloads and drawing of secondary weapons and smart use of terrain. Use airsoft weapons and air guns for this training, practice hitting targets on the move as well as quick access to ammo and secondary weapons, use replicas which as closely represent the real weapons you have to hand and also wear all of the clothing and gear you would be expecting to for real.

To lead untrained people to war is to throw them away
Confucius

GROUP TACTICAL TRAINING

You need to learn to work effectively with your team mates, how to move and fight together. Developing group skills is not just about maximising your combat effectiveness in terms of number of zombies killed, but also safety to all survivors, bases and vehicles which you work around. So let's have a look at a few drills you can run through together.

ADVANCING

In a Zompoc scenario it is possible to advance together as a team whenever you please, rather than providing support from the rear, this is due to the fact that you are not at risk from gunfire or other military hardware. Despite this, always have people allocated to protecting both your sides and rear. Zombies can be hiding anywhere, this is especially a concern in built up urban areas. Ideally never stay far from your vehicles, having them advance with you beyond a few hundred yards, in order to maintain radio and where possible visual contact, as well as a potential bug out option.

RETREATING

The manner in which you retreat from combat will vary depending on your foe. Against shamblers you can simply jog without major defence, but against runners it is very different. The chances are a runner will be able to run faster than you, especially if you are weighed down by weapons and equipment. Retreat a single person at a time whilst the rest of the team fights. If a team member is bitten or infected, leave them behind.

TARGET ACQUISITION

This primarily relates to the use of any projectile weapon, though you should of course develop you awareness and perception skills as well as peripheral vision no matter what. Target acquisition is about safely getting a target in the sights of your weapon as quickly as possible. This can be done by setting up paper targets and running in to the room not knowing where those targets are. If practicing with BB guns you can also get some of your team mates to stand in as the zombie targets, just be sure they have eye protection! When you acquire targets, be sure to know what other potential targets are around you and also friendly's which could be in the line of fire. Practice all of these scenarios where possible, or at least give them consideration before going in to combat.

HITTING MOVING TARGETS

Most people learn to shoot against static targets, but this is no good when your opponent is on the move. Shambling zombies will be moving quite slowly which will help, but runners can often be extremely difficult to hit on the move. Hitting moving targets is accomplished by 'leading your target'. You can expect to have to shoot zombies walking or running towards you, that is the easiest moving target to strike. But what if you need to shoot a zombie from the side who is trying to intercept a survivor whilst you fire from safety? To hit a moving target you need to follow its projected path and 'lead' it slightly, which means aiming slightly ahead of its current position into its projected path. As you pull the trigger do not stop tracking, continue to move the weapon through the arc that you were following.

Hitting moving targets with a gun, bow or crossbow is extremely difficult but not impossible. You can practice this with BB guns and other survivors, but the low muzzle velocity of the ammunition will have a different effect. It may be a reasonably good representation of a crossbow though, where velocity is roughly similar in many cases.

A good way to practice hitting moving targets is with a stream. Get a piece of wood, throw it in, do your best to hit it as it moves quickly downstream. Try not to do this too often as to waste ammunition. Ultimately hitting a moving target, unless they are coming directly at you, will always be difficult. It will often be easier and more reliable to wait until your target slows or stops, such as reaching an obstacle.

USING CONFINED SPACES

In modern warfare confined spaces can be a real problem because large numbers can be wiped out with automatic weapons or grenades. But you do not have to face modern weapons. Confined spaces for you means that the enemy cannot make maximum use of their numbers as they are bottlenecked and you can make maximum use of your firepower, or, if you do not have guns, formation fighting. Corridors, streets and buildings are all going to be relevant here. Be sure that you do not limit your friend's arc of fire, also ensure that you always have eyes in every direction.

FIGHTING IN OPEN SPACES

When outnumbered, which you almost always will be, open spaces can get you killed quickly, for you can be attacked in all directions with no means of channelling the enemies numbers.

Against slow moving hoards you are best staying on the move and punching a hole through the enemy's forces until you can get clear. But against the running hoards, this may not be an option. Fighting back to back will enable you to fight without risk from behind, but severely reduce your combat effectiveness as a team. You never really want to get caught up in this situation, but if you do, run where you can. Fight like hell if you can't, read about Gatka!

BOARDING VEHICLES

Seeing as you will hopefully have nicely modded up zombie proofed modes of transport, there will likely only be one main entry point. This bottleneck will mean that you have to be wary of your surroundings when boarding, which you should be anyway. Board like you would retreat, always having at least one or two people guarding your position as the others get on board. If the vehicle allows, those on board should then provide cover from the vehicle so that the last of the team can get in.

ROOM ENTRY

This is a subject covered in huge detail for police and military purposes, fortunately you only need know a simplified version. Room breaching or entry against zombies is far simpler due to the lesser degree of variables, such as opponent's weapons, hostages, traps etc. When you want to enter a room, not knowing what lays on the other side, stack up either side of the door, ensure that all weapon muzzles are in a safe area as to not endanger

your fellow survivors. Also be sure to have those at the back protecting your rear. When you open/breach the door, you should enter in a crisscross fashion, as it is the fastest way. If the man in front of you goes the wrong way, do not hesitate, just go the opposite direction to him and it will work.

Room breaching needs to be done with speed. The faster you move in the faster those behind you can get through and support those at the front. Where possible, never have your team leader as the first to enter. At all times have 'muzzle discipline' (not pointing your weapons at fellow survivors). When entering, continually scan for danger, do not stop until you know for sure that the room is clear. Stop and guard any potential non cleared entrances or doors.

SNIPERS AND SPOTTERS

Both of these categories can be great for supporting teams in terms of both firepower and observation, however their own safety must be considered. In the Zompoc snipers and spotters want to be as high up as possible, for they have no risk from enemy weapons as they would in modern combat. Snipers and spotters should never work alone, as they cannot focus on their task and be aware of their surroundings at the same time. Always have them work in groups of two or three, ideally, a sniper, a spotter and a guard.

In cases of retreating and fast extraction sniper teams can get cut off from vehicles and teams. For this reason, be sure to keep them as close to your vehicles as possible. Beyond normal group tactical training, be sure that the sniper gets regular target practice. When the group works together, always ensure that the sniper's surroundings are protecting, ideally by the guard, if not by a spotter.

FIGHTING IN SHIFTS

When in combat troops suffer from fatigue fairly quickly. This is especially true of hand-to-hand fighting, meaning combat effectiveness is severely reduced. Prolonged fighting with projectile weapons can also increase fatigue as well as reduced combat effectiveness as ammunition is spent and weapons jam or clog up. If you can fight in sets, whereby there are always some of you resting. Often this will not be possible as to you survive you will need everyone in action. But when you are fighting in confined spaces such as doors and corridors, or from vehicles, this will be doable. Allowing people time to rest and recoup will keep them at maximum combat effectiveness, ensuring they stay nourished, re-supplied and on form. When you have smaller numbers in your group or are against the wall this will not be an option, but having many people capable of doing the same job with regular experience and team skills will greatly increase the effectiveness of the whole group.

FRIENDLY FIRE

This issue has been discussed in several sections in reference to different elements to it, but this is specific to combat and tactics. The chances are that most if not all of the survivors in your group will have no military experience, working effectively as an untrained militia. When using guns and projectile weapons you should always be careful of friendly fire and this is taught frequently to anyone who uses a gun, such as gun club enthusiasts. Don't aim guns at your friends, but what of close combat weapons? When trying to decapitate and destroy the brain you will likely be swinging around big heavy weapons in close formations, something few have any experience of today. Injuring other survivors is another reason why destroying the brain rather than decapitation is a better and more reliable method. Destroying the brain will typically be done with a vertical strike with some form of blunt or heavy instrument. It is comparatively safer than swinging a sword horizontally with speed and force when your fellow survivors are nearby.

AIR ASSAULT

This is unlikely but if you do have access to aircraft then you can consider using the Air assault tactics pioneered in the 1950s and 19060s to deliver military units directly into action. You can make use of aircraft such as helicopters to seize and hold key terrain which has not been fully secured and rarely, to directly engage and destroy the enemy. If you wish to be able to carry out this kinds of operations your people will need additional training in rappelling and air transportation, and their equipment is sometimes designed or field modified to allow better transportation in helicopters.

There are a few key differences between conventional air assault operations and those used ion the Zompoc. The main difference is that you are not likely to have more than a couple of suitable vehicles. The second is that you are not conducting operations against other humans, so the shock and surprise part of these operations will be lessened. This does not reduce the potentially for tactical flexibility though and sometimes an air assault is the quickest and most reliable way of securing a target.

A good example of the use of an air assault operation would be to secure a bridge or other vital building or structure. Let us assume that a hoard of zombies (undead or infected) is heading towards an area occupied by people. There are two bridges that connect the zombie side of the area to the living. An air assault could move a dozen people right into the bridge location literally minutes before the zombies arrive. One they arrive there are a variety of tactics they could use as described previously. Just remember that air assault units tend to be lightly equipped and in small numbers so are not designed for prolonged and heavy combat. Don't waste them!

In this example one of the most basic and obvious uses is to set up defensive positions and fight the zombies them off. Another would be to set up traps, mines and charges to break up the zombies advance. Another might be to rig the bridge for demolition. Another use would be for them to set their traps and then move to an overwatch position to scout and report zombie movement back to your base.

CHAPTER 9: OPERATIONS

I am more afraid of our own mistakes than of our enemies' designs.
Pericles

Before you jump into your truck and race off to kill a load of zombies it might be an idea to actually think about what you are doing so that you last more than 10 minutes. Operations does not include an overall strategy. It is designed to cover specific operations that you are likely to conduct during the Zompoc. These can range from scouting a petrol station out to staging large-scale military operations against zombie-infested towns. These operations are designed primarily against the zombie enemy but can be adapted against the living if they prove more of a threat to you under dangerous times. Refer to the other sections on convoys, vehicle preparation,

tactics, training, weapons and equipment to assist with these operations.

This section consists of mission planning along with detailed information on potential operations that you will need to carry out. Yep, this goes especially for you Americans! Real life soldiers plan their missions down to the last detail...you can do the same.

PLANNING

This is a rather important part of your missions and each stage needs to be looked at carefully. It is easy to just grab the nearest gun and race

off to raid a nearby town only to end up surrounded with your friends dying and your one vehicle crashed into the windows of the local Mc Donalds. Planning is critical!

INTELLIGENCE

Before the start of a mission you need to review any intelligence or information you have on the target. The target does not literally mean something you have to destroy (note for any Americans here), it is literally the target. Maps, information on the surrounding area, identifying marks, structures and objects need to be noted here. The more information you have the better you can plan your mission. Your first job is to look at the overall target area. Use maps and target photos if available or verbal information to get the 'big picture'. This is very important, especially if your mission takes place at night.

THREAT LEVEL

Use previous reconnaissance to gauge the level of threat from the environment, zombies and any potential surviving humans. Are you expecting a heavy presence or are you expecting there to be no contact with the enemy? This will determine the capabilities you will need and help you formulate an effective plan.

EQUIPMENT SELECTION

Once you know your target and your objective it is time to choose appropriate weapons and equipment. If you are expecting large numbers of hostiles then weapons, explosives and vehicles will need to be chosen appropriately. For reconnaissance missions you will want light, fast vehicles with good protection and basic weapons. For a rescue mission or raid you will need the capacity to haul supplies plus transports for workers and rescue personnel.

COMMUNICATION PROCEDURES

Establish communication procedures, call signs and fail safe signals for the mission. Make sure the team knows who is doing what and how to contact each element. Fail-safes are critical if or when kit breaks down, is damaged or lost. Obviously radios are the best form of communication. There other methods though and backups are critical. Lights, torches and flares can work at nights. During the day smoke, fire and sound can all be used along with the traditional signal cloths or flags. Just make sure all your people know how the system works!

SUPPORT FORCES

Support units are those units not directly

involved in the mission but provide assets additional to the mission. This might include several spare backup vehicles, sniper teams or reconnaissance units. Make sure you have enough options in case things go wrong. Remember the old adage, 'no military plan survives beyond its first encounter with the enemy'.

WHEN THINGS GO WRONG

You must know what to do if something goes wrong. Plan built-in redundancy for this. For example, if you need three trucks for a raid, bring four. Make sure you standardise as much as possible, for example, don't use vehicles with different fuel types and capability unless you have a specific reason to do so. There is no point in trying to move all the spare fuel from a petrol truck to a diesel one if there is a breakdown in hostile country! Think of likely things you might have trouble with.

Overheating vehicles is one quite common problem so make sure you have plenty of water on you. The benefit of water is that you can drink and use it for cooking, eating and many other uses. Another common problem is tyre punctures and blowouts. This is very common and is pretty likely to occur in the unmaintained roads of the Zomoc. Throw into the mix all the kinds of debris and junk on the roads and you have lots of reasons for tyre trouble.

Remember, the leader may be the one to get killed or stopped in some way, what happens then? Make sure somebody can take over at this point and that there is a quick, effective procedure to carry this out. At some point, you may not have enough members to complete the mission. Decide upon an abort plan and be ready to use it. It is foolhardy to press on if you do not have enough munitions, people or equipment.

MISSIONS

Missions are planned procedures carried out with a number of your fellow survivors with a particular objective in mind. It is important to carefully choose one of the following plans or to create your own using the same principles.

There are five main types of missions that you will conduct during the Zompoc. These missions include reconnaissance, supply, combat, personnel and demolition operations. In some circumstances you may want to combine some of these missions or carry several out in sequence. For example, a tactical reconnaissance followed by a raid or cull. Remember that these mission plans are frameworks for you to work from, feel free to modify them according to your own

requirements and resources. Each mission is numbered and includes critical information such as briefing material, objective, required vehicles, equipment, personnel and an additional notes section where relevant. Check the relevant vehicles, personnel, equipment and training sections of this book for further information. All of these missions with the exception of airborne specific missions assume you will have no airborne component. If you do have access to helicopters, gliders etc. Then you can obviously use this to provide additional capability as long as you can fly, maintain and operate them effectively and safely. There is no point whatsoever in flying a rescue mission in a helicopter if you crash into the people you should be saving!

All missions should include the following basic equipment:

1. Rations including food, water plus emergency supplies
2. Communications gear, radio
3. Basic medical supplies

RECONNAISSANCE

This is possibly one of the most valuable missions you will ever perform. These missions may be conducted to provide long-term information but most likely they are designed to provide vital intelligence prior to launching any of the other missions. It is even more important to carry out reconnaissance prior to raids or military operations. Your ability to carry out these missions will reply upon properly equipped vehicles, working communications and trained personnel. These missions may also be carried out as part of another ongoing mission, such as a raid so you may want to combine personnel and equipment into the entire operation.

SUPPLY

Finding, collecting and moving supplies will be one of the most important types of operations you will ever have to carry out. From day one

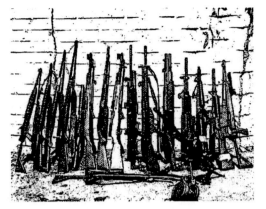

you will be raiding shops and stores for goods. Initially you will start out on foot but later on will be much better served by the use of vehicles, these can range from horse and quads through to trucks and possibly even trains! Supply missions are likely to be very common and you should therefore spend plenty of time and resources setting up these missions to be carried out frequently and reliably.

COMBAT

Combat operations are those conducted with the express object of attacking and defeating the enemy. The enemy is primarily Zombies but be in no doubt, during the Zompoc you will face all kinds of dangers and this will include other people. You may end up fighting similar groups to yourselves; you may even intentionally attack them for supplies or materials. These operations are essential for both general survival and also for expansion or obtaining supplies. Combat operations always require the use of your trained soldiers along with the best militia you have to hand. Make sure your people are trained for combat as well as you possibly can. Also make sure you use stage 3 modified vehicles, if possible, as these are best equipped for combat. Combat missions may also include aircraft and this adds

an extra dimension to the tasks that you can carry out and also carries the potential to cause all manner of new problems.

PERSONNEL

Personnel missions are those that involve collecting, retrieving or otherwise working with friendlies. These missions are critical as the living are your greatest assets. Though these missions may seem simple they can easily go wrong and then you'll lose irreplaceable people. It is very important when dealing with new people that you have procedures in place for checking their health both when you retrieve them through to when you get them back to your base. It is a good idea to provide some form of quarantine new people for a set period of time in case there are hidden symptoms of infection. Never, ever just accept the word of people, even your own people regarding the health of status of new people. You quite simply cannot ever take a chance like this with your own health!

DEMOLITION OPERATIONS

These are quite close to a mobile offence operation in that you need to travel fast and light to a particular location. The big difference is this operation is about the destruction of structures or objects. These structures can include bridges, buildings and supply stores. There are various reasons why you may conduct these operations. For example, destroying certain bridges can slow down or stop some zombie types or alternatively reduce the number of places you need to defend. For these operations you will need the same resources as a mobile offence along with those that have explosives training. It is pretty obvious but please do make sure that the people you are using for demolition work actually know what they are up to. At the very least you don't want people losing fingers and toes. Even worse would be substantial damage to your people and or equipment.

PLAN STRUCTURE

- ❖ **OBJECTIVE**. Each plan must have a clear and obvious objective. This is simple and each member of the team needs to understand its importance. Ensure your term do not go off mission by ignoring the objective.
- ❖ **BRIEFING**. Each mission will have a detailed briefing that outlines the location, the mission plan, escape procedures, timing and anything else pertinent to the mission.
- ❖ **VEHCILES**. Which vehicles are best suited to the mission and how many do you need? Here you will list in as much detail as possible what is required. If the vehicles need any special equipment or modification it will also be mentioned here, such as armour or extra fuel tanks.
- ❖ **PERSONNEL**. Which people and what number do you need? How many solders do you need and what kind of training?
- ❖ **MISSION EQUIPMENT**. This is where you list anything special and important to the mission. For example, a demolition mission will require the use of demolition charges of some kind.
- ❖ **NOTES**. This section is for anything else that needs to be known for the mission but did not fit into the previous sections. This section is also handy for going over the most important points, especially escape procedures.

MISSION PLAN 1 - TACTICAL RECONNAISSANCE

OBJECTIVE

To observe the target area, note terrain, access and escape routes, possible route and transport problems, hostiles and zombies.

BRIEFING

This is close-up reconnaissance and will require you to get your people in close to town, cities and supply locations to see at first hand the number of hostiles, to check for resources and potential strong points and vehicles. This is a very dangerous mission and is often conducted prior to carrying out other more involved missions, such as raids and culling. Expect any kind of terrain due to the nature of the mission and choose your vehicles accordingly.

VEHICLES

The best vehicles are light scout vehicles such as motorcycles, quads, trikes, convertibles and horses. Speed, stealth and reliability are more important than armour, weapons and load carrying capability. Take at least two vehicles for scouting.

PERSONNEL

Each vehicle needs a driver, if capable add one spotter per vehicle too. These must be your trained people and able to take over if needed, use communication gear and weapons. Always use your best people for scouting.

MISSION EQUIPMENT

Equipment for reconnaissance consists of two main categories, survival and scouting equipment. Make sure you have the following:

- ❖ Emergency communication gear, flare gun
- ❖ Close range and long range weapons
- ❖ Binoculars, pen, paper, notepads

NOTES

You must ensure you have multiple escape routes; fast vehicles and also backup units ready to extract you in case of emergencies. Items such as notepads, telescopes and binoculars will be critical for these missions.

MISSION PLAN 2 - STRATEGIC RECONNAISSANCE

OBJECTIVE

Observe the specified locations for both current problems and also potential problems in the future. Look for weak or damaged fencing, damaged roads, areas likely to flood and also whether zombie infestation is likely in the future. This is also a good opportunity to put signs up to help or warn other survivors, mark for supplies, paint danger symbols etc.

BRIEFING

You will investigate and monitor areas for signs of potential danger or change. You might not be looking at conducting operations in these areas yet but will still want to keep a watch on things. For example, you may send out daily patrols to watch the main highways. If danger is spotted this news will give your people time to prepare for defensive operations or to prepare a heavy convoy to break and escape.

VEHICLES

As you are looking at long-term reconnaissance the time issue is less important. Also, you are looking at wider areas and trying to spot potential future problems. For this you will need more people and thus some extra carrying capability. Take a scout vehicle with plenty of space or a pickup truck with escort bike.

PERSONNEL

You will need drivers plus as many trackers/spotters as you can safely take. If you plan on putting up signs or marking buildings take militia along with you. Make sure they are guarded and being careful at all times.

MISSION EQUIPMENT

Equipment for reconnaissance consists of two main categories, survival and scouting equipment. Make sure you have the following:

- ❖ Emergency communication gear, flare gun
- ❖ Close range and long range weapons
- ❖ Binoculars, pen, paper, notepads
- ❖ Paints, posters, hammers, nails, wood

NOTES

As with all missions make sure you have a backup unit in reserve, just in case.

MISSION PLAN 3 - RAIDING

OBJECTIVE
Collecting these supplies will require careful reconnaissance before sending on convoys to extract the goods.

BRIEFING
Raiding is basically shopping with weapons in hand. This will be especially important in the early days, as you will need to forage for supplies to keep your people going. Supplies will include everything from food and water to tools, ammunition and fuel. The recommended system is to start with a reconnaissance operation, follow this up with a mobile offensive operation to clear out the zombies from the area. Next send in your supply vehicles to extract the goods.

VEHICLES
At least two stage three prepared transports plus as many extra support vehicles and transports as required.

PERSONNEL
You will need drivers for all mission vehicles.

On top of this you will need armed guards for the vehicles plus militia members for loading, unloading and additional defence. Raids will use all manner of people and skills.

MISSION EQUIPMENT
You will require equipment for defence, possible offence, emergencies and loading. Some of the key equipment includes:

- ❖ Ropes, bags, sacks, boxes, cases
- ❖ Lifting gear
- ❖ Axes, crowbars, demolition charges
- ❖ Emergency communication gear, flare gun
- ❖ Close range weapons

NOTES
Have a backup unit stationed nearby in case people need to be evacuated. This unit needs to be capable of carrying all personnel from the mission, so it will be rather substantial.

MISSION PLAN 4 - LIGHT RAIDING

OBJECTIVE

Small scale supplies collection. Either due to lack of resources or because you want to be more discrete.

BRIEFING

This is similar to a normal raid but uses far less people, vehicles and planning. The primary use of light raiding is that you send only a small number of people or vehicle to the area. This would be either due to design or lack of resources and assets.

Setup a collection point a reasonable distance from the supplies and then send small scout units of two or more vehicles to sweep in and grab small numbers of supplies. Race back, load them up at the collection point and then head back in. This can be less risky by will take much longer to achieve your operation objectives.

VEHICLES

At least one transport is needed to wait at the collection point. You will then need an additional retrieval vehicle, something like a pickup, van or small 4x4. Use extra retrieval vehicles and transports as needed. A small number of armed scouts would be very useful for this very fluid raid.

PERSONNEL

You will need drivers for all mission vehicles. On top of this you will need armed guards for the vehicles plus militia members for loading, unloading and additional defence. You are travelling light for this mission so take only your best people.

MISSION EQUIPMENT

Keep equipment to a minimum, as you want to travel light and fast.

- ❖ Ropes, bags, sacks, boxes, cases
- ❖ Lifting gear
- ❖ Emergency communication gear, flare gun
- ❖ Close range weapons

NOTES

Make sure the collection point is well guarded and has flares or other ways of drawing attention if attacked.

MISSION PLAN 5 - TRANSPORT MISSIONS

OBJECTIVE
Transport materials from point A to point B.

BRIEFING
These are where you move supplies from one place to another. This could be the movement of a truckload of food from a recently raided shop right through to massive convoy operations to resupply bases and compounds. Refer to the convoy section of this book for information on conducting safe convoy operations. Ensure you conduct reconnaissance prior to a convoy mission and ideally a running reconnaissance mission as you conduct the actual transport too.

VEHICLES
At least one transport is needed. A small number of armed scouts would be very useful. Add extra transports, assault vehicles and scout vehicles depending on the size of the convoy. Refer to the convoy section for more specific information. For longer range transport add extra fuel tanks or include refuelling vehicles, tankers or tanker trailers.

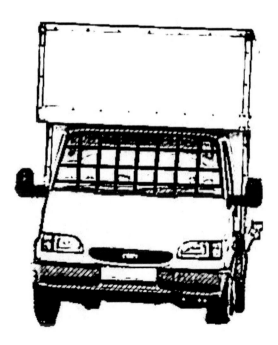

PERSONNEL
You will need drivers for all mission vehicles plus extra-armed personnel for mobile firepower and guard work. Loading unloading can be undertaken by the convoy crew or by crew waiting at points A and B. For extra firepower add militia members in pickups or transports like buses and minivans. If required add extra crew for loading work at each end.

MISSION EQUIPMENT
- ❖ Emergency communication gear, flare gun
- ❖ Close range weapons
- ❖ Extra ammunition
- ❖ Loading and unloading equipment if required
- ❖ Extra lamps, searchlights, flashlights

NOTES
Communications gear and weapons are very important for convoy work as are a sufficient number of people for the variety of tasks. Lookouts will be needed along all points on the convoy.

MISSION PLAN 6 - DEFENSIVE CULLING OPERATIONS

OBJECTIVE

The objective is to clear a specified area or region of zombies.

BRIEFING

Culling entails the permanent destruction of the enemy, not just the immobilisation of them. This means extra tools and equipment will be required. These operations are carried out in the immediate vicinity of your safe areas. These may consist of nothing more than shooting the odd zombie that stray too close to your compound to sending small parties out to clear the streets or fields near your base.

VEHICLES

Not required. Transports, assault vehicles or scout vehicles may be used if required. The simpler the operation the better.

PERSONNEL

Militia are perfectly suited for these missions when led by a soldier, especially when they do not have to venture outside your safe areas. For more dangerous operations include additional soldiers to add extra experience and skills.

MISSION EQUIPMENT

- ❖ Emergency communication gear, flare gun
- ❖ Close range, medium range and long range weapons
- ❖ Extra ammunition
- ❖ Materials/fuel to burn bodies
- ❖ Igniters

NOTES

Keep a few light vehicles ready on case an immediate evacuation is required. Also, spotters and snipers in your base in a position where they can provide covering fire would be of use. For culling operations it is important that you remember that the mission is to 'kill', not to just put out of action. This means fire or head shots so make them count!

MISSION PLAN 7 - OFFENSIVE CULLING OPERATIONS

OBJECTIVE

This mission is all about heading to a specific area and removing all threats. Culling entails the permanent destruction of the enemy, not just the immobilisation of them.

BRIEFING

These are simply about reducing the numbers of zombies in a given area. You should carry out these operations as frequently as possible. The more you do this the safer a given area will be. These make good training missions as the geography should be well known and your people are a short distance from your safe areas. Refer to the convoy sections and missions for extra advice on how to travel to the combat area. This means extra tools and equipment will be required. As you are moving into an area you must prepare for the unknown.

VEHICLES

This is an important combat mission and will require the minimum of 1 transport, 1 combat vehicle and 1 scout vehicle. Ensure you carry varied ordnance and plenty of ammunition for this mission.

PERSONNEL

This mission is exactly the kind if thing your soldiers train for. Make sure you use a solid core of good fighters backed up with a group of the best militia. Do not take anybody that is a poor fighter or poor shot.

MISSION EQUIPMENT

- ❖ Emergency communication gear, flare gun
- ❖ Close range, medium range and long range weapons
- ❖ Extra ammunition
- ❖ Materials/fuel to burn bodies
- ❖ Igniters

NOTES

As with other missions, make sure you have a rescue squad on standby. For these missions use your best weapons. Items such as Molotov Cocktails and improvised flamethrowers are handy for these missions. Fire based weapons can disable and destroy zombies at the same time.

MISSION PLAN 8 – MOBILE OFFENCE

OBJECTIVE

To perform a culling operation whilst remaining on the move in your armoured vehicles.

BRIEFING

This is where you use your vehicles in offensive culling operations. These are fast moving operations that are perfectly suited to stage 3 vehicles plus soldiers and militia. If you lose vehicles to accident, damage or lack of fuel you will need to use the mobile defence operation. Both vehicle mounted weapons and those carried by your people come in handy here. This is a much less effective version of the offensive culling operation and is designed as a vehicle mounted raid. These are good at reducing the numbers of zombies on the streets or to help clear out parts of an area. You will still need to conduct mission 7 if you want an area completely pacified. Ensure you have a specific route to follow and a time to extract to a safe area before returning home in an armoured convoy. Start the mission by selecting a start place to ensure all people and vehicles are present. Start the attack either as a single fighting column or split up into several groups and spread out in the area to cause maximum damage. Keep a reserve group for the latter option in case you need to help or rescue units in trouble.

VEHICLES

This mission requires the use of your best combat vehicles. Make use of assault vehicle, personnel transports, gun vehicles and scout vehicles. More than any other mission this one cries out for stage 3 modified vehicles. Weapons, armour and protection are all key for this mission.

PERSONNEL

You will need drivers, soldiers and militia for this mission.

MISSION EQUIPMENT

- ❖ Emergency communication gear, flare gun
- ❖ Vehicle mounted weapons
- ❖ All personal weapons
- ❖ Extra ammunition

NOTES

Have a backup plan for damaged or broken down vehicle plus a signal for immediate withdrawal. Also, for these missions do not stop, speed is your friend!

MISSION PLAN 9 - MOBILE DEFENCE

OBJECTIVE

Your units have been ambushed whilst travelling in vehicles and are unable to continue further. You must defend yourselves from a static position.

BRIEFING

This is where your mobile units are attacked in large numbers. This might happen for example when your raiding party is ambushed and surrounded or perhaps when your nomadic column is surrounded. In these situations we will assume that escape is not an option, perhaps you are out of fuel or you are in the middle of re-supplying when it happens. There are several important considerations. First, you need a solid defence that can defeat the attack allowing your escape and second, you need a way to escape if you are unable to defeat them in a defensive operation. Refer to the tactic section for ideas such as the defensive vehicle laager. Obvious weaknesses are zombies climbing underneath vehicles and through gaps between vehicles. You are safest when fighting either on top of or inside the vehicles. If you are conducting this operation at night then make sure you cannot be surprised, this mean light! Either use vehicle-mounted lights or send flares up to light up areas. Do not fight at a disadvantage in the dark!

VEHICLES

This is an emergency mission and you will therefore have to use whatever is to hand. Form up the slower heavier vehicles into a laager and keep a small reserve ready to break out if you find you are unable to defeat the attack.

PERSONNEL

Whichever personnel happen to be in or on the vehicles.

MISSION EQUIPMENT

❖ Whatever equipment you are carrying

NOTES

This is a dangerous situation and one that you will not usually intentionally create. The only time this is likely is when you want to rush an armoured column into an area to control. You will smash through any zombies present and then form a strong vehicle-based fort. If the fight is going to be long then you will need lots of ammunition, food and medical supplies.

MISSION PLAN 10 - RESCUE MISSIONS

OBJECTIVE
Rescue a number of personnel.

BRIEFING
These are usually launched to recover those remaining after a botched operation. The biggest problems suffered by these missions are that they suffer from a limited timeframe. This reduced time means you have little or no time to perform adequate reconnaissance or maybe even mobilise a sufficient number of resources. You want your best people, vehicles and equipment for these missions. Fight your way in, rescue them and then fight your way out. You will need to perform medical and Zompoc triage, especially with new and unknown people. If they are infected then carry out your standard Zompoc procedures.

VEHICLES
Use your best, most reliable vehicles with the space to carry people and supplies. In an emergency you can use light vehicles but make sure you have the capacity to recover all those found. Ensure you can quickly enter and leave these vehicles quickly and easily.

PERSONNEL
You need your best people for these missions. You need a small number as you will need the space for the rescued. Ideally you want people with multiple skills in driving, combat and first aid.

MISSION EQUIPMENT
- ❖ Emergency communication gear, flare gun
- ❖ Close range weapons
- ❖ Heavy weapons for suppressing fire
- ❖ Medical supplies
- ❖ Stretchers
- ❖ Extra weapons and ammunition for rescued personnel

NOTES
Rescue missions are sometimes carried out after hearing distress transmissions but most of the time it is for when a raid or mission goes wrong. Be careful as it is very easy for a rescue mission to be caught up or surrounded. Quick thinking and speed are the essence, hence using your best people for these missions.

MISSION PLAN 11 - COLLECTION OR RETRIEVAL

OBJECTIVE

To rescue or retrieve personnel with a planned and co-ordinated response.

BRIEFING

These missions are similar to rescue missions but have one big advantage, that of time. Time is your friend and allows you to organise and muster forces for safe and efficient operations. You will often need to organise these operations as a backup for when things go wrong. Raids, reconnaissance and combat operations can always go wrong. When this happens you will need to send in the cavalry to the rescue. Retrieval operations need to be conducted by those with experience, with your most well maintained vehicles. This is not a rushed rescue but a carefully planned operation.

You will send in scouts to find your people, use light vehicles to rescue them and load them into your transports. If you have time conduct a reconnaissance mission first. If numbers or vehicles are limited then use the light transports to both collect the people and to transport them.

VEHICLES

You need a mixture of vehicle to perform a safe collection or retrieval mission. The vehicles are split up into three main categories. The first of these is the recon unit, this might be one or two motorcycles to help locate the exact extraction point. The next part is the retrieval vehicles, these are small to medium sized armed vehicles with enough space to carry the people and equipment. The third and last part is large armoured transports. These act essentially as mother ships for the mission and will bring back the people in larger numbers.

PERSONNEL

You need your best people for this mission along with the best-trained fighters.

MISSION EQUIPMENT

- ❖ Emergency communication gear, flare gun
- ❖ Close range weapons
- ❖ Heavy weapons for suppressing fire
- ❖ Medical supplies
- ❖ Stretchers
- ❖ Extra weapons and ammunition for rescued personnel

NOTES

You have time and resources on hand for this mission so take no chances and make sure you get everybody out alive and uninjured.

MISSION PLAN 12 - DEMOLITION

OBJECTIVE

To destroy a structure.

BRIEFING

Demolition missions are simply those missions designed with destruction of structures, buildings or other large objects to clear the route for yourself or to deny access to the enemy. These operations will usually combine the use of other missions including tactical reconnaissance, transport and culling. Start by selecting your target, then send in a reconnaissance team and culling operation. Follow this with an armed column, secure the area and then set your charges. Load up your people and supplies and head for home.

VEHICLES

For a demolition mission you will need a varied selection of vehicles including transports for the demolition people and guards. You will need several escort vehicles to perform reconnaissance and scouting work. Make sure your transports are well equipped and armoured in case of a forced defence.

PERSONNEL

You need your best people for this mission along with the best trained demolition specialists.

MISSION EQUIPMENT

- ❖ Emergency communication gear, flare gun
- ❖ Close range weapons
- ❖ Demolition charges
- ❖ Heavy weapons for suppressing fire
- ❖ Medical supplies

NOTES

You have time and resources on hand for this mission so take no chances. Ensure that you both destroy the target structure and also protect your people from both hostiles and also injuring your own people with the charges or debris!

MISSION PLAN 13 – AIRBORNE ASSAULT

OBJECTIVE
To attack a zombie infested area or to perform airborne based culling operations.

BRIEFING
Equip your aircraft with aircraft mounted weapons or with crew armed weapons to provide offensive capability. You will head into the target area and provide heavy firepower to cleanse it of zombies or to support ongoing operations. These missions are much more effective when combined with ground troops as an air assault will find it tough to eliminate all hostiles. This is especially true for fixed wing aircraft as helicopters are capable of hovering or concentrating on a particular region for periods of time or even by hovering at them.

VEHICLES
At least one aircraft such as light fixed wing aircraft or helicopter. More basic machines such as air balloons can also be used though they are slow and less capable in an assault scenario.

PERSONNEL
Aircraft trained crew as well as supporting gunners. Crew need communication training and ideally one medic per aircraft.

MISSION EQUIPMENT
❖ Emergency communication gear, flare gun
❖ Close range weapons
❖ Heavy weapons for suppressing fire
❖ Medical supplies
❖ Aircraft mounted weapons

NOTES
Air assault missions are always heavy on the expenditure. Make sure you have a backup mission planned for airborne transport in case anything goes awry.

MISSION PLAN 14 – AIRBORNE TRANSPORT

OBJECTIVE
Transport materials from point A to point B via air.

BRIEFING
These are where you move supplies from one place to another. This could be the movement of a truckload of food from a recently raided shop, right through to massive convoy operations to resupply bases and compounds. Refer to the convoy section of this book for information on conducting safe convoy operations. Ensure you conduct reconnaissance prior to a convoy mission and ideally a running reconnaissance mission as you conduct the actual transport too.

VEHICLES
At least one aircraft, ideally more than one to spot for problems and to assist with rescue and recovery if one is lost. For transport most light aircraft will not be suitable. Passenger or cargo aircraft are required or most types of utility helicopters.

PERSONNEL
You will need pilots, navigators and trained armed guards. Loading/unloading can be undertaken by the aircrew or by crew waiting at points A and B. Carrying crew to load and unload will restrict the space available for cargo. If required add extra crew for loading work at each end.

MISSION EQUIPMENT
- ❖ Emergency communication gear, flare gun
- ❖ Close range weapons
- ❖ Extra ammunition
- ❖ Loading and unloading equipment if required
- ❖ Extra lamps, searchlights, flashlights

NOTES
Communications gear and weapons are very important.

MISSION PLAN 15 – RIVERINE OPERATIONS

OBJECTIVE
Transport, reconnaissance and combat operations.

BRIEFING
Riverine operations are fundamentally the same as land based missions but have the caveat that water based vessels are usually of little use for actual operations other than transports. Basically use water based craft to ferry goods, people or weapons to an area to conduct an operation as per earlier mission. Upon completion return to the water based vehicles. Essentially the boats become a mobile base.

VEHICLES
At least one boat, ideally more than one in case you hit any problems. If you have access to larger craft then use these as bases and then load people and equipment into smaller boats as required.

PERSONNEL
You need crew for the boats plus additional crew for loading materials and also for defence purpose. Make sure they can swim!

MISSION EQUIPMENT
❖ Emergency communication gear, flare gun
❖ Short, medium and long range weapons
❖ Extra ammunition
❖ Loading and unloading equipment if required
❖ Extra lamps, searchlights, flashlights
❖ Dinghies, lifeboats, motorcycles, trikes etc

NOTES
Make sure you have a plan and equipment in place for any loss of power, equipment or damage to your water based craft. If your hull is holed or you have to abandon ship - what is the plan?

CHAPTER 10: SUPPLIES/LOGISTICS

*Generally management of the many is the same as
management of the few. It is a matter of organization.*

Sun Tzu

During the Zompoc it will be critical to the survival of the living to be able to obtain supplies and distribute them amongst your people. Even in the very first hours of this disaster you will start accumulating the things that you will needs for the next few hours, then days and then into the future. In the short term you will be able to raid to accumulate what you need. Ultimately you will need to produce, grow and maintain supplies of food and materials to keep your people alive. This chapter is designed for the short to medium term goals of raiding, foraging and distributing supplies. For information on growing and making food and consumables please read the appropriate section. For information on transporting supplies please also see the section on travel and transport.

SUPPLIES

Supplies are simply all the goods and materials that you will use and consume during the Zompoc. These supplies consist of short-term items right through to items that will help you continue civilisation on into the future. Without supplies you will be dead in a matter of days! As well as identifying items that will be of use to you also need to think about items that will be of benefit to others in your party as well as future situations. For example, in the short term you will need batteries for radios and torches. After a few days these will run flat. Do you stock up on thousands of batteries

or do you get equipment that will allow you to recharge them yourself? How about shotguns, what do you do when you need more shells? You can look for more in sporting good shops or you can hunt down the reloading equipment and become self sufficient. Obviously on the day the Zompoc breaks out you do not want to be playing around with charger - the week after though...

WHAT YOU NEED

Food is the number one item and you'll be needing lots of it. We need to make sure that we are taking in everything our bodies need, not only to survive, but to thrive and help promote the living. For a balanced diet we need equal parts of protein and grain as well as fresh fruits and vegetables in nearly equal parts. It is important to know how to get and store the different types of food as most long-term food storage requires cold storage. Some products will even need freezing. If you live in Norway then this isn't a problem, for those of you in California it may be more difficult.

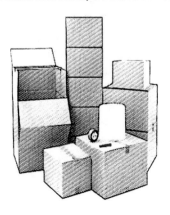

SHORT-TERM FOOD

When travelling either on foot or by vehicle or if you are going to be forced to travel long distances space and weight will be an issue. Know your nutritional requirements before you embark on an expedition. As was stated

before, having fresh food is a good plan, but also knowing what kind of travel food to carry is a must. Taking some less perishable produce is fantastic, but also considers taking with you

travel cakes made of dried meat, dried fruits, nuts/seeds and something that gives you a lot of calories. Today, we see a lot of energy bars on the market, but a method that was used long ago (as unappetising as it sounds) was rendered animal fat. Animal fat provided the high caloric intake that was required when travelling all day and there was very little storage space.

Pre-packaged food, be it in cans, bottles, jars, bags, wrappers or boxes is often the least good food you can eat. Though many of the pre-packaged foods we have come to know and love will provide you with that caloric and fat intake that is needed, they will be short term solutions that won't give you long term energy and will provide little (if any) nutritional benefits. That being said, pre-packaged foods aren't all bad and there are some benefits. Many of the MREs (Meals Ready to Eat) that you can buy and that the military uses can survive for 5-10 years and have substantially more nutritional value than the snack cakes or bars we often think of when we think of pre-packaged food. If you plan on getting these military supplies make sure you get them from a supplier that sells good that are well in their dates. Don't bother buying foodstuff that will go bad a few weeks or months after buying them.

Similarly, there are some energy bars common in the market that provide much more complex carbohydrates and less sugar which will provide you with long-term energy. Many pre-packaged food, if you know what to look for, can contain large number of vitamins and minerals as well.

LONG-TERM FOOD

Long term food is the kind of stuff that you can store or stash for use at a much later date.

There is not point is rushing off to the mountains with a boot full of fast food. Actually, there is probably not much use in going anywhere with fast food. These supplies might not seem important at the start but believe us, you will want these goods for the coming weeks and months to come. The more long-term supplies you stash the less contact you will need with people and locations. Less contact means less time for zombie problems. These are the kind of problems you can do without.

- ❖ **Meat,** though a staple diet item it is important to cure and store the meat so that it lasts more than a few days. Drying and/or curing so as to remove the moisture or make the meat itself inhospitable to bacteria, mould or other organisms is the most common and easiest method. Liberally salting and seasoning the meat will make the flesh more palatable.
- ❖ **Salt Curing,** Salt is a common ingredient when used to store meat, but in the salt or brining method, there is little else used. Salt curing preserves the meat in a way closest to its original state, but it also has the shortest shelf-life.
- ❖ **Canning,** Canning meat will allow you to store the meat up to a couple of years if stored properly, but is a slightly more complicated method of preservation than the other methods.
- ❖ **Drying,** By far the easiest method, and one of the easiest to store, is simply drying the meat. Nearly everyone is familiar with meat dried into strips, usually after being seasoned, this, of course, is called jerky.
- ❖ **Fruits & Vegetables,** Vegetables and fruits can be dried and cured similarly to meats, but the easier method for these is canning. The key thing to remember with fruits and vegetables is this: spoilage is caused by moulds, fungus and bacteria being fed by the sugars in the produce, but the only way the mould/fungus can take hold are by having moisture.

SUPPLY GEOGRAPHY

There are many places to obtain supplies, though as you might expect, some are better than others. Depending on where you live in the world you will have access to dense urban areas right through to the open countryside and deserts.

The single biggest problem that you will have with most locations is that where you find supplies you will also find people. This means that the supplies you need and zombies could be found in the same place. Always think about what a location looked like before the Zompoc. If the place was full of people then it is a fair assumption that those same people, if now zombies, will be lurking in the same place. Be careful! It would be awful to head off to collect some food and clothing only to get jumped by a couple of dozen crazed zombie shoppers! Stores are usually found in these types of places, each has pros and cons and it is very important that you study them carefully.

Don't forget that it isn't just the building you need to think about, it is also the area around the shop. Is it likely to be full of zombies? What is access like and is it also likely to be the target of any other survivors? Plan for meeting both the dead and the living whilst looking for supplies and have a plan to deal with both. It is quite likely that you will find a zombie, lurking in the back of a store just waiting to spoil your day!

MALLS

Shopping malls are very common throughout the world and have many useful futures to the survivor in the Zompoc. The best thing about a mall is that rather than just one shop you will actually find all kinds of stores selling a bewildering number of products. Expect everything from food and clothes to electronics goods and hunting supplies. Shopping malls are also handy in that they are based outside of many city centres on the main access roads. This makes a shopping mall a handy place to raid as you can park your large transports directly inside the parking areas.

There is a downside to malls though and this is that they are always full of people; this could translate into huge numbers of zombies during the Zompoc. These places are also likely to be popular destinations to any other survivors, especially those that have watched the classic Romero film, 'Dawn of the Dead'. Make sure you have an escape plan and don't delve too deeply into the mall as you might end up trapped and be unable to escape back to your transportation. Caution is advised!

TRADING ESTATES/RETAIL PARKS

Retail parks offer many of the advantages of a shopping mall in that they contain a variety of stores offering all kinds of products. Retail parks also offer lots of parking and good access via main roads. They also suffer from the same problems in that they attract large numbers of people. One added benefit of the park over a mall though is that each of the stores is separate, this allows you to work on one area at a time and are thus less likely to be overwhelmed. There is also more space between stores which will make it easier to spot potential threats and to defend yourselves.

CITY CENTRES

These are dangerous places to obtain supplies as this is where you will find the most people and also the most chaos. You can expect a large to massive zombie infestation plus possible partially infected. On top of this it is easy to become trapped in cities and towns where people have abandoned or crashed their vehicles trying to escape. You may have no choice in the early days but in the end you must get out. The thing city centres have going for them though is that you can find many different types of shops and stores offering most of the items you will need.

The main thing to always remember about city centres is that they have a high density of everything; people, zombies, supplies and danger. Smaller towns are a much better alternative as they will often have the same or similar stores to the larger towns and cities but feature small populations and also a much shorter distance between the main shopping centre and the access roads. Raiding a city like London could mean hours before you can escape to the open roads, whereas raiding a small town like Caerleon in South Wales would be a matter of seconds from the shops to the countryside and main roads. It is probably a fair assumption that any small towns and cities will be full of the insanity and chaos that you can expect would follow the early outbreak. Shops will be broken in to, there may be fires and who knows what else in the streets.

STREETS

Shops are found on streets, street corners and off the main roads. These places can offer any kind of goods from food to shoes and hats. Though you are away from the city centre you must remember that houses, flats and homes all used to be occupied by the living and they are now your enemy. There might be one really handy shop but if it is surrounded by five hundred houses you could find it seriously dangerous.

NEAR HIGHWAYS

Highways or motorways as they are known in the UK are the large, major transport arteries that are scattered through the country. There are various places that you can obtain supplies from that are situated right next to main highways. These places include service stations, petrol stations, retail parks and farms. The great thing about stores and garages near the main highways is that they are less likely to be locations heavily populated by people or

zombies, yet feature good road links and the ability to move your transports directly to the location. The only real problem you might face is that a highway could be easily jammed with smashed or abandoned cars. Access on these rounds is therefore uncertain.

STORES AND SHOPS

There are many types of stores available at these five main locations. Each of them offers differing types of supplies, some of more importance than others. Here is a comprehensive list of possible stores and outlets to raid for useful and important materials. Make sure you check with the locations section listed above to compare risk versus opportunity. It might be better to make extra trips to out of town areas for important supplies rather than drive into a city centre to pick up some fishing line only to be surrounded by twenty thousand zombies, all after your ass!

SUPERMARKETS

This mega-store is the ideal place to pickup all manner of goods, not only under one roof but also in one actual store. The supermarket features many of the same problems of a mall in that there are limited exits and almost certainly large numbers of zombies hanging around. Like a mall you will find good parking plus handy access to main transport links.

DIY STORE

These shops are now more common than the traditional hardware store in the UK though you can still find the latter more often in the US. These places are a goldmine for the

Zompoc survivor. Expect to find tools, fixings, plumbing and piping, wood, weapons such as axes, knives, blades and poles, sheets of metal, ropes, chains and more. Expect pretty much anything here except for food and medical supplies.

GARDEN CENTRES

Garden centres are big business in the UK due to the exciting obsession people have with playing with plants and shrubs in their gardens. Thankfully the garden centre now has a use as they are well stocked on supplies for getting you self-sufficient. Want seeds to grow fruits and vegetables? Want feed for your animals? Garden centres nearly always have these!

PETROL STATION

Also known as a gas station in the US or sometimes simply as a garage in the UK. These locations are obviously good places to find fuel for your vehicles and other machines. Remember that refining fuel is difficult and in

the long term you will need access to stored fuel. In later months and years petrol and diesel will become the dominant currency. In the short term you can obviously siphon off fuel from all the abandoned vehicles you will find littered about.

POUND SHOPS

These are known as Dollar Stores in the US for obvious reasons and are an excellent source of general odds and ends for your survivors.

Expect to find lighters, batteries, flash lights, first aid, basic vehicle maintenance items and water. The only real downside to pound stores is that you are never 100% certain as to what they might actually have in stock!

PHARMACY/CHEMIST

Also known as drug stores in the US, here you will find food, medical supplies, soaps, batteries, torches, water etc. These stores often carry a bewildering array of other items such as water, drinks, sweets (candy), gum and cigarettes. The great thing about medical supplies and cleaning materials etc, are that they last for so long. The shelf life times can be in years.

FARMS

They are a great source of fuel, generators, hand tools, solar fence chargers (to charge car batteries), clothes and vehicle batteries. Even better they have relatively few people though watch out for zombie sheep! If you live in the UK you will probably find a farm is one of the few places you can actually find a working gun! As in gun shops just be careful, you don't want to get shot by an angry farmer!

SHOE SHOPS

Shoe stores are very important in keeping your poor feet looked after. Ditch dress shoes and go for sturdy boots and shoes for men and women. Heels are definitely out. Also, remember that most stores only keep one shoe on display, the rest are in the storage area where it is usually dark and secluded. As

always be very careful when out shopping in the Zompo!

ANGLING SHOPS

In the UK you don't usually find hunting shops, rather angling shops. These places still sell

handy items such as fishing line, weights, knives and tools. Don't forget the obvious angling equipment too; you can always fish for food too!

HUNTING SHOPS

These are usually only found in the US. They contain all the good stuff found in angling stores plus more exciting kit like archery gear,

gun powder, primers, reloading supplies, guns- if any left, ammo and camping gear. Be careful though as this is likely to be a popular place for survivalists and other living to rush to. Some US hunting stores also carry a decent selection of weapons though they are obviously

optimised for hunting. Saying that though, there are still those that think the .50 calibre Desert Eagle pistol is well suited for this task!

GUN STORES

These handy places go without saying! Here you will find weapons, ammunition and hopefully reloading materials so you can continue to produce your own ammunition! In the UK you will only find hunting rifles, air guns and shotguns. In the US you will find pretty much anything! Be careful though, you are equally likely to find the shop owner barricaded inside with a veritable arsenal of weapons. Don't get shot on the way in!

CAR PARTS STORE

If you have vehicles then you will need parts and tools to keep them going. Yes, you can cannibalise other cars but at some point you will actually have to fit a new part or maybe find somewhere with a 14mm spanner. These places also sell oil, anti freeze, oil filters, belts,

alternators, spark plugs and wires, starters, and gas treatment. You will find many of these places in out of town shopping centres but be careful as some are much more about sound systems and exhaust tips and than actual car stores. If you can try and get an idea where your local car parts place is, if you have a less than reliable car you may already be a regular customer!

FURNITURE STORE

On the face of it you might think these places are a waste of time, they do however carry items that are very handy, especially later on and there is a good chance that other survivors will not appreciate the items these stores have to offer. Some of these choice items include mattresses, couches, tables, sheets, pillows, and blankets. Everything a growing zombie proof community needs! Furniture shops can also prove a handy place to obtain extra material for clothing and repairs. There will also be a good amount of wood and other

burnable fuels. You will also find a good quantity of cabinets and sturdy storage units that could be use as they are or smashed for their materials.

CLOTHING STORES

It might be shocking to note that yes, we do need clothes and during the Zompoc you will initially not have a lot of time to wash and iron clothes. Expect to find clothes for the entire group, coats and boots etc. These items can be stored for ages and are thus a great item to collect and stash for another day. Try and go for stores that sell decent quality clothing that is study and will last. This doesn't mean go for designer brands, it means go for clothes that you know work.

The stuff you really want is outdoor clothing and sturdy work clothes. They may not be the most fashionable but they will be of great help in the Zompoc. Make sure you have clothing suitable for life outdoor as you are going to find creature comforts hard to come by. Don't discount hats and gloves too. The winter can be cold!

OUTDOOR SHOPS

These stores are very common in the UK and sell all types of goods that would be of use for outdoor pursuits. You will find boots, coats, thermal clothing, camping stoves, torches and maps. Most stores also carry pocket knives and GPS systems too. The only real downside

is that they are found in city centres and sometimes shopping malls so can be risky to visit during the Zompoc. These stores are also a handy place to kick up spare batteries and maps. In the UK you will also find that many of these stores sell long lasting, high energy food bars that are great for storing and using in emergencies. These foodstuffs are much like the lembas bread carried by the hobbits in Lord of the Rings!

ARMY SURPLUS

Army surplus stores in the UK carry all kinds of handy stuff but they do lack one important item....weapons! You will however find excellent outdoor gear that is strong, durable and weather proof. Stock up on everything from trousers and socks through to sleeping bags, hats, tents, gloves and knives. Army surplus clothing is much better than pretty much everything else you will found out there

for use in the Zompoc. Military clothing is strong, long lasting and designed to dry out quickly. This clothing Is perfect for pretty much any occasion. One added benefit is that you can get decent camouflaged kit. One to not get attacked is to not be seen in the first place!

EBAY AND ONLINE SHOPPING

One of the most popular way to buy products these days is to pop online with your computer or mobile phone and simply click You are

kidding right? Assuming there is still Internet access and that you can find a working computer with an active connection there is absolutely no point, none at all in trying to buy goods online. It doesn't matter if it says the item is in stock, you won't get it! If you are not convinced then simply go ahead, you are not worth saving!

RAIDING

This may sound more like something you would expect a Viking to do but during the Zompoc it is sadly something you will have to rely upon. Raiding is essentially shopping without permission and usually armed. Raids can consist of one or two people popping inside a shop to grab supplies right through to a full scale armed raid with multiple vehicles and lots of people. Either way you will find raiding will be the only way you can supply yourself and people with food, water, fuel and weapons in the short term. It is important when raiding to know what to look for so you don't all come back with loads of perishable apples, when you could have brought back dozens of types of items to last both long and short term. Always ensure you are armed when raiding and that people never, ever travel off alone.

STORAGE

Assuming you are not living out of a car you will need somewhere to store your supplies. This in effect will become a storage depot of sorts. You have a variety of options with regards to storage and this will completely depend on the number of people that you have as well as how many locations you have under control. Initially you will probably find that your safe house is also where you will store all your supplies. This is fine to start with but eventually, as you get more people and start collecting more goods, you will have to expand. When you set up store houses it is important that they are safe, secure and organised. Stores should have one way in that is always guarded. This guarding is not just against zombies but also against other people that might look to steal your hard earned food and water or maybe even to barter it on with other people.

One simple and secure method of storage is to make use of sealed and secure vehicle containers. Many large trucks have storage area and they usually only have loading from one side. The benefit of vehicle based storage is that you can move it if required. This is especially handy if your depot is hit by a Zombie attack and you need to get away fast. There is nothing worse than escaping with your life to only find that all your food, water and other critical supplies are stuck in some building you can never get near again. For vehicle based storage makes sure the sides and doors are secure. Don't use a soft backed vehicle for obvious reasons.

Another possibility for storage is to make use of the railway system and associated railway buildings. The buildings themselves are usually pretty sturdy to protect them from vandals and thieves. The tracks obviously link areas together and will be very difficult for a zombie to stop a train rolling towards them. You can also make use of the trains and their wagons to create an armoured supply base that is full mobile, just make sure you Havre the means and knowledge to move the train!

See the vehicles section for more information on using trains for combat, transport and offensive operations.

DISTRIBUTION

Distributing your supplies is much more difficult than you might think. You might have a trailer full of tinned food but what stops your people eating it all in one week? How long will your fresh food supply last and who gets to eat them? Distributing these vital supplies will be dangerous, as hungry people can quickly become desperate people. This means you need to use reliable and trustworthy people that will not let others take advantage of them to help with this.

EARLY DAYS

In the early days you can just hand out to people what they need, when they need it. Make sure that the people in charge of the supplies have a good inventory of the supplies they have and that they use supplies in a sensible manner. This means giving out realistic quantities based on supply, rationing valuable or rare items and ensuring that perishable items are used before they go bad. Later on, as you expand your territory base and numbers you will need to carefully hoard and ration supplies for the long-term survival of your people. You can use a variety of measures from a fixed ration of items per person, per day through to a ration card type idea. Make sure that the person in charge of handing out and sorting rations is not the same person that physically moves the good around and to your people. Get them an assistant to do this so they can always keep an eye on the goods.

MEDIUM TERM PLANS

Once you start to get yourself established and have a few decent outposts created you will need to ensure that you can move supplies, materials and food to where they are needed and at the correct time. You may find that you will have several decent, defensible bases as well as access to a port or harbour a few miles away. On top of this you might raid the nearby towns and villages for supplies on a regular basis. If you are moving food and perishable items, especially over longer distances there are some very important considerations.

The first of these is a working transport infrastructure, such as roads, vehicles, rail transport, and ports. If you only need to move materials a short distance then paths, dirt roads and tracks are acceptable. If you need to move several trailers worth of goods twenty miles then something better suited to the task like main roads, waterways or railways will need to be considered.

Contaminated or spoiled food is a big problem. You definitely do not want a large number of sick people because you made some stupid decisions with regards to the handling of food. Food handling technology and resources such as refrigeration, and storage, warehousing will also help keep your good safe and also allow you to make use of them for longer period.

Lastly you will need an adequate source of materials based on demand and need. If you end up with one hundred people you are going to need decent access to large amounts of clean water, food, clothing and cleaning materials. There is no point setting up your new home in an area next to a massive steelworks that is fifty miles from any source of supplies as you could easily end up with a lot of people and no food within a safe distance.

LONG TERM PLANS

For long term distribution you need to review the 'Rebuilding' chapter as this covers other related areas such as bartering and stockpiling goods to trade with other survivors. If for example, you have good access to certain supplies in excess of what you need you can trade them for items that you do need. Once you are at this stage you should have perfected the idea of storage, transport and logistics to a sufficient level. It would make sense that at this point you will be obtaining supplies by means other than just raiding towns and stores, as this is a very short-term approach. Food supplies will only be available for so long before you will need to grow your own or possibly find other that are growing food and then trade for it. If you are looking at trade then you have to introduce the idea of supply and demand and start to consider the idea of basic economics to make the most out of your fledging economy.

THEFT

With distribution comes the chance that your goods will be stolen or attacked by other survivors. This is very dangerous as the loss to you will be in people, vehicles and supplies. There is also the possibility that your own people will be tempted by the goods they are hauling and may make off with the lot to a safe place of their own. This is where your core of dependable and trustworthy guards comes in. It is their job to think of the collective and to get the supplies back in one piece.

PUNISHMENT

With theft and mutiny comes the requirement of punishment. If people are found stealing your materials it is very serious, much more than in the days prior to the Zompoc. The loss of supplies could mean death to all your people. Those found breaching your rules need to be punished. The worst possible punishment is execution or banishment. In theory banishment is more human but it will send them out on their own where they will have to fend for themselves in zombie country. Another problem is that a banished person is a person with a grudge. This banishment could come back to haunt you sometime in the future. Consider your punishment carefully and always think to the future!

CHAPTER 11: WEAPONS

Among other evils which being unarmed brings you, it causes you to be despised.

Niccolò Machiavelli

The Zompoc is not time to being a tree-hugging, vegetable eating pacifist. You have one responsibility and that is to yourself. Stay fit, alive and healthy. To do this you are going to need an edge over the zombies. They may be able to match you in strength or stamina but they surely won't be able to match a bullet! Quite simply, get some weapons or die a painful death. Whether you intend to hide in a hole or go on the offensive, you're going to have to get your hands dirty at some point, so

be ready for it. Organise simple and easy ways of carrying weapons where possible, utilising sheaths, scabbards, holsters, slings and packs. Depending on where in the world you live there will be restrictions of some kind on equipment that you can buy or items that you can use. Obviously once the Zompoc kicks in rules will fly out of the window, until then it it important that you follow the laws of your region.

PROJECTILE WEAPONS

Everybody thinks of a gun first. If you're a trigger happy yank you likely have one in your truck and one in your trousers, but if you're a Brit, you probably don't have one at all. You can find guns in gun shops, police stations and army barracks, all of which probably got the idea to hold up near the ammunition already, so don't expect to be welcomed in and given supplies. Projectile weapons come in all different flavours from target pistols and crossbows up to sub-machine guns, shotguns, rocket launchers and bows. Like most items you will be using in the Zompoc you will need spare parts, supplies (in this case ammunition) and the knowledge to use them.

HAND GUNS

Easy to carry and use, but typically short on range and accuracy. Handguns of any sort are very hard to find in the UK, unless you're a 'gangsta'. If you do find any handguns, they will probably be blank firers or BB pellet guns, great for holding up banks, not so much for shooting zombies.

9mm Automatic – If you can find a handgun in Britain, through police or military sources, it will almost certainly be a 9mm automatic, such as the Browning High Power, Sig Sauer P226/P228 or one of the many such guns in the Glock family. All of which will feature a good, semi-automatic rate of fire, reasonable ammo capacity and quick reload times. Sadly the 9mm round doesn't have as much stopping power as you would like, accuracy is key here, consider these pistols as sidearms only.

HIGH POWER HANDGUNS

Big Power handguns are really popular for film use as they look great, massive hand cannons, such as .50 Desert Eagles and big Revolvers. In the real world you will find these monstrous guns to be of little practical use in a fighting situation, whether fighting zombies or humans. Big power handguns feature low ammo capacity, are heavy and cumbersome and also typically difficult to find ammunition for. The chances are that zombies will have to be shot in the head, meaning 9mm, .45, or anything in the typical range of pistol calibres will be fine.

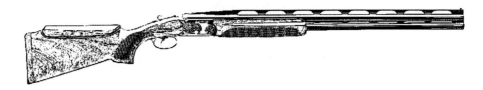

SHOTGUNS

The most common firearms to be found in Britain are double barrelled, over and under or side by side. You may also be able to find the odd pump actions which are a big improvement, more popularly used by criminals, but also by sports shooters. Shotguns are simple to use because they require little training and accuracy when used

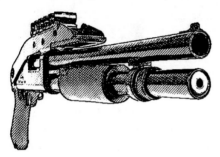

up close as they were intended, however, ammo capacity is very poor, especially in Britain, and reload time is slow. A shotgun will take a head clean off, ammunition is also more common than any other in Britain, a shotgun is

mister reliable. Ash used one, it worked for him, groovy. Most shotguns that you find will have wood stocks as seen below, this is good, as it will help your accuracy with clean head shots as well as be useful for clubbing zombies at close range should the need arise. If you have to face runners, do not put too much faith in double barrelled shotguns. The pump action shotgun is a big step up in terms of rate of fire, though reload times is still not great, as well as the fact that many British pump actions only have a capacity of three, (one on the chamber and two in the tube), making them little better than a double barrel. Shotguns are always depicted in films as hugely powerful weapons, but do not be fooled by this and forget their weaknesses. A sturdy hand to hand weapon will frequently be better suited to the job than these. The one big advantage that shotguns have over any other gun in Britain is that ammo is relatively common compared to all others, which are very rare.

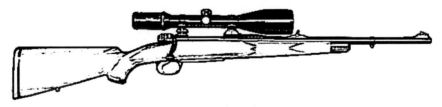

RIFLES

Hunting and target rifles are mostly high power with very high accuracy, but lots of skill required. Slow rates of fire mean they are great if you are camping on a rooftop, not so good when you have to deal with the rabble. A high power hunting rifle is the camper's best friend. If you can find big enough supplies of ammunition they can be used for relaxed and

casual culling of the undead at your own pace. However, the use of these weapons involves a good location and preparation. Making effective use of a rifle such as this requires more skill than most realise, as they are too accustomed to playing Counterstrike and Quake, in reality sniping is a fine art.

SUB-MACHINE GUNS AND ASSAULT RIFLES

Only available through police and military routes in Britain, high rates of fire along with typically high accuracy and good power. Ammunition is scarce and you will burn through it quicker than you can imagine. If you do have access to large ammunition stores great, if you don't, forget it. Considering the rarity of these weapons in Britain you will have difficulty finding enough ammunition to last more than a single fire-fight, if you do find one, keep it for the darkest of days. If you find any military supplies then you might get access to the SA80, with the latest revisions its now a decent rifle, but use its accuracy, not rate of fire.

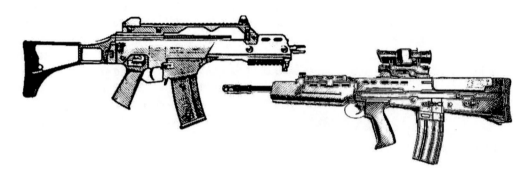

In Britain you would likely see the SA80, the standard rifle of the British forces, it has gained a horrific reputation for reliability over the years. Fortunately, since Heckler and Kock made a host of improvements to the weapon it has become widely regarded as an excellent peace of kit; just tainted by its reputation. The SA80 is an incredibly accurate rifle, one of the finest of its kind in the world and its bullpup layout makes it excellent for use in vehicles and confined spaces. The only weakness of this rifle is its close quarter abilities, being bullpup it is poor for use with a bayonet and clubbing zombies in the head with the stock. In Britain, the only place you can find an assault rifle is through military or police armouries, however, there are some rifle owners who own something similar, typically with a single shot bolt action design due to the countries laws. In America you are far more likely to find weapons such as this, and whilst they will often be only semi-automatic, that is all you want.

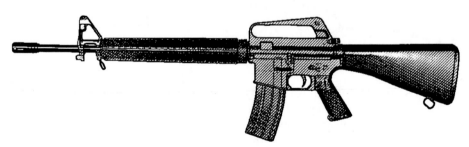

In America you are likely to find some variant of the M16 rifle, for all intensive purposes it is the same as the SA80, same calibre, ammo capacity and comparable accuracy, the only difference being the more traditional layout, as opposed to the bullpup SA80. The SA80 also has SUSAT optics as standard (typically). The SA80 can be used on semi and full automatic, whereas the standard issue US army M16 have semi and three shot burst. All of that is pretty irrelevant to our purposes, never use burst or full automatic. These weapons should be used as close range sniper rifles, carefully aimed single headshots; anything else will be wasteful and have you out of ammo quickly. It is possible that you could get your hands on military assault rifles, but this will very much depend on the speed of the outbreak and availability. If the outbreak takes a few days then it is likely that the army will have time to deploy and you may get access to their equipment, if it is rapid, the weapons will be locked away from easy access.

ANTI-MATERIEL RIFLES (AM)

These super power sniper rifles are in fairly common usage by military units around the world, most commonly characterised by the Barrett M82, also called the 'Light-fifty'. These monster killer rifles will rip anything apart at quite incredible ranges, but is that really necessary? You will never need the power and range that this rifle is capable of to fight zombies, with its weight and size being a massive fuss to lug around. It could only be potentially useful against monstrous mutations, which isn't that likely.

RECOMMENDED GUN

The Shotgun is extremely common throughout the developed world, as well as ammunition for it. Reliability is typically excellent with very little maintenance needed. The beauty of shotguns is there ease of use, they may not be the best gun, but with all things considered, most people will do much better with them than any other projectile weapon.

MACHINE GUNS

High power, high rate of fire. Machine guns are heavy and unwieldy things, best kept mounted to vehicles and defensive positions of your base for rainy days. Ammo will run out almost immediately if you attempt to use them regularly. The only place you will find such weapons in the UK is in military stores, where they use the M249 (as seen by the man on theft side of the image above), a 5.56 chambered, belt or magazine fed support gun, the smallest of these weapons. You may also be able to find M240's, a larger calibered and much longer weapon, as well as .50 Calibre Browning Heavy machine guns, for use on vehicles and fixed positions only, these all sound very nice indeed, but good luck finding one. The machine gun is the ultimate carnage machine, continuous sustained fire with large ammo capacity. Sadly, even if you do find one, your ammo will run out quicker than your wages on pay day. If you are lucky enough to get your hands on one of these babies, mount it as base defence as a last resort tool, as it won't last long.

ROCKET/GRENADE LAUNCHERS

As with machine guns, these are a military store find only, very rare, as is ammo. Fortunately zombies don't drive armoured vehicles, so don't waste your time, a Molotov cocktail will be just as useful and eminently more findable and replaceable. If however you do stumble across one, don't leave it behind, keep it in your vehicle for those times when you need to really get things done quickly.

.22 RIMFIRE WEAPONS

This calibre is kept as a separate section to all other guns as it is incredibly common compared to other ammunitions and should be considered in its own right for that reason due to its characteristics. .22 rimfire is a very small calibre round with a very low velocity and effective range. It is very cheap to buy and has little recoil, making it extremely popular for target shooting, as well as hunting of smaller animals such as rats and squirrels and occasionally slightly larger game. This round is very commonly found in bolt action and semi-automatic rifles (depending where you live), it is small and light, making ammunition easy to carry. The big downside to this cartridge is that it has no stopping power at all, and due to the low velocity is more prone to ricochets than larger calibres, when hitting hard targets, such as the skull. This lack of stopping power, short effective range and tendency to ricochets mean that .22 rimfire weapons should only be used from secure positions or as a last resort on the ground.

PELLET GUNS

In terms of BB guns, forget it, but pellet guns can be very powerful. High power pellet guns are used by some for hunting. An accurate shot to the head could be enough from the best of these weapons to do the job; you will have to experiment to see if this works. Some people modify these beyond legal limits to be classed as firearms; they may be good for a headshot. Ammunition is easily carried and replaced, but stopping power of even the best is inadequate, keep them for target practice if in doubt.

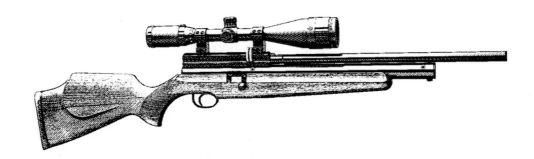

HOME MADE FLAME THROWER

You're not going to find an actual production model flame thrower, at least not in Britain, but you can however make your own very simply. This is the super soaker flame thrower, made from just a few cheap and readily available materials. Get a super soaker water gun, fit a zippo type lighter on to the front with some kind of clip (or gaffer tape). Fill the gun with petrol or another flammable substance, light the zippo, pump the gun to build the pressure, you're ready to go!

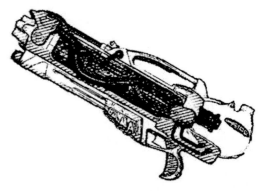

As you can see, this flame thrower can be made with just a common kid's toy and an easy to find lighter. It is easily replaceable and easily refuelled. When using flame throwers a few things must be remembered. Initially, friendly fire can be a big problem, be very careful you don't roast your own friends and allies. Next, a zombie might keep coming at

you until the flames eventually destroy the brain or incapacitate their limbs, so be ready to run or shoot from cover. The flame thrower is a very available and realistic weapon to use in the fight against zombies, especially in Britain where guns are rare. With its weaknesses in mind, the flame thrower is fantastic against shamblers but suffers badly against runners, unless you fight from a secure position.

NAIL GUN

These are easily available in DIY stores and therefore both simple to acquire as well as supply ammunition for. Nail guns can potentially be used as a close range gun, similar to a handgun, but easy to re-supply. Pneumatic nail guns (which most are), typically run off an internal magazine, making ammo capacity reasonable and reload times quick. Just like using a regular gun the nail gun can kill a zombie by destroying the brain. You may

have to fire several shots to take them down, but it's better than not having a gun at all. Most nail guns are powered by mains electricity; these can be run from vehicles if necessary (with an inverter) and can be good for that purpose. The other option is to use a wireless nail gun which will come with its own battery pack. You do of course need to have a means of recharging it, but that is not a major problem short to mid-term.

The one hurdle of using a nail gun in the UK is that they legally have to have a safety feature which means they will not fire unless the nose of the gun is compressed in. This is to stop the nail gun being used in a projectile fashion as well as avoiding major accidental injuries. Sadly, this rather sensible safety feature makes the nail gun useless as a weapon. The safety feature can be bypassed if you have access to tooling, but that is best left to those in the know. Be warned, converting a nail gun in to a projectile weapon in the UK is highly illegal, so do not attempt to manufacture this in preparation for the Zompoc. Despite the nail guns weakness of this safety feature, they are of course a fantastic tool for DIY work, they will come in handy, if you have a wireless model or means of powering.

BOW

The great thing about the bow is its simplicity, it is also available legally and easily in the UK, so there are a fair number around. A bow is fairly simple to learn to use, sadly it is very difficult to be good enough to consistently hit a target as small as a head, especially when that target will frequently be moving. Ammunition is fortunately far less of a problem than a gun, but with the skill requirements and lack of stopping power, they are best reserved for those already experienced with them and for culling operations from a safe position.

IMPROVEMENTS FOR GUNS

In fight for survival, your equipment needs to be the best it can possibly be with the tools and options available, this is about optimisation. A key to remember here is that gaffer tape is your best friend, its the solution to many problems.

TORCHES

By choice you never want to be fighting in the dark, but choice is not always a luxury you will have. Sometimes you will be forced to travel outdoors in the dark and even when indoors, you may not always have much, if any light at all. A gun mounted torch is the best option, as you want your gun to hand at all times and need to be able to see where you are going as well as shooting. In the world of 'tactical' equipment, many a complex device has been created to solve this problem, but you are unlikely to have access to them, your solution is a hand torch and gaffer tape. Be sure not to block the sights of the gun or space needed for pump actions or slides to move

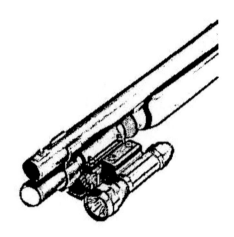

QUICKLY ACCESSIBLE AMMO

Many people have been killed throughout history because they could not reload their gun in time, do not be caught out! Whatever ammo you do have make sure it is accessible, this may be as simple as having webbing or jacket with pockets such as a fishing vest, but the gun itself can carry additional ammo.

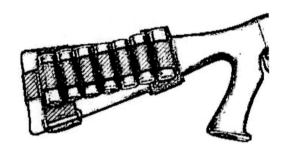

SLINGS

These are not to look dashing, it is about practicality. A sling on any longer weapon will allow you to take one or both hands off the weapon at any time to use for other things such as opening doors, changing ammunition, or drawing a secondary weapon. Slings also allow you to do things like climb ladders and jump over walls easily without losing your weapon. Ideally you want high a grade police or military sling such as a three point sling, available at airsoft and army surplus shops. If that is not available make your own from study belts and gaffer tape.

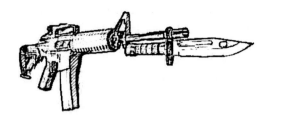

BAYONETS

For hundreds of years soldiers have been using bayonets, so they are useful then? Sort of, but they suffer the same problems as a spear. No blunt trauma to strike with, only a thrusting strike which would have to be well placed and accurate. Fit a bayonet if you like, but you'd be better off making sure your rifle was sturdy enough to smash them in the head with.

SILENCERS

This is probably one of the best accessories you could get as it will not alert zombies from afar to your presence when you have to fire your weapon. Sadly, they are incredibly rare in the UK. Unless you know a well equipped hitman, don't expect to find one.

LASER SIGHTS

Lasers are simple pointer devices which allow target acquisition quickly without the necessity of using sights. Whilst they are a matter of personal preference; never become wholly reliant on them. To be remotely useful, the laser must be fitted with perfect alignment to the barrel of the gun, so no bodging with gaffer tape! You will generally find a torch is far more useful to you.

RECOMMENDED UK PROJECTILE WEAPON

Guns are sadly quite rare in Britain, and those that have them will guard them well, the crossbow is the next best thing that you can acquire easily. Whilst the crossbow is not any good in a stand up fight against serious numbers, it will keep you out of infection distance when fighting small numbers or from a secure position, it is by far the best readily available projectile weapon in the UK.

CROSSBOW

The crossbow is the poor man's sniper rifle, easy and legally obtainable without a licence,

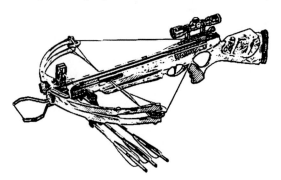

but sadly quite rare. The crossbow is much easier to use well for accurate shooting than a bow, as well as power being typically higher. The trade off is that crossbows are much slower to reload than a bow and have a more complex construction, sometimes needing more maintenance. The crossbow is best used in the same fashion as a sniper rifle, from a safe and secure position for some relaxed plinking.

Despite the drawbacks the crossbow is findable and is easier to use, easy to supply ammo for and will likely keep working. As long as you know where to find one, great, get one. There are many types of crossbow from traditional medieval models to modern composite versions with rifle style stocks. Despite the visual differences, little has changed on crossbows over the last few hundred years other than the composite pulley systems allowing for quicker and easier reloads.

Ammunition for crossbows are called bolts, as opposed to arrows for a bow. The only difference being that crossbow bolts are often shorter than arrows, meaning they can be carried more easily and in greater numbers. Modern high power crossbows with rifle stocks and telescopic sights can be used the same as a sniper rifle, up to a certain range, but do not rule out the use of smaller pistol crossbows. Pistol crossbows are cheaper and easier to carry, still putting out plenty of power for a killing shot as well as quicker reload times for some of the rather excellent reload cocking handles. Pistol crossbows are also excellent for use in a vehicle from loopholes or other firing positions.

The only consumables typically required for crossbows are bolts (ammunition) and strings. Occasionally strings wear out or break, so keep a few handy. Crossbow bolts should be kept in large numbers if you have a crossbow, but making your own is quite easy. Ammunition can be improvised simple from wood or metal dowel from your local DIY centre. It will not have the accuracy of professionally made ammo, but perfect for close range work. Crossbow bolts can also be used for target practice against a boss (shooting target), and re-used over and over, as opposed to guns, which cannot easily re-use ammo.

The last important note about crossbows is that use them according to your enemy and situation. They are no good against hordes unless you have cover to fight from, nor running zombies in a similar situation.

Whilst guns are rare and difficult to obtain, as well as find ammo for, crossbows are not constrained by any purchase laws other than the necessity to be over 18 to buy one. With a quick search online you will find hand crossbows of good quality and around 80lb draw weight for under £40, buy it!

HAND-TO-HAND COMBAT WEAPONS

When guns aren't available or ammo is nowhere to be found, you can always rely on your own two hands to do the work. The key weakness of hand to hand combat weapons when fighting the undead is initially that close contact with them increases the risk of injury and prolonged contact will fatigue you quickly. Only engage in close quarter combat if you have the best gear possible or have no other choice. When looking at hand to hand weapons you have two choices, some form of edged weapon that can decapitate the creature or some kind of blunt trauma implement that can destroy the brain. These two ideas can be combined, such as a long hafted axe. So, which is the best option? The issue with many edged weapons, such as swords, is that you have to be skilled at decapitation and able to continually do it well. A blunt trauma instrument is a simpler bet, it will also be easier to maintain.

THE KNIFE

A knife is a standard survival tool, no doubt you will want to keep one on you at all times for the day to day necessities. However, do not consider it a key weapon in your fight against the undead. Few knives can easily deliver a clean simple decapitation or deliver the blunt trauma to destroy the brain. Keep your knife handy for utilities, not fighting.

MACHETE

A big step up in the zombie fight from your utility knife, it delivers a much heavier cutting blow as well as heavy hitting power. Despite this, the machete should be considered a backup weapon; it isn't meaty enough for stand up fighting. Despite this, machetes are fairly easy to find in most countries, or something similar, such as the kukri, when combined with a shield it can be a good useable combination.

FIRE AXE

For those who want to go old school the fire axe is readily available in hardware stores, in fire fighting kits in buildings and a host of other places. The fire axe is a good length, best wielded in two hands. It is fast, powerful, capable of strong cutting strikes as well as heavy blunt trauma strikes with the back of the head. Any decent fire axe will be robust and its use comes naturally to all those with enough aggression. The fire axe is also a great all purpose tool, helpful for breaking into supply stores and making doorways wherever you need them. There are other types of axes such as camping axes, tomahawks and various other single handed axes, but none match the fire axe for sheer power and versatility.

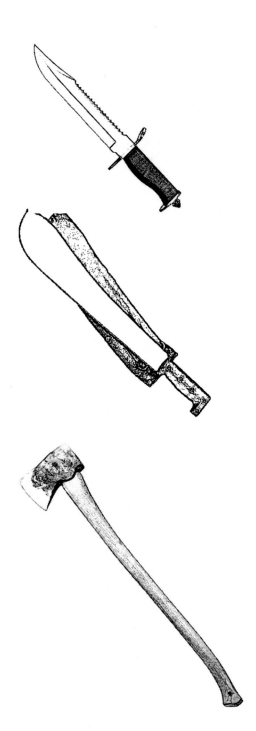

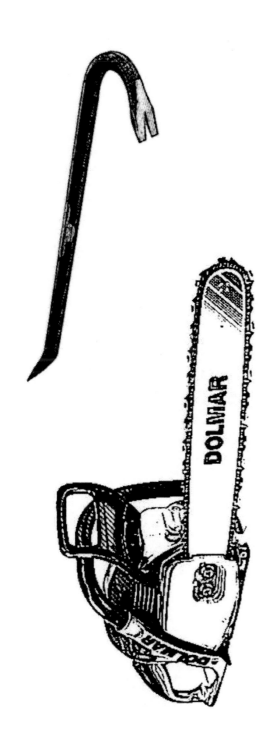

CROWBAR/TYRE IRON

You have played Half Life haven't you? Of course you have, this is an excellent starter weapon. The crowbar has good hitting power for caving in the skull or piercing it. Sadly, crowbars aren't always to hand, but what is readily available and does a similar job is a tyre iron. Almost every car in the country has one, not a great weapon but quick to hand and better than your own hands. Wheel wrenches are normally found under the spare wheel in most cars in the boot/trunk.

CHAINSAW

A chainsaw is a portable mechanical, motorized saw and is used in logging activities such as felling, limbing, and bucking, by tree surgeons to fell trees and remove branches and foliage, to fell snags and assist in cutting firebreaks in wildland fire suppression, and to harvest firewood.

If you follow the movies then the chainsaw is the ultimate weapon when up close and personal. Sadly the chainsaw is big, heavy, unwieldy and noisy, all things to be avoided when establishing your load out. The chainsaw may look fantastic, but the fire axe is better in all other ways. The chainsaw will not only draw every unfriendly flesh eating monster to you within a matter of minutes, it is also big, heavy and difficult to use in hand to hand. It is certainly useable and if you have one to hand, use it if you have to, but don't go looking for one.

Those that have seen Zack Snyder's Dawn of the Dead remake will understand how the chainsaw can pose a serious threat to those around you, especially when used from a vehicle. It really is best avoided, even a simple club is preferable to it.

SHOVEL

When the violence kicks off and you need something quick, shovels are in most people's garages or sheds. They are tough and hit with enough force to take out the brain. The thin edge can also be used for decapitation; the shovel is the poor man's fire axe. Be sure that the shaft is in good condition, strong and not rotten. This is a great general purpose tool to have anyway. Be sure to keep one around, such as on your vehicle. These tools are actually pretty heavy and if you have any problem swinging it around you are probably better off with a lighter weapon that you can actually use.

SWORD

When it comes to hand to hand, nothing looks as sexy as a sword, but fashion isn't everything. Good quality sharp swords are a rarity, they need a lot of skill to wield effectively and require maintenance. If you do have a nice sharp sword and have the skills to use it, do so, you'll be the envy of all other zombie fighters. If however you run into combat with a cheaply made, typically rat tail tanged, stainless steel monstrosity, you will likely meet a sticky and rather embarrassing end. If however you have access to decent quality swords, here is an overview of what is available and how useful they are:

SINGLE HANDED

This is a broad category of anything intended for single handed use that is capable of good cutting and thrusting, arming swords, Chinese broadswords, sabres, basket hilt broadswords and backswords, scimitars, tulwars etc. These weapons can be carried with relative ease on the body and are quick to handle, are capable of decapitations as well as limited brain destruction through medium blunt trauma deliverance. A decent quality single handed sword can be very useful. Do not however use certain specialist one handed swords such as the rapier, it's very stylish but simply doesn't cut it against the undead. Any relatively short single handed sword with good cutting ability can be remarkably useful.

TWO HANDED

This category covers anything from longswords and katanas, up to renaissance zweihanders. All of these swords have great cutting ability, many can also be half-sworded when things get too close for comfort.

Popular culture would have you believe that the Katana, or 'Samurai Sword' is the ultimate sword, that it can cut through all other swords, metal armour and concrete, and be faster than any other sword known to man. Without a doubt the Katana is a fine sword and excellent at what it does, but try and stay objective. In reality, its hard edges will take a lot of damage against zombie skulls and its short reach may have you closer to them than you want to be. No doubt it's an effective tool for decapitations but will need skill to wield, but the then same could be said for most swords.

POLE WEAPON

There are all sorts of pole weapons about. The most obvious is a plain shaft, known as a quarterstaff. Historically, Eastern Martial Arts bo staffs will do the job as will any study hardwood pole, or even a metal weightlifting barbell. The spear is a simple development that can be built very quickly with a small knife, a long pole and some gaffer tape.

Generally simple pole weapons such as this are excellent against humans, but sadly inefficient against the undead. The blunt force trauma of a blow from a pole weapon will have to be well placed with good power to destroy the brain. At the same time thrusts are very dangerous with a spear because unless they strike the brain the zombie will keep coming at you! This problem can be resolved by modifying your spear in to a boar spear, with additional hooks to stop the beast in its tracks. The boar spear is excellent at keeping a zombie away and perhaps could be useful when working as a group to subdue a zombie whilst your friend finishes the job.

HEAVY BLADED POLE WEAPON

Pole weapons such as pole axes, halberds, naginatas are powerful pole weapons and a big step up from a staff or spear, however, they require space to wield them. Against shamblers they can be useful, against runners, think again. These weapons can be especially useful when used from secure fortifications or vehicles. The advantage of heavy bladed pole weapons is that the ferocity of their cuts can dismember or decapitate with relative ease. Always be sure to carry a smaller backup weapon however, for when the zombie passes the point, you are in trouble.

HAMMER/MACE

Heavy iron, now we are talking. A heavy, ideally spiked object on the end of a short strong shaft is a simple, reliable and easy to wield tool. If you have a mace to hand, great, if you can weld, make one, otherwise, get a hammer, such as a club hammer. These

FLAIL WEAPONS

A flail weapon can be anything from a motorcycle chain to a full reproduction medieval implement. You can also build your own. Flails are fantastically effective against

weapons are great in confined spaces and can destroy the brain in one simple, smooth stroke. These weapons are super reliable, require no maintenance, are easy to carry, great in confined spaces, a great all rounder. Just be sure to wear a high level of protection if you are fighting with a mace due to the close nature of the combat.

As far as how to use a mace it is very simple. You swing the mace and let the mass of the head keep the weapon moving. Simply use it as a heavy and very mean club. It may not be subtle and it will require you to get close to zombies. You will find it to be a simple and highly effective weapon though.

humans because they cause a lot of surface damage that can put your opponent on the floor. Flails which feature heavier ball ends can also cause similar damage as a mace, but what against the undead? Any type of flail can be an unwieldy weapon. A large part of why they work so well is that the threat of them is enough to keep your opponent at a distance whilst you continue to strike them. This is not the case against a zombie. Against the undead you may only get one good strike in before they close the distance and then your weapon is useless. Flails are also a major hazard to any other survivors that you fight alongside, they are best avoided. One potentially good usage of a flail would be for vehicle usage from a high position with a purpose made or converted long chain flail that would allow you to strike from safety.

VEHICLE SPECIFIC HAND HELD WEAPONS

There is plenty of crossover between weapons you use out on the street and from defences to those used from vehicles, but there are a few tools that are specifically suitable for vehicular usage. The main things to remember when using weapons from vehicles is that you will need extra reach. Quite often you will be fighting from a raised platform and this will require several extra feet in the end of whichever weapon you are using. As you lengthen a weapon you will find it will become heavier and also harder to move. Swinging a ten foot pole is very hard whereas swinging a two foot pole is a lot easier. It is therefore important to select the correct weapon and to also keep short-range weapons as backups incase the enemy get a little too close or you lose your main weapon. Historically weapons such as lances, spears, long bladed swords and large aces were used from horseback.

RAMMER

These may go by different name in different areas, but they are readily available in DIY stores, intended for compacting ground and tarmac. A rammer is a heavy square metal block attached to a long shaft of wood or metal. The rammer is excellent for use from high sided vehicles; you can strike the tops of the head of zombies surrounding your vehicle from safety. A well placed strike from a rammer will easily destroy the brain; you may however consider lengthening the shaft, depending on the height of your vehicle. Due to the extra mass at the end of the rammer you will find it swings through the air very well

and can thus be used as a striking weapon also. Handy in an emergency just be very careful that you don't swing the weapon into your nearest friend! As with most weapons it is a very good idea to practice beforehand. On the job training with zombies only gives you the chance to make a single mistake!

DEMOLITION CROWBAR

Typically around five feet long, all metal with a pointed spear tip, excellent for using through convenient weapon slots in vehicles. These are incredibly tough and easily found in DIY stores. Use these to stab into the face the torso (if infected zombies). You can also use the edge

of the bar to strike against the neck and head if you have enough space to swing the weapon. These weapons are a good bit heavier than their wooden counterparts but if you are using this in a vehicle you have somewhere to lean it.

THROWN WEAPONS

Fighting from afar is always preferable to getting your hands dirty. Though they should not to be used as a core weapons they are a great way of cleaning up with as little fuss as possible. These weapons are especially useful for fighting from a fixed defensive position or when on a mobile weapons platform. Traditionally thrown weapon were often carried along with close quarter weapons so that they could be hurled into battle and then followed up with blades and spears.

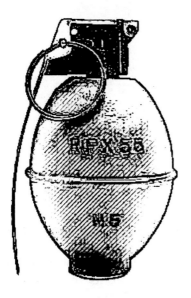

GRENADES

The most difficult to obtain of all thrown weapons, only available through military stores, chances are, you won't find any, so forget about it. If however you do find one, they are nice and simple to use. Pull the pin out, the bit that looks like a keyring, and throw. The grenade will not begin its timed ignition until you release the bar on the side, hence you can pull the pin and then wait 20 seconds until you throw it if you like. Pipe bombs are a make at home version of these, but they are not efficient against zombies. Shrapnel will rarely hit the right spot to kill them.

Grenades and pipe bombs are wickedly effective against humans, but when zombies feel no pain and have only a small number of target zones that will stop them in their tracks, their usefulness diminishes. If you want something that does a better job with less hassle all round, go for a Molotov.

THROWING KNIVES/AXES

There are a surprising number of these weapons around, and many not originally designed for it can be used as such anyway. The biggest problem of these weapons is that you have to be very skilled to get head shots with them and will likely run out of ammunition very quickly, just don't bother.

JAVELIN

The javelin dates back to ancient times and was considered to be a powerful and deadly weapon in the right hands. These weapons were used en mass as well as used by individual heroes in one-on-one combat. Because of its sport usage you will find at least some of these about, they are also easier to make yourself. Javelins have all the problems that throwing knives and axes have, as well as being even more unwieldy to carry in any sort of numbers. If you want something that does this job, get a crossbow. These weapons take lots of training and practice to get right. If you happen to be an Olympic javelin thrower then great, get lots!

MOLOTOV COCKTAIL

Named after Vyacheslav Mikhailovich Molotov, a Soviet politician who was the People's Commissar for Foreign Affairs, or the Foreign Minister, of the Soviet Union to Finland. The Finns named the cocktail after Molotov in the winter war of 1939-1940, but the idea had been borrowed from the Spanish Nationalists during their Civil War. The very existence of the Molotov came from the need for a quickly made and effective incendiary device, when military grade options were not available, perfect then for when you as a civilian need a quick and simple to produce weapon using only readily available materials. The creation and use of the Molotov under currents laws is

highly illegal, so do not manufacture them in advance and risk being in a cell when the apocalypse begins.

The Molotov is easy to find the materials, quick and easy to make, this is the fighter's friend, sit back safe and sound and watch them burn! A Molotov cocktail consists of a glass bottle partly filled with flammable liquid, typically petrol. When petrol is used as the main ingredient, motor oil or sugar is commonly added to help the gasoline cling to the target. A petrol soaked rag is placed in the neck of the bottle, extending out of the neck. The bottle must then be corked in order to ensure that the rag stays in place when thrown. When you are ready to use the Molotov, light the end of the gasoline rag and throw it at your target, the bottle will smash at whatever you throw it at, spreading its contents over the target and surrounding area. The lit rag will cause the petrol to ignite.

ADDITIONAL WEAPONS

Some weapons are just an obvious choice such as a shotgun or an axe, but there are a huge variety of possibilities, including many items which weren't intended or built as a weapon but can be used as such. All potential weapons should at least be considered. Establishing what works quickly and safely can make all the difference, be open to ideas, but also quick to develop good solutions.

ACID

From a fighters perspective acid is dangerous to use. It requires time to work, close proximity to apply and is dangerous to the user. Acid can be used to purify areas of dead zombies, but it is still an overcomplicated step when fire is generally just as good and much

easier to acquire and use. If for some reason you have access to large amounts of acid it can make an excellent barrier to zombies in terms of shallow moats. Acid is guaranteed to kill al know forms of zombie.

FIRE

The use of fire has already been considered with the flame thrower and Molotov Cocktail, but those are projectile and thrown weapons in their own right. Fire itself will completely destroy a zombie and completely remove the body, making for a clean and effective kill. Despite this, fire brings with it many inherent risks. Zombies do not feel pain nor fear anything, and cannot therefore be deterred by either of those elements which would normally

be used against humans. Fire therefore can be very dangerous to the user, as much as it is to the zombie. A zombie will keep coming at you until the fire eventually removes their capacity to walk, crawl and move, which could take

quite some time. Fire also has other risks, such as friendly fire and the potential damage to useful buildings, supplies and vehicles.

When using fire as a weapon, consider the situation carefully ideally use it from a fortified position, but even then be aware of its risks. If you use fire in any form from a static vehicle or weapons platform, the zombies will still come out you and the flames can cause damage to the vehicle or building that you are in. Fire can be created by throwing petrol/gasoline over zombies (though its a bit close for comfort) and lighting them up. It can be used in traps or to burn down occupied buildings.

POISON

This is an ancient way of killing people or for taking your own life. It exists in many forms but sadly poison is intended to shut down the body's functions, something that will have little to no effect on the undead. You also need specific poisoned for specific targets. Keeping poison around is typically more of a risk to your fellow survivors than it is to the enemy, leave it alone.

TRAPS

Mankind has been using traps for thousands of years, both for food and for pest control, as well as the killing of dangerous animals. Traps can come in many forms depending on their purpose; you must establish which are best suited to your needs. Traps can be used to ensnare intruders, they can also be used in person to catch and kill creatures. Using traps as a defensive system, rather than relying on solid defence measures such as walls and guards is not a safe or good option.

Using traps offensively however can work, though might be considered overly complicated. Common traps include the pit trap, where you disguise a pit and have zombies run or walk over the ground that collapses under them. These pits typically feature spikes at the bottom, this may keep the zombies there for a while but is not a final solution. Other traps such as cages or rooms can be used with bait. For the most part traps are overly complicated and involve too many variables. Be aware that most traps will not kill a zombie and not necessarily stop them in their tracks, do not rely on them to save your life.

A barbed-spike plate is a basic non explosive booby traps. The plate, a flat piece of wood or metal, is used as a base to fasten any number of barbed spikes. The spikes, ranging in length from several inches to several feet, are fastened securely to the base. When a man steps or falls on the spiked plate, or is struck by one, the spikes will penetrate, producing a serious wound.

A spike trap box is a simple wooden box made of boards joined together with four corner posts. The box has a lightweight-top but the bottom is removed. Barbed spikes are placed in the ground at the bottom pointing upward. This trap is usually set up on dirt roads and trails to take advantage of favorable camouflage and frequently used paths.

A trap pit is a large trap box with a bamboo top. Stakes are made of sharpened wood or bamboo or barbed spikes and used to line the box. When a zombie steps on the trap he will fall into the pit. The top turns on an axle; therefore, the trap does not need to be reset to work again. The pit is often prepared as a defensive obstacle and then made safe by locking it in place with a crossbeam until the desired time of use. Note that the pit is over 2 metres deep.

One last thing on traps is that even if do not stop a living zombie such as an infected creature it will cause substantial damage that will slow down and potentially kill them hour or days later. By setting up traps on main access route you can weaken and slow down zombies and give yourselves a much better chance of fighting those that either gets through or those that are already weakened through injury.

ANTI PERSONNEL MINES
Mines and explosive booby traps employed by the enemy against friendly personnel are limited in type and quantity only by the availability of explosive materials and the imagination of the enemy. Anything that can be made to explode and cause injury can be rigged as an antipersonnel mine or booby traps. Antipersonnel mines and explosive booby traps are very successfully against enemies that are not familiar with the devices. Against enemies such as zombies they will prove devastating.

MUD BALL MINE
The mud ball mine consists of a hand grenade encased in sun-baked mud or clay. The safety pin (pull ring) is removed and mud is molded around the grenade. After the mud dries it

holds the lever of the grenade in the safe position. The mud ball is placed on trails or anywhere troops may walk. Stepping on the ball breaks the dried mud apart and releases the lever detonating the grenade. Any lever-type grenades may be used.

TIN CAN MINE

A tin can mine is constructed from sheet metal or any discarded metal container (beer, or soft drink can). The firing device for the explosive is an improvised fuse with zero delay action. A hand grenade fuse may be used by removal of the delay element. The mine functions by a tripwire attached to the pull ring. Pressure on the tripwire pulls the pull ring, activating the mine in the same manner as a hand grenade.

BOUNDING MINE

The bounding mine is improvised from expended trip flare cases. A wooden cylinder slightly smaller in diameter than the mine case is hollowed out so that a standard grenade can fit inside. The wooden cylinder (with enclosed grenade) is then fitted into the mine case and the grenade's safety pin is extracted. When the mine is detonated, the cylinder and grenade are propelled upward. As the wooden cylinder and grenade separate, the handle flies off the grenade, activating the fuse.

This mine is fabricated of cartridge cases or pieces of pipe of various sizes. It is loaded with a charge of black powder, a primer, and a variety of fragments for missile effect. When the victim steps on the mine, the igniter detonates the black powder charge and propels the fragments upward.

ELECTROCUTION

Electrifying a human body with enough power can reduce it to a burnt crisp; the effect on a zombie will be the same as that on a human. In theory currents approaching 100 mA are lethal if they pass through sensitive portions of the body. In terms of low voltage devices such as stun guns and tasers, don't bother, they will not do enough damage. The problem with electrification is it involves harnessing huge amounts of electricity, which is neither easy nor very safe.

Death to an infected zombies can occur from any shock that carries enough amperage. Small amperages (40 mA - 700 mA) usually trigger fibrillation in the heart which is reversible via

defibrillator, but large amperages (> 1 A) cause permanent damage via burns, and cellular damage. The heart is most devastated by foreign electricity, next is the brain. Women are more susceptible to macroshock electrocution than men, but men are equally susceptible to Microshock electrocution. As to the effect electrocution would have on the undead it is uncertain as much more power if required to cause sufficient failure to the body or to damage the brain.

If you are thinking of doing this you could really do with a few test subjects. Make sure they are expendable!

CHAPTER 12: PERSONAL EQUIPMENT

If you can accept losing, you can't win.
Vince Lombardi

When you initially have to defend yourself the first thing that will occur to you is to get a weapon to strike with. The next thing will be to find protection to reduce the risk of injury. You will then look to additional items such as load bearing and useful items. Personal protection is far more important in zombie warfare than when facing human beings, for zombies cannot just hurt you, but also turn you. Physical contact with the undead should be avoided at all costs, but when the time comes, or the situation requires it, you must be prepared. Fortunately human beings have spent thousands of years developing ways to protect the human body, there is a wealth of kit out there waiting to be used.

To understand what kit is best you must first understand what it is you are protecting against, then you can decide what best fits those needs. You approach to survival and job within a community will also affect the kit you should attain.

IMMEDIATE IMPROVEMENTS

You can go searching for better gear later, first look at what you have in your own home, work or car. The initial task is to cover bare skin, scantily clad busty women may look good in the movies, but function must come before fashion. The most basic concern initially is just from abrasions and cuts to bare flesh which can lead to injection, including from blood. After this, zombie bites are your main worry. Find the strongest materials you have in your own home and put them on, leather is one of the best materials available in the battle against bites. Most people have some kind of leather coat of jacket, many also have leather gloves, put all this on. Put on sturdy boots, the higher the ankle the better, it's all extra protection. Hiking boots, army boots or Goth boots can all do this.

WEATHER CONSIDERATIONS

The Zompoc is a scary possibility but you must also consider the elements, for they can equally be dangerous to you in your new life. The advice on equipment assumes a relatively mild climate, as is seen in Britain, you must however give more thought to your surroundings. Consider the possibilities if you were in a desert, a freezing climate etc. Even if you do not live in these climates it is not impossible that you will be in one of them when the Zompoc starts or end up in one through no choice of your own.

Weather conditions are not something that work in your favour as the undead no longer need their bodily functions. Heat and cold will no longer affect them, at least only extreme example would. In a very hot climate you will have to give major consideration to your protective gear, as it will have far more effect on your stamina. Colder climates mean you will be able, and in fact want to wear more gear which is great for protection. Normal survival will be much harder.

PROTECTION FROM OTHER HUMANS

Just because you have to fend zombies off on a daily basis it doesn't mean that humans are no longer a threat. They have successfully killed each other on a regular basis for their entire history. Having a common enemy, the undead, should result in the least amount of hostility between surviving humans, but this isn't always the case. Below is a list of risks from humans that should be considered:

SUPPLY OWNERSHIP

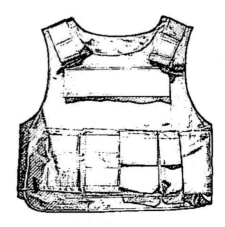

From the minute the zombie attacks begin everything becomes a finders keepers situation. No laws, no ownership (initially), every man for himself. Do not fight your fellow humans for supplies, share where possible and avoid violence at all costs. There are too few of you as it is and no risk of your life is worth taking unless absolutely necessary. In the beginning supplies will be plentiful, so take what you can without stepping on toes.

Later, when supply searches by organised groups become common place, hostilities between groups will become an ever growing problem. The risk here will come from how your opponents have equipped themselves with items from the weapons section. You may therefore have to defend yourself from guns, axes, swords, all manner of items. It is not realistic to equip yourself with protection against all types of attacks from both zombies and humans, so equip for zombies and try and avoid conflict with humans.

FRIENDLY FIRE

Even in the most professional of armies in the world friendly fire still exists. When civilians form militias and are fighting at their wits end against terrible foes, this will become worse. Protecting from friendly fire is initially about special awareness and peripheral vision, stay out of the reach of your friends axe swing! Relatively untrained people using guns will also panic quickly are fire quite randomly, group

training can begin to address this. Thrown weapons should be used with particular care to where your allies and equipment are. Do not bother with bullet proof vests for this purpose, it is too much additional weight and

its usefulness is outweighed by its negative points.

THEFT

In desperate situations humans will scavenge anything they can, including your supplies. Such deliberate attacks could come in the form of an all out assault with guns, right down to a night raid with knives, or even no contact at all. Theft of vehicles and the supplies they hold when in the field is also a concern. The simple answer to this is guard duties at all times on facilities and vehicles. Show strength to those that see you with items and ensure you are able to back it up if the time comes, ideally show enough strength so that potential thieves will move on.

TERRITORIAL CONTROL

When a group of people establishes control of a building, a street, a village, town or even region, they often will not want to share, they may also try and oust anyone currently on what they consider their territory as well as attempt to expand into yours. This is best avoided by having a larger and stronger group than those around you, attempt to ally where possible. Try to avoid territorial wars with humans at all costs, but if they happen fight for your lives, and win.

USEFUL ITEMS FOR CONSIDERATION

There is a huge array of potential gear you have accessible in the world around you. What you have to figure out is which is best and how you can get it. Just because one item offers excellent protection in the current pre-Zompoc world, it does not mean it will be well suited to the Zompoc itself.

MOTORCYCLE ARMOUR

This is by far one of the best all round options in terms of availability, protection offered, weight and manoeuvrability. There are many motorcyclists on the road today, they almost all own good quality bikers jackets due to this demand, supply is also high and readily available. All towns and cities will feature shops in which you can buy bikers jackets, but also make note of where the out of town shops are that will be better and safer for access. Ideally, keep a bikers jacket at home. There are also many 'biker inspired' jackets available in more common high street stores, do not dismiss them outright, but use common sense. Many biker lookalike jackets have nothing in common with the biker jacket other than style,

fashion, means that you may well have access to some or know someone that does. Mail is a made up of continuous metal rings woven and interlocked together. Some modern versions are made of aluminium, lightening items massively, whilst still offering generally good protection against bites. Mail (unless aluminium) is typically a lot heavier than you would think, many are also poor grade quality that could easily be bitten or torn apart in a fight.

this is especially true of women's fashion. Biker jackets should be robust, difficult to bite through and without obvious gaps.

Motorcycle equipment is actually a good overall kit for many parts of the body. Gloves, trousers (pants) and boots all provide excellent protection. What you have to consider here is that comfort, manoeuvrability and stamina are all important factors in the Zompoc, so choose which bits are comfortable and appropriate for your task. Always weigh off protection against movement and decide which is best for you.

MAILLE

Maille, also known as chainmail to the uninitiated is not what you would call common, but the number of re-enactors, as well as SCA and LARP followers around, as well as its growing popularity is goth/grunge

Mail has excellent coverage (depending on item) and flows with the body, making movement excellent, but it is too heavy for the protection it gives, only consider its use if you do not need to move around an awful lot, also look into the quality of construction, riveted being much tougher than butted for example.

PLATE ARMOUR

Ready to get some heavy iron? Hell yeah! Plate armour looks godly in the protection stakes, full body protection that cannot be penetrated or smashed, it even looks cool, you'll be a walking tank surely? The reality of plate armour in a zombie situation is that its overkill in many aspects and in that it is heavy, slow, cumbersome and will hit your speed and stamina greatly.

Coverage of plate armour varies greatly upon the period in which is was made or styled upon, as well as how costly it was, some may cover just vital areas, others the entire body, with mail to protect joints and gaps. Lesser armours that have many gaps will be a real concern. The quality of armour varies greatly from one manufacturer to another. Straps and fittings are of particular concern, as they will be taking the brunt of the attacks. A lot of re-enactors, SCA and LARP members own plate armour, you could of course also 'borrow' from a museum. Sadly plate armour is in reality too cumbersome for realistic usage, but at least some people do have it to hand.

RIOT ARMOUR

You might think that this is so specialist that it is unrealistic, but fear not. During a Zompoc situation riot armour would be broken out across the country, as well as many other people owning it for personal usages. Riot armour is typically built along the same lines as medieval plate armour, but with modern materials. Riot gear is incredibly tough and does not suffer from the weight problems of plate armour. Sadly, riot armour typically has many gaps as it is only intended to stop blunt trauma. Bikers' gear will generally serve you much better than riot equipment, though the gloves are good. Also consider making use of the police riot shields.

SECURITY PROTECTIVE GEAR

Various forms of protective gear exist for security uses, from doorman to police and bodyguards. You can get Kevlar stab resistant shirts and jackets and stab-proof vests. Anything vest based is useless to you due to coverage. Shirts and jackets could potentially

be useful, but whether they will stop a zombie jaw is a matter of pure speculation. A thick leather jacket is a far safer bet.

SPORTING SAFETY EQUIPMENT

Specialist equipment exists for hundreds of different sports. What is available to you will depend on where you live and what sports/martial arts you practice. The wealth of various sportive protections cannot be covered, so follow simple rules. Use protective gear that does not have gaps or selective protective areas. Only use sportive equipment that will stand a good chance of stopping the penetration of teeth. Make sure you can still move and fight effectively in it. Equipment for the modern sport of fencing, often called

Olympic Fencing could be very valuable, as all jackets and breeches are made to be puncture resistant and not leave gaps. Fencing equipment is available to cover most of the body, it could be excellent light armour or at least a base layer. Coaching equipment is preferred.

HOMEMADE ARMOUR

There are lots of possible 'off the shelf' options for protective gear as has already been discussed, but what of making your own? Gaffer tape is your friend, if you don't have any in the home, you aren't even prepared for normal life, let alone the Zompoc. Go and buy some! With a supply of gaffer tape and

everyday materials in your home you can make all kinds of protective gear. Historically many cultures have used various forms of quilted armours, typically called gambesons in western culture. These garments are made from stitching many layers of material together, or stuffing fabric between stitched layers. Quilted protection has provided protection from all kinds of weapons for thousands of years, so why stop using it now? Okay so you may not have access to a nicely tailored and fashionable medieval gambeson, it doesn't matter. Using household items such as duvets, towels, old clothing, sofa covers and a little

gaffer tape you will be able to quickly make something very effective.

This principal of homemade protection can also be applied to improving off the shelf items or repairing them. With enough material in quilted armour you will prevent even the strongest of bites, hence why police dog training teams still use the principal for training their dogs for combat today. Just always beware that mobility is always important, take care not to impede articulation and movement.

Quilted armour has only one major downside, it insulates you. In Britain this should rarely be a problem, but in hotter climates it will be and may be a severe handicap.

HELMETS

In a modern military, police, work and sportive context helmets are very valuable, but how suitable are they for the Zompoc? Most helmets are intended only to stop blunt force trauma or protect certain target zones, they will protect the face but almost never the throat and neck. Most helmets are to be avoided due to the cumbersome nature and relatively little protection against zombies. However, helmets can be useful for fighters and soldiers who are at more risk from their environment and fellow fighters.

There are times when a helmet can be useful , however if you are fighting infected 'Fast style' zombies they will not just try to bite you but also beat you senseless. In this scenario, keep an eye out for riot/security helmets, fencing masks, lacrosse and American football helmets. Also, if you ride a motorbike or bicycle, or fight from an open top vehicle, a helmet can protect you from potentially being knocked unconscious which could have fatal consequences. Despite this, the helmet should not be considered part of your regular load out unless for specific reasons.

GLOVES

The hands are a very vulnerable target on humans, even more so when facing the undead. The key to gloves is to have full hand coverage, as long a cuff as possible and hard wearing material. Leather is a fantastic hard wearing material that will give varying levels of

protection depending on the glove. Many fashion leather gloves, such as typical ladies gloves and driving gloves, will feature only a small amount of abrasion protection. The best gloves for this job are motorcycle gloves, police riot and any other substantial long cuffed style. Don't forget that you are not just looking for a glove to protect against zombies, you also need something to keep the cold away, to protect against abrasions and to stop broken glass cutting your hands. The Zompoc will change the world around you and your hands and feet need to be secured against all kinds of threat. A cut hand can soon become infected and this is a big problem for you and your people.

USEFUL ITEMS TO CARRY

Now that you have established your weapons and protection, sort out what else you need to be carrying. It is entirely possible that you will be carrying your survival kit initially, so there may be some items you can carry over. With any luck you will have a vehicle and be able to carry most of what you need in, or on that

vehicle. Of course, this may not be a luxury that you have, as well as needing the ability to survive, if your vehicle is lost through damage or being unreachable at any time. On top of this, many tasks will need to be done on foot, such as foraging for supplies. During specific jobs your kit load out may change, below is a list of items that could well come in useful if you carried them on your person.

- ✓ Torch
- ✓ Filled Water Bottle
- ✓ Snack to keep energy levels up
- ✓ Ammunition
- ✓ Utility Knife (fixed blade ideal)
- ✓ Flares or Glow Sticks
- ✓ Close Range Radio
- ✓ Bandages and Tape

Depending on your situation, and how many of you there are, you may be forced to carry more. Give plenty of thought to items that could come in handy, but also do not carry more than you need. Having the right tool for the job could save your life, but having too much junk weighing you down could bring it all to an end, so personally tailor your equipment to your scenario and requirements.

LOAD BEARING

In everyday life you have likely become accustomed to carrying little more than your keys, wallet, a phone, and handbag for women; that's all going to change. As seen above in the useful items section, you will likely want to carry a good number of useful items, above all, plenty of ammunition or spare weapons where available. Carrying all of this can be difficult, and if doing so compromises your speed and stamina it could all be over. So sort out a way of carrying everything you need, there are a few simple solutions.

HANDBAG/SHOULDER BAG

Almost all women own handbags, they are at least an improvement over having nothing but your pockets. Only use handbags with shoulder straps, if they are hand held, forget it. Shoulder bags, for men and women, are also common, they serve the same purpose. These bags are a basic option with limited capacity and not particularly good for fighting in, look to upgrade quickly. The one advantage that these bags do have over a rucksack is that they are more easily accessible. If you cannot find other load bearing equipment for your ammunition and utilities, consider using one, potentially as well as a backpack. Other bags such as gas mask bags do the same job. Hand bags also get in the way of your arms and are thus of little use when you need to use weapons. Consider their use carefully.

COMBAT TROUSERS

These have become extremely fashionable over the last few decades, which is a good thing as this is something you are going to want to get hold of. Combats feature much better load bearing ability than normal clothing, they are also typically excellent for movement and durability. Do however beware of fashion combats, which will often not be as good on capacity or durability. The best combats are genuine military combat trousers and these are easily found in army surplus shops in pretty much all major towns and cities.

BELT POUCHES

In the 1990s carrying things on your belt was still cool. Money pouches, Swiss Army knives, and mobile phones but not anymore. Typically the only people with anything held on their belt anymore are police and security forces. This equipment is intended to carry a small selection of very specific items, such as tear gas, handguns, cuffs, torches, truncheons etc. You may well consider this as a good option, especially as many of the items will be useful to you too. Utility belts such as these are available from army surplus stores. It is also possible to buy utility belts as used by tradesmen every day. These are usually hard wearing leather belts with pockets and loops to hang various tools off from.

BACKPACK

This is the way to carry the largest capacity possible, depending on the size of bag of course. Backpacks are easy and comfortable to carry, with very little restriction on movement. Try and get the best back support available and a waist strap if possible. Backpacks are excellent for foraging for supplies due to their capacity, but storing ammo and important utility devices in them can really slow you down when you need speed the most. Make sure you get a decent bag, ideally from surplus shops. Make sure the straps are in good

condition and that the zips are all working properly.

FISHING/UTILITY VEST

A simple vest with many different pouches to carry different items, they allow quick access to smaller items. A fishing vest is a simple and effective way to carry extra ammunition as well as torches, flares and utility items. Utility vests are available in many shops including camping stores, army surplus and fishing shops

etc. The one downside to a fishing vest is that they are usually quite a relaxed fit, allowing more movement than you would like when running or fighting.

ARMY WEBBING

Called the PLCE (Personal Load Carrying Equipment) in Britain. Webbing is a belt system with a selection of utility pouches attached to it which in turn has a harness going over the shoulders to take the weight off of the waist and hips. Webbing is intended to be used both standalone and with a backpack, meaning you can carry ammo and essential equipment within easy access, whilst still carrying a backpack for non-essentials. Webbing can be found at army surplus stores, as well as among many airsoft players and cadets. Webbing is robust and comfortable to use and is a great way of carrying extra equipment as comfortably as possible. There is a reason the military use it!

COMBAT/ASSAULT VEST

These vests are essentially a military or police grade version of a fishing vest, stronger, better fitting and better suited to moving quickly and fighting. Just like webbing, combat vests are available in army surplus stores, some camping stores, as well as common among airsofters, police specialists and other enthusiasts. Some vests today are also what is known as 'plate carriers'. These vests are intended to work both as load bearing and body armour at the same time. As previously discussed, bullet proof vests serve very little purpose and will weigh you down. If you get one of these load bearing vests remove the plates from it. Most plate vests have simple removable plates, consider putting the plates to better usage such as on your vehicle.

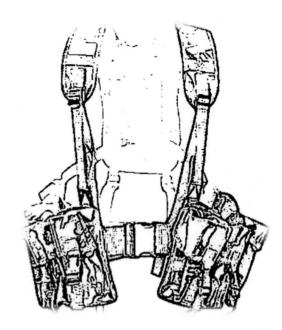

FASHION CONSIDERATIONS

When the Zompoc strikes, function will always be required over fashion, with this in mind there are a few changes to be made with

regards to personal grooming, clothing and fashion. This applies to both men and women, especially as many men are now using products similar to those used by women. The one good thing about the Zompoc is it might stop this trend!

NAILS

If you have long nails, cut them, same goes for false ones. Long nails can only get in the way of the necessities of life and can also cause further pain in certain situations. The fact is you should have found yourself some decent gloves anyway, so no one will see your nails much anymore!

HAIR

In today's society many women have long hair and it has been for a number of decades popular with many men too. Cut it off. You don't have to become a Marine and shave it all off, but cut it short. Long hair can be pulled in a fight and it can also get in the way of your vision and equipment, as well as getting caught and entangled in various objects. Short hair is also easier to keep clean, which is vital during the Zompoc.

COSMETICS

Do not even think about giving consideration to cosmetics, at least not until the worst of the Zompoc has passed and rebuilding has started. Time spent searching for and applying cosmetics is wasted time, use what time you have well.

CLOTHES

Everyone likes a bit of variety to what they wear together with some interest to this degree and this is unlikely to stop anytime soon. You can of course still choose what to wear and personalise your own gear, but only whilst it fits in with your rules of your equipment load out. All clothing must cover as much as possible, ideally all skin if possible. Clothing should, where possible provide bite protection. It should also be easy to move and fight in and perform all tasks necessary. The traditional route with clothing was to add layers as and when needed. If you look at historical precedent it was common in the middle ages to wear maille beneath your main clothing for extra protection. Maille can be bough very cheaply and even the lightweight aluminium maille that is made these days would provide decent bite protection. Stick with traditional fabrics and go for sturdy, hard to tear materials. Lycra is not the material to be wearing!

IDENTIFICATION

Armies throughout the world make use of different means of identification for personnel, vehicles and equipment. This is not without reason as advanced communications, code signs and friend or foe equipment is sometimes not a reliable and simple as a basic armband to let people know who the friendly people are. Knowing quickly who is friendly, who is enemy and who is an unknown is extremely important and could mean death for

your survivors. In terms of the Zompoc, it is quite likely that many survivors will look bedraggled and fatigued to the degree that it will often be difficult to distinguish between them and the infected, compounded further by zombie blood on their clothing if they have fought in hand-to-hand combat. Also, it is a good idea to rotate your identification marks periodically for security reasons.

COMBAT

One of the most basic ways of identifying survivors is adding something to your clothing which signifies that you are not infected. This can be as simple as a coloured armband which is clearly visible. The important element here is that everyone uses the same form of identifying mark and that you as quickly as possible let other survivors know what it is and why you are doing it.

STANDARD KIT LOAD OUTS

Here is a selection of standard kit loads outs based on what is available and later what your intentions are. There are a huge number of different weapons types available to you depending on the country and area you live in. The character's listed kits are just typical and good examples of potential choices equipment.

UNEQUIPPED CIVILIAN

This is how most people start when the apocalypse begins. The chances are when all goes to hell, you will be wearing simple

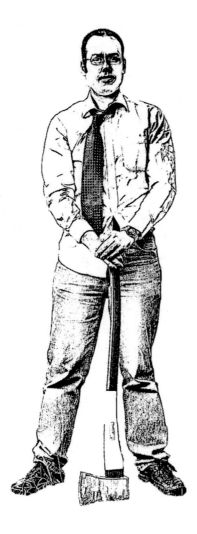

everyday clothes or equivalent. This character equipment assumes that the Zompoc has just started and that you had no time to prepare, or no time to access what you had prepared.

Due to fashion, many people wear relatively restrictive clothing on a daily basis, whether that be a form fitting suit, or a pair of high heels. Due to the limited access to firearms in the UK, you will have to grab anything to hand, axe, shovel, barbell, hammer etc. With this in mind, fighting is not the object, only survival, focus on getting out of danger quickly.

Skin coverage goes a long way, remember, leather is not just for bikers and Goths, it is your best friend in the zombie war. This is the default class for everyone; no one should ever be without some kind of weapon and basic protective gear, no matter what their position in the new world is.

Nobody should stay at this level of kit for more than a day or two, establish better equipment as soon as possible!

FORAGER

These are equipment and supply hunters and gatherers. You need your hands free and ability to move quickly and easily, someone else will do most of the fighting for you. Foragers must always work with other more heavily armed colleagues. If you do not have enough people in your group or are forced to work alone then you will likely have to merge this role with that of the soldier and spotter.

The forager needs load bearing capabilities; a decent sized pack back is a good solid standard, available from hiking or army surplus stores. In more controlled and larger

KIT LOADOUT

❖ **Light to Medium Armour.** You do not want to be in a stand up fight, stamina and speed are more important.

❖ **Free Hands.** Your hands need to be free to forage, holstered, slung or sheathed weapons are important.

❖ **Load Bearing.** A medium to large pack is best to keep you agile but useful.

❖ **Gloves.** Dealing with an infected world, zombie and otherwise, is a huge risk.

❖ **Crowbar.** Essential for breaking your way in to anything.

operations the foragers may be able to use trolleys or sack barrows, but only when you have enough spotters to protect them. A large rucksack is useful in that is leaves your hands free to climb and fight, as well as manoeuvre over any sort of terrain. In terms of weapons, your job is not to fight, you need both hands free to forage. However, in an emergency, you need to defend yourself.

Holsters and sheaths are an excellent way of carrying small self defence weapons whilst keeping your hands free.

If you are forced to merge this class with spotter or soldier, consider the usage of rifles, shotguns or crossbows on slings.

Choose the least combat-capable people to be foragers, whilst they are guarded by those who are eminently better suited to fighting. What is a priority for foragers is the ability to run when need be.

SPOTTER

This class is a medium equipment level. The spotter works alongside foragers as well as vehicles, their job is to lead the way in supply hunts and protect others whilst they work in dangerous environments. A medium level is required as spotters need to be effective in a stand up fight but also able to run both quickly and for prolonged periods of time if need be. In this job you do not need your hands free or the ability to carry anything other than your weapons and ammunition. Substantial enough weapons for a fighting retreat are necessary,

KIT LOADOUT

❖ **Light to Medium Armour.** Vary your protective requirements on role.

❖ **Primary Weapons.** Your job is to look out for others, keep a good primary weapon on a sling.

❖ **Comms gear.** You have the most important job for communication, a radio is ideal to keep in touch with base/vehicles.

❖ **Binoculars/telescope.** As a spotter, you keep others safe by ensuring there are no surprises.

but nothing to heavy that it will slow you down. A spotter may be able to work at a distance, on vehicles or a rooftop, or may have to be within a few feet of a forager at all times.

The spotter class can also take the role of a sniper, though would in an ideal world work alongside a sniper and assist and protect them.

Whilst your role is that of observation and prevention, you could at any time be embroiled in an all out stand up fight. For this reason, be sure to carry a good amount of spare ammunition with you at all time, as well as a good secondary weapon.

If due to a lack of people you spend more of your time on the ground with foragers, consider upping your armour, taking ideas from the soldier or guard load out. The spotter may well be a group's leader and organizer, so be sure they are very capable people.

SOLDIER

When your group gets large and well developed enough that you can hunt the zombies in packs, you will need the soldier class. The solder has only one interest, combat. With this in mind, they need the best protective gear available that will allow them to move and fight for prolonged periods. Weapons need to be plentiful and ammunition even more so, this is not about hiding and running for your life. Soldiers will need to work together in at least groups of four, ideally more. If fighting running zombies the number of soldiers required to be safe and effective will increase.

Fighting zombies from vehicles is generally preferable, and against runners, pretty much essential. Despite this, the luxury of a well protected vehicle is not always one that you will have. The soldier ranks should be made up of the strongest and best fighters that you have, there may be some carry over between soldiers and spotters, depending on how many people you have and requirements.

Soldiers are the elite of your group when it comes to fighting ability and combat proficiency, be sure they get the best equipment.

With the amount of equipment needed and expectation of sustained fighting, fitness is a high priority. Additionally, be sure to have soldiers supported always by well prepared fighting vehicles/platforms.

If guns are not available to you, close combat is not a great option as an intentional culling measure, put more emphasis on using vehicle fighting platforms, however the equipment load out does not change.

GUARD

A guard is able to be the heaviest equipped of all, expected to stay in one place or move very small distances. Guards therefore do not need speed, only the best protection possible. Consider using any bullet proof vests you have for guards, as they are most at risk from rival humans.

When you have enough people and have developed your group structure to the point that you have an organised base of operations, even if that is your home, it will need to be

guarded. When foragers, spotters and soldiers are out looking for supplies and fighting the hordes, the base must be defended. The base is at risk from zombie infestation at all times, as well as threats from other rival or desperate humans.

Guards should be intelligent and logical, reliable people. They do not necessarily need to be the fittest or strongest of your party, in this respect, the elderly can fulfil this task, providing they are still relatively able. In an ideal world you would have excellent fighters as your guards, but they will likely be needed for more hands on tasks. If you are not yet at the stage where your base is in relative safety the majority of the time, let the soldiers fill this role.

Guarding is often a boring job, but at least it doesn't require lugging lots of kit around. You will not need to be carrying anything more than weapons and ammo. If you are able to use strongly fortified positions, which you should, consider the use of crossbows, Molotov cocktails and flame throwers, as they are easy to keep supplied and great from protected positions.

DRIVER

Like foragers, drivers are best kept lightly equipped, with their hands always available. Any weapons need to be single handed and easily carried and drawn from a seated position. A driver can double up as a spotter or forager. Make sure you have equipment available to them for this if necessary for when they are not driving. Where possible a driver is best left as a fixed spotter for the vehicle they drive, with radio access to the rest of the team. In this respect, a driver can handle small operations. Consider keeping easily accessible larger weapons on board for when the driver acts as a spotter to the vehicle as others forage.

KIT LOADOUT

❖ **Light Armour.** You should in theory not need any protective gear if your vehicle is prepped properly.

❖ **Light Weapons.** Only carry something that is small and easily carried on your body.

❖ **Comms gear.** You need to keep in contact with everyone, but this equipment should be vehicle based.

Drivers do not need to be particularly fit and able, nor good in combat; only cool headed and practical. A handgun or machete is all they should really need and will be best suited to their time spent in the seat. Cross draw tactical vests, or shoulder holsters are best suited to this purpose.

As a driver will often to have to work as a spotter or guard for their vehicle, they will need to know how to use heavier weapons, if not to carry them. Vehicle mounted weapons are best suited to this purpose, as they are ready when required and within the safe confines of the driver's vehicle.

Consider keeping heavier armour and weapons onboard with easy access if you need to improvise at any time, or your vehicle gets compromised in anyway.

If your role as a driver is on an open top vehicle or motorbike, consider upping equipment to the levels of a spotter. Whilst the driver class can be merged with others, it is always best to maintain a separate driver who is responsible for and stationed at their vehicle at all times during operations.

240

CHAPTER 13: VEHICLES

Those who live are those who fight.
Victor Hugo

Here is a pretty detailed list of the main types of vehicles you could make use of along with their strengths and weaknesses. Remember, you may need several different vehicles, especially if putting together a decent convoy. Before you start grabbing all the vehicles you can it is important to consider what you need them for and what is available to you.

WHICH TO LOOK FOR?

NUMBER

How many vehicles will you need to meet your needs and those of your team? Obviously the number and type of vehicles required is based heavily upon what you have access to and what your plan is. Initially you may just want one vehicle that you can escape the city in. Afterwards you will want spares in case of break downs and also different types of vehicle. When it comes to raiding and convoy organisation you will find the required number will go up.

PURPOSE

This is more important that it probably sounds. For fast escapes, getaway or cross country performance you may find light, fast vehicles like motorcycles, horses and sports cars are great. For hauling supplies though you will need large cavernous vehicles that are sturdy and reliable to move your goods. For combat operations you will need a mix of strong vehicles with passenger and equipment

carrying capability. Decide what you need a vehicle for, then look for something to fill that need, not the other way around!

PROTECTION

Your primary enemy is zombies. Yes, this is obvious but you need to consider your enemy before you start thinking about protection. Protection covers several areas, primarily the protection of people and then protection of the vehicle. There is no point crashing into a zombie to find the front of your car crumples or the engine cuts out. Look at the types of zombies you will face and then plan protection based on the threat. For the slow, shambling undead you want horsepower to push your way through the bodies whilst making sure the doors, windows and locks are secure from being easily opened on the outside. If you are fighting against infected zombies then do you need to avoid getting blood on you? If so there is no point sticking mesh and spike everywhere, it will just make it more likely you will get hit at some point. Choose the right level of protection for the task required. For example, don't choose a low to the ground sports car as your primary raiding and assault vehicle. It will get stuck on the bodies, is easily damaged and provides a poor fighting platform.

STEALTH/NOISE

No, this doesn't mean you need a stealth mode button and black radar absorbent materials. This section refers to the noise that your vehicle makes and how discrete it is.

Obviously a small engine petrol car makes a good, quiet scout car whereas a V8 powered monster truck is rather less discrete and likely to draw attention to your activities.

CARGO CAPACITY

Again, look at the role your vehicle will be expected to carry out. If you are collecting supplies, picking up wounded or operating a large fighting platform for your troops you will need something strong, powerful and sturdy to carry the amount of kit required. Certain vehicles such as vans, pick up trucks and buses all have substantial load carrying capability. Remember, this is not just based on space but also the vehicles design. Pickups and buses all feature heavy duty axles and suspension as they are designed for this kind of work. The main consideration is the type of cargo. For people you need decent access, ideally in more than one place. Door, large windows etc are essential for the safe deployment and extraction of personnel. Sun roofs or anything removable on the roof all help here.

SIZE

The size of your vehicle is like all the other considerations and based entirely on the required job. You will need all size vehicles, sometimes large for supply work, some smaller for military support, guard work and scouting plus a variety of sizes for combat operations. Remember, the larger the vehicle the greater the liability if something goes wrong. What if it tips over, blocking a road or breaks down? A larger vehicle though can play the part of a moving fortress that will protect your people as you are on the move.

OUTFITTING

This refers to kitting out your vehicle for particular operations. A combat vehicle may have reinforced sides, firing ports, spare weapons, mesh on the glass and a plough on the front. This obviously makes it slower, heavier on fuel and less suited for quick discrete operations. Some vehicles are better suited to outfitting than others. For example, older trucks feature ladder chassis that are massively strong and perfect for welding extra armour, spikes and ploughs too. A modern family car with its shell construction is much less suited to this role.

TRANSMISSION

This is less a problem in Europe as most vehicles are driven with a manual gearbox. In the US and some other countries there are many people who have never driven 'a stick' before. It really isn't that complicated but it is worth considering. If you don't know how to drive a manual car then jumping in one will probably result in you failing to move or stalling right away. Think carefully about this one and choose wisely!

FIGHTING FROM VEHICLES

Fighting from a vehicle has its advantages and disadvantages. By vehicles very definition they are generally faster and also more durable than you are. They are therefore extremely mobile so hit and run, and sweeping tactics are easy. Driving in quickly, shooting or running down a few zombies and then retiring works well. You need to consider how you will fight from particular vehicles so you can get the most out of them. Slower, heavier vehicles make excellent mobiles fortresses and you can equip them with armour, weapons, medical supplies and food to keep moving for a while. Converted four-wheeled vehicles can prove handy here, especially as they tend to be raised slightly higher giving better line of sight. Lighter, less powerful vehicles can also be used as fast hit and run vehicles. Carry a few extra people with weapons and you can keep on the move whilst fighting away. Lighter vehicles do have a weakness though in that they are more easily tipped over or can be stopped with weight of numbers. The danger from being swamped is also greater, so watch out!

LAND VEHICLES

Here is a comprehensive list of vehicles that you may be able to find and make use of during the Zompoc. Please remember to re-read the previous sections to ensure you are looking for the right vehicles to do the right job. Some of these vehicles are more likely in one country than another. For example, throughout Europe vehicles tend to be smaller and offered with smaller capacity engines. The larger trucks and vehicles will be much easier to find in the US along with the wider, straighter roads to use them on.

ROLLER-SKATES

Roller-skates come in the form of inline skates or quad skates and provide a stable, fast platform for a single person. They are not suited to rough terrain but allow great speed on flat surfaces. They are good on pavements, roads and in urban areas such as shopping centres and malls.

BICYCLE

A bicycle is actually a pretty handy vehicle to have. You have faster speed than a human on foot and the maintenance is minimal. There are many types of bicycle and the only real problem you face in their use is damage to the tyres. Make sure you have spare tyres, inner tubes and a puncture repair kit to hand. The obvious weakness to a bicycle is the lack of armour or protection and the fact that it is powered by you. Therefore if you are lazy or hungry your progress may be impaired. Nothing motivates you more though than a hoard of zombies on your ass!

SKATEBOARD

The skateboard is not quite as useful as items such as bicycles. If nothing else by the fact that they are difficult to use unless you have already had a fair bit of practice on them. The great advantage over roller-skates is that you can jump off and fight on foot or simply run. This gives you options and options we like!

SHOPPING CART

Why would you use a shopping cart? Well, for a starter it has wheels, has basic bite proof armour and is available in massive numbers. The main problem is that once inside you cannot control and power it. You can use a trolley as a ram though and it can be used to protect the front of a person or group of people. Also handy is its ability to carry supplies and weapons along with a midget or small child with a weapon!

HORSE

A quiet means of escape or travel to safer and more secure areas. Can carry somewhat large amounts of equipment. No fuel required,

except for vegetation and water to feed the horse. These supplies are easy to find if not in an urban area. Horses are not for inexperienced riders, as the horse may become startled and throw the rider. It may require special care. A horse will not attract attention like a motor vehicle, but if zombies are encountered on a horse you will have a problem. An untrained horse will not stand a chance in a fight and it would be best to continue riding away. There are many types of

horse and if you really want to you can train a horse to stand when faced with danger and even to fight back. The creation of warhorses is probably best left as the subject of another book!

CHARIOT

The chariot is the earliest and simplest type of carriage, used in both peace and war as the chief vehicle of many ancient peoples. If you have access to basic supplies and horses then the chariot or carriage could prove cheap and handy. Basic designs include fast, light, open, two or four-wheeled conveyances drawn by two or more horses hitched side by side. The car was little else than a floor with a waist-high

semicircular guard in front. One or more crew control the chariot and also handles weapons and equipment. The chariot can be used simply as a supply and scout vehicle or as a true war chariot. For the ultimate in combat power add scythed wheels and carry quivers for spare arrows. Start dicing up those zombies!

MOTORBIKES& QUADS

Motorcycles and quads are small, easy to find vehicles that are both quick and agile. These make great scout vehicles as well as handy items for escape and hit and run attacks. They are poorly protected from attacks and are not great platforms to fight from. Motorcycles are a very quick way of getting around in areas that don't have roads, or have bad roads. They can get into places that almost no other motorised vehicle can and they make great scout vehicles. If you fall (which you will at some point, it's inevitable) you could be badly injured and left an easy target for the zombies. Either bring friends on other bikes or even better, don't act like an idiot and be careful! Pulling wheelies and jumping over fences might make you feel cool until the moment you mess up and are left for zombie food. Weapons suitable for use with these vehicles are small firearms and close quarter combat weapons. If you want to go old school couch a spear and use it as a lance, become a knight on a bike!

OFF ROAD BIKES

The majority of scramblers/dirt bikes in the US and the UK are two-stroke and therefore very loud, especially at open throttle. If any kids have got near them you might be lucky to even find an exhaust pipe still fitted to them! Scramblers have a very limited load carrying capability, but expect no more than a small

rack on the front and panniers on the back. Obviously you can also carry supplies on your person in a rucksack or bags. Some films such as the 80s Delta Force with Chuck Norris.

SPORT BIKES:

Sport bikes have many of the advantages and disadvantages of the dirt bike. The biggest single difference is that these are designed for super high performance. These bikes have razor sharp handling, brutal acceleration, good top speeds and incredibly short braking distances. This makes them great for whizzing around and getting in and out of trouble very quickly. These bikes are likely to have even less carrying ability than the dirt bike, especially on the front, though you can still fit smallish panniers to the rear to carry something. Small modifications will allow the fitting of extra weapons and equipment.

ATV's

ATVs (All terrain vehicles) or quads are the dirt bike's four-wheeled brother. They have outstanding off-road ability and also are better

able to carry loads, extra equipment and in an emergency passengers or a small trailer. The ATV is far heavier, so if it falls on you it can do very serious damage or certainly pin you down for zombie feed. The extra weight makes them very unstable if you get one or more wheels off the ground. It is all too easy to flip an ATV over, so you should be very careful when riding them. These are better suited for combat and for carrying more equipment thus making them a handy all-rounder. They are reasonably economical and easy to carry on other vehicles, on trailers or towed behind light vehicles.

GO-KART

A go-kart is an open-wheeled motor vehicle with small, simple wheels. These vehicles are usually raced on scaled-down circuits. Karting is commonly perceived as the stepping stone to the higher and more expensive ranks of motor sports. The go-kart usually comes in two formats; either the more professional racing version or the much smaller version used at fun fairs for children and youths. The racing variant usually makes use of small petrol engines and is both fast and manoeuvrable. Karts can reach speeds exceeding 160 miles per hour while go-karts intended for the general public in amusement parks may be limited to speeds of no more than 15 miles per hour. Don't go for the latter! The kart is essentially a road orientated version of an atv or quad.

TRIKE

The trike is simply a three-wheeled motorcycle. The configuration is a single wheel at the front with two at the rear, usually joined with an axle. The reverse configuration is usually considered to be a three wheels car. Combines many of the features of the atv quad but with additional speed and also the possibility of carrying more equipment or people on the rear. Treat it as a motorised chariot!

CARS

Cars are a wide category of vehicles that are designed to carry small numbers of people, usually from one to eight with single engines, four wheels and designed for use on roads. In the UK the term car also includes the smaller end of the scale that is known as trucks. They are the most common vehicle and will therefore be easy to find during the Zompoc.

CITY CARS

A city car is a small, moderately powered automobile intended for use in urban areas. It is comparable in size and features to a neighbourhood electric vehicle (NEV), has four seats, and is typically 3.4–3.6 metres (11–12 ft) long. These cars have been sold in Europe since the 1960s, and now are an official car classification. They are also known as A-Segment cars. These cars are very handy in tight spaces and make good scout and raiding vehicles. They are surprisingly agile and nippy for their size too. You can even find convertible versions of them that make great little gun cars for mission support. Popular city cars include the Fiat Panda, Austin Mini, Daewoo Matiz and Fiat 500. Due to their light weight and small engines it is probably best not to waste too much time modifying these vehicles with anything but the most rudimentary add-ons.

FAMILY CARS

Family cars are very common and include home grown brands and imports of all shapes and sizes. These cars are plentiful and these days are pretty reliable. They can carry an adequate amount of supplies and people.

They have no special feature and are not good at impacts or for use in combat, especially compared to trucks and muscle cars. Possible modifications include escape hatches, reinforced windows, external stowage and communication gear.

RALLY CARS

These cars are actually variants of the common saloon cars. These vehicles at first glace appear relatively uninspiring but they feature reliable mechanics, powerful turbocharged engines and very effective four-wheel drive. These could make useful attack or escape vehicles or even operate as assault vehicles, though they will not be strong enough to smash through obstacles unscathed. Useful modifications include escape hatches, weapon mounts, additional light armour, reinforced windows, external stowage and communication gear.

CONVERTIBLES

Convertibles are cars that have the ability to change to an open top configuration. They are also known as cabriolets or rag-tops. These include cars with soft tops and those that feature solid roofs with mechanisms to open them. The soft tops usually have more space for people but are of course very vulnerable to zombie attack in either mode. The hard top variants carry less people or supplies but do have the advantage of a sealed down secure mode. This could prove very handy in a Zompoc environment.

SPORTS CARS

These are the fastest, most agile vehicles after the sports bikes and are great at racing around. They are not particularly strong, guzzle the fuel and can carry very little. They are best kept for recon, escape or any scenario where speed is critical. They do have the benefit of being able to carry a little more than bikes and are a more stable platform due to their four wheels. Maintenance is frequent and not easily carried out unless you happen to have a Porsche or Ferrari mechanic to hand. If you really need a

sports car then stick to Japanese or German vehicles. Doing this will at least give you a decent chance in terms of reliability. Popular reliable sports cars include the Toyota Supra, Porsche 911 and Nissan 300ZX.

MUSCLE CARS

Muscle cars are the utmost in comfort and style plus they have the ultimate soundtrack

with the roar of a mighty V8. These cars may not be in the pinnacle of modern engineering but they are big, heavy and powerful. They are strongly built and can easily smash through zombies, leaving burning rubber and the sound of a growling V8 in its wake. They are not as fast or manoeuvrable as sports cars but then again, you are not on a racing track, you are in the Zompoc. Due to the strong chassis and powerful engine they are perfect to be up armoured and equipped with extra storage and weapons. These are the perfect hunter and support vehicles for the people. Muscle cars are easy to find in the US but sadly in the UK a muscle car is usually considered to be something over one litre. Pretty shocking! In the UK look for Australian import cars like the Holden Monaro or imported US cars. At a push you can use some of the higher end BMW cars. If you can get a US car then any of the classics like the Camaro, Mustang, Firebird, GTO from the 60s onwards will be perfect for you.

MPVS

These are the epitome of domesticity and have no real use in the world other than for the people who are convinced that they need to carry 7 people everywhere they go. When the seats are installed they have next to no load carrying capacity, are overly large and probably the most boring car on the road. Luckily, during the Zompoc there is finally a reason to make use of the humble MPV. They can make handy troop transporters and with their reasonable economy (diesel models) they can prove good for medium to long-range hauling. Rip out the useless rear seats and you will still get a few people in plus a decent amount of supplies. A minibus is better but the beauty of the MPV is that the mundane masses have bought them in their droves and they are thus easy to find.

TRUCKS

Truck actually means different things in the UK and the US. Here we will use the US idea of a small to medium sized, sturdy vehicle, often a pickup or 4x4. There are many different types of trucks and most of them have uses during the Zompoc. There is a big difference between utility trucks and luxury vehicles. We would definitely recommend choosing the more spartan utility vehicles like Land Rover Defenders, Jeep Wranglers and Toyota Hi-Lux pickup trucks.

SMALL 4X4

A small 4x4 combines the benefits of a sturdy truck with off-road ability. This off-road ability comes in handy for driving over the heads of the undead.

Brands such as Land Rover and Jeep produce very affordable and easy to maintain vehicles. They've gone just about everywhere and can be modified for an amazing number of purposes. The models have hardly changed in years so would be pretty easy to modify and maintain long-term. Some of the great features of these vehicles are that they can be stripped down, their doors removed, windscreen folded down and a myriad of other changes. They feature strong chassis, engines with plenty of torque and easy access to spare parts. Even better, these vehicles car provide almost any function needed from transport to assault or reconnaissance.

LARGE 4X4

The large 4x4 includes primarily five door vehicles with decent passenger and storage space. Big brands that are worth going for include Land Rover, Jeep and Hummer. This category includes the larger capacity 4x4 trucks. These are often knows as the long wheelbase vehicles and common ones include the new Jeep Wrangler 5 door, the Land Rover Defender 110, the Hummer H2 etc. The Defender is used worldwide as a military vehicle, especially popular with the British SAS (Special Air Service). The H2 Hummer isn't a purpose built vehicle like its namesake, the H1 Hummer. This means that it isn't quite as tough as the real Hummer though for civilian use it is still pretty solid. Civilian Hummers feature all the modern comforts, powerful engines and automatic transmissions, so ideal for Americans or those that are gearstick

challenged. All of these larger 4x4 vehicles are available in pickup truck configuration. These versions are very common and easily modified with weapon mounts or for carrying loads. Pickup versions are usually equipped with strong springs on the rear axle to help carrying heavier loads, so bare this in mind for the jobs you need the vehicle to undertake.

PICK-UP TRUCKS

The difference between pick-up trucks and large 4x4 vehicles is that they are designed for load carrying, not off-road driving. This usually means they are 2-wheel drive and are surprisingly quick on the road. Common models include Dodge Ram, Ford F-series, Toyota Tundra, Nissan Titan, Toyota Hi-Lux,

Defender 110 pickup etc. Full-size pick-ups are the biggest civilian use pick-ups out there. In the US most of these trucks are rear or all-wheel drive, V8 powered vehicles, so performance is surprisingly decent. In the UK these vehicles are almost entirely diesel powered, so will lack the speed of the V8's but will have lots of torque. Some pick-ups may feature some form of off-road ability, ideally with permanent four-wheel drive and good ground clearance. If you need the off-road ability though it is best to stick with the pick-up variants of the common 4x4 vehicles.

LUXURY SUVS

SUV (Sports Utility Vehicles) such as the BMW X5, Cadillac Escalade, Lincoln Navigator, VW Toureg and Porsche Cayenne fit into the luxury

4x4 category. These vehicles are not at the top of your list when the Zompoc arrives. Most are not all that tough, when compared to dedicated utility vehicles, and their off-road capability is usually basic at best. On top of

that they have far too many electronic gizmos, bells and whistles and gadgets that will most certainly break during hard usage. This includes advanced engine management and navigation integration that you will be unable to modify or fix easily. The biggest plus though is that you will find hundreds of these vehicles all around the world. They are very, very popular and because of this you may actually find it easier to take and simply ditch it when you hit a problem.

RECOMMENDED UK VEHICLE

Land Rover Defender - formerly known as the 90 or 110 depending on wheelbase pre-1990, Defender afterwards. The Defender is neither a comfortable nor luxurious vehicle, but it is exceptional at what it does. Most defenders are diesel and good on economy for their size, featuring excellent torque to move through objects at slow speed. The low ratio gearbox will allow for excellent grunt from a standing start and the ground clearance good to keep the running gear out of danger. Off-road ability is outstanding, and load capacity great, they are very common and easy to maintain and find parts to. The Defender is the ultimate all-round vehicles for many different roles, as a bonus, many already have useful modifications, such as roof racks, bull bars, under body protection etc.

UTILITY VEHICLES

These are vehicles found outside of the home/family sector and are used by companies, agencies and corporations to provide a job or function. These machines tend to be stripped of any unnecessary complication and are also sturdy and well constructed. Whilst less common than cars or SUVs you will still find plenty of them about. Remember that most of these big machines run on diesel, yes, even in the V8 loving United States! In the long term you will find these machines will provide the backbone of your combat and transport capability. Due to their simple design and larger sizes they are often easier to work on and maintain, just make sure you have a toolkit equipped with big tools!

TRUCK/LORRY

In the United States "truck" is usually reserved to describe commercial vehicles larger than normal cars, and for pickups and other vehicles having an open load bed. These might include a variety of smaller 4x4 vehicles or pickups. In the United Kingdom and Ireland, lorry is used instead of truck, but only used for the medium and heavy types. Smaller vehicles such as vans, a pickup or an off-road four-wheel drive vehicle are never considered to be a lorry in these countries.

A lorry is a great vehicle of use in the Zompoc and it comes in very handy for moving large groups of people and supplies around. They can also be used as substantial personnel transporters, perfect for getting 20-30 armed people to pour out the back of a truck to the centre of the city to raid for supplies.

The biggest problem with these large vehicles is that they are hard to navigate around corners and not meant for city travel. With these large vehicles you may have some trouble getting around, but it will bring you in a main road to the centre of town, and back again. Designed for long distance travel these large machines will allow you to carry lots of

provisions and ammunition for tens, hundreds or even thousands of miles! Perfect for travelling down motorways, highways and main roads with a decent escort.

Anybody that has seen Mad Max II, The Road Warrior will know the potential uses for big, powerful trucks. In that film they use trucks for goods and people transport as well as a mobile fortress. They also use the truck as a moving barrier in their fort! So, if you have one, you can also use it to barricade your fortress in the same way! These big vehicles are not so great off-road even though they have powerful engines, large wheels and reasonable ground clearance. If you get stuck or tip over then you will have to abandon the trucks as you won't be pushing it over anytime soon!

Larger trucks are sometimes known as semi-trucks in the US or articulated lorries in the UK. These vehicles can be given a wide variety of trailers giving you lots of trailers, giving you lots of options. This means you can have a few tractor units (the front bit) and a selection of trailers back at your base. These trailers include liquid storage tanks (perfect for carrying water, fuel, milk, gas), standard box trailers for bulk transport/living space (standard cargo carrying variant) , flat beds for transport of large items or vehicles, car transport ramps (for carrying collected, damaged or salvageable vehicles) and lastly bus-style trailers for personnel transport. The personnel transport trailers are pretty unusual and you are much better off just getting hold of a bus.

MINI-BUS

A minibus is a passenger carrying motor vehicle that is designed to carry more people than an MPV, but fewer people than a full-size bus. Minibuses have a seating capacity of between 8 and 30 seats and make a really, really useful people and equipment haulage vehicle. They are kitted out with reliable and economical engines and perfect to be up armoured and equipped with extra load carrying capacity. Every convoy should have at least one of these useful general-purpose vehicles. If you have the choice you should always pick one of these over the more numerous but less useful MPV class of vehicle. These are simple and there is much less to go wrong with them.

SCHOOL BUS

The school bus is a vehicle used extensively in the United States. The handy thing with these vehicles is they are stored together so you can either pickup a couple at once or simply head to the depot for spares or to get a replacement vehicle. These vehicles are solid, reliable and good for moving large groups of people around. They are designed to carry substantial weight and because of this you can easily

modify and add armour and weapons to these buses and still carry people. These vehicles suffer in terms of off-road ability as they are almost always two-wheel drive and fitted with wheels optimised for on road usage.

BUS

A bus is a road vehicle designed to carry passengers, any number from eight to a hundred passengers. Buses are widely used public transportation. The most common type of bus is the single-decker bus, with larger loads carried by double-decker buses and articulated buses. You can use the commercial bus for the same jobs as the school bus, plus they are easier to obtain outside of the US. A luxury bus is called a coach and often features less seating but increased storage and additional facilities such as televisions and toilets, perfect for long distance travel!

HORSE TRANSPORTER

A horse transporter is actually a modified lorry and is designed to carry a number of horses safely and securely for long distance travel. The beauty of the horse transporter is that the cargo area is large and secure making it ideal for a variety of tasks during the Zompoc. Use it for secure haulage of supplies or use it as an armoured troop transporter. Do not confuse a horse transporter with a horse box, a trailer designed to be towed behind cars or trucks to carry one or two horses.

VAN

A van is a kind of vehicle used for transporting goods or groups of people. It is usually a box-shaped vehicle on four wheels, about the same width and length as a large car, but taller and usually higher off the ground. Larger vans in the UK are classified as lorries (trucks). Vans are best used for medium to long-distance cargo transport. They have excellent load carrying capacity and are relatively economical.

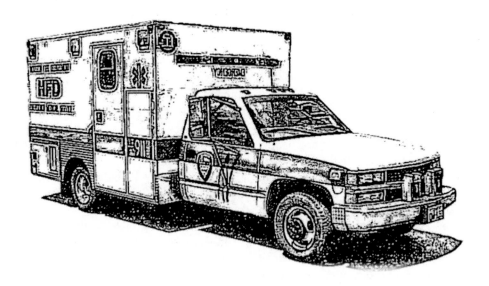

AMBULANCE

An ambulance might not feature off-road capabilities but they are rather tough vehicles, designed for continuous service in all manner of circumstances. The greatest asset of this vehicle is that it features lots of room for storage, and when found may carry emergency medical supplies that will prove very handy later on. The load capacity is high and also very secure from the outside. Most ambulances allow transit from the crew section to the transport section in the rear. In terms of fuel economy this vehicle is best suited for shorter-range travel as they tend to be rather heavy and often fitted for speed, rather than economy. This vehicle would be perfect as a rescue vehicle, fast assault vehicle or even as an ambulance. The biggest downside to the ambulance is that to get one you will almost certainly have to head to a hospital and this is a place not to be taken lightly. A hospital could be teeming with infected, especially as this is where they would be likely taken during the early days of the Zompoc.

DUSTBIN LORRY

Officially known as waste collection vehicle (WCV) this is a truck specially designed to pick up smaller quantities of waste and haul it to landfills and other recycling or treatment facilities. They are designed to carry heavy weights and are very strongly built and are a common sight in most urban areas. Uses for these are as armoured transports as they only need the cab to be reinforced. The only downside is that you will need to find either a brand new, unused truck or will have to do some serious cleaning unless you want to drive round in a vehicle that stinks of rotting waste...nice.

COMBINE HARVESTER

These are massive vehicles designed to harvest crops in a field. They feature decent off-road performance, large wheels, good ground clearance and are pretty well armoured. The front part of the vehicle is known as the cutting bar and is usually equipped with very sturdy cutting wheels. This could allow the combine harvester to be used as a zombie assault vehicle, the bar slashing through any zombies that get in the way. Test the theory on a few zombie strays first though! The big downside to the combine harvester is speed and fuel economy. Also, due to their size, they are awkward to use on roads.

TRACTOR

A tractor is a vehicle specifically designed to deliver a high tractive effort at slow speeds, for the purposes of hauling a trailer or machinery used in agriculture or construction. This basically defines the primary benefits of the tractor, its pulling power and slow speed. This makes the tractor useful to use but only in certain circumstances. There is very little that will stop a tractor. It has bags of power, big wheels and is very heavy. If you need something pushed or pulled somewhere then the tractor is the machine. One variant of the tractor is a digger like a JCB. This is essentially the same as a tractor but fitted with a digger on the rear and a large plough on the front. With a little armour on the crew compartment you have the perfect assault and support vehicle. Also, the utility function of the digger is that it can be used to help fortify your base and move heavy materials around.

SNOW PLOUGH

A snowplough is a tough, sturdy vehicle found in colder climates that is very well suited to the Zompoc. The most important part of these vehicles is their excellent grip in poor weather as well as the massive armoured plough on its front. The plough, whilst designed to move snow, is equally adept at smashing aside zombies or rubbish and debris that get in your way. The only difficulty is actually finding these powerful trucks, especially in areas with a moderate climate. You will be likely to find them in council depots unless the Zompoc hits during bad weather, in this case expect to find them abandoned on the main routes where they should be clearing the streets.

FIRE ENGINE

The biggest disadvantages of a fire engine during the Zompoc are its size, fuel consumption and noise. The lights and sirens are not particularly useful in the early days as they will do nothing other than attract zombies. The fire engine is large and hard to turn, but relatively speedy, and should be very well cared for as they need to be guaranteed to work in an emergency (for obvious reasons). Fire engines are very sturdy and can carry lots of supplies providing you strip it of its fire fighting equipment. The water carrying capacity of a fire engine is massive and this could be handy to you for a variety of reasons. Some fire engines come equipped with substantial extending ladders or platforms. You may have a use for this capability, if not look for the water carrying appliances rather than the ladder based vehicles.

AIR VEHICLES

Here is a comprehensive list of aerial vehicles that you may be able to find and make use of during the Zompoc. There are some major advantages and disadvantages to using aircraft, most of which come down to the complications of using them. Some of the aerial vehicles are able to avoid these problems though and it is these that you may want to try and add to your vehicle list as soon as possible. Due to the fact that weight is always an issue it is not of much benefit to modify vehicles with the exceptions of lights, communication gear and possibly weapons.

UNPOWERED AIRCRAFT

Unpowered aircraft are simply aircraft that carry no method of propulsion. This means no engines or fuel to burn. This makes them relatively simple and in the long-term they could be of great use in the Zompoc. Their lack of propulsion does however create other problems that will limit their usage. Because they have no powerplant they need assistance to launch trough the use of winches, hilltop launches and rockets. This lack of power plant also means limited use in load carrying as well as range.

GLIDERS

Gliders, hang gliders and paragliders do not employ propulsion once airborne and are therefore quite handy methods of transport in a world where fuel, airports and resources are limited. Take-off may be by launching forwards and downwards from a high location, by pulling into the air on a towline, by a ground-based winch or vehicle or by a powered "tug" aircraft. Vehicle launch or winches on vehicles would allow aerial reconnaissance and support aircraft to be launched relatively frequently with no use of power or fuel. Paragliders are especially useful due to their small size, ease of storage and ability to insert people and their personal kit into a location by air. The big disadvantage of gliders is their reliance upon air and thermals to keep airborne and this can easily reduce the range.

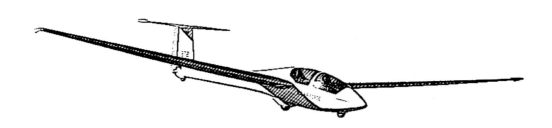

BALLOONS

Balloons come in a variety of shapes and sizes but they all drift with the wind. Though normally the pilot can control the altitude, either by heating the air or by releasing ballast, giving some directional control. A balloon can also be tethered, ideally to a powerful winch and then anchored down firmly. You can use these for observation or for emergency escape. The real benefits are that they require far less training and knowledge to use, though it is still easy to mess things up and crash into a zombie filled city. Balloons can be filled with helium or you can use fuel to heat the air. The latter is probably easier to come by as filling a balloon with helium is not as simple as it sounds.

KITES

Kites can provide some uses in a Zompoc scenario. They are aircraft that are tethered to the ground or other object that maintains tension in the line. To stay airborne they rely on virtual or real wind blowing over and under them to generate lift and drag. Without wind the kite will lose lift and fall straight to the ground. Kites can be used to lift weights, cameras or even people which can all be of use during the Zompoc. The kite can also help reduce the gross weight of a load when provided with sufficient lift. Another feature of a kite is that it can be used as a method of propelling a land vehicle like a kart or buggy. A kite is therefore of no real use in terms of air transport but it can provide a variety of utility uses where items need to be lifted.

POWERED AIRCRAFT

These are aircraft that feature some form of power plant. These are more complicated than the non-powered aircraft and generally require much more maintenance and also the skills and knowledge to fly them. The added weight of the power plants and fuel to drive them tend to make powered aircraft heavier and thus larger. The big upsides to these aircraft is they are the most common and most useful of all aircraft. They exist in a variety of power plants and excel at range, height and speed. The last three factors of of utmost important in the Zompoc as you will want to be able to travel to safety whilst being out of the clutches of the zombie threat.

PROPELLER

A propeller powered aircraft comprises a rotating propeller that creates aerodynamic lift or thrust, in a forward direction. These are very common aircraft and range from single engine Cessna type places through to larger multi-engine planes like a C130 Hercules or a twin engine Beechcraft. The benefits of these types of aircraft is that they usually feature short take off and landing capability, especially the smaller planes. Propeller powered aircraft are also slower than jet powered aircraft making them good for observation or for use as attack aircraft. These aircraft are ideally suited to short and medium range usage and need less advanced maintenance and knowledge to keep them flying. They are also slower than jet aircraft, but usually faster than helicopters.

JET

Jet engines can provide much higher thrust than propellers, and are naturally efficient at higher altitudes. Nearly all high-speed and high-altitude aircraft use jet engines. If you can find one of these that is working, and you know how to fly it, you will find it is great at hauling people and goods great distances and

at a fair speed. Jets come in all shapes and sizes but are rarely used as light private aircraft. Expect to see either executive jets or military aircraft at the lower end of the scale. Anything larger will be for freight or passenger transports. These planes all require airports to operate from, along with supplies, fuel and maintenance - all of which must be provided by those with knowledge and experience.

HELICOPTER

A helicopter is an aircraft that is powered by a vertically mounted rotor usually powered by an internal combustion engine. These handy aircraft can take off and land in all manner of

locations. They require massive amounts of maintenance, are hard to learn to fly and very heavy on fuel. If you don't have a pilot and crew then forget it. If you are in the fortunate position to have access to a helicopter though you will find it useful for a plethora of uses. Be careful flying into dangerous areas, as any kind of failure will put you in the ground...hard. Always carry medical supplies, water and communications gear.

WATER VEHICLES

Water based transportation is actually of great use in the Zompoc. Please bear in mind that access to watercraft will be determined by your location in the world. Most people live within reasonable access to the sea or to a major river of some kind. If you don't then spend a little more time in the land vehicles section! Obvious exceptions to this are for those living in heavily urbanised areas or areas lacking in waterways! Here is a comprehensive list of water vehicles that you may be able to find and make use of during the Zompoc. This section is divided up into classes of water vehicles and also by propulsion type. These include boats, ships, stationary platforms and other forms of watercraft.

BOATS

A boat is a watercraft of modest size designed to float or plane and to provide passage across water. Usually this water will be inland or in protected coastal areas. Most navy's define a boat as a vessel that can be carried onboard another vessel, with the exception of submarines. Boats come in all shapes and sizes, some powered, others not.

UNPOWERED BOATS

These are watercraft that are usually propelled through the labour of the people in the boat. The normal method of movement is using paddles or oars to push the boat through the water. The benefit of this type of boat is that they are usually light, relatively small and can be used when there are no sources of fuel or wind to move the craft. Obvious problems are reduced cargo space, small size, slow speed and a complete reliance upon manpower to move the boat. These vessels are handy to have onboard larger boats or ships and are commonly used as lifeboats. Common craft include kayaks, Canadian canoes and rowing boats.

SAILING BOATS

A sailing boat is a vessel propelled partly or entirely by sails and is a common method of propulsion for small vessels, even today. The term covers a variety of boats, larger than small vessels such as sailboards and smaller than sailing ships, but distinctions in size are not strictly defined and what constitutes a sailing ship, sailboat, or a smaller vessel (such as a sailboard) varies by region and culture. The boats have the benefit of using a free source of motive power, wind and can thus travel vast distances without the need to carry or burn fuel. Many sailing boats also feature auxiliary engines to provide backup power or an additional form of propulsion. Larger sailing yachts would make excellent vessels as they are spacious, well equipped and perfect for long distance travelling. Couple a sailing boat with additional small boats and you have a vessel that is most effective and reliable for the continuing months of the Zompoc.

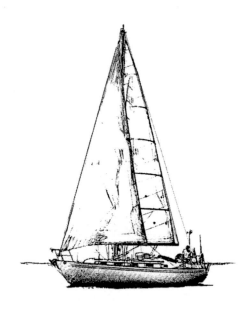

POWERED BOATS

These craft contain a power plant, fuel and gearbox and are found all over the globe. Be careful with powered watercraft as they are reliant upon a fuel source and will require maintenance to keep them operational. If you are checking a boat's engine just remember that they are generally water cooled, so don't test run them out of the water!

SPEEDBOAT

A speed boat is a small craft, optimised for speed and agility, hence the name. They are perfect for high speed escape or insertion missions but cannot carry large amounts of supplies or fuel, so keep this in mind when planning operations. Expect to find these vessels at marinas in coastal areas. Speedboats can also be found on trailers and at boat marinas.

FISHING BOATS

Fishing boats are generally small, often little more than 30 metres (98 ft) but up to 100 metres (330 ft) for a large tuna or whaling ship. They usually have nets or rods on board and could provide useful fishing facilities. Don't just assume that a fishing boat will have all its nets, rods and tackle on board though. Many fishermen will bring in these valuable items and lock them away securely. Fishing boats usually have some kind of crew area but use most of their deck space for storage and fishing. The other really useful benefit of fishing boasts is that they tend to be very

DINGHY

A dinghy is a small boat that is often towed or carried by a larger vessel. These boats may be powered by oars, sails or a small outboard motor. A dinghy is handy to travel from boat to shore or to move small numbers of people stealthily.

Be careful to ensure that small boats like this have auxiliary propulsion devices, such as oars or paddles, in case the main motor suffers a failure, runs out of fuel or jams on something. The main disadvantage is the size of the vessel. Relatively little can be carried making them suitable only for auxiliary use or as an escape craft. They are usually sturdy craft and likely to last some time.

reliable and sturdy and that they can work in all weather conditions, day after day.

JET –SKI

A jet-ski is a personal high speed watercraft. These machines are essentially the motorcycle of the waterways. They are not quiet but feature great speed and manoeuvrability. These vehicles are not great at carrying loads and will use fuel pretty quickly. Use a jet-ski for specific reasons and ideally carry them on other vehicles when distance or load carrying capacity is required.

SHIPS

Ships are large vessels that float on water and are generally distinguished from boats based on size and passenger capacity. These critical and numerous vessels may be found on lakes, seas and rivers across the globe. They allow a variety of activities, such as the transport of people or goods, fishing, entertainment, public safety, and warfare. Ships usually require larger crews with specific skills, knowledge and responsibilities. Modern ships feature large degrees of automation, but this places even more dependence on the ability of their smaller crews to manage them effectively.

MILITARY SHIPS

There are many types of military naval vessels currently in service around the world. They have major advantages and disadvantages over other vessels for use during the Zompoc. The major advantages are that they are usually designed to be sturdy, long-lasting and relatively simple. The latter is obviously not true when looking at the more major vessels such as aircraft carriers, but it is probably fair

and the fact that they can be very effectively sealed down against the elements or attack, they can make excellent floating bases. A navy frigate moored in a harbour, whilst not invulnerable, will almost certainly be tougher and easier to guard than most buildings.

Modern naval vessels can be broken down into three main categories: warships, submarines and support and auxiliary vessels. Submarines are dealt with later in the other vessels section. Modern warships, though powerful even in the smaller classes, are generally going to be overkill for the Zompoc. They feature limited space and are usually designed for specific purposes. They are generally divided into seven main categories, which are: aircraft carriers, cruisers, destroyers, frigates, corvettes, submarines and amphibious assault ships. Even the small corvettes and frigates are still big vessels that need hundreds of crew to operate them. Most navy's also include many types of support and auxiliary vessels such as minesweepers, patrol boats, offshore

to assume you won't be sailing around in one! The big disadvantages of military vessels are that they are generally quite large and require trained crews to operate them. They may also feature equipment and hardware that will be hard, if not impossible, to control for the layman. Due to their difficult nature to board,

patrol vessels, replenishment ships and hospital ships. If your long-term strategy can make use of these vessels then they can prove very tough and reliable. A military transport ship is a great long term base from which to launch raids and perform a variety of missions. Smaller vessels such as patrol boats are also much beefier versions of civilian motor launches with all the benefits of a military boat.

COMMERCIAL VESSELS

Commercial vessels or merchant ships ply the worlds shipping lanes and can be divided into three broad categories: cargo ships, passenger ships and special-purpose ships. Cargo ships transport dry and liquid cargo. Dry cargo can be transported in bulk by bulk carriers, packed directly onto break-bulk, packed in containers as aboard a container ship or driven aboard as in roll-on roll-off ships. Liquid cargo such as oil is generally carried in oil tankers and chemical tankers. These cargo vessels are large, sometimes massive, and require large amounts of fuel and space to travel. For travelling large distances with lots of supplies they are unsurpassed but for anything else they are an awful lot of fuss in the Zompoc. You are better off sticking to the larger boats and coastal vessels in most cases.

Passenger ships range in size from small river ferries to giant cruise ships and in some circumstances could provide you and your

fellow survivors with a strong, secure and long lasting floating island. Just don't become too complacent. Some are suited specifically for sailing coastal routes whilst others are designed to travel the world. This type of vessel includes ferries, which move passengers

and vehicles on short trips; ocean liners, which carry passengers on one-way trips; and cruise ships, which typically transport passengers on round-trip voyages promoting leisure activities onboard and in the ports they visit. These vessels share many of the characteristics of the cargo vessels but are obviously optimised for passengers rather than cargo. They feature many sealable rooms that whilst handy for defence could also harbour a large number of zombies for a long time. Use these for much the same uses as the cargo ships in the Zompoc. Other commercial vessels include tugboats, pilot boats, rescue boats, cable ships, research vessels, survey vessels and ice breakers.

INLAND AND COASTAL SHIPS

There are many types of ships that are designed for inland and coastal waterways. These are the vessels that trade upon the lakes, rivers and canals and are built with these waterways in mind. These vessels are specially designed to carry passengers, cargo or both in the challenging river environment. One of the long-term benefits of inland watercraft is that freshwater lakes are less corrosive to ships than the salt water of the oceans. This means they tend to last much longer than ocean freighters. Lakers older than fifty years are not unusual. Due to the flatter shape of the ship's hull, coastal ships will be able to stay much closer to shore and find it easier and safer to navigate more shallow waterways.

This type of vessel is therefore perfect as a coastal base where you can sail or moor a vessel in a major estuary or channel in safety. They can carry decent supplies and equipment and can also be retrofitted with weapons for additional protection. Be careful taking these ships too far out to sea though, as they are not intended to traverse oceans and rough seas. The last thing you want is to escape from a few thousand zombies only to drown in the middle of the Pacific!

STATIC WATERCRAFT

These are vessels designed to be used and operated in a static environment. They are anchored or fixed to the sea or riverbed with the intention of being used as a working or living space. Most static watercraft are unable to move easily, such as house-boats but may have their own power and be able to move to other locations if needed. There are advantages and disadvantages to having a water based home, the most obvious being that they are harder to reach. This complication also makes it more difficult for you to keep them resupplied. Another major problem is that water based fixed bases cannot be easily altered in size, making them a problem if you wish to expand in the future.

HOUSEBOAT

A houseboat is a boat that has been designed or modified to be used primarily as a human dwelling. These boats are common throughout the world and can be found on rivers, lakes and canals. Some houseboats are not motorised because they are usually moored, kept stationary at a fixed point and often tethered to land to provide utilities. However, many are capable of operation under their own power and some may look like ordinary river craft from the outside. A houseboat of sufficient size would be an excellent base of operations, providing it is not too close to land and is not in shallow water. With secure door and windows this could be a handy haven. It is important with a houseboat to make sure you have enough space for people and supplies and that you can use smaller vessels to move people and goods to and from your new home. Make sure your houseboat has procedures in place for scenarios such as leaks, deliberate sabotage and even worse, a successful breach by zombies. If this vessel is somehow surrounded by zombies and is static you will either have to fight off all assailants or will have to escape. Make sure you plan for this, don't wait until the fateful day when they knock on the hull!

OFF-SHORE PLATFORMS

An off-shore platform, often referred to as an oil platform or an oil rig, is a large structure usually used to house workers and machinery needed to drill wells in the ocean bed and ship or pipe them to shore. There are also defunct offshore platforms that are designed for military use or smaller scientific platforms used for research. Depending on the circumstances, the platform may be fixed to the ocean floor, consist of an artificial island or may float. These structures are designed to withstand all sorts of weather and are massively sturdy and strong. Some have now been standing for scores of years and will be standing for many more. As they are isolated they are already equipped to be self sufficient and can manage on their own for some time. They will have facilities to generate power and also feature a variety of amenities for food preparation, cleaning, preparing food, creating heat etc. This makes them great for the Zompoc as a sturdy, zombie safe haven in the ocean. In many ways they are more like a large static houseboat but with far more real-estate. You can resupply either by watercraft or if you have the skills, aircraft and resources by aircraft. Some of the older military islands are also useful possible storage sites, but they are relatively small and hard to make even partially self sufficient. Use them for storing fuel, spare ammunition or perhaps set them up as temporary medical facilities.

OTHER WATERCRAFT

HOVERCRAFT

A hovercraft is a craft capable of travelling over relatively smooth surfaces supported by a cushion of slow moving, high-pressure air. These unusual vehicles are used throughout the world as specialised transports. Because they are supported by a cushion of air, hovercraft are unique among forms of ground transportation in their ability to travel equally well over land and water. Small hovercraft are used for sport or passenger service, while giant hovercraft have civilian and military applications and are used to transport cars, tanks, and large equipment in hostile environments and terrain. Hovercraft are not as complex as they might sound and in the right locations can prove excellent vehicle for use in the Zompoc. You can travel over the sea and then straight up onto the land to grab supplies or rescue survivors and then turn back to the sea. The main problem with hovercraft is where will you find them? Some countries use them as short to medium range ferries, but in other parts of the world they are very rare.

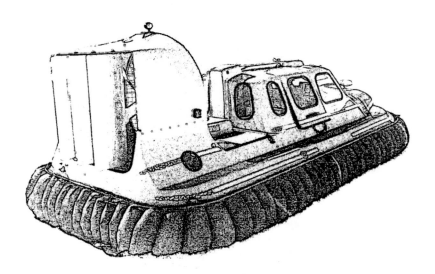

SUBMARINES

A submarine is a watercraft capable of independent operation below the surface of the water. These vessels are mainly used by the military, though civilian vessels are in use amongst the scientific community. These are generally launched from other surface ships though and are more accurately described as a submersible, which has only limited underwater capability. The term submarine most commonly refers to large crewed autonomous vessels and in the case of nuclear submarines can remain at sea for long periods of time. A submarine is hard to crew and will need a base to operate from. The ability to submerge is not that much help in the Zompoc and there are great risks when sailing in this way. Our advice, unless you are in the Navy and happen to be in a submarine at the start of the Zompoc, don't bother.

CHAPTER 14: VEHICLE PREPARATION

Know your enemy and know yourself and you can fight a hundred battles without disaster.

Sun Tzu

This section concerns all the fun work and modification you can make to your vehicles to make them better suited to the Zompoc. This ranges from disabling the airbags and adding luggage racks to armour plating 18-wheelers and fitting them out with flame throwers! This chapter deals primarily with the modifications you can make to create level 3 vehicles.

Let's divide preparation up into three key stages based on the time available to you:

STAGE 1: OH SHIT, LET'S GET OUT OF DODGE!

This is where you have, at the most, minutes to get ready and go. Maybe you have just woken up to find the dead at your door. Don't go looking for your toolkit, just grab your family or entourage and your basic survival kit. If you need to escape do it now! Don't think, just follow your basic survival plan and do it. What plan? Checkout the plan section of this book! If you have more than a couple of minutes go to stage 2.

STAGE 2: A-TEAM

This stage is where you have some time, maybe minutes, maybe an hour to prepare and ready your vehicles. You will not have the time to make major modifications but you can do a few simple things to make your vehicles better suited to surviving the Zombie Apocalypse. The first thing is to make sure you carry anything and everything you think you may or may not need if you can never return to your home. Read the survival kit section for more information. The next thing is to protect your vehicle from being forced open. This means ensuring you can lock the car from the inside and make sure it works. Get the child locks on for doors you don't want to use so people don't freak out and leave your car when you are in trouble. If you want to stay alive, stay in the car till you find somewhere safer. Grab a brick, rock, anything that can break the glass to get out. If you have more time them move to stage 3.

STAGE 3: THE LONG HAUL

If you have enough time for stage 3 then you were either already in a safe place or you have followed stage 1 or 2 to escape and are now looking to something a little more permanent. The main things you will want to do to a vehicle are adding greater protection, adding offensive capability, cargo expansion, escape hatches, communication and survival equipment. Vehicle modification comprises a bewildering array of welding, electrical, electronic and mechanical work. Some of these jobs can be carried out by the non-technical, others require the use of those with decent tools, skills and knowledge. If your only knowledge of weapons comes from playing Counter Strike don't even think about welding machine mounted hardware to your vehicle. Keep and simple and only fit the things you can cope with!

DEFENCE

Defensive modification of your vehicles includes wide varieties of upgrades that are designed to protect both the vehicle and the people within. These modifications may include metal, plastics, wood, car tyres and more. You need to protect the vehicle first and then the people. If after hitting a zombie the airbag goes off and you stop then you are royally screwed. First job is to rip out anything you don't need, this means anything soft and fluffy, furry dice, spare seats, DVD players, parcel shelves and air-bags. The more you take out the more space you create for the important stuff.

ARMOUR PLATING

This can be made of various metals and can provide handy protection to all parts of your vehicle. Remember to protect key parts of the

vehicle first, these will include the windows, engine radiator, wheels etc. Iron or steel offers great protection from a variety of threats but will increase the weight and bulk quite quickly. Aluminium offers great protection when fitted in large block and is substantially lighter than steel.

WINDOWS GLASS PROTECTION

Car window glass is very, very strong. Contrary to what Arnie can do a zombie will not be able to punch through one. One problem you will find though is that when the window does smash it can often shatter into pieces. This is dangerous to you and also makes it easy for them to get at you. To help resolve this you can start by attaching film to the inside of the cars windows. This film is often used to tint or darken the glass of the car. The main benefit is that if the glass is cracked or damaged the film will stop the glass shattering and falling inside the car. Chicken wire or mesh can also be fitted to protect the glass.

WINDOW STEEL SHUTTERS

These can be fitted to either the interior or exterior of the car. On the outside of the car they will provide maximum protection but will be awkward to raise or lower unless you lower or remove the windows. Internal shutters can be used no matter the state or condition of the windows. Internal shutters have one downside in that they will reduce the amount of internal space. One place to find these type of shutters is to use the ones fitted on shop doors.

Obviously avoid the larger ones fitted over the display windows as they will be much too large for most vehicles.

SHARP SURFACES

One handy little modification is to make climbing or grabbing your vehicle in any way a painful and damaging affair. Yes, as a general rule zombies will not shy away from injuries it will damage hands, cuts veins and make it harder for them to get you. Useful materials for this are broken glass set un a glue, ideally something like epoxy resin. Fit this on all the edges of your vehicle and you'll find plenty of zombie fingers and hands getting slashed or badly injured if they get too close. You can also add sharpe metal edges and blades to the climbable surface of the car to encourage hands and arms to drop off!

BUMP AND CRASH PROTECTION

This is also important to stop taking damage when you hit objects, especially zombies. Car

tyres can prove perfect for this as they are easy to find and last for ages as a defensive barrier. Attach then to the sides, front and back of your vehicles for great defensive protection!

STEERING AND AXLE PROTECTION

This is actually the most common part of an off-road vehicle and therefore relatively easy to find. Most good off-road shops sell aluminium mounts to protect the vulnerable underside of your vehicle.

OFFENCE

These modifications will provide additional damage dealing capabilities to any of your vehicles. These range from spikes and blades to rams, guns and other projectile weapons. In countries where firearms are more common you will want to add more weapon mounts and ammunition stores. Elsewhere you will be looking for fighting platforms, rams and spikes. You will need to be able to survive head-on impacts with the undead and keep moving, this means a sturdy vehicle and some basic modifications. First is to disable or remove any safety equipment that will stop you in a crash. Second is to protect the crumple zone of the front and rear of your vehicles. Things have changed, the crumple zone is now the zombie's head, so let's add metal to the right parts of your cars and trucks.

RAMS

These are simple reinforced objects attached to your vehicle to be smashed into other objects. It is important to attach these directly to the chassis of your vehicles so this will usually mean fitting them to older cars and trucks. The most important part of the vehicle to modify is the front. Fit something sturdy to the front, a cow catcher is great but so are bull bars or anything else that is metal and sturdy. Ensure you attach it directly onto a solid part of the vehicle. This is where traditional 4x4 vehicles like Jeeps and Land Rovers with solid chassis come into their own. Any item from metal barrels to heavy timber or snow ploughs will work well here.

INTEGRAL WEAPONS

These weapons are attached to your vehicle and are either aimed by pointing the front of the vehicle at the enemy or by being turned and crewed by those on board. It is best to add your heavier and more powerful weapons directly onto the body, such as large calibre machine guns and flamethrowers. For the latter you can add additional fuel either onboard or in a towed bowser or trailer.

LOOPHOLES

Originally loopholes were arrow loops or arrow slit passes through a solid wall and were originally for use by archers. For your purposes they are slots and holes cut into the

outside of your vehicles to allow the use of projective weapons such as firearms. The more you add armour the more likely you will need to incorporate loopholes into the design.

FIGHTING PLATFORMS

These are parts of your vehicle that are designed to give your people sufficient space to move around and fight effectively. This ranges from use the bed of a pickup truck to adding flat sections on top of trucks for your people to fight from. Make sure you have side barriers to stop zombies reaching your people. Add weapon pintle mounts to the sides for additional mounted firepower.

BOARDING PLANKS

These are simple devices and allow you to perform various operations without having to step on the ground. You can extend a plank from part of a truck onto a house window frame. An added benefit is that you can use the planks to move materials between vehicles. Don't believe the movies though and attempt to do this on the move. This is guaranteed to end up with you dropping people or supplies into the street!

SPIKES

These are sharp, projecting objects designed to impale zombies that you either crash into or those that try and get inside your vehicle. These range from sharpened wooden spikes to heavy-duty steel spikes used for demolition work. Like rams it is important to anchor these firmly to the chassis of your vehicle.

SCYTHES

These are cutting edges and blades fitted to the sides of the vehicle or directly to the wheels. These were used historically on the sides of chariots and can provide a handy extra weapon that protects the sides of the vehicle and also stop zombies getting too close, providing you are moving. These are great to use on vehicles that are carrying people or

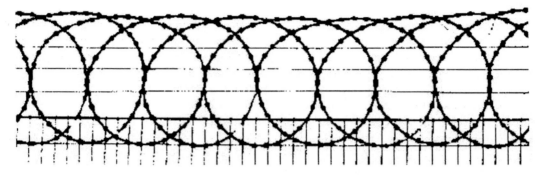

supplies as they make it difficult to access parts of the vehicle by the virtue of having cut away the legs of the offending zombies!

RAZOR WIRE

This is a more modern and more vicious version of the traditional barbed wire. It is quick and easy to fit and will slash and injure anything that try to move past it. Razor wire is also great at entangling people and zombies. Remember this as it is possible you can get stuck in your own wire or even worse, give the zombies something to hold on to.

GUN PINTLE MOUNTS

These are used with guns as the mounting hardware that mates the gun to a tripod. Essentially the pintle is a bracket with a cylindrical bottom and a cradle for the gun on top. The cylindrical bottom fits into a hole in the tripod while the cradle holds the gun. These mounts can be attached to various points on the vehicle, make sure they can be accessed quickly and easily from inside.

SPONSON WEAPON MOUNT

This refers to the aspect of the vehicle body directly over the wheels and includes layers of hardened, bulletproof or reinforced materials to protect the occupants. The sponson can also be used as additional storage space for both vehicle equipment and components, and either ammunition or crew belongings.

WEAPON TURRET

The turret is a rotating weapon platform that can be fitted to a vehicle. The turret protects the crew or mechanism of a projectile firing weapon and at the same time lets the weapon be aimed and fired in many directions. The beauty of these mounts is that they allow you to install heavy weapons whilst offering a completely sealed firing platform. The big problem of course is that a turret is no easy piece of equipment to find, fit or build. It will need to be strong and able to rotate freely. To be truly effective the turret needs to be motorised so that it can move quickly whilst the gunner concentrates on the targets.

CUPOLA MOUNT

A small turret, or sub-turret on a larger one, is called a cupola. The term cupola also describes rotating turrets that carry no weapons but instead sighting devices, as in the case of tank commanders. A finial is an extremely small sub-turret or sub-sub-turret mounted on a cupola turret. The protection provided by the turret may be against battle damage or against the weather, conditions and environment in which the weapon or its crew operate.

POWER AND PERFORMANCE

There are a variety of modifications that can be made to boost the power of your vehicle. Power can refer to simply more horsepower or possibly reducing weight or drag for better performance. General engine upgrades such as air intakes and exhausts are not really worth bothering with as they take time, reduce the lifespan of your engine and offer no real benefit in the Zompoc environment.

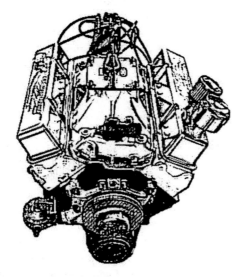

NITROUS OXIDE

Nitrous oxide (often referred to as just "nitrous or NOS") allows the engine to burn more fuel and air, resulting in a more powerful combustion. The gas itself is not flammable, but it delivers more oxygen than atmospheric air by breaking down at elevated temperatures. While NOS is pumped into the

engine you will receive a substantial boost in power. The downside is that you can actually develop enough power to damage or destroy the vehicle's engine. Be careful and make sure you add a red 'boost' button.

WEIGHT REDUCTION

Though normally only done for sports cars or those being modified for track days, there are still many uses for this modification during the Zompoc. This is a handy procedure for scouts and reconnaissance vehicles. Remove items such as sound systems, door interior inserts, redundant seating etc. This will also free up space inside if required.

TRANSPORT

This includes any modifications designed to improve the cargo or passenger carrying capabilities of your vehicles. You will need the capability to add lots of spare supplies, food, fuel, weapons, tools and more on your vehicles. This can be done internally and externally. With the space created by ripping out non-essentials you can add cargo nets, boxes, crates and more internally. Bolt or weld roof racks, safari racks and jerry can holders to the outside to increase your load carrying capability.

LUGGAGE MOUNTS

Luggage mounts are an easy to make modification and of great use during the Zompoc. These can include luggage racks, roof bars and roof boxes and will massively add to the load carrying capacity of your vehicle. The more you can put on the outside the more internal safe space you create for your most valuable supplies and people. Be careful about placing too much on the top of your vehicle though as this will shift the centre of gravity and make it less stable and increase the risk of tipping.

CARGO NETS

These can be added inside or outside the vehicle to hold down supplies or to add extra capacity for all manner of goods. Just remember, a net can be used to pull yourself up and onto your vehicle, handy for you but also for the enemy. Many vehicles such as Land rovers and MPVs now come supplied with small cargo nets to stop items from rolling around in their boots (trunks).

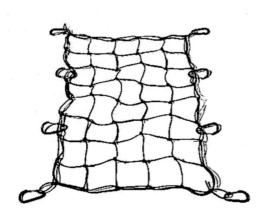

JERRY CAN HOLDERS

These are for carrying additional water and fuel and are commonly used by off-roaders, military vehicles and those heading out on overland expeditions. You never know when you will find more, so make sure you always have the capacity to carry as much fuel as you can find. These are easily purchased at most hardware and 4x4 shops. These can be fitted to any vehicles.

Be careful that you know what was previously used in the jerry can as you do not want to put drinking water in a can that previously help oil or petrol. Either paint them different colours for different liquids or put a marker of some kind on each can. The other way to check is to remove the cap and take a whiff. Be careful when checking fuel filled cans as the fumes can be pretty unhealthy!

TRAILERS

A very simple modification of fitting a towbar will allow you to pull trailers, fuel bowsers and other items. You will also find having a dedicated point like this will be handy for pulling other vehicles if required. An added benefit is that the towbar can be used as a rear mounted ram. This will provide additional protection to the rear of your vehicle as well as a last resort weapon.

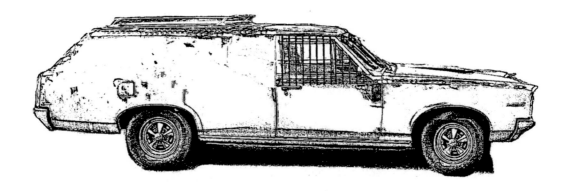

MISCELLANEOUS

There are other modifications that don't easily fit into the above categories. Some of these modifications may actually also exist in some of the other sections but for other reasons, such as the horns or speakers. These items also include both modifications and also handy tools and equipment that you will not want your vehicles to be without. You will probably find that you will want most of these fitted to your vehicles so keep on the lookout for the parts on your travels.

ESCAPE HATCHES

You are doing your Mad Max bit, racing down the freeway when your tyre blows out and you end up in a ditch on your side. Zombies are getting closer and the doors are buckled and jammed. How do you get out and away to another car? What, you're on your own? Never mind, you are now dead! If you have friends with you though you need to get out. The basic bare minimum is a tool to cut belts and to smash windows. Escape hatches are simple modifications than can be made in places other than the main doors for access and escape. They need to be secure so that they are not easily opened by the Undead but easy enough to escape through in an emergency situation. Make sure the sections that are cut are covered to avoid cuts and abrasions.

SPARE TOOLS

Shovels, hammers, axes and crowbars can all be carried externally on your vehicle. These items are useful in all manner of scenarios and by carrying them on the outside you avoid cluttering the interior. Carry extra, small tools like saws, knives, hammers and wrenches internally also. They are handy for both repairs and for combat! Also, if you need to get out in a hurry, especially from a damaged vehicle you may need to smash or cut your way out.

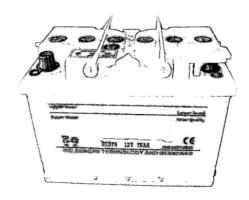

POWER

Spare hardware for providing additional power is very important. These items include extra car batteries, charging circuits and the means to charge the batteries. You can fit wind or solar generators on your vehicles or more realistically carry this kind of equipment in your resupply vehicles. You can then recharge your equipment using the potential of the environment, rather than your limited fuel. Dynamo type equipment for power low voltage radios is also a good plan. Solar cells can be fitted to the roofs of your larger vehicles. In this case make sure you are always storing this power, whether on the move or not.

SURVIVAL KIT

This can include materials for starting fires, purifying water, erecting shelters and food preparation materials. If you go hiking or camping you will probably already have this kind of equipment. Make sure you know how to use the stuff too!

INTERNAL REFUELLING

Add auxiliary fuel filling spots on the inside of your vehicles so that you can refuel your vehicles without having to expose yourself. Do not disconnect the external fuel filler though as this will still be handy! Keep spare piping, siphons and tools inside so you can improvise and move fuel as needed. Remember the way siphons work, the item you are filling needs to be lower than the source or else you will be waiting a long, long time!

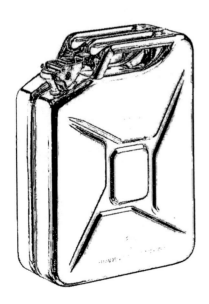

COMMUNICATION

Communication will be very important between both vehicles and your bases. Mobile phones may work for a while. Ultimately you will need to reply upon yourself and this means loudhailers, megaphones, loud speakers and radios. These modifications can range from simple lights or flags through to more advanced electronic communications.

FLAGS

Flag signals can be various methods of using flags or pennants to send signals. These can range from a simple red flag for danger, green flag for okay, right through to a full, detailed signalling system as used by ships and the military. The important thing is to ensure that you have an adequate supply of flags. Also ensure that your people understand the messages being conveyed.

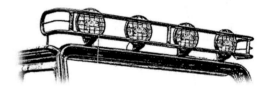

LIGHTS

Lights can be used to provide communication in a similar way to flags. Simple flashing of lights can be used to signal the start or end of an operation. More complicated usage can include Morse Code for detailed messages using a full alphabet. Obviously torches can be used for this purpose but they do have an annoying habit of going missing or the batteries run down. It is pretty easy to add extra lights onto vehicles and either run them from the 12v accessory socket or even better, run them from a feed direct from the battery.

EXTERNAL SPEAKERS

These have a variety of uses and are thus very handy devices to fit onto your vehicles. By connecting these speakers to your vehicle's sound system and microphone you can shout orders, send signals and play music. Music is important; it keeps the spirit up and also announces to friendlies in the area that help is on the way. Do not underestimate the benefit of loud rock music! If you are leading a twenty truck convoy into zombie infested territory there is nothing like some classic rock or metal to fire up your people into a zombie crushing fever.

Adding exterior tannoy speakers will help with this and can also assist with communications if you need something done fast. Make sure you have a good selection of classic rock on hand, perhaps a few select playlists or mix tapes. Avoid at all cost hip-hop, pop and soft Emo music. You want hardened zombie killers!

RADIOS

Fit radios into all vehicles and establish standard procedures for their use. These radios can include a wide variety of models and types. Just make sure you are all using the same frequencies and types of equipment. Don't have some on VHF sets and the rest using UHF for example. Ideally have a radio system mounted in the vehicles, connected directly to the main battery. Also have a few spare emergency portable sets,

FIREARMS

This is a very simple method but has the advantage of being loud and perfect for those nasty surprises. The most common signal is three shots fire as a warning that there is danger. Extend this as required.

FLARES

Flares are limited in number and thus best used as danger or emergency signals. They can be left burning outside buildings or near dangerous drops or falls. Just remember that they only last so long and cannot be re-used.

FLARE GUNS

These can be used in the same way as normal flares but have the advantage in that they can cover distance and height. In theory you may be able to use these to distract zombies with the pretty lights. Try it out and see if it works. A flare launched from a gun can also be used to light up areas further away from your vehicles. Even better, use the flare gun as a signal for assistance in emergencies or as a weapon.

HORNS

Ensure car horns or similar work and establish simple procedures for communications with simple horn blasts. For example, one continuous tone means all hell has broken loose, or else you are dead and fell onto the horn. As with lights and flags you can use your own more detailed code for communication with the horn or simply opt for the international recognised Morse Ccode. Basic car horns can be supplemented or improved by adding electrically powered air horns. Whilst a little bit fiddly to fit for the novice they do add a massive boost to your emergency communication and sound cool too!

CHAPTER 15: REBUILDING

To cherish what remains of the Earth and to foster its renewal is our only legitimate hope of survival.

Wendell Berry

Assuming you and your group of survivors has stayed alive for the first few days and weeks, you will need to start planning on rebuilding your lives. This section assumes that you have reached a relatively stable period that could follow any of the following scenarios:

❖ You have destroyed or damaged the zombie population sufficiently that they are no longer a threat.

❖ You have found a region or place that is safe, strong and secure from the Zompoc.

❖ You have a safe region plus the ability to remove the affects of the zombie infection, such as an antidote.

If you have not reached one of the above stages then please re-read the 'Fighting Back' chapter as it is not wise to start thinking about farming when you are stuck in a basement in the centre of New York surrounded by over a million zombies and nothing but your bible!

The rebuilding phase is essentially the post-Zompoc phase and a time when resources are minimal. Survivors will be grouped together in small communities, assuming your group isn't the last one left, and you will need to look to the future. On top of the ever present zombie threat there is also another threat, one that may be even bigger...other people. You can be sure that if you are building a safe place to live,

farming, hoarding supplies and operating a successful defence you will be a tempting, juicy target for any other survivors that are left. Eternal vigilance will be the price of freedom to your people. There are two approaches to rebuilding. The first is to operate a nomadic lifestyle with your people constantly on the move with a well equipped and armed convoy. By doing this you can live off the land, collecting supplies as you go and always keeping on the move. This may or may not work. Ultimately though, one mistake could cost you your convoy and then all your people. The other option is to re-establish some semblance of civilisation, to do this you will need to do two things:

1. Keep the living alive and help them thrive
2. Destroy or cull the zombies to allow the above

EARLY DAYS

During the early days, months and years of the initial outbreak you will find yourself hiding out in a variety of safe house and fortresses. When you move around you will make use of a well protected convoy. You must anticipate long periods of time without commerce in the future and must place a strong emphasis on logistics. Amass stockpiles of supplies for your own use, for charity and for barter. Key areas of planning include long-term storage of food, common ammunition, medical supplies, tools, gardening seeds and fuel.

Your first basics tasks will include:

❖ Initiating culls to protect your safe area (see the strategy section)
❖ Finding, protecting and organising your most important resource, living people
❖ Establish safe compounds and storage depots
❖ Raid and forage for supplies

In the short term this is ok but ultimately a more permanent arrangement will be needed, with a fair allocation of resources and responsibilities. It is unlikely that this will happen quickly as zombies will be too plentiful at that time to be able to venture out of your fortresses and feel safe. Also, unless you are well prepared you will not have your initial resources ready at the start of the Zompoc. You will need to find them first, this creates many problems that you will have to overcome with careful planning

LONG TERM

Assuming you survive long enough you will need to establish, run and decide on a form of social organisation suitable for survival and expansion in the remnants of an undead world. Either you will do this or somebody else will do so. Your government (for want of a better word) would be more like the size of a village or town at most. You would be establishing a government based on survival and furthering the human race. You would not need all the land you can find. Your goal is to survive and therefore you need enough to survive and then to expand.

WHO IS IN CHARGE?

If you are at the stage of creating a form of structure and government how will you do it? This may not be as easy as you might think as you will need to get people to join you and your way of thinking and contribute effectively to the cause. You can essentially create your main core of people using a more forceful, 'I am in charge' structure or alternatively try and go for the more inclusive caring and sharing liberal approach. One thing I would remember from history is that in time of crisis it is usually best to choose one man to lead, even for a short time. Often action, any action is better than inaction.

Now let's assume that you have a secure base or fortress. To keep this guarded and supplied you will need a number of people, realistically at least two dozen with no upper limit. You will notice that this follows more of a clan or

PROS
* ❖ Obedience of the citizens
* ❖ Easier to instil system change where the structure is dependent upon you
* ❖ Large pool of potential recruits for military, policing or defence force
* ❖ Control over resources and allocation

CONS
* ❖ Higher chance of being assassinated
* ❖ Can lead to major problems if the leader dies or is killed
* ❖ Less likely to be able to ally with someone else
* ❖ Desertion is possible, especially from those forcibly drafted

family group to start with. First decide on a form of government structure for your renewed society.

FORECEFUL APPROACH

The forceful approach doesn't of course mean you go around cracking skulls to get your own way, though you may have to of course. When we say forceful we mean you form a small, elite core of competent and experienced people and from this core all decisions are made. For example, you might find half a dozen people, who have survived for six months on their own will prove tough, experienced and ready. These people are the ones you want to help run your new system. By all means initiate new people into your group. Just remember, your core people are in charge and new people (newbs) need to know this. This system will look a lot like a military structure. This isn't a bad thing though ultimately you will probably need to enfranchise the rest of your people, perhaps moving into the more liberal system below.

LIBERAL APPROACH

This less forceful system is the belief in the importance of individual freedom. This belief is widely accepted today throughout the world, and was recognized as an important value by many philosophers throughout history.

Once you have chosen a basic approach it is time to then elect/appoint officials, write out the laws and rights of everyone, and then begin building. It is important to establish rules, rights and responsibilities very early on to make the best use of all your resources. For example; letting people retain ownership and trading of items can help innovation and

PROS
- ❖ Obedience of the citizens
- ❖ Better Morale
- ❖ More motivation to work and get involved
- ❖ People more likely to voluntarily join you

CONS
- ❖ Less money/supplies for yourself
- ❖ Potentially less obedience from citizens
- ❖ Chance of someone more charismatic taking your place

private enterprise but can also eat into limited resources and lead to profiteering.

RULES AND RESPONSIBILITIES

Once you have decided upon some kind of a system of governance you will need to create a basic system of rules, laws, rights and responsibilities so everybody knows their place and what they can and cannot do.

EXAMPLE CONSTITUTION

RIGHTS
- ❖ All citizens are entitled to an equal share of rations for people doing the same type of work
- ❖ All citizens have the right to carry weapons

RESPONSIBILITIES
- ❖ Citizens are responsible for the safety of the state
- ❖ Any citizen that is found to be infected, must be immediately euthanised

LAWS
- ❖ No attacking other citizens
- ❖ No disclosing information to foreigners
- ❖ No theft from other citizens
- ❖ No zombie like motions or sounds
- ❖ No hoarding rations
- ❖ No breaking curfew

NOTES:
As you can see, the laws and rights are simple but fair, everyone is treated equally and everyone is kept safe.

WHAT YOU WILL NEED

For a thriving and successful society to grow you will need all the facilities you would expect in a small town. It is best to try and make use of existing structures and materials rather than building or sourcing materials from scratch. To start with your need storage and distribution structures. These need to be manned and guarded against all enemies, external or internal. In the early days you will be surviving on supplies gathered outside your base but later on you will need to become self sufficient. You will also need safe, guarded barracks for your people. These buildings must be well protected, more so than any others. Watch towers, communication systems and guards must be well co-ordinated. Ideally a large bell or alarm that can be triggered from anywhere will be critical. Ensure all citizens are trained in what to do when they hear it. After moving past the foraging, collection and storing phase you will need to move on to modification, adaptation and manufacturer of certain items. To do this you will need workshops, power, tools, garages etc.

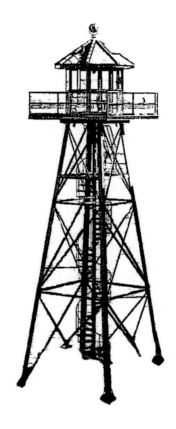

SELF SUFFICIENCY

At some point your system will need another push to allow it to expand and thrive for years to come. For this to happen you will need to become self sufficient. This will either happen because you choose it or it will be forced upon you by necessity, either from lack of food or supplies or because it is too dangerous for you to obtain them anymore. You will need ready supplies of clean water, power and food as well as ways to remove waste and rubbish.

FOOD

Food is somewhat important as you need it to live. There are many ways to obtain food apart from living on the supplies you have raided over months and years. At some point you will need to farm and harvest food in various forms to keep your people alive and well. Apart from a sufficient amount of food you will need to

consider nutrition and a balanced diet. You want healthy, productive people! What kind of food then, can you farm or harvest? Well, with the farming route you can consider sweetcorn, potatoes, squash, tomatoes, beans, lettuce, peppers, carrots, apples, cucumbers, onions,

zucchini, peas, grapes, cauliflower, broccoli, garlic, celery, eggplant, pumpkins, watermelon, rhubarb, radishes, yams and wheat for starters. Produce such as wheat requires additional work afterwards so this must be considered in terms of time, space and experience. Animal products such as meat, milk and eggs can also be considered, though meat requires feed for animals plus much more land. Basic estimates on growing your own food with small farms suggests

approximately one acre of land per person. If you want chickens and, cattle then you will need more space for this. It is already easy to see that a small community of around one hundred people would require one hundred acres of land in constant use just for food production. Add cattle and the number can double or more. On top of this you need a fair number of people to work the land, clean and prepare the food, cook it and distribute it. For meat you will need butchers, cooks etc. Expect the bulk of your people to be working on this.

WATER

Planning for an adequate supply of water is most important. Allow for predicted extremes in weather due to climate change with increased droughts and floods. Pumping of water is very energy consuming. Placing of the house and garden below the water source can save considerable energy with gravity being used to reticulate the water. For drinking water, always check the quality of the water in regards to the mineral content and the presence of herbicides and pesticides.

Ways to source water include:

❖ Rain water - The collection of rain water is dependent on the area of the collecting roofs and rainfall. It is usually of high quality with little contamination, requiring regular cleaning of the roof guttering.
❖ Bore water - Drilling a bore-hole is expensive and is a hit or miss affair. If water is found to be of a useable quality and of sufficient quantity, there are the costs of purchasing a suitable pump and its installation and plumbing plus the ongoing costs of pumping the water for use.
❖ Dam water - Often requires pumping, so positioning is important. It requires regular maintenance. Adequacy in times of flooding, is dependent on rain and surface run off. It loses much water through surface evaporation on hot windy days. For healthy dam water, it requires a "clean" collecting basin in respect of fertilisers, herbicides, pesticides and no direct stock usage.
❖ Spring water - Before human consumption check quality as above and reliability in summer and droughts.

- ❖ River and stream water - Quality as above needs to be checked regularly if used within the house along with the ongoing monitoring of what is happening in the water catchment area.
- ❖ Well water - A shallow four metre deep well can be placed adjacent to a "dry" stream bed.

POWER

We all live in an age of electricity. There is no reason why you will have to manage without it, providing you can find or create basic machines and a source to power them. Natural fuels such as coal, petrol, gas and wood should be plentiful, especially as most humans are no longer using them. Finding and storing energy will be very important, as will guarding them. If you have access to massive quantities of refined oil then you may want to consider building a security compound around the site and post people on rotation to guard it. Power can be created by using water or wind to drive turbines that then produce electricity or by burning fuels to create heat that is then used to power devices through steam movement.

Solar cells, water and wind turbines can all be used to drive turbines and then create electricity. This power can be used either immediately or stored for later use. Storage can be either through batteries or by creating potential power such as pumping water to high ground so that it can be let back down to power turbines when required. If you are sourcing supplies for power use, be very careful and use armoured convoys to bring fuel supplies back as frequently as possible. The extraction points should be guarded and secure.

WASTE

Disposal of waste is important and potentially dangerous. Waste can be dumped, buried or burnt. Whichever way you choose make sure it is away from your habitation and that those involved in waste disposal are protected from the material and that they follow hygiene procedures to the letter.

EDUCATION

We will need future engineers, farmers, mechanics, teachers, soldiers and drivers in the future. These skills will need to be passed on. The ability to read, write, understand basic mathematics and to be able to improve our lives will not stop just because the Zompoc is over. Store books and materials for future generations. Computers, CD-ROMs and long term storage devices should all be kept, ready for when they will be needed again.

MEDICAL

Medical training, supplies and equipment will be critical to keeping your people healthy and thriving. Dedicate a portion of your resources to this very important task. Don't rely upon one trained medical person, either find more

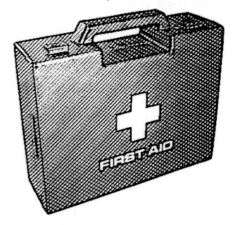

or start training up others. If you lose your only doctor you are going to be in trouble later on.

TRANSPORT

Transport will be necessary for both people and goods. Transportation will be dependent on available vehicles, materials to transport and the environment. Read the 'Vehicles' section for more information on this and also the 'Travel & Movement' section. If you have access to grazing land (for horses), petrol or water then use these to ease your transportation needs. As in any society, both ancient and modern, you will find it much easier to move people and goods from place to place if you have some form of infrastructure set up that is capable of handling both vehicles and goods. This can include waterways, roads, tracks and rails. Note that rails can be used even without trains and provide a low maintenance way of moving items.

SECURITY

Security is a word you will have been taking seriously from day one and is presumably one of the reasons you are still alive. Security includes the defence of your hard won new territory from all kinds of threats, not just the zombie threat. You will need to protect against zombies that may be created within your base, external attack from other humans, internal revolt plus other potential threats. Security is going to be very important and something that your resources need to be made available to.

Due to the fact that resources will always be limited along with manpower you will always need more people producing food, supplies, materials and equipment than you will have for combat. This doesn't mean you will have no security, it just means you will need to be careful in how you organise yourself. A good model would be to base your security around the system set up by the Later Roman Empire. Unlike in the good years where people, money and resources were plentiful and enemies were small the Later Roman Empire faced dwindling manpower, reduced resources and masses of well organised enemies at the border. They made use of a multilayered security system and it worked pretty well for them (for a time!). You should use some of their ideas along with a little common sense based on your situation.

Your security system will be made up of three main kinds of people; civilians, militia and soldiers. This three way system will be heavily biased towards civilian and militia as you cannot afford to have all your people running around totting guns. Give it a few months and you'll be dead from starvation.

The security system is operated by the militia, with support from the soldiers, as and when they are needed. Each day will be split up into watches, the militia will take turn during these intervals to take part in security operations. All guard towers, internal patrols and guarding buildings will be done by the militia during their allocated watches. Additionally, if the

security alarm is raised all militia will head to their allocated places ready for security operations. This means that the militia essentially form a security service and police force. The soldiers will be the hard core of the security system and will not take part in basic security operations. They will be available during emergencies to provide backup and leadership when needed for defence. Raid operations, culling and attacks outside the region will be conducted by the soldiers, with additional support if needed by the militia. It is wasteful to use the soldiers for basic security as their numbers will be spread thin and give them no time for more dangerous work that could take their toll on the less well trained militia. Any soldiers that are forced to retire from age, injury or other reason will provide leadership or the militia. They will become militia members also, but will make their main profession based on security support such as education, weapon manufacture, training and vehicle modification. Though they are less able than before, they still have valuable skills and experience that are vital to the survival of your people.

SOLDIERS

As you are setting up your long term system you will find most of your people will work on all manner of tasks, from driving and collecting supplies through to combat operations. As time progresses and you start to develop a more long term system you will need to invest time and resources into producing an effective military system. This is based around the role of the soldier. Unlike the rest of your people, the soldier has only one job, that of military preparedness. Like the Spartans of old, their profession will be one of physical training, equipment maintenance and combat and tactical training.

These people must be carefully selected will be your most proficient and capable fighters. As well as preparing themselves and their units for combat it will also be their responsibility to train and prepare the militia and civilians for combat operations. This training will consist of regular physical training classes for all members of the military and militia as well as hand to hand combat training and the use of weapons.

Soldiers must ensure they are always prepared in terms of training and equipment. They are usually needed in emergencies and can expect to have to deal with zombies both at a distance and up close. We recommend that soldiers train in the use of modern and traditional weapons so that they are able to keep fighting no matter the level of supply or equipment. Good weapons to practice with are all firearms, bows and crossbows, knives, machetes plus whichever specialist weapons they have an aptitude for.

MILITIA

These are all the people in your territory who are capable of working or fighting. Age, sex or ability is not so important here, only that they can physically stand and fight when the time comes. These people are the backbone of your society and include farmers, mechanics, teachers, miners, drivers etc. Being in the militia does not mean that you are less important than the soldiers, it means that you have other skills, knowledge or specialism that are of more value than using you in the frontline.

It is important that the militia are trained by the soldiers as they will have the knowledge and experience to pass on to the militia.

Militia will obviously have their 'day jobs' but must ensure that they have basic combat training and will be expected to fight when needed. Unlike soldiers, the militia will not normally be carrying full combat equipment, armour and load outs so keep this in mind when they are called up for action. Keep militia out of hand to hand combat as much as possible and get them used to following order, staying in groups and practicing ranged fire with whatever long range weapons you have access to. Militia should always carry at least one weapon no matter what job they are working on. This weapon needs to be reliable and also one that the person has trained with.

One way to keep militia training on top form is to make the end of the week a communal training session where all militia practice and compete against each other. Completion is an excellent way to promote practice and also help you identify individuals with an aptitide3 for combat.

Don't forget than the militia are likely to be less reliable than the soldiers in a dangerous situation and you cannot completely rely upon their staying power or morale. If one is injured, captured or killed it could spark a panic amongst the less experienced. This is why it is important to try and involve militia in patrols, guard duty and convoy work so that that receive regular exposure to the dangers outside. At the other end of the scale you may find certain individuals lose control and may rush off doing their Rambo bit, thus risking all your people for a foolish few kills.

CIVILIAN

These are the population that are unable to perform regular combat and supply operations for your fledgling society. This does not necessarily mean that they are infirm or too young or old it simply means they are not best suited to the continuing rigour of this kind of work. If you have injured militia, those that are a little older or those that are simply not best suited for operations will fit into this category. This isn't a problem though as there is still much to do and they will be critical to assist in the running of your state.

Young children are obviously required to continue the progress of your people whilst the older or less physically capable can still offer education, training, political office and many other important jobs. There is actually a strong argument for getting more mature and experienced people involved with positions of management, decision making and leadership as they should be working from a greater pool of knowledge and hopefully, wisdom.

It is important that civilians are trained to move to safe houses whenever the region is in a state of emergency. The intention is that civilians will rely upon militia and soldiers who are training regularly to protect and defend them. Though they will have no active part to play in normal security operations it is still important though that they are taught to handle firearms and from the earliest age how to call for help in emergencies so that the soldiers and militia can be mobilised. Panic buttons, if you have power, are handy for older people. As for children, don't bother, they are more likely to create false alarms. You can always get more children!

TRADING IN A POST APOCALYPTIC WORLD

A currency based system relies on a relatively stable world, as well as a guarantee from banks or governments to backup their currencies as they are only promissory notes. For a currency system to be successful, you must know that you will always be able to use this currency everywhere, and must have a way to prevent counterfeiting. Some items such as food, fuel and weapons will become very important and potentially a new baseline for trade.

Bartering is a method in which goods or services are directly exchanged for other goods and/or services without a common unit of exchange such as money. Barter usually replaces money as the method of exchange in times of monetary crisis, when the currency is unstable and devalued by hyperinflation. This section relates to trading outside of your own compounds, convoys or regions. This means you will be dealing with people who will almost certainly be more interested in themselves than helping you. So remember, your priority is your people, you are not a charity!

GUIDELINES FOR MERCHANTS

It is very important to sell your goods in a populated place, ideally one set up specifically for trade. Keep in mind that there may be infected or undead about as well as thieves and other undesirables. More organised trading posts may be armed and safer than trying to trade in back alleys or from the boots of trucks. If you have a dedicated place for trading make sure it is secure and accessible from one place that can be guarded. Merchants should always have a guard, or carry a weapon that they are highly skilled with. If you can't hire a guard, travel with someone who has one. It is easy to be distracted when making a trade and then forfeit your goods or even life.

TRADE SUPPLIES

These supplies are items that are important to store, maybe not for yourself, but items that can be very useful to trade at a later date. For example, medical supplies will always be n demand as will alcohol and cigarettes. When people are stressed they smoke, zombies will sure push up demand.

ADDICTIVE SUBSTANCES & STIMULANTS

These will become more important as people supplies run low. They take up relatively little space and people will give almost anything to get their fix, and this can be beneficial to you. Stimulants like sugar, caffeine and stronger stuff will be desirable by the living as when they are asleep they are vulnerable to attack.

TOBACCO AND ALCOHOL

These goods last a long time and in this situation will be in great demand. Alcohol also has other uses, especially in its stronger forms for cleaning and for fuel.

FOOD

If you are able to cure or store food to last a long time you will be able to trade for many high value items.

FUEL

There are many types and forms of fuel and those that stock-pile them can do very well with trading. The disadvantage with fuel trading is that petrol, diesel and aviation fuel take up large amounts of space. Commandeer fuel containers, Lorries and bowsers to provide a mobile supply service!

MEDICAL SUPPLIES

These will be in high demand and will hold great value. Simple things like aspirin, Bacitracin or Neosporin, saline solution or hydrogen peroxide will be in demand. Bandages and materials for making casts will also be in great demand.

WEAPONS & AMMUNITION

Projectile weapons, including firearms require ammunition. Even with things like a bow, the arrows will eventually break and get lost. It's not as easy to manufacture arrows or bolts as people think. In countries with limited access to firearms, such as the UK, these items will fetch a very heavy price!

BATTERIES

Many things require batteries and once they run out they will become useless. Recharging gear and solar chargers will be worth a small fortune. Keep them, charge the batteries and sell these on instead!

LITERATURE

Books, both fictional and non-fictional, will not initially be in much demand but as time moves on there will be interest in science, technology and entertainment. There are plenty of places to source these materials, so don't waste too much time on them in the early years. As you start to set up power systems, repair stations and the like it is a good idea to either stockpile non-fiction literature yourself or destroy what you cannot use. There is no point in spending a fortune building a steam engine to run milling machines to hire out, if your competition has a book showing them how to build something even better.

SERVICES

Goods are not the only thing to be traded. If you have skilled mechanics, medical workers or soldiers you can hire out their skills in exchange for other goods and services. It is very important to ensure your people do not get cherry picked by other groups so keep an eye on them and ideally leave them guarded by your most trusted people. Be careful about hiring out people as opposed to their actual services as they can be easily kidnapped or held for ransom. If you have to lend them your people either send guards or even better, get them to hand over something as security. This security can be in either goods such as food or fuel or in people. Some of the services you can offer up include:

REPAIR

Machines, generators, doors, weapons, vehicles, tools and equipment all need maintenance and repair. There are two options when something stops working, either get it repaired or replace it. You need to fit the cost your services somewhere in the middle so replacement is more expensive than using your people's skills to repair or service the items your customers already possess.

MERCENARIES

The payment of people from other areas for combat and military operations has been known for millennia. Those that have the skills throughout have earned much currency through many periods in history. Those with skills and the ability to use them will be in high demand during the Zompoc. People with weapons plus military training will be at the top of the list. You can hire out their time for bodyguard work, scouting or any of the operations listed elsewhere in this book. Make sure you have a good enough incentive to keep control of your mercs so they don't wander off to join other people, else you'll be forced to hire mercenaries yourself.

One of the biggest problems with mercenaries is that they can be very useful, dedicated and loyal. There is one proviso, you must pay them and pay them on time! Don't make the mistake the Carthaginians made by deciding not to pay their mercenaries. They rebelled and ended up costing a fortune as the Carthaginians had to hire a new army to fight them!

COOKING & FARMING

Cooks are one thing, farmers are another. The ability to hunt, farm or butcher animals is not an easy one, neither is the ability to grow field after field of good quality crops. You can hire your people out for labour though you would

be better of selling their knowledge in running farms and related operations.

MEDICAL

People will always need treatment for illness, accidents, childbirth etc. Your services along with desirable drugs, painkillers and medical supplies will be a major selling point. Be careful that your valued personnel are not exposed to dangerous infection or zombies as they will be unarmed and unprepared.

MANUFACTURERS

This section includes any of your people that can provide skills to create and modify items and equipment or supplies. These can include blacksmiths, ironmongers, carpenters, builders, joiners etc. Make sure you charge extra for supplies and materials!

MESSENGERS

The ability to send, receive and understand message is important. You can hire out services of postmen to hand deliver notes and letters to outposts and convoys throughout the land. These people may also be experts in operating radio and communication equipment. You can set up communication points with their own power and then charge to send and receive messages.

ELECTRICITY

People will pay for electricity, especially when they find all their valuable and life saving equipment no longer function when nothing comes out of the wall sockets. People who have rechargeable batteries will want them recharged. Some people who have electric vehicles and use them for short distances will want electricity. The ability to create and manage electricity will be of massive use and though you can hire out your services to provide the same service to others you can also hire out the actual power. Charge people to recharge batteries or to provide a certain amount of power over a certain amount of time. Be very wary about building power

generation facilities for your competition, as once built what can you really offer them? The only upside to this option is that if they cannot maintain the equipment themselves. If this is true then you get paid to run and to fix the machines providing the power. Even better!

ENTERTAINMENT

Eventually people are going to need entertainment. Initially the ability to provide power will be important but the advantages of live performances should not be underestimated. If you have access to actors, musicians, singers and poets you can finally find a use for their somewhat lacking skills in the Zompoc. Hire out a singer with a few musicians or maybe put on a show with some actors. Ideally work from existing information, the time for writing new songs and plays is probably not yet!

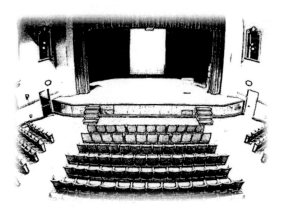

CHEMIST

Certain types of steel require chemicals to create, these are not usually knows by most people. Gunpowder can be made with a simple recipe and common chemicals. Toothpaste will be useful and many medical supplies can be made with access to chemicals and some tools. The ability to source chemicals is very important and in just this task alone you can hire out personnel. You can then charge for teaching skills to produce certain compounds and compositions for all manner of tasks. The knowledge required as a chemist should be guarded and only small parts of this sold for a good price. Better still, you can hire out the work of your chemist, get your customers to supply the materials, you can then create what they want less a percentage to yourself.

TRAINING
The more skilled a person is, the easier it is to survive and also the more valuable they will become. A common youth with the skill to play a football videogame is just one more mouth to feed. Train the youth to perform a basic task and they suddenly have value. The ability to turn the valueless to the valued will

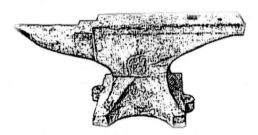

be a very useful skill. Turn unskilled workers into farmers, soldiers, cooks, teachers, blacksmiths - but make sure your competition pays a damned good price for this critical knowledge. Also, make sure you keep a few secrets to yourself, always maintaining an edge!

POSSIBLE USES FOR ZOMBIES
Some people feel that after the Zompoc, when resources and labour are limited, we may need to look to the remaining zombies to help us. There is a possibility that zombies may have a use as opposed to simply burning and destroying them. This is certainly unlikely but is for some it still worth understanding. Be aware that keeping zombies around is very, very risky and should therefore be considered as a last resort where you have no other choice or if you have a guaranteed safe way of keeping them at arm's length.

MANUAL LABOUR
Manual labour is the most obvious use for zombies as they should still have some form of basic motor function remaining. Their use as crude slave labour where repetitive or dangerous tasks need to be carried out could have some uses. For example, zombies could be fitted with explosive charges and then sent into mines to blow holes and expand tunnels. They could also carry items, even ones that might damage a living human. Their use for demolition work would also be a possibility, just make sure that in all these tasks they are restrained and can be halted to be destroy immediately if required.

ENTERTAINMENT
Zombies can prove an interesting and possibly amusing diversion for your entertainment starved populace. Use zombies to run around mazes, taunt them with meat, have your photo taken with them or stage mock fights. You can

even use them to put on some kind of macabre show, though what the story might be, who only knows.

MILITARY

Zombies can provide a few uses for your combat forces. These uses include target practice, for training squad tactics against a real enemy or even better; use them for mine clearing or bait.

RESEARCH

To defeat zombies you will first need to understand them, this will come either from experience or from detailed study. Be very careful as a zombie outbreak in your research areas can make the problem start all over again!

ZOMBIE RIGHTS

There are some who feel that the terms undead or infected or even the living dead is not a politically correct term. Some argue that they should be called the living impaired. These zombie liberals also feel the living impaired they should eligible for government care during these trying times as they find it hard to maintain work due to their condition and require special care. This may sound weird but it is important to remember that zombies used to be humans. Depending on the type and how they were altered they may still bare some of the ideas, knowledge, skills or memory of the human. The idea of human rights refers to the basic rights and freedoms to which all humans are entitled.

Examples of rights and freedoms which have come to be commonly thought of as human rights include civil and political rights, such as the right to life and liberty, freedom of expression, and equality before the law; and economic, social and cultural rights, including the right to participate in culture, the right to food, the right to work, and the right to education. Most, if not all of these rights will be waived based on your understanding of the material in this book. It is up to you if you want to try and help zombies through political, emotional or religious rights. Our basic advice though is that if you want to worry about zombie rights simple trigger the right to food and ask the nearest zombie what they would like to eat. Therein lies your answer.

INDEX

Perhaps catastrophe is the natural human environment, and even though we spend a good deal of energy trying to get away from it, we are programmed for survival amid catastrophe.

Germaine Greer

USEFUL INFORMATION

ZOMBIE ABOLITION SERVICE (ZAS)

The ZAS is a worldwide organisation dedicated to the eradication of the Zombie menace and the survival of the living. They are establishing units throughout the world to gather knowledge, plans and ideas in readiness for the Zompoc. Join them and help form your local ZAS militia and ensure the survival of humanity before it is too late!

DEPT OF HOMELAND SECURITY

The United States Department of Homeland Security (DHS) is a Cabinet department of the United States federal government with the primary responsibilities of protecting the territory of the U.S. from terrorist attacks and responding to natural disasters.

They work in the civilian sphere to protect the United States within, at, and outside its borders. Its stated goal is to prepare for, prevent, and respond to domestic emergencies, particularly terrorism

This organisation has loads of useful and helpful information on disasters planning, organising supplies, travel, communication and much more. Though it is designed for the United States, much of its information is very helpful and practical to people in any country.

CONTACTING THE AUTHORS

If you have questions with regards to Zompoc preparation or have suggestions or ideas for the improvement of this manual please contact us directly. We will read all e-mail and will do our best to reply to as many as we can.

Email: info@zompoc.com
Website: www.zompoc.com

ABOUT THE AUTHORS

Michael G. Thomas, is a writer, martial artist and military historian. He has written books on European martial arts and military history and is co-founder of the prestigious Academy of Historical Fencing. The Academy has over 100 members all training in traditional armed and unarmed European martial arts. His specialist subject areas are teaching the use of the medieval two handed longsword and the German long knife in both the UK and other parts of Europe. He has degrees in both Computing and Classics and has undertaken substantial research in the fields of machine learning and artificial intelligence as well as Ancient Greek and Byzantine military history. This diverse and detailed background is of great use in preparing the array of different topics covered by this book.

Nick S. Thomas, is a writer, martial artist and European fencing champion. He has written books on European martial arts and is co-founder of the prestigious Academy of Historical Fencing. The Academy has over 100 members all training in traditional armed and unarmed European martial arts. His specialist subject areas are teaching the use of the renaissance rapier and companion weapons, 19th century military sabre and medieval and Renaissance dagger fighting. Nick has taught both in the UK and around Europe and won two European martial arts Tournaments in 2009. He has a degree in Film Production and a keen interest in civilian fighting forms.

ZOMPOC
HOW TO SURVIVE A ZOMBIE
APOCALYPSE

MICHAEL THOMAS & NICK THOMAS

Meticulously researched and vigorously detailed this important survival manual is the most detailed and up-to-date book you will find to keep you and your family safe during the zompoc (Zombie Apocalypse). This book is unique in its coverage of all zombie strains from the viral infected fast zombies through to the shambling re-animated undead. All subjects from zombie identification, first-aid, escape techniques, household defence, combat techniques and raiding through to bartering, supplies, vehicle modification, weapons and convoy structure are all covered in great detail.

With this book you can prepare for the day the Zompoc strikes and be ready to fight back and eradicate the Zombie menace from our streets. This book is illustrated throughout and even contains full plans and instructions for a post -Zompoc rebuilding of civilisation!

WWW.ZOMPOC.COM

ISBN 978-1906512330 -0

9 781906 512330 >

ZOMBIE ABOLITION SERVICE